Publisher's note

C000061644

This is the fourth of t
Martin Archer's great military saga about a young
American enlisted man who remained in the army,
received a battlefield commission and promotions, and
became a professional soldier. This particular novel
follows "War Breaks Out" which described the war as it
might have occured if the Soviets had decided to fight
instead of allowing the Berlin Wall to fall.

Now the Soviet Union is gone. This novel is the story
of what might have happened, and still might happen, to
the men and women who were and are on active duty
after the Cold War ended. It is a novel set in a real war
that is likely to happen sooner or later between China and
Russia - when China attempts to reclaim the lands in the
Russian east that it lost to Russia when China was weak
and distracted by the Chinese revolution.

Readers can find the other action-packed books in this
great military saga by going to Amazon.com and searching
for *Martin Archer military stories*.

There is also an interesting alternative good read for
those who enjoy military fiction. Michael Cameron Adams
found the last three novels of the *Soldiers and Marines*
saga so eerily accurate in their likelihood to occur that,
with Martin's permission, he has rewritten *War Breaks Out*
to set it in the near future when America's military

become involved when a new war breaks out in Europe as a result of a refugee crisis and Russian meddling.

War in the East

Tensions were already high when Sergeant Willy
Williams stood up and increased them even more by firing
a round from his flare pistol. Then he dropped down
instantly and hugged the ground as his flare flashed
upward and lit the night above us with its distinctive click
and pop.

Everyone else, meaning me and the eight Russians
troopers Willy and I were camping with, were already out
of our little two-man tents with our weapons ready. We'd
been out of them and flat on the ground with our weapons
loaded ever since we first heard voices in the distance.
Hopefully we are in a circle and facing outward so we do
not shoot each other if push comes to shove.

There was a streak of light from our little camp as
Willy's flare went up—and it ended about two seconds
later with a loud pop; and suddenly it was so bright around
us that it was as if the sun had suddenly come out. *Jesus,
they are all around us. We are in the middle of a bunch of
Chinese.*

The Chinese infantrymen streaming down the slope on both sides of us could see the streak of light as the flare went up. So they instantly knew exactly where we were even before the flare lit us up and let everyone see everyone else.

"Hold your fire," Lieutenant Bao instantly shouted. "Do not fire."

He was too late. The nervous Russians opened up on the suddenly visible Chinese and the Chinese instinctively began firing back. There was a lot of screaming and shouting that could barely be heard over the roar of the AK-47s we were all carrying.

The result was inevitable. The heavily outnumbered Russians were annihilated and the Chinese took heavy casualties, much of it as a result of their own friendly fire.

I fired a few rounds at a couple of Chinese soldiers near me and heard the first few seconds of the firefight. Then a tremendous punch hit me in my left side.

Chapter One

The beginning of trouble.

The war with Russia and the Eastern European countries ended almost as quickly as it had begun. The Soviet Union fell apart and the survivors of the Eastern European armies returned home. Hungary and Czechoslovakia were immediately occupied by forces from the United States and Britain. The Germans stayed in Germany to avoid inflaming local tensions; besides, they had more than enough on their plate as a result of taking over East Germany and its devastated and corrupt economy.

But then things began to change. Hungary and Czechoslovakia quickly renounced their pact with the Russians and applied to re-join NATO and the European Common Market; so did Poland which had defied both the Russians and the west by remaining neutral during the war. The other Eastern European countries quickly followed suit and East Germany reunited with West Germany once again.

Two weeks later everything went to hell in a hand bucket. The peace deal fell apart—because the Soviet

Union fell apart. We had a peace treaty with an entity that no longer existed.

The collapse of the Soviet Union had been long predicted but the speed at which it occured was totally unexpected. The Warsaw Pact's military defeat in Germany turned out to be the straw that broke the camel's back of a political system already overburdened with corruption and an unworkable economic system.

Whatever the cause of its collapse, the Soviet Union came apart at the seams. It happened quickly and caught everyone by surprise. One after another, over a period of little more than a couple of days, the non-Russian members of the Soviet Central Committee flew back to their original homes and proclaimed themselves to be their country's new president "until elections can be held."

As a result, all of the nations that were part of the Soviet Union are free and independent states from Latvia and Lithuania in the west to Uzbekistan and Tajikistan in the east. And Russia continues to occupy millions of square miles of land east of Lake Baikal which the Chinese say belongs to them.

In fact, the same old Soviet bureaucrats are still in power throughout Russia and in many of the newly independent states of the old Soviet Union. And they still do not have a clue as to what to do.

******

Militarily things were really a mess. The Soviet Union's large and technologically obsolete military was quickly divided up among its nation states, even its nuclear weapons and rusting naval fleets. There was no rhyme or reason to the division. Each of the former Soviet states ended up with whatever military equipment and nuclear bombs were in its territory when the Soviet Union fell apart.

The result was inevitable: Russia became a failed and repressive state with a much weakened military and a slowly collapsing economy run by the corrupt remnants of the Soviet bureaucracy and KGB, a party of crooks and thieves according to Russia's political dissidents.

Even worse, today Russia is still totally cut off from its vast eastern territories bordering China and North Korea. In a way I was responsible for Russia being cut in two. I was the one who ordered the destruction of the bridges over the rivers in the middle of Russia so the Soviet armies attacking Germany could not get reinforcements from the east as they did years ago to help Moscow win World War Two.

Being cut off from its eastern provinces is significant for Russia. It means that if war comes in the eastern half of Russia, the Russian military will have to fight it out with the Chinese with the troops and equipment it has on hand at the border and what it can airlift in with the decaying remains of its battered air force.

Russia's only alternative would be to ship reinforcements and supplies all the way around the world to the Port of Vladivostok on the Sea of Japan or to one of the small fishing ports immediately to the south of Valdivostok and even closer to North Korea. All those ports are served by Russia's single east to west transportation system, the Trans-Siberian Railroad and the roads and power lines that run, or used to run, along its right of way. That service remains important in the east even though the Trans-Siberian was destroyed in the middle of Russia—it means Russian military supplies and reinforcements can still arrive by sea at Vladivostok and be sent inland to the eastern half of Russia via the railroad.

Unfortunately, both the Trans-Siberian Railroad and the road along side of it run close to the Chinese border. That is important because if there is a war with China both the railroad and the road are virtually certain to be cut before meaningful amounts of reinforcements and supplies can reach Vladivostok. Once that happens, the entire eastern half of Russia, everything east of Lake Baikal, will be totally cutoff from Moscow and on its own. And that is the crux of the problem—if there is a war with China, the Russians will have to fight with whatever they have on hand with no hope of getting reinforcements and supplies.

1969 was the last time the Chinese invaded Russia. It was an attempt to retake the land China claims Russia illegally seized in the disputed Ussuri River area. The Soviets fought them off by moving some of their then-modern military equipment and more than a dozen additional army divisions and a number of naval infantry brigades eastward across Russia on the Trans-Siberian railroad.

But now the Chinese aspirations and abilities are significantly greater and Russia's ability to counter them is significantly weaker. And because NATO took out so many of the Trans-Siberian bridges in the recent war, Moscow can no longer send reinforcements and supplies to the eastern half of Russia by road and rail. Today Moscow can only send help by air and via the Vladivostok docks and hope it will be enough.

There is one ray of hope. The dozen or more additional Russian divisions sent east in 1969 to fight the Chinese are still there with all their equipment and so are the Russian Marines; they are there because that is where the West German teams of airborne engineers stranded them by blowing up so many of the Trans-Siberian railroad and road bridges in central Russia west of Lake Baikal.

Russia's basic problem is simple. Another war with the Chinese is coming and this time it's not going to be a mini-war fought over a relatively small amount of land in the Ussuri River basin.

At least I think it is coming; the Chinese have got to be looking at the lands they claim in eastern Russia as low lying fruit with not much in the way of a Russian army or air force to defend it.

******

The collapse of the Soviet Union and the Warsaw Pact should have been the end of Russia as a military problem for the United States. But the American Secretary of State, fifty six year old former senator Barbara Hoffman, a statuesque woman with rigidly coiffed hair, quickly negotiated a replica of the deal with the Russians which included a lot of nuclear disarmament promises neither side had the slightest intention of keeping. Then the Senate hurriedly ratified it in late night vote in exchange for the withdrawal by the President of several of his Supreme Court nominees.

"A reasonable price to pay," exulted the Secretary of State at the time. She saw her efforts to obtain an agreement to begin nuclear disarmament talks and establish peaceful relations between Russia and the United States as her crowning achievement. It will be the basis for her presidential campaign next year when the current President's second term ends. *And she is touted to win even though, according to my old army buddy and now Secretary of Defense, Dick Spelling, who obviously does not like her, no one should ever vote for a woman who has her hair done by welders.*

Our Vice President, former Marine Captain Bernard B. "Bernie" Carey, will likely be Hoffman's opponent in the primaries. At least that is what the media pundits are saying. Carey split with the President and signaled his opposition to the new treaty by refusing the entreaties of the White House to speak out in support of it.

The United States has another problem, and it is a big one: All of the former Soviet states and their Warsway Pact allies and most of the NATO countries, except Britain are refusing to sign Secretary Hoffman's new treaty. Only the United States, Britain, and Australia are committed to help the peace loving Russian communist crooks and thieves in the event the peace loving Chinese communist crooks and thieves send the Chinese army to retake the lands Russia seized years ago with various one-sided "treaties" when the Chinese were weak and distracted by internal strife. *It certainly makes life interesting.*

******

Our new treaty with Russia and its rapid ratification created a great deal of political stress and even a brief flurry of impeachment talk by a couple of publicity seeking congressmen. It all started when I was dumb enough to allow a CBS news reporter to interview me when I was visiting Campbell Barracks, the Heidleberg headquarters of the American Forces in Europe.

I was there to see how the repairs were going. As everyone now knows, Campbell Barracks is the American army's peacetime headquarters and got heavily damaged when Russian Spetsnaz troops infiltrated West Germany and stormed it at the beginning of the war. They hit the virtually empty building in the hope that it would remain an important headquarters after the war started. It was not. *I may be dumb but I am not that dumb.*

* * * * * *

Campbell Barracks was still reverberating with the sound of hammers and filled with the smell of fresh paint when the CBS reporter and her camera crew found me talking with the German contractor supervising the work. I was there because we were about to begin moving back in. When we do, because the head of the United States' European Command automatically becomes the NATO Commander, the current NATO headquarters in Brussels will return to once again being a ceremonial headquarters filled to the gills with self-important generals and politicians holding meaningless meetings and issuing insignificant orders and memos.

Actually, now that our army is without a real enemy in Europe, Campbell Barracks won't mean much either. It really does not matter. I will keep an office there but I certainly won't spend much time there. Brussels is closer and has better food—and I do not intend to spend much time there either.

In any event, the CBS reporter asked me why I supported the new treaty with Russia. I told her I did not support it; and then I foolishly shot my mouth off by going on to say that no one had asked me about it and that it just does not seem right to help a vicious and undemocratic government stay in power, particularly one which is grossly incompetent and started a war to distract its people from its economic failures.

Well, goddamn it, that is the truth. Those self-serving sons of bitches killed and wounded many thousands of our fine young men and women and traumatized hundreds of thousands more.

CBS ran the interview on *Sixty Minutes*, the talking heads said it was important, and the proverbial shit hit the fan. It seems the Secretary of State and the former congressman serving as the President's Secretary of Defense, without the President's knowledge, had privately led key members of the Senate to believe that America's military leaders had been consulted, and that we had agreed that using such a treaty to establish a permanent peace between the United States and Russia was the right thing to do. The senators are well and truly pissed, thankfully not at me.

I sure as hell was not consulted and I am pretty sure Dick Spelling, my old army buddy and the soon to retire Chairman of the Joint Chiefs, was not consulted either. At least that what Dick told me over hamburgers and beer at his place the other night.

But who said what hardly matters to those of us who are in the military. For better or worse, the new treaty has been ratified by a well-meaning Senate whose members did not want either another war with Russia or a couple of political activists as Supreme Court justices. That their ratification of the treaty in exchange for the President withdrawing his nominees made it quite likely we'd end up sucked into a war with China seems to have escaped them.

Me? I have got everyone concentrating on getting our troops back home from Europe. Even more importantly, I am trying to make sure our casualties get the best medical care and our troops do not get kicked out on their asses by our politicians and military bureaucrats when the American military downsizes—as has always been the case when a war ends and the military's bureaucrats can make their lives easier by getting rid of those who did the fighting.

What's my plan? I am going to retire when my term as the American Forces Commander is over and spend more time at home with Dorothy and the kids and maybe do a little writing. It's time to get the upstairs bathroom fixed and go shopping for a new car.

Chapter Two

The reception.

There was quite a crowd waiting outside the new military passenger terminal on the tarmac of the Bonn airfield on this wet and overcast summer morning—and rightly so. It has been a couple of months since American and British troops moved into the Warsaw Pact countries and the shooting stopped. Things have settled down a bit and at the moment I am watching Dick Spelling's plane, a big shiny Boeing 747 with the "United States of America" painted on its side, as it taxis up to the terminal. Literally hundreds of dignitaries and officials are on hand to greet him.

Dick is the Chairman of the Joint Chiefs and the German military is going all-out to welcome him. Little wonder; America's armed forces played a big role in the defeat of the Soviets and the reunification of Germany. A German military band has been tuning up for the past ten minutes and, as the big 747 taxied up to the waiting crowd, a long red carpet was in the process of being unrolled in front a substantial honor guard.

Dick's arrival was a sight to behold. The German President, its Chancellor, and a band and honor guard were waiting in the empty hangar at the end of the red carpet. Waiting with them are numerous German and NATO generals and admirals, more than I had ever known existed. Then Dick and his wife, Marjorie, came down the stairs and everyone saluted, clicked their heels, and shook hands while the band played German military marches and various national anthems. Dorothy and I gave Dick and Marjorie big hugs.

I almost upset the dignity of the occasion when one of the welcoming speeches was droning on, the one by the elderly German President with the absurdly dyed black hair; I leaned over and whispered in Dorothy's ear "I think I must have some German blood in me—when the band was playing those marches I had an irresistible urge to pick up a weapon and march eastward." She giggled and a little old German lady with bluish hair standing behind her gave her a very stern look of disapproval.

******

After the welcoming speeches concluded, and many hurried trips to the hangar's clean but rather spartan toilets were enjoyed, a long cavalcade of black Mercedes and Cadillac limousines carried everyone to a reception and dinner at the Excelsior in downtown Bonn.

Yes, Cadillacs. This is an important affair and Cadillacs are still thought to represent the peak of American automobile elegance. At least that is what GM's advertising has been claiming for years and the State Department seems to have accepted.

It was an altogether happy occasion with lots of smiling acknowledgements and mutual congratulations exchanged by high ranking officers and dignitaries of various countries. And that is as it should be—their troops, at least those of some of the countries whose senior officers and political leaders are here tonight celebrating the victory, fought and died together and quickly won. Some of the officers and officials present, but damn certainly not all of them, even contributed to the victory.

The reception and banquet that evening went on and on in the Excelsior's grand ballroom. First there was a long reception line in which Dorothy and I had to stand for almost an hour along with the NATO Secretary General, Dick and Marjorie, and a host of German generals and dignitaries. That was followed by a sit down dinner in an ornate and smoke filled hotel ballroom and many warm and friendly speeches in German and English.

As far as I am concerned formal receptions and dinners are inevitably boring. Perhaps the most significant thing about the reception, at least so far as I am personally concerned, is that it is one of the few times I have ever worn my medals and decorations. Actually, it was the only formal dinner I have ever attended other than when Dorothy and I got married and her mother insisted on holding a big wedding. Being in the little detachment near

Riems and forgotten all those years did have a few benefits.

"It turns me on to see you wearing all your medals." Dorothy whispered into my ear as the desert was being served."

"I am so glad," I whispered back.

"It also turns me on when you are not wearing them."

"I am even gladder."

She took my hand and squeezed it so I leaned towards her and gently squeezed back. *Of course I squeezed back.*

******

It was not until much later that evening that Dick and I finally had a chance to talk privately in his hotel suite at the Excelsior Hotel Ernst, the big downtown hotel across the street from the Bonn Cathedral. Dorothy and I were staying in the suite next to Dick and Marjorie's. *Tomorrow night it will be the American military's turn to host a reception and dinner in the very same Excelsior ballroom— Bonn is a small city and does not have many alternatives.*

"You know, Chris," Dick said to me, "I think one of the reasons I got such a big welcome is that the Germans are about to tell us that they will be so busy expanding

Germany to include the East Germans that they will be unable to help us if the Chinese attack Russia."

"Unfortunately you are right. They are not going to ratify Hoffman's new treaty. Not a chance. Klausen said as much yesterday when we met to go over the provisioning of our troops in Hungary and Czechoslovakia. He is a bit embarrassed because of all the help we provided during the war, but not enough, and the message is clear."

"What do you think the odds are?"

After thinking about it for a moment, I replied. "Well, I'd say the odds are zero that the Germans will help the Russians. They hate them now more than ever; hell, they are more likely to help the Chinese if it comes to a war between China and Russia. And I do not blame them. I do not know what the odds are that the Chinese will attack. I really do not."

"Join the club. Neither does the CIA nor any of our other intelligence agencies."

"But Dick, I hope I am wrong, but my gut instinct is that we weakened the Russians so much that the Chinese will attack. It's their big chance. The question is where and how soon and with what?

And then I added, "and the even bigger question is what the hell are we going to be ordered to do then?"

******

"Can we talk here?" Dick asks as we picked at a complimentary room service snack of cheese and crackers in the living room of his suite. It was something that neither of us needed after the big dinner at the reception. Our wives, and particularly Marjorie Spelling who had flown for hours just to attend the dinner, were tired and already in bed.

"Yeah," I told him. "One of my guys ran a bug detector and left us a jammer."

So I turned on the jammer. It's sort of a radio-looking thing in a small grey box and it immediately began making the rising and falling buzzing noises that indicate that it's okay if we talked. So we did. First we talked about what matters most—our troops in Germany, Hungary, and Czechoslovakia and how soon we get them home. They all want to go home and I am still a bit pissed that the President returned the commercial planes to the airlines before I could them all back to the States.

Then we sat around the table in the suite's sitting room and talked about the new treaty with the Russians. One thing we agreed immediately is that, because of the new treaty, the Detachment in France, the little group of planners and doers which I'd organized and led for so many years, should stay open and focus on helping the Russians fight off the Chinese if it comes to a war. If it was up to me, I suggested to Dick, I'd say fuck them both and let them fight it out. But it is not up to me, and that is probably a good thing since they have both got nukes.

So now, instead of German officers helping our guys quietly plan and gather equipment and supplies to defeat a Russian invasion, we will probably have Russian officers helping our guys quietly plan and gather equipment to defeat a Chinese invasion. Sheesh.

Keeping the Detachment open raises a minor and easily solved problem. My surprise appointment over hundreds of more senior officers to become the Commander of American Forces in Europe, which automatically made me the NATO commander during the war, has more than three years to go. Someone else will have to run the Detachment instead of me.

Dick and I talked it over and it was a no-brainer. We quickly agreed that Dave Shelton was the right man for the job. Dave's the long time Special Forces colonel who had been with me at the Detachment from the beginning. He took it over, and finally got promoted, when I was bumped up three ranks at the last minute and got the European command. Another of the original Detachment guys, Mike Morton, the SEAL who almost got thrown out of the navy because he never finished his college degree, will be his number two.

Many of the original team will probably stick around simply because they won't know what else to do. Our biggest gap will be replacing the handful of German officers who functioned as our armor experts. This time we will use Americans. Dick and Mike are already scouting for the right guys.

******

Dorothy and I were snuggled up in the big king size bed when the bomb went off in front of the hotel.

Chapter Three
The terrorists.

Dick and I both jerked open our doors to the green carpeted hallway at almost the same time and looked at each other. We were both wearing pajamas and the hotel's fire alarm bells were clanging. The security detail assigned to us to keep gawkers and reporters from bothering us, a young Marine captain and a sergeant, were standing in the hall. They looked extremely nervous. I was not exactly yawning with boredom myself and neither was Dick.

I wanted to see what was happening so I rushed back into the room and pushed the drapes open. A crowd of people was beginning to stream out of the front of the hotel and into the little park across the street in front of the cathedral. They were dressed so they must have been in the hotel bar or lobby. The street itself was empty except for a big garbage truck parked right in front of the hotel.

Something did not feel right. *Oh Shit.*

"Out into the hall," I shouted at Dorothy who was struggling to get one of her arms into a bathrobe sleeve. I did not wait for a response - just grabbed her much too roughly by the arm and dragged her out into the hall in her flimsy nightgown. We were both barefoot.

"Dick," I shouted. "Heads up. I think we are being hit. Get Marjory out of that room. Now." It was a command even though he ranked me. "And you two," I shouted to the wide-eyed captain and sergeant, "stay alert. I think we are being hit."

A few seconds later Dick and Marjorie rushed out their room. The Spellings and the two Marines, now with their pistols drawn, were close behind us as I rapidly pulled a very confused and barefoot Dorothy down the hall. I was desperate to get her away from the front of the building.

"Run," I shouted over my shoulder at the others, "Run."

There was "exit" sign over a hallway door that opened on to a stairwell with metal stairs. I ripped the door open. "In here and hurry," I shouted as I pulled Dorothy through the door. It was an emergency exit onto a metal staircase in a concrete block stairwell. The hotel lights flickered off and its battery powered emergency lights had come on a few seconds after the explosion. The stairwell was lit by a single emergency light fixture over the door.

"Give me your pistol," I ordered the captain as he dashed in behind us. "And go help General Shelton get his wife down the stairs. Hurry, goddamnit, hurry."

Dorothy was standing on the landing just inside the exit door as I took the captain's pistol, grabbed her arm, and started down the stairs. And then I stopped on the first landing below my floor. I could hear people running *up* the metal staircase. And they were wearing shoes. *Too soon for rescuers and they are coming the wrong way.*

* * * * * *

Leaning against the staircase wall was the best place I can find to wait to see who is coming. I crouched a bit and held Dorothy back around the corner with my left hand while I aimed the captain's pistol at the landing below with my right. I put it at waist level and about three feet ahead of the turn in the stairs. Just as I aimed, a machine gun carrying figure in a ski mask bounded up the stairs and into view. I shot him twice. Two taps. "Stay here," I said to Dorothy as he was falling.

His gun clattered as it dropped on to the concrete landing. He bounced off the wall and fell flat on his back on the stairwell landing about ten steps below me. I could hear more steps coming up fast. *At least two more*, I thought as I bounded down the stairs three at a time and swept up the stubby little submachine gun the guy had been carrying. I dropped the Marine captain's pistol as I picked up the submachine gun and kept going until I reached the next landing. It looked like an ancient Uzi from Israel.

The stunned would-be shooter was obviously wearing a vest. He was already gathering himself to get up as I passed by on my way down to the next landing. So as I dropped the pistol and picked up his weapon I made it a point to step on his neck instead of jumping over him. I stepped as hard as possible and I think I might have felt something snap. *Probably just wishful thinking.*

It was a really old Uzi and I was already aiming it and ready to fire as I bounded on down the stairs. The man in the ski mask coming up next was not quite so ready. When he came around the corner below me, I hit him with a three or four round burst right in the ski mask; and he got off a two round burst into the wall as his finger instinctively tightened when he got hit. The wall behind him was instantly splattered with blood and body parts.

And I suddenly realized I could not hear anything. *Shit. I am deaf.* So I bounded on down past the almost headless shooter and hunkered against the concrete wall a couple of landings down. All I could do now was wait and be ready to shoot.

"Captain, I need you down here now," I shouted up the stairs. "Hurry.".... "Hurry."... "Dorothy, you stay there."

It seemed like forever and time was standing still but it was actually only a couple of seconds later that the Marine captain slid in behind me like a ball player stealing second base.

"Grab that Uzi" I shouted over my shoulder just as I realized he had already scooped up the second shooter's weapon. "Good man." The name on the captain's uniform was Solomon.

"Watch the front, Solomon. They have got vests. Be ready to fire. Can you hear anything? Footsteps?"

I was looking back up the stairs towards Dorothy when Captain Solomon suddenly fires an ear shattering sustained burst. There was no answering fire. *Christ, I sure heard that.* Then there was absolute quiet. I could not hear a goddamn thing.

"Sergeant," I shouted up the stairs. "Watch our rear. Cover our rear."

There was an answer but I could not make it out.

"Dick, any casualties? There was another answer and I could not make it out either. *Shit. I am really deaf now.*

Then I followed Captain Solomon as he slowly crept down the stairs to the third shooter. He obviously was not wearing a vest—Solomon virtually cut him in half. Then I watched as Solomon moved down past the guy he shot to take a position on the next landing further down. *Very smart move.*

After a couple of seconds I shouted, "No casualties here. Everyone stay down."

Seconds later a wide-eyed and red faced Dick Spelling inched down the stairs towards me. He had a questioning look on his face and a blood covered Uzi the third shooter no longer needed. I shook my head. Then the staircase and the entire building literally shook from what was obviously a massive explosion.

Ceiling tiles rained down on top of us and the emergency lights flickered and went out. Almost instantly the battery powered emergency lights came back on again. They were in the corner of the staircase above each floor's emergency exit door.

"Time to hunker down and wait," I told Dick. "Can you cover the rear and send Dorothy and Marjorie down a bit so they are between us?"

"Right," Dick snapped as he nodded and began to move cautiously back up the stairs. *I heard him faintly. Good.*

"Captain Solomon, are you okay? Can you hear anything?"

"No Sir. Nothing" I could barely hear him even though he was only about ten feet away on the next staircase landing and shouting. "I think it's clear in front of us."

"Do not take any chances," I said in a stage whisper. "Hold your position."

It was quiet as I cautiously started to move back up the stairs towards Dorothy and the Spellings. Then suddenly the door on the landing started to open two feet away from me. I whipped the Uzi around and a young woman in a hotel bathrobe screamed and leaped back as the gray painted metal door slowly began to close. It was obviously a self-closing door.

I stepped to one side as I pulled the door open and darted a quick look. The hall was rapidly filling with terrified people and some of them had multiple cuts and were bleeding. They must have been looking out the window when the second bomb went off and got hit by the glass. *Oh fuck. What if there's another or the damn building collapses?*

"Get in here...Hurry...It's safer inside the staircase," I ordered loudly with a beckoning motion at the walls of the stairwell. Then I repeated the explanation and command in German and French. *I know about collapsing buildings from Alaska and its earthquakes. Stairwells are the safest place to be.*

A dozen or more very confused people poured into the narrow stairwell between me and Dorothy. Many of them appeared to be stunned. Then a woman screamed a short little scream and began sobbing deep choking sobs, almost hiccups; she was looking up the stairs to the next landing and saw the blood running down the metal stairs from what was left of the mostly headless shooter who'd supplied Solomon with his Uzi.

Then everyone started talking at once. "Silence," I roared in my best drill instructor's voice. The talking abruptly stopped. For a few seconds there was no noise except for two women who were quietly sobbing. A couple of steps up the staircase two absolutely terrified children with bright eyes and tears streaming down their faces were holding on to a white-faced woman with bleeding cuts on her face. She looked to be in shock and so did the kids.

Several of the men looked like military types. *Probadbly came in for the reception.*

"Who is military?" I aske loudly in English and then in German. Several hands waved. I pointed to the one nearest the door, a stout fiftyish man with very short graying hair.

"Open the door just a little and watch the hallway," I ordered in German. "Shout and move away from the door if you see an enemy."

"Captain Solomon," I shouted. "I'm going to check things out up above." *I am going to get Dorothy and Marjorie...* "Hold that position," I ordered. I could smell smoke; electrical wires were burning somewhere.

* * * * * *

I walked quickly up the stairs through a rapidly widening puddle of blood from the almost headless shooter. Dorothy and Marjorie were two landings up with Dick crouching on the stairs just above them with his Uzi aimed upward.

Dorothy and Majorie were watching me anxiously as I climbed the stairs up to them. Marjorie looked particularly haggard and confused. I could see the Marine sergeant further up. He was crouched on the landing above the one Dick was on with his pistol pointing up the stairs. Our rear was covered. *Dorothy's okay. Thank God.*

"Okay," I said loudly so the sergeant could hear me. "I think we are good to go. Time to start down. Let's go."

I led the way and we began moving down the stairs towards the group of new arrivals who were jammed together on the landing below. I pushed right on through them with Dorothy and Marjorie following right behind me. We all began to walk down the stairs together.

Dorothy was horrified and began trembling as I her and Marjorie down past the two attackers I had killed and then past the man Solomon killed. Unlike the two I killed, the third guy did not appear to be wearing a vest. The long burst Solomon fired literally cut him almost in half and messed his face up pretty good too. *And rightly so.*

I looked back as Marjorie gagged and threw up against the stairway wall after she stepped over what was left of him. The next time I looked back Dorothy was holding Marjorie by her arm and carrying a child.

I was not taking any chances on the walk down. We became a compact little military unit on the move. Dick and the Marine sergeant, Willow according to his name tag, brought up the rear walking backwards with their guns pointing up the stairs behind us.

Captain Solomon and I took the lead, leapfrogging each other from one staircase landing to the next, each time waiting for the other to get into position and nod. Dorothy and Marjory were walking down behind us along with the people I originally ordered into the staircase.

Almost immediately terrified and injured people start entering the staircase both ahead of us and behind us and the shouting and noise in the narrow little stairwell got louder and louder. *Or maybe it has always been that loud and my hearing's starting to come back.*

About four floors down we were able to relax slightly as we began to run into more and more people and could hear others moving down ahead of us. So I began helping an elderly lady who seemed to be confused and let others go past me as I waited for Dorothy and Marjory to reach me.

Many of the people on the staircase seemed to have been injured—lots of bloody faces and upper bodies cuts. It was quickly apparent from the loud conversations and the type of injuries I was seeing that most of the casualties were the result of the second explosion.

People heard the first explosion and opened the drapes of their rooms to see what was going on when the second and much bigger explosion occurred. *Just as I had done moments earlier.* The second blast took out most of the windows in the front of the hotel and sent shredded glass into the rooms and the people in them.

Despite the increasingly crowded staircase we continued to move down the stairs cautiously even though the staircase has become so crowded that Solomon and I were no longer alternating in the lead. It was a real mess with those who were not seriously injured trying to do their best to help those who were. There were lots of groans and sobs and much loud talking. Most of the children were crying hysterically and so were several of the women.

After a while, I do not know how long, there was a lot of shouting and police with their pistols drawn came puffing up the stairs. I heard them coming and put my Uzi down on the step I was standing on. As soon as I saw them on the stairs below me I shouted up to Solomon, who was on the landing above me, that police were coming up the stairs and he should put his weapon down so they do not mistake him for a terrorist.

"And go back up and make sure General Spelling puts his weapon down and before the police reach him," I shouted. *We do not need any accidents to make things worse than they already are.*

A policeman coming up the stairs, an anxious looking tall skinny gray haired guy in a green uniform with a pistol in his hand, saw the Uzi on the stairs and looks at me carefully for a split second. But I was in pajamas, barefoot, and with Dorothy on one arm and using the other to hold up an elderly woman wrapped in a blanket with blood streaming out of a bad scalp wound.

Two floors later I turned the unknown woman over to a big German fireman who promptly swept her up into his arms and began carrying her down the steps ahead of me. We followed him down. The smell of smoke was getting worse.

Dorothy and I stopped and stood back against the stairwell wall to let others pass until the Spellings reached us. Dorothy and Dick were now each carrying a crying and totally naked young child. Girls. There was an anxious and bloodied woman in a nightgown clinging to Dick's arm who looked like she might be their mother. Marjorie Spelling had wild eyes and seemed to be clutching Dick's other arm for dear life. The two women were using the staircase railings to steady themselves as they came down with Dick in the middle carrying the child and the women hanging on to his arms for dear life.

I started to take the child Dorothy was carrying but she was clinging so desperately to my wife that I stopped trying and satisfied myself by taking Dorothy's arm to help hold them both up and guide them down the stairs. I left the Uzi on the stairs. Hopefully no one will trip over it.

As we got down towards the bottom of the stairs I could see over the heads of the people in front of me and saw periodic puffs of smoke coming in from an open door leading to the outside. As I got closer to the bottom I could see the people coming down the stairs ahead of me exiting through the door into a narrow smoke-filled and dimly lit alley.

We slowly and gingerly walked in the crowd through the doorway to what we hoped would be safety. It was not.

As soon as Dorothy and I cleared the door we could see by the flickering light of a light somewhere above us that people were having trouble walking. Little wonder. The alley was filled with debris and broken glass and most of us had bare feet.

For some reason, as I went out the door and started down the alley an image flashes through my mind of my experience years ago when I tried to walk out of the Mekong River barefoot to get into Laos. Probably because the first thing I did was step on something sharp. Goddamn it.

"Watch where you walk but keep going," I shouted unnecessarily to caution everyone as I tried to pick my way forward in the jostling crowd. "The damn alley is filled with glass and debris."

We could somewhat see the ground in the red and flickering glare of a fire somewhere above us. We were engulfed in smoke in a dark and dingy alley running between the hotel and the building next to it. The shouts and noise were almost overwhelming.

It was absolute chaos as we hobbled down the alley towards the sidewalk and the relatively fresh air in front of the hotel. Firemen and rescue workers were flooding past us in one direction to enter the alley and get into the building from the alley door we came out of; fleeing guests and hotel workers, those with shoes on, were going in the other direction and desperately pushing past us in an effort to escape.

What we saw when we finally limped out of the alley was enough to make me want to turn around and go back inside. A police emergency truck with mobile lights was illuminating a scene of unspeakable horror. Bodies and body parts, injured people, and rescue workers were everywhere. The distinctive rising and falling whooping sound of German police and fire sirens was overwhelming and growing louder and louder amidst the shouting and the screams and cries of the injured.

The second bomb, the really big one, had obviously been in the garbage truck. It caught the hotel guests exiting the hotel and assembling in the street and the park in front of the hotel. The truck had disappeared and so had some of the guests; replaced by a hole in the road.

Dorothy suddenly screamed and sat down in the middle of the street still clutching the child as the rest of our little party gathered around her. Her foot. I run my hand over it and felt a protruding shard of glass.

"Hold on," I told her as I pulled it out and nicked my hand in the process. She gasped as I pulled it out but did not say a word. "Sorry," I grunted.

We were about ten yards out of the alley and I could hardly walk due to the cuts and punctures on my bare feet.

"Captain," I said to Solomon as he came up behind me, "You and the Sergeant go on with the children and their mother. Get all three of them to a hospital.

"But whatever happens, you two stay together and do not let the kids be separated from you or their mother or from each other. Not by anyone for any reason. Go with them in the same ambulance and stay with them until you are absolutely sure they have been treated and won't be separated. I do not care how long it takes.

"When you are absolutely sure they are together and safe, I want you two to report to me or Colonel Peterson at my headquarters at Brussels as soon as you are able. Both of you. Together. And call me or my aide, Brigadier

Hart, instantly if anyone fucks with you or tries to separate them."

Solomon nodded as he reached down and gently took the crying child out of Dorothy's arms. Then he hurried on towards the ambulances and their flashing blue lights. Sergeant Willow was carrying the other child and holding their mother by the arm as they followed close behind.

We sat there for at least a minute with Dick and Marjorie standing next to us—Dick leaning over to catch his breath with his hands on his knees and an obviously shocked and disoriented Marjorie clinging tightly to his left arm and looking like she might keel over. My feet hurt and Dorothy could not stand up because of her foot. *Well we cannot stay here.*

I pulled myself to my feet and picked up Dorothy and, in one big move, swung her over my shoulders in a fireman's carry.

"Up you go, Love. It's time to get your foot fixed. Hold on. We are almost there."

Dick grabbed my arm to steady me and help hold me up as we staggered off to the less congested left side of the little park where we could see a rapidly growing number of ambulances, fire trucks, and police cars. Marjorie was clinging to Dick's other arm. For a few moments I could see Captain Solomon and the children ahead of us until they disappeared into the growing crowd. My feet felt numb. *What happened? Who are they and why?*

That is what I was thinking when off somewhere off in the distance I heard Dick. "We made it, Chris. Let them take her."

Things were a bit hazy at first but then I realized Dorothy was holding my hand and we were careening through the streets in an ambulance with a whooping siren. Dick and Marjorie were sitting opposite us with some kind of attendant on his knees in front of Marjory. Dick had his arm around her and she had a blank and almost relaxed look on her face.

* * * * * *

Chaotic is the only way to describe the hospital emergency room. Dorothy's a doc and her terse words of medical jargon to a harried German nurse caused her to turn away to find someone more seriously injured to help. We had been triaged and rightly so.

Dorothy and I sat on the floor with our backs against the wall with Marjorie between us while Dick rushed off to find a phone. He needed to report our whereabouts and, more importantly, find out whether this was an isolated incident or something else.

Five minutes later Dick returned.

"Isolated incident so far," he reported as he squatted down to hold Marjorie's hand for a moment. "But I raised the alert level just in case."

We still had not been treated, and rightly so, when almost an hour later a dozen or more medics from the Eleventh Airborne's base hospital on the outskirts of Bonn poured into the room and begin putting us on stretchers. They were all business and seemed to know what they were doing.

"Stay and help them here," I ordered the master sergeant who appeared to be in charge of the medics as they loaded us on their stretchers.

"Leave your medics here to help with the wounded as long as they are needed. All we need is a driver."

Marjorie and Dick rode with us in an Eleventh Airborne ambulance as we rushed out of the hospital's parking lot with its siren screaming so loudly that we could barely talk.

******

A huge staff and a large group of armed guards and obsequious officers were waiting as our ambulance rolled up to the base hospital's emergency room door; the word as to who was being brought in had obviously reached the hospital before we arrived. They were prepared to treat us for everything from cancer to athlete's foot and fight off a sustained enemy attack while doing it.

Men and women in green smocks put Marjorie and Dorothy on their stretchers first and zipped them inside. Then they helped Dick step out so they could get to me. As they lifted my stretcher and began to pull it out of the ambulance, I heard the words and an unforgettable unique rasping voice that brought a big smile to my face—and absolutely appalled looks to the faces of the hovering colonels and generals.

"Jesus Christ, it's the dumb sonofabitch who always forgets to duck. What the fuck are you doing here?" *Big Joe! All five feet two of him.*

I am smiled and tried to roll over and sit up as a couple of orderlies leaned in to pull the stretcher out.

"Wait a minute."... "Lemme see his feet"... "Shit, that is nothing"... "Well kiss my ass. You mean I got out of bed in the middle of the night just for those piddly little scratches?"

I know damn well what Joe was doing even if most of the people standing around us do not. He is a combat medic reassuring a wounded guy he is going to be okay. I have heard it from him before and said it myself, even when it was not true.

"Big Joe," I say as I leaned forward and we beamed at each other and shook hands warmly, "I pulled a big shard of glass out of Dorothy's foot. It may have broken off in there."

"Got it. I will go tell the techs. She'll need an X-ray. Be right back."

******

They had my feet under an X-ray machine by the time Joe came back. "Dorothy's fine except she may need some painful stitches if we cannot close up the big cut with the new sticky tape we are using. X-rays came up negative. No glass. And we have General Spelling's wife resting in a room with a nurse watching. She is really beat. Maybe in shock."

"Gonna a tough night?" I asked.

"Looks like it. We are starting to get a lot of casualties. Mostly wounded civilians, the triage overflow from the German hospitals. Lots of lacerations. What the hell happened?"

"Some kind of attack. Bombs and guys wearing vests and carrying old Uzis. I have no idea who or why but they sure as hell meant business."

"Russians you think? Pissed because we cleaned their clocks?"

"I don't know. Maybe, but I don't think so. It just does not figure."

"Well somebody is seriously pissed at somebody. The TV in the lobby says there are hundreds of casualties, many dead and seriously wounded. Says there are reports of a shootout and dead terrorists. You see any of that?"

"I sure did. On our way out we met three of them coming up a stairwell carrying Uzis."

"No shit. What happened?"

"Got the first one with a borrowed pistol and then picked up his Uzi and hosed the second with it. A fast thinking young Marine captain, guy by the name of Solomon, did a good job on the third."

"Sonofabitch. You're still picking up guns!"

Then, because we had not seen each other since Dorothy and I got married, we caught up on what we've been doing while the X-Ray technicians dithered about and decided to take another picture. After the war the army sent Joe to nursing school for a bachelor's degree and turned his warrant into a major's commission when he got his RN and some kind of practitioner's license. He is a lieutenant colonel now and the hospital's administrator, and the very proud father of two teenage boys.

******

Dave Shelton showed up the next day to take us home. He brought an ambulance, two army plainclothes sedans, and four husky Marines from the Detachment's guards to "carry luggage and stuff," by which he meant me and Dorothy being picked up in the wheel chairs we were in and carried down the front steps of the hospital. It seems Big Joe called him and told him we are going to have trouble walking for a few days.

Dorothy and I rode home together in the back of one of the sedans and dozed most of the way holding hands. I had spent much of what was left of the night on the phone to Brussels and Washington and I was suddenly really bushed. *Hmm. I Wonder how Big Joe knew to call Dave?*

Susan and John Christopher come bounding out of the house as we drove up and were literally jumping up and down and into our arms before we could even get out of the car. Marlene and Ingrid, the two Swedish au pairs stood beaming in the background along with a smiling and relieved Jackie Shelton. She had rushed over with Mike Morton's wife, Shirley, and moved into the guest bedroom as soon as she heard the news. Mike had come over and stuck around with a couple of his shooters "in case there might be a problem." *Jeez, I am glad to be home.*

Marlene and Ingrid were a treasure and we needed them more than ever. For the next couple of days or so Dorothy would have to use a crutch to stay off her damaged foot and I could hardly walk at all; both my feet were too sore to stand on, particularly my left foot which apparently got been rather thoroughly cut and punctured by glass and other crap as we walked through the alley and the chaotic square across from the hotel.

We had a lot of help in addition to Marlene and Ingrid. Dave left a couple of the Marines to provide any "heavy lifting and help around the house" that might be necessary; and Big Joe sent a nurse lieutenant in the ambulance. She would stay in the guest bedroom.

The Detachment's Marines are carrying their MP5s and will stay outside and be periodically relieved until we are sure what happened and why. Dave is no fool. Even after all the calls no one knows what the hell is going on.

******

"But why did it happen?" That was the question I put to the two deferential German police inspectors after I had gone through a very complete step by step description of what I did during the attack. After speaking to Captain Solomon and Sergeant Willow, the inspectors had driven down from Bonn to visit me at home rather than wait until I got back on my feet.

I am still at home because it hurts like hell to walk, my left foot particularly. And I want to stay home with Dorothy and the kids. I can tell she is still upset and her foot's still sore and inflamed. A couple of the Detachment Marines help me get down the stairs so I could sit at the kitchen table and meet with the inspectors.

According to the German police inspectors, they are part of a massive investigation into one of the worst terrorist episodes in Europe in many years. *If you do not count any of the wars.* Almost a hundred people were killed and several hundred more wounded, some terribly. Most of them when the garbage truck exploded. Coming as it did so soon after the war, it raised all kinds of questions.

NATO, the FBI, Germany's Federal Police, and half a dozen or more other agencies appear to be running parallel investigations and everyone is, so they all claim to the news readers and talking heads we've been watching, cooperating with everyone else. Even the Russians are reported to be cooperating according to the talking heads on CNN.

The German police inspectors arrived promptly at ten in the morning along with a couple of bleary-eyed FBI agents who had flown in last night from Washington and an equally weary colonel from the Pentagon's legal branch who said Dick Spelling sent for him "to assist you with any legal questions."

"We are not yet sure why they did it, Herr Generaldoktor, but it increasingly appears to have been directed at the Chief of the Turkish General Staff, General Bezman. He was in a room on the floor below yours."

"Turkey? Why do you think so?" I ask quizzically.

"We have identified two of the three attackers you killed. They were guest workers from Turkey working in a German factory that manufactures light fixtures. The Turkish government has identified them as religious fanatics who belong to a militant Islamic group dedicated to overthrowing Turkey's secular government."

"Both have been in Germany for several years and are wanted by the police in Turkey. We are still trying to identify the third." *I bet they are. Soloman really wasted him. Acted fast. Did a fine job.*

"So far as we can tell, the plan appears to have been to cause an explosion in the park in front of the hotel. Then slip up the back stairs and kill General Bezman in the confusion when the second and bigger explosion went off."

"And their plan might have succeeded in all the confusion, Herr General, if not for your reaction to seeing the garbage truck parked where it should not have been."

The two FBI agents and the Pentagon lawyer just sat in on our kitchen chairs and recorded the police inspectors' interview. They did not ask a single question or say a word after they introduced themselves. *Weird.*

Chapter Four

A Moscow surprise.

It was about three weeks after the terrorist attack and I had just finished spending three excruciatingly hot summer days in Washington getting carefully briefed about the new treaty. The briefing was okay in that it was complete and I think I understand things a little better. What was not okay was enduring the mindless thoughts of the profane ex-congressman serving as the President's Chief of Staff. In any event, it was August 31st and I was bored to death and on my way to Moscow on an old air force Starlifter.

Major Terry Martin, a tall black Air Force Academy grad from Detroit and the Starlifter's pilot, knew all about the plane and its interesting history. According to Martin, Lockheed built the Starlifters for the air force to use as military cargo planes. But then someone in the company had the bright idea of also selling them to the airlines as passenger jets. So it built this one as a demo model with passenger seats and passenger windows.

Martin smiled, and I smiled back, when he explained that the plane flew but Lockheed's commercial sales did not. So the Air Force accepted it as part of their cargo plane order and uses it for either cargo or passengers or as a "combi" carrying both. Carrying both cargo and passengers at the same time makes it a rare kind plane, according to the major. He is obviously quite proud to be flying it.

I did not have the heart to tell him that it was not rare to me. I had seen many a "combi" when I was growing up in Alaska. Alaska and Wien Airlines both had 737s set up to simultaneously carry both passengers and cargo. It was quite common to see people getting off the rear of the plane in a village hundreds of miles from the nearest road while a fork lift simultaneously unloaded snow machines, pickup trucks, and pallets of Coca Cola and groceries from the front.

On the Starlifter with me are my old friend and long time deputy at the Detachment, and now its new commander, Dave Shelton; an army colonel by the name of Arnie Miskin who will be our interpreter; and my new aides: Colonel Jack Peterson, Captain Ari Solomon, and Staff Sergeant Andy Willow. Mike Morton was holding the fort at the Detachment while Dave was traveling with me.

There were also three signal corps warrant officers on board who were experts at using the plane's satellite communications equipment, two brigadiers from the

Pentagon Dick Spelling insisted I bring along "for their expertise," and a protection detail of a half dozen or so Marines from the Detachment under the command of Gunnery Sergeant Robinson.

Miskin is no more a military officer than I am the man on the moon.

Also on board was an English-speaking Russian navigator in the cockpit who sternly announced that we were about to enter Russian air space and therefore must close the window shades and not take pictures.

The Russian security measures are surprising in that they are seriously out of touch with reality and modern technology—the war is over; we are now supposed to be allies; and the United States and Russia abandoned aerial photos in favor of satellite photos many years ago.

Our reception in an isolated aircraft parking area of Moscow's Sheremetyevo airport was quite formal and correct. On hand to meet us were a couple of Russian generals and an American army brigadier named Selden, the recently reestablished embassy's senior military attaché.

The stony faced Russians saluted, shook hands with obvious distaste, and escorted us to a line of waiting limos. *The Russians obviously do not like the idea of working with us any more than we like the idea of working with them. Unfortunately our masters have spoken and there's not much we can do about it.*

I immediately got some idea of how well we were going to work together when the Russians began arguing with the Russian-speaking American brigadier who was the military attache at the newly reopened embassy; they wanted us to ride with them in the Russian limos instead of with Brigadier Selden in the embassy limos.

Everyone was talking and arguing at the same time so I raised my hands for silence and rather loudly said, "Everybody shut the fuck up. I will ride with the Russians and the rest of you ride with General Selden." Then I tromped over to the Russian limo and got in before the driver could run around and open the door.

It was my first visit to Russia and the ride through Moscow was a real eye opener. The summer air in the "people's paradise" was foul; there were long lines of poorly dressed people in front of some of the stores; and the streets were jammed with dilapidated cars and trucks belching smoke.

Traffic just inched along. Not us. We zipped down one of the several empty lanes in the middle of the road all the way to the hotel where we would be staying, the Metropole.

My entourage showed up thirty minutes later. The embassy cars traveled on the crowded lanes used by ordinary Russians and had to stop for the lights and traffic cops.

******

The two stony faced Russian generals marched with us into the Metropole's ornate lobby, waved us towards the front desk, and promptly disappeared. We checked in and were totally ignored for the rest of the day except for a number of obvious "minders" camped out in the hallway and in the hotel's lobby.

Exactly at eight the next morning there was a knock on my door and one of the minders informed me that we have been invited to visit to the Russian Military Ministry. I took Dave Shelton and the two Pentagon brigadiers with me. I also brought along the Air Force Colonel, Arnie Miskin, to act as our translator. *Arnie may be wearing a uniform and a colonel's chickens but dollars to donuts he isn't military.*

We were met with a great deal of military formality and ushered without delay into the office of Marshal Petrov, Russia's newly appointed defense minister. He was a large and affable elderly man with lots of medals from the "Great Patriotic War" and a cigarette constantly in his hand.

According to Miskin, Petrov was brought out of retirement when his predecessor was removed as a result of losing the recent war with NATO.

It became quickly obvious that Petrov did not have a clue as to what to do with us. At first I was not even sure he knew why we were in Moscow. After a few banal inquiries about our flight and accommodations he offered us coffee. I accepted with a polite nod.

After finishing our coffee we were ushered into to a smoke filled conference room for a totally useless briefing. We sat on wooden chairs around a long wooden table with the briefers standing at a podium next to the end of the table. Colonel Miskin was sitting next to me to be my translator. He constantly whispered into my ear whatever was being said by the Russians.

A group of Russian officers and a couple of eagle-eyed civilians in shabby suits were also in the room. They just sat there staring at us and puffing away as the briefer provided even less information than a stateside television newscast. It was mostly a political history about how peace-loving Russia has successfully developed Russia's far eastern lands by following the correct path of socialism and the evil Chinese failed to develop theirs because they deviated from the superior Russian path which is, obviously, the only way to go.

Can these guys really mean this bullshit? I don't know whether to be worried because these guys are so stupid or be insulted because they think I am stupid enough to believe them.

There were two briefers and they took turns saying nothing about the Russian forces on the border and the Chinese forces they face, and then dodging or filibustering the questions I tried to ask.

This is useless. I am going to fall asleep if this nonsense continues. These people have either been ordered to tell us nothing or are totally ignorant about the state of affairs along the Chinese border and do not want to admit it.

Finally, I have enough of the briefers' historical reminisces and stories of Russian superiorities and interrupted, rather sharply.

"We are not asking about the latest official version of Russian history, Colonel, We are asking about the Chinese forces you face and how you think they might attack and, much more importantly, where and when and how the Russian General Staff thinks Russia will need our help in responding.

"And even more importantly, much more importantly," I emphasized, "what military preparations and support can we and our allies contribute that will discourage the Chinese from attacking Russia in the first place?"

After a brief pause and a wave my hand to disperse a plume of smoke that was drifting in front of me, I continued.

"If you do not know the answers, say so. But stop the bullshit about how your bureaucrats and political theories are better than theirs and everybody else's. It has nothing to do with your military situation and, quite frankly, no one in the world, including me, believes a word you are saying."

I know a lot of soldiers smoke but this is really carrying things too far. I have been in smoke filled rooms before but never like this. Is this a deliberate effort to drive us off for some reason or are these guys just crude and rude?

Then I added a somewhat sarcastic comment. "Listening to you two," I said while shaking my head in disgust at the two briefers, "I am beginning to think that there is no reason for me to be here and I am insulted that you think I am so stupid. What you are doing is convincing me that Russia's new treaty with America is of no importance to Russia, just the best excuse you could find to end a war you were losing badly and never should have started. If that is the best information you have for me, I am going to call it a day and go home.

"Marshal," I said, turning and addressing a now somewhat disturbed Petrov who is sitting across from me with a translator constantly whispering in his ear. "Don't these officers understand that my government, at the request of your government, has ordered me to find out what America, and particularly our forces in Europe, can do to help Russia prevent a Chinese attack and defeat it if it occurs?"

Then I leaned forward and continued very pointedly before he could answer.

"We can not do that unless we know how you think the Chinese will attack and how Russia would like us to help if they do. And why are we even sitting wasting our time if Russia does not want us or need us to help discourage the Chinese from attacking?"

I spoke harshly because I was more than a little pissed at the Russian rudeness and having my time wasted. Prior to leaving Washington I had sent a request for a Russian briefing as to how the Russians evaluated the ability of the Chinese to invade Eastern Russia and how and where they thought such an attack would occur. I also asked how the Russian military thought we might be able to help them prevent it or repel such an invasion if it came.

What I had been handed by one of the minister's military aides when we arrived is a folder containing a sightseeing schedule for our visit to Moscow's tourist attractions and a long shopping list of supplies and equipment the Russians would like us to provide "to help deter the Chinese."

I scanned the Russian shopping list again when I finished speaking. *It looks more like a list of office equipment and consumer electronics that would make life more enjoyable for some bureaucrats and their wives rather than what the Russian military might need to fill in their supply gaps so they can fight the Chinese.*

Then I quickly scanned the list again, and sort of shook it at Petrov a little, and rather sarcastically asked him a question.

"If we provide this, and I am certainly not saying we can or will since it does not seem to have much military significance and looks more like a shopping list for your wives. But if we do, how and where will it be used and by whom and what are the priorities for its delivery?"

"That will have to be worked out by General Sholakov and his staff," was the elderly marshal's answer through the young Russian officer doing the translating. "He is in command of our forces in the East."

Okay, that makes sense. He is the general who will lead the fight if the Chinese invade. I nodded in agreement.

"Okay. That makes sense. But then why am I here listening to this bullshit and being offered guided tours of Moscow's tourist attractions instead of having a meeting to discuss military matters?"

******

Our schedule suddenly changed. There was a knock on my door and one of the minders in the hall, the bald one, handed me a new schedule. Tomorrow morning, instead of taking us to see Moscow's tourist attractions, the Russians are flying us out to visit General Sholakov at his headquarters at Khabarovsk in Russia's Far Eastern Military District. It is Russia's biggest military district because it covers the entire eastern half of Russia, everything west of Lake Baikal including Russia's borders with China and North Korea.

So much for touring Moscow to see stuffed communists.

And then the plan change again when I called everyone into my hotel room and informed them that the Russians would be flying us out in the morning to meet General Sholakov, their commander in the east.

Barry Goldman, the air force brigadier, shook his head negatively and strongly advised against flying in any Russian plane with Russian pilots. He was quite convincing.

"The damn things are not safe; they are poorly built and poorly maintained and their pilots are badly trained. You can go if you want to but I have still got a couple of children at home and I am not going. I will resign first."

A response like that from a pilot who twice flew combat tours of more than a hundred missions over North Vietnam is more than good enough for me; we would either go in the Starlifter or we won't go.

******

Our minders pretended to be quite upset and astonished when I informed them the next morning at the hotel breakfast buffet, without saying why, that we would either fly out to Khabarovsk to see Sholakov in our own plane or we won't be going at all. The minder who could speak English immediately assured me that their planes are well built and their pilots' training is excellent and so is their aircraft maintenance.

The briefers in Washington were right. The hotel rooms are bugged.

Things got resolved when I put a face saving spin on it for them.

"Look at it this way," I said to the interpreter of the seedy looking guy with the chin stubble who seemed to be the most senior minder of all. "Our plane is relatively large and part of the interior is configured for passengers. We have seats available and can take some Russian troops with us.

"That means you can take some pictures of the United States Air Force carrying Russian troops to the border and use them to let the Chinese know the treaty is in effect."

Five boring hours later about sixty Russian officers and half a dozen photographers arrived at the Starlifter. They had been bused in from a military field south of Moscow to go with us. They would be flying with us to Khabarovsk instead of going there in their own transports.

It is probably my imagination but I think some of them are greatly relieved to be flying with us in addition to being extremely curious.

Our old air force Starlifter was ready to go as soon as the Russian photographers stopped flitting about taking pictures and got on board. It was going to function as our office with its crew and our protection detail sleeping on board in sleeping bags even if other accommodations are offered. The Air Force was emphatic about the crew never leaving the plane. The story I got from Goldman is that the Air Force does not want the Russians to get a look at its avionics.

Why the Air Force is so concerned about the plane's avionics escapes me. The Russians got more than enough samples of them a couple of months ago when more than a hundred of our planes went down on their side of the battle line. Must be something else.

It was a long and boring trip except for the absolute astonishment of the Russians when they discovered the Starlifter's toilets actually work and our flight attendant sergeants brought them hot meals from the galley. They were also totally amazed and did a lot of chattering and pointing when they realized that all the Americans, even the enlisted men in the aircrew and the Marines, had cell phones and were talking to their families in America.

******

Our reception at the Khabarovsk airport was very different from Moscow's. General Sholakov, the Commander of the Far Eastern District, all of Siberia east of Lake Baikal in other words, showed up with a band and honor guard at the airport. He appeared to be truly pleased to see us. Two hours later it was abundantly clear as to why he was so pleased—his army was literally falling apart.

Sholakov's problem is simple: The Russian army in the east, which is primarily dispersed all along the Chinese border, has not been paid or resupplied for months. Sholakov was running out of food and many of his men and their families have been reduced to eating their awful combat rations. *If you think ours are bad, and they are, you ought to try eating the Russians' sometime.*

Sholakov could not get any food for his men and their dependents because nothing has been shipped in from Western Russia for months because the Germans cut the Trans-Siberian Railroad during the recent war. They cannot even truck it in because the road system, even after all these years, still has unbuilt gaps in it in the middle of Russia. And he cannot get food from the China because the Chinese never reopened the border after the 1969 Sino-Russian mini-war over the Ussuri River islands. *In other words, his command is truly fucked up and rapidly disintegrating.*

There was still some food left in the stores and warehouses of the civilian sector, Sholakov reported. But he cannot buy any because no one will accept the Soviet rubles he has.

"My men," Sholakov reports with a resigned sigh, "are beginning to trade their fuel and their trucks and Jeeps for food and cigarettes."

The only thing the Russians have in abundance is ammunition and very large quantities of diesel, gasoline, and aviation fuel located in a number of large underground storage depots that were scattered about in the Russian East.

"And that is the only thing that has saved us, Christopher Ivanovich—my men along the border are trading gasoline to the black marketeers for food and cigarettes for themselves and their families; my men in the interior and their families cannot even do that. They have been reduced to eating old combat rations which date back to the Great Patriotic War."

Jesus, the situation is much worse than we thought. The Chinese can just waltz in here and these people will fall apart if even half of this turns out to be true

First things first. I immediately sent off an encrypted report to Dick Spelling describing the situation with a request that he have his staff begin a full court press to come up with a fast fix for the Russians' food and payroll problems.

I also forwarded a copy to Mike Morton with a request that the Detachment work the problem of a Chinese invasion from the perspective that the Chinese will probably have to use the railroads in northern China, the ones that used to connect to the Trans-Siberian, to move their tanks and heavy equipment up to the border.

Our signals team, a couple of warrant officers headed by a Mr. Liska, sent the report via satellite and seriously scrambled to avoid any possibility of a Chinese or Russian interception. I labeled it preliminary and tentative. *Mentioning a possible Chinese use of their railroads is enough to tell Mike what needs to be planned and organized.*

****** *China*

Meetings of the Military Committee of the Chinese Communist Party are going better these days, Li Ping mused to himself, as the speaker droned on. It all began to change when Mao died and his successors finally retired. Now, under the party's new leadership, China can finally begin to take its rightful place as the leader of the world. *And I, as the Chairman of the party, will show the way and be famous forever.*

Our tool, of course, will be the Red Army. And the first step will be to regain the Chinese territories the Soviets illegally occupied years ago while we were busy fighting to make the revolution, all of them.

Victory will be doubly sweet because it will avenge the defeat we suffered in 1969 when Lin Biao ordered our army to retake some of the Russian-occupied lands along the Ussuri River. I had to go along with that moronic decision despite it being doomed to failure because we were too weak and the Soviets too strong.

Yes, this time things will be different. Then it will be India's turn in the Himalayas and America's turn in Korea and Taiwan.

"Oh…. I am very sorry, comrade Bo, I was distracted by thinking very deeply about what you said about our wheat supplies. Would you repeat that last bit about the Russians please?"

****** *The Russian east*

On our first evening in the Russian east, Generals Woods, Goldman, and Shelton and I along with our interpreter, Colonel Miskin, had dinner with General Sholakov and his deputy, General Turpin. We talked for hours. Miskin and a young Russian lieutenant named Basilof, who looked about fifteen and has incredibly bad teeth, acted as the interpreters. *I wonder how Miskin learned Russian.*

It was an interesting evening. Sholakov laid on quite a spread for someone who claimed to be running out of food, and there were several bottles of vodka and packs of cigarettes on the table and more on a sideboard. The Russians chain smoked; the Americans did not smoke at all except for Woods—he matched the Russians puff for puff.

All the vodka and liquor on the table surprised me. That is because before we left Washington I made it a point to have our embassy inform the Russians that I was unable to drink due to a recent medical problem. Obviously that word did not reach Khabarovsk.

Sholakov apologized when I explained my problem. "I am sorry, my friend, I did not know."

"But do not let my problem stop you, Yuri Andreovich," I said. "Here, let me pour a glass for you."

Everyone except me drank a lot and the Russians and General Woods smoked until a smoke-filled haze filled the room.

It isn't true that I have a medical problem and do not drink. But the Russians' consumption of alcohol is legendary so before I left the States I decided that, if it turned out to be true, it would be better if I kept a clear head while everyone else was losing theirs.

After a bit we settled into a long discussion of the Chinese order of battle Sholakov expects to face and the Russian troops and planes he has available to counter them. As you might imagine, we were particularly interested as to where his units were currently located and where and how he thinks the Chinese will hit him and with what.

There was no question about where Sholakov and Turpin think the Chinese will attack: They expect to be hit right here in Khabarovsk where their headquarters and the administrative offices for the Russian East are located. And, because they know all the Chinese officers are taught to be followers of the strategies and tactics of Sun Tzu, just as the Russian officers are, they think it will be soon because their defenses and logistics are so weak.

At one point Sholakov drew himself up into a pose of fake pomposity and laughed and poked fun at himself and Turpin.

"And we are sure it will be here because, being splendid military men who remember exactly word for word what they taught us at the military academy, Eugene Eugeneovich and I have been able to apply the superior aspects of Marxist-Leninist reasoning to foretell the future even better than Gypsy fortune tellers."

He and Turpin respond to his speech by absolutely roaring with laughter at each other and clicking their glasses. Even Basilof smiled. It was contagious and we all smiled with them.

Then, after a pause for another sip, Sholakov continued with a sigh and a disgusted shake of his head as if he could not believe it.

"Fortunately, we also have spies in China who say they are coming and satellites that sometimes work long enough for Moscow to take pictures of their preparations and send them to us.

"There is no doubt about it, Christopher Ivanovich, the spies and the satellites are right — the Chinese are coming."

Then he told us how he intended to respond.

Sholakov's basic plan was simple and classically Russian from the days of Napoleon and World War Two—hold them as long as possible at the border and then retreat along the railroad leaving a couple of divisions at Kharbarovsk to be another Stalingrad and a couple at Vladivostok to be another Moscow. Then, when the heroic defenders and the partisans he leaves behind bleed the Chinese invaders enough, he'll counterattack and try to wipe out the Chinese armies when they get far enough from their depots and run low on supplies.

According to what Colonel Miskin was translating, the Russians expect the Chinese to initially hit their forces somewhere near Vladivostok in the hope that they will move some of their forces down from Khabarovsk to protect the port.

"But I won't move them and weaken our defenses," Sholakov said somewhat drunkenly, "and they know it. But they will try anyhow.

"Vladivostok and the region around it will have to hold them off on their own," Sholakov told us. "The admiral there has enough naval infantry troops and sailors because of our 1969 war with the Chinese. So I am in the process of withdrawing the four army divisions that are there to support them. I am bringing them here to fight the Chinese when they come.

"Our illustrious navy and its naval infantry should be able to hold Vladivostok because the navy can resupply it by sea".... "if the navy has any ships left and if it can find enough fuel for them," he added with a sigh.

"Here," he says, "right here in Khabarovsk where we are sitting is where the main Chinese attack will come—because of the Trans-Siberian Railroad. They will try to cut it here or south of here because it is the railroad, not the port at Vladivostok, that is the key to keeping the Russian lands that are south of the Amur River.

"My problem, my dear American friends, is that the Chinese are desperate to get some of the Russian lands in the Amur drainage that I am supposed to defend. They do not need the port because they have plenty of ports; they need the land because the population they have to feed is so large. So they will keep coming and coming and coming and we won't be able to stop them even with the help of your America—unless we use our nuclear weapons." *Nukes?*

That was the bad news. The good news was that Sholakov has a lot of firepower to use before he and his generals have to decide whether or not to go nuclear:

twenty five infantry and air assault divisions and about a thousand planes of which, he estimates, three or four hundred are not operational at any given time for one reason or another. He also has twenty or so isolated and mostly off-road "independent brigades" which are the Russian equivalent of the American National Guard. "We are bringing them in now," he told us.

It sounds like a lot, but it means the average division has to defend more than a hundred and fifty miles of border. Worse for him, the average Russian division is not anywhere near as big or well-equipped as ours; about twelve thousand men.

Then our discussion turns personal. Sholakov admitted it was hard to know what tactics the Chinese will employ when they attack. They have, after all, never been in a real war against a real army except for Korea. Then General Woods piped up.

"Well Sir, General Roberts here is a real expert on how the Chinese behaved there and lost the war."

Then Woods turned to me and explained.

"Yes sir. At the War College we studied the way you defeated the Chinese army you faced. Defeated them repeatedly. It was masterful."

"And we speculated in class as to whether the Chinese would learn from their defeats and adopt new tactics or keep their defeats a secret and repeat them. Either way it would seem to apply here."

Sholakov got so excited he waved the cigarette in his hand about and sprinkled cigarette ashes onto the bread and sausage slices on the table.

"Please General, tell us what happened." He was very drunk and very insistent.

So I did. With the young lieutenant constantly translating as I spoke, I explained how battlefield casualties and the lack of officers resulted in a young enlisted man ending up as a task force commander—and how he got ready to fight the Chinese even though the old general trying to direct the war from thousands of miles away denied they would enter the war.

Sholakov and Turpin sat absolutely enthralled as I explained how I placed my men at a choke point some distance from the border through which I thought the Chinese would have to pass—and then fortified the hell out it with everything I could lay my hands on, including the men and equipment I gathered up from the fleeing and disorganized troops who reached us after the Chinese broke through their lines.

Sholakov and Turpin listened with intense seriousness.

"It is amazing," I told them, "how fast the morale and fighting ability of exhausted young men recovers when they reach prepared positions and are given lots of weapons and ammunition along with a good night's sleep, a couple of hot meals, and clean clothes."

Sholakov literally gasped out loud and puts his drink down when Woods told him how my little force of about a thousand men, and a couple of thousand more I pulled out of the retreat and placed into positions my men had prepared for them, had suckered the Chinese into repeated human wave attacks that we were able to chop up and destroy.

General Roberts' men, Woods explained with drunken satisfaction, so devastated the seventeen divisions of the Twenty First Route Army that the Chinese high command ceased trying to take the transportation corridor General Roberts and his men were defending—and then took so long to reroute its invasion force to the only other corridor that it was defeated there also.

"Fuck your mother. Can it be true?"

"And there's more to it than that," General Woods said emphatically and more than a bit drunkenly.

"When the Chinese abandoned their attack on his troops and withdrew them to attack elsewhere, General Roberts promptly counterattacked by personally leading some of his men and armor on a three day raid through the Chinese lines and into the Chinese rear. It destroyed several more Chinese divisions and so disrupted the flow and timing of the Chinese troop movements that they could not get together a large enough force to break through in the other corridor."

Sholakov and Turpin get increasingly enthusiastic as I spent the next couple of hours reliving those desperate days and describing them step by step.

When I finally stood up, exhausted and jet lagged and ready for bed, a now totally sober Sholakov jumped up and gives me a great manly hug.

"If I believed in God, Christopher Ivanovich, which of course as a good communist I could not, I would say a prayer thanking him for sending you to us."

******

Later the next morning we met again for another briefing and to ask each other a good many follow up questions. We had gotten up early to prepare the questions and we had a lot of them. So did the Russians.

Three hours later we boarded the Starlifter and flew straight to Washington over Alaska and Canada with a midair refueling along the way. Miskin, Woods, Goldman and the Signal Corps warrant officers stayed behind in Kharbarovsk as observers.

It was a long trip and I spent most of it writing a report for Dick Spelling and the President. But before I sacked out on the floor in a sleeping bag for a few hours I was able to have a long conversation via the satellite phone with Dorothy and the kids before they went to bed. *They are back to the States for a short visit and are staying with Dorothy's mom and dad. I really miss them.*

Washington and the media seem to have finally awakened to the very real prospect we may soon be involved in another war and it may turn nuclear. As a result, even though it is July 4th, as soon as we landed I was taken to the White House to brief the President and the National Security Council. Spelling himself met me at the airport so we could talk privately on the way in.

"The President's beside himself, Chris. He and everyone on his staff are now afraid Russia will start a nuclear war if the Chinese attack and they cannot be stopped by conventional forces."

Then he got really cynical.

"It's so bad even the President's Chief of Staff is worried; he told me yesterday that he is terribly concerned that if there is another war the President's standing in the polls will go down." *It escapes me why that is important since he is in his second term and cannot run again.*

"Well," I responded, "I do not get it why his standing in the polls matters but the President's certainly right to be worried about a war and so is everyone else. As it stands, Sholakov has control of the nukes in the Russian Far East and probably will not be able to hold the Chinese without using them. He is spread too thin and the morale of his men is terrible. Christ, they have not been paid in months and their troops and families are running out of food."

"Is it really that bad?"

"Worse, so far as I can tell."

"Any chance Sholakov was deliberately exaggerating his problems to get more help from us?"

"Maybe," I replied, shaking my head, "but I do not think so. I just do not know."

******

We reached the White House in time to make the regular morning meeting of the National Security Council. All the Service Chiefs were present and the session started about an hour after we arrived. The atmosphere seemed tense and I got the impression of serious disagreements and lots of hostility and anger between some of the members. There was a lot of nervous smoking.

The President, on the other hand, was his usual affable self, quite warm and welcoming. He just sat there and ate jelly beans and listened. *Yes, jelly beans.* Fortunately, he seemed aware of seriousness of the situation and the possibility we might get dragged into another war.

On the other hand, according to Spelling, he is not like so many of our politicians who seem to think that making a speech expressing concern about a problem is the same as actually doing something about it. This President, Dick told me at the beginning of the recent war, actually thinks there is more to his job than just making speeches.

"Good to see you again, General Roberts. We are all looking forward to the big victory parade this afternoon. Seems appropriate that we are having it on the Fourth of July, does not it? But first, we liked to hear your report and recommendations about the situation in Russia. What do you have for us?"

"Thank you, Mr. President. I wish I was the bearer of good news. But I am not." Then I laid it all out.

There was an appalled silence and everybody just looked at everybody else when I finished. Then I decided to offer some suggestions.

"But I do have some suggestions as to how we might get out of this mess and reduce the chance of being pulled into a nuclear war."

Everyone sat up and leans forward. *That got their attention.* The President was interested, very interested. "What do you recommend, General?"

"Well Sir, I think we should try to break the scenario that leads to a Russian nuclear attack on the Chinese that drags us in. We can do that, I think, by officially abandoning the Russians and unofficially giving them a lot of help.

"The scenario we do *not* want probably goes something like this," I explained, emphasizing the 'not.'

"The Chinese invade to reclaim the lands they say the Russians stole from them; the Russians try to fight them off and we honor the new treaty by helping the Russians; our aid is not enough so the Russians concentrate their forces and retreat down the Trans-Siberian Railroad; the Chinese then concentrate their forces to fight the concentrated Russians; the Russians then use tactical nuclear weapons to eliminate the concentrated Chinese forces; and then China responds by nuking Russia and, God forbid, Russia's new allies, the U.S. and the U.K. and Australia.

"So the question," I continued, "is how do we break that terrible scenario?"

Then I explained that appealing to Moscow not to use nukes should certainly occur and, unfortunately, is almost equally certainly not going to work or have much impact on the final decision. When push comes to shove, I explained, Moscow is not going to have much to say about whether or not Sholakov and the Russian generals in the east use their nukes.

Russia's big problem, I explained to the President, is that a few months ago, during the war, we helped the West Germans totally cut the Eastern half of Russia off from the rest of Russia. We did that by helping the Germans destroy the Trans-Siberian Railroad bridges west of Lake Baikal. As a result, the Russians can now only supply their forces in the east by air or by extremely long sea voyages around the world to Vladivostok.

Unbelievably, I told the President and the council members, there are no roads, absolutely not a one and there never have been, connecting the eastern half of Russia with western Russia and Moscow, only the railroad. All they have got in the middle of Russia are unconnected road segments running along the railroad right of way in some places.

"I know it sounds unbelievable, Mister President, but it's true—they never finished filling in the gaps in the road system so that a truck could drive all the way from Moscow to the Chinese border.

"In other words, Mr. President, all the Russians have is a road system that cannot be used and a railroad that is going to need years to rebuild the bridges we helped the Germans destroy; it is either an airlift and sealift or nothing."

Worse, I explained, the old communists in Moscow, the guys the Secretary Hoffman's been dealing with, do not have much power to affect what happens in east. Probably little or none; they have effectively left Sholakov and his troops out there on their own and the Russians in the east do not appreciate it or think much of Moscow.

Sholakov made it pretty clear while we were visiting him that he and his commanders will do whatever they think they have to do to stop the Chinese no matter what the bureaucrats in Moscow may want them to do.

"Sholakov was quite specific about Moscow's lack of authority in the east. He told me flat out that he and his officers do not intend to go down in history as the men who lost the east because they blindly followed the orders of a bunch of corrupt and far away party bureaucrats."

Then I gave the President a summary of how I saw the situation.

"What all that means is that the key to solving our riddle is not in Moscow— it's in the east." ... "So the question is, how do we discourage the Chinese from coming across the border, and if they do, which seems likely, how do we prevent or discourage Sholakov and his commanders from using their nukes?"

"There are two basic answers to our problem, one in the east and one in Moscow."

"In the east, as I see it, we need to help the stranded Russian generals be more effective—so they feel they can win, and can win, without using their nukes. One way we can do that is by helping them feed and pay their troops; another is by supplying them with whatever supplies and equipment they will need to tear up the Chinese railroads just as we supplied the Germans so they could tear up the Russian railroads a couple of months ago."

Then I turned to Moscow.

"In the west, I think we need to seriously consider disentangling ourselves from Russia in the eyes of the Chinese—by repudiating the treaty. Accordingly, it is my strong recommendation that we junk the treaty as soon as possible and certainly before the Chinese actually invade."

Then I leaned forward in my chair and spoke slowly and deliberately to give weight to my recommendation.

"As I see it, Mister President, our best bet is to help the Russians do to the Chinese what we helped the Germans do to the Russians. That means providing General Sholakov and his men with the food and money they need to sustain themselves and help them cut the Chinese railroads and highways so the Chinese cannot bring in enough supplies and reinforcements to defeat them." … "We do not need the treaty to do that. We can junk it."

There was a long silence. Then the arguing began.

The arguing lasted, and periodically got quite heated, until we had to break to get ready for this afternoon's big Fourth of July victory parade down Pennsylvania Avenue. It was scheduled weeks ago and it's a beautiful summer day. I am going to wear my battledress and march with the troops carrying my faithful old MAT-49. *It's the first parade I ever marched in and marching in a parade is one of the things on my bucket list.*

But first things first: Dorothy and the kids flew in for the big parade two days ago and were waiting at her parent's house in Georgetown. *And I cannot wait to see them.*

Chapter Five

Homeward bound.

Our flight from Andrews back to Reims on July fifth was long but enjoyable and full of domestic bliss. John Christopher sat on my lap and helped me read Doctor Seuss out loud for a couple of hours while his big sister and mother talked and laughed as they played cards—"go fish" and Monopoly. Finally, both the kids both fell asleep. Then Dorothy and I played bridge with Dave and Jackie until we landed

We were finally back home, the kids were asleep upstairs, and Dorothy and I are sitting together and talking. It was late in the evening and we were all seriously jet-lagged from the trip, especially the kids. Our home-coming fire is in the fireplace even though it was a warm summer evening. It felt good, really good, to get back to our own home after the trip to Russia, the big parade, and a visit with the grandparents.

I know. It's summer. But somewhere along the line it became a family tradition to light a fire in the fireplace whenever we come home from a trip.

"Do you remember when you told me the members of a family are like the cars on a freight train—all hooked together and going in the same direction?"

That was the question Dorothy asked as she leaned her head against my shoulder. We were sitting together in front of the old stone fireplace watching the flames flicker lower and lower as the wood burns down.

"Sure. It's true," I replied with a question in my voice. *Strange question.*

"Well, my love, in about six months we are going to add a caboose to our train."

******

After breakfast the next morning Dorothy was driven off to see patients at the Reims clinic and I drove out to the Detachment for a visit. It had not changed much since my last visit just before the war started. The only thing missing were the German officers. They got promoted and reassigned when the war started. They won't be back.

What suddenly changed was the Detachment's mission. Now it will try to help the Russians against the Chinese instead of helping the Germans against the Russians. *That is got to be the fastest about face in history that did not involving betraying someone.*

It was like a school reunion at the Detachment. Everyone was given the option to return after the war and almost everyone decided to continue, except the Germans who had served as our armor experts. They have gone on to bigger things and been replaced by two highly decorated American lieutenant colonels, Jack Marshall and Will Rutherford. Both of whom had distinguished themselves commanding tank battalions during the recent war.

Dave and Mike were the senior guys and had been with me at the Detachment since the very beginning. The good news, according to Dave and Mike, was that their wives and the other Detachment wives were tremendously pleased about the Detachment continuing to operate.

All the wives, like mine, obviously like living in slow and comfortable France despite its godawful bureaucracy and high prices. *Beats the hell out of living in military housing in the States, that is for sure. And both the local French school where Susan and Little John Christopher go, and the service school at Reims where most of the Detachment kids go, are a lot better too—more school days, more hours, more content, and teachers with academic degrees.*

In any event, we spent the morning eating donuts and drinking coffee and tea, looking at maps and aerial photos, and brain storming as to how America's military might help save Sholakov's Russian troops without putting

Americans on the ground to fight, and certainly never into or over China.

Some of the ideas were quite imaginative and worked well in the war that just ended. They might be useful if we have enough time to implement them, which we do not. The problem, of course, is that we do not have a clue as to the Chinese objectives or their order of battle or where their attacks will be concentrated. The CIA and NSA are working on it. So, it is safe to assume, are the Russians. *And they better hurry; we are rapidly running out of time.*

After listening to everyone, and reviewing what had worked and not worked against the Soviets, I ordered Dave and Mike to concentrate on identifying targets and preparing pallets of supplies and equipment for whatever engineers and swimmers the Russians can provide. Put it together, I told them, on the premise that the Russians will have no more than the next five weeks to get ready.

Our emphasis at this point, I explained, will be on helping the Russians cut the railroad and road bridges the Chinese will have to use to bring up supplies and reinforcements. That means both the bridges on the Chinese side of the border when the invasion starts and then the bridges on the Russian side behind the advancing Chinese. *Although I did not say it, that is probably all we can do to help the Russians hurt the Chinese when and if they attack.*

We will also, I told them, need to think about what we can do to help strengthen the Russians by bringing in supplies and reinforcements by air. What was left of the Russian navy can carry or convoy supplies from Russia and elsewhere to Vladivostok which, if Sholakov is right, may end up being rather quickly cut off and isolated with unusable airfields.

Most of the other responses will take more than five weeks to prepare. But we may want to prepare them just in case the Chinese delay their attack for some reason.

Everyone agreed that helping the Russians cut the railroads and roads the Chinese will have to use to get their supplies and armor into Russia seemed like the best place to start. So Dave and Mike were told to start gathering supplies and identifying which of the bridges the Russians will most need to cut and which they will need to protect; the new armor guys, Marshal and Rutherford, will work with the photo interpreters headed by Jack Riley to identify hiding places where Russian armor and partisan units can hide—and then emerge from them to cut up the Chinese rear.

Mike asked the sixty-four dollar question. He wondered if the Chinese know how we cut the Russians sector of the railroad and will take precautions against a repeat? Or will they, he asked, God forbid, run the same type of bridge cutting operation back against Sholakov and trap his forces between their cuts. *That, of course, is truly*

*the sixty four dollar question and something the Russians
will have to guard against.*

It was settled. Dave Shelton will be the Detachment's
liaison both with me and with the joint-services team Dick
Spelling is setting up in the Pentagon to work the problem.
*I have established a relationship with Sholakov so I am to
be his American point of contact. I will coordinate directly
with him via Colonel Miskin and our signals team, the three
warrant officers we left at his headquarters under the
command of Mister Liska.*

I only stayed at the Detachment for the meeting. Then
it was a helicopter ride to Brussels for a late lunch and a
briefing on how the troop withdrawals are going; then,
finally, it was another helicopter ride back home for a
family dinner and another round of admiring crayon
pictures, playing Monopoly, and reading *Doctor Seuss* out
loud.

*It was a wonderful evening and spaghetti with meat
sauce is my favorite meal. We watched television for a
while. Then both of the kids fell asleep on the couch and I
carried them up to bed.*

******

Only a few days had passed since I got back home and
it seemed we might already be running out of time. NSA
and the CIA both reported the Chinese have gone beyond

aggressively planning an invasion; they are beginning to stage massive amounts of troops, armor, and railroad equipment in the Chinese railroad towns along the Chinese railroad line that runs along the border near Khabarovsk. A similar staging of troops and equipment was also occurring on the Chinese border opposite the Russian forces on the Ussuri River, and there were reports of Chinese troops infiltrating over the border just as they did so many years ago in Korea.

Dick Spelling called me at home last night to give me a heads up. Both NSA and the CIA now say the Chinese plan to begin moving even more of their troops up to the border within the next thirty days, and, according to their analysts, will most likely try to cross it west of Khabarovsk and perhaps additionally somewhere between Khabarovsk and Vladivostok.

Both the CIA and the NSA say the Chinese will attack sometime before September first. According to the intercepts and intelligence analysts the Chinese have decided to go for a quick victory before winter really sets in and the Russians can get their act together.

But what is their ultimate objective? According to Dick Spelling, the CIA and military intelligence analysts are divided. Some think the Chinese are merely going to run a repeat of 1969 and once again try to take the Ussuri River lands whose ownership fell into dispute years ago when the river channel changed; others think the Chinese will go in south of Khabarovsk to cut off Vladivostok; and one or two that the Chinese may try to go all the way and take both Khabarovsk and Vladivostok and all the Russian land south of the Amur River. *What they all agree is that there is going to be a war and it's going to start soon.*

The big news, Dick said, was that in a couple of hours the President and the British Prime Minister would jointly announce that the United States and Britain are going to ignore the inevitable Russian protests and end their mutual defense treaties with Russia. Privately, according to Dick, this morning the President will call the Russians sometime today and assure them that we will continue to do all we can to help them so they won't have to use their nukes.

Dick says the President and the Secretary of State still do not get it that Moscow may not have much to say about whether or not Sholakov will use his nukes.

Sure enough, the President's Chief of Staff called about thirty minutes later to let me know the President will announce the repudiation of the treaty. The Secretary of State was with him and she assured me that she and her staff would all be working to prevent the use of nuclear weapons.

"How do you plan to do that, Madam Secretary?" I inquired in a very polite voice.

Secretary of State Hoffman promptly and rather proudly assured me that within the next three or four days she will personally fly to Moscow to meet with the Chairman of the Russian Communist Party.

"Assuming the Chairman agrees to do everything you ask them to do, how will that stop Sholakov and his generals from using their bombs?" I asked.

There was a long silence. Then she sayid "Well that is their problem, isn't it?"

I almost start to say something sarcastic. But then I thought better of it and did not. So all I ended up saying was "I certainly hope you are successful, Madam Secretary. And please do not forget to ask Moscow to send General Sholakov more reinforcements and supplies. If Moscow sends him enough, he might not feel it necessary to use his nukes." *Maybe I am learning how to be a politician.*

Interestingly enough, a few minutes later the head of the CIA called with the latest information on Chinese troop movements and, oh by the way, did you hear that we are cancelling the treaty with Russia and how do you think the Russians will react? *What was interesting was that the Vice President was sitting in his office and chimed in with a happy hello. I wonder what that means?*

"Well, Director, if you are asking how the Russian government will react, the answer is that I do not know and it probably does not matter very much. The important question is how will Sholakov and the generals in the Far Eastern Military District react?"

"And my answer to that," I said, "is that it will depend on whether they get enough assistance so that they think they might be able to defeat the Chinese with conventional weapons without having to use their nukes."

Then I continued and tried to explain.

"I think Sholakov will only use his nukes when he comes to believe he cannot defeat the Chinese by holding them at the choke points he has established, and then cutting the railroad and road bridges behind them so the Chinese cannot get supplies and reinforcements.

"On the other hand, what we have accomplished so far may be significant. *I hope.*

"Our willingness to actually help the Russians, instead of just making idle promises, has convinced Sholakov and his generals that it may be possible to defeat the Chinese without using nukes. At this point the Russian generals in the east seem willing to at least try to use conventional means to defeat the Chinese and push them back across the border".... "but it is likely that their willingness to forego using their nukes will last only so long as there is a chance their conventional arms will be successful."

"Do you think General Sholakov and his men can defeat the Chinese with conventional weapons and push them back to the border?" The Vice President asked.

"Yes Sir, it will be real close but I think they just might be able to pull it off—but only if Moscow does everything it can to help them and we provide enough additional support; and I do not mean troops and planes."

Then, after pausing for a moment to gather my thoughts, I added a thought.

"If the Russians can defeat the Chinese again, as they did in 1969 when the Chinese attacked in an effort to regain the Ussuri River territory, it may cause China to quit trying to use military force to expand and look for another way to go such as improving their economy. The problem, of course, is that this time the Chinese attack may succeed because its efforts will be much more massive and the Russian defenders much weaker and more isolated.

"Worse," I said pensively, "if the Chinese succeed they will undoubtedly be encouraged to go again. Perhaps against Taiwan or India. That is the real reason we have to help the Russians."

******

According the latest message from Woods and Goldman, Sholakov has just assigned several of his divisions to guard the key bridges and other potentially vulnerable points along the Trans-Siberian, the ones identified by Dave Shelton and the guys at the Detachment. He also has his men digging in on the approaches to Khabarovsk and is moving a significant amount of troops, three full divisions and almost all the engineers under his command, back to two choke points in the mountains on the railroad's main line to Khabarovsk and one "just in case" choke point on the branch line of the Trans-Siberian that runs down towards the Chinese city of Heihe.

Additionally, Sholakov is assembling most of his helicopters and the troops of his one and only air assault division at the Podovsk airfield. The field is far enough from the nearest Chinese base that the Chinese planes may not be able to reach it with a surprise attack before they are intercepted.

The airborne troops will be his mobile reserve. He'll rush them by helicopter to whatever turns out to be the hot spot and try to contain it until he can bring up reinforcements.

Hmm. It's a smart move for Sholakov's to use his air assault division as a rapid response force—he can beef it up with whatever additional helicopters and troops the Russians fly in from Western Russia. We destroyed a lot of the Russian helicopters and elite units before Moscow threw in the towel a couple of months ago, but we did not destroy them all.

According to NSA and our team on the ground, Sholakov was constantly calling Moscow asking for all available helicopters and Spetsnaz companies and he is evacuating his dependents on the supply planes when they go back to get more men and supplies. *Smart move. I am glad this guy was not making the decisions a couple of months ago when we were fighting the Russians.*

Separately at my suggestion, and without informing Moscow, Sholakov has directly contacted the Russian navy's base and fleet commanders and asked them to very quietly and secretly send to as many of the navy's frogmen as they can spare for six months of temporary duty "to help defend naval assets in the east." Those who come will "earn a premium pay in dollars for themselves and for the bases that send them."

I know—it's an overt effort to bribe the Russian navy's base and fleet commanders. It's also a real gamble to ask for the frogmen because it may leak to the Chinese and alert them to what we have been suggesting to the Russians. I need to speak with Sholakov and caution him never to tell anyone, not even his deputy, General Turpin, how he plans to use the frogmen. Hopefully, if the Chinese find out they will think the frogmen are being sent to defend the ships at the Vladivostok naval base.

The reason I so strongly recommended to Sholakov that he ask for the Russian swimmers and Special Forces troops was simple. If the Chinese invade, Sholakov may be able use them to sever the Chinese supply lines by cutting the roads and railroads behind the Chinese lines even if it means blowing up bridges in Russia. Then he can try to use his air assault forces and his "left behind" armor units and partisans to destroy the Chinese trapped between the bridge cuts.

If Vladivostok and Khabarovsk are able to hold and Sholakov's various response forces destroy enough of the Chinese rear, the Chinese forces in front of his chokepoints will wither and die for lack of support. Then Sholakov won't have to use his nukes. *That, at least, is the plan. It better work because it's all he is got.*

* * * * * *

Our aid was beginning to flow to Sholakov. Dave Shelton had already sent two planes full of demolition team pallets and explosives to Arkhara, the Russian airfield where Sholakov's air assault division and its helicopters were presently located. It is about midway between Karbarovsk and the key city of Podovsk—and just west of where a branch line of the Trans-Siberian leaves the main line and runs south to the Chinese city of Heihe.

In addition, Mike Morton and some of the veterans from the swimming and penetration teams are going out on a third supply plane to act as trainers and mission planners. It will leave this afternoon carrying explosive packs for any Russian frogmen that happen to show up.

Mike and his swimmers will be there as unarmed instructors. They will be based at the Arkhara airfield and are under strict orders not to participate in any operations or get anywhere near the Chinese border.

******

Everything was cooking right along at the Detachment with additional troops having been drafted in from the Metz garrison on temporary duty. The Detachment's permanent staff were working with them around the clock to load pallets and truck them to the Reims airport.

So far the pallets have been going out of Reims on regular C-130s. But, because of a combination of slow arriving supplies and a shortage of tankers for aerial refueling, not enough pallets have reached the Russians to have much of an impact.

That is about to change. The supplies we want to send to the Russian east have finally begun pouring in and, starting as early as tomorrow morning, we will begin using the planes of two newly assigned squadrons of extended range C-130s. Some of the new C-130s are already en route to Reims with equipment and supplies for the pallets; others are flying direct from California and Alaska to the Russian Far East with food and payroll money for the Russian troops.

Although their crews do not know it yet, six of our extended range C-130s will have their American markings painted out and turned over to Russian crews. Sholakov will use them to fly in reinforcements and materials from Russia.

The American air crews delivering the planes will stay with them for a while as instructors to help the Russian air crews transition into them. *But they will sure as hell be ordered to never fly with the Russians on actual missions once the war starts.*

That we are actually doing something to support the Russians so they would not need to use nukes was the good news. The bad news was that Dorothy was a really pissed. I just told her I would be going out myself as early as tomorrow afternoon. *I need to scope out how the situation is shaping up and the one thing I damn sure know is that it cannot be done from thousands of miles away.*

******

"Please wake up General. We are about thirty minutes out of Khabarovsk."

"Oh. Right. Thanks Bobby."

"There are some messages for you, Sir. And Jerry's got a hot breakfast you can eat while you read them. Everyone else has already eaten."

According to the messages, both the American and Russian airlifts were gathering momentum and moving into high gear. The Russian planes were bringing in Spetsnaz, various handheld and vehicle mounted missiles from what was left of Moscow's inventory, and volunteers anxious to earn dollars to support their families; they were taking out Russian dependents as well as Russian civilians with sufficient foreign currency to bribe the gatekeepers and the Russian plane crews.

American planes were bringing food supplies, particularly meat, fruit, and dairy products, into various Russian airfields. They were also bringing in money, green American twenty dollar bills, and American Special Forces troops to pass them out. Every Russian soldier in the east is going to get an "eastern allowance" of an additional five hundred dollars per month regardless of his rank; the frogmen who volunteer as swimmers will each get an additional four years pay, a gazillion worthless rubles, and twenty thousand dollars for each successful mission. It was immediately payable on their return.

It was sort of like a combination of the extra pay our soldiers get if they are in a combat zone and the extra cost of living pay they get if they serve in Alaska. The big difference is that Alaska is prosperous, beautiful and relatively safe; the Russian East is poor, drab and dangerous.

Our planes were also carrying out Russian dependents. We were carrying them to the States and putting them on civilian carriers to carry them back to Russia. That was already turning into an unexpected problem. Some of the Russian military wives were defecting rather than continuing on to Russia. *Wonder how their husbands will respond when that word gets out.*

And, miracle of miracles, the Russian grunts and junior officers were actually getting their pay, even the sailors and naval infantry at the big naval base at Vladivostok; Spelling was sending the money, all in twenty dollar bills, with a number of two-man Special Forces teams for each Russian division to guard it and pass it out each month.

Dick Spelling made a smart decision when he assigned the Special Forces guys from the Group at Fort Bragg to handle the delivery of the food and money to the Russian troops. Many of them served in Viet Nam and the middle east and have experience paying and feeding foreign troops—and they totally understand the importance of not letting the senior officers and government officials get their hands on the money.

One of the messages I leafed through as we prepared to land was about the money. It seems Moscow wants the money being sent to pay the soldiers routed through Moscow and the Secretary Hoffman thinks that doing so would be "an important gesture."

My response to the inquiry from the President's Chief of Staff was probably not well thought out: "Fuck the gesture. It's more important that the troops be paid than meaningless politicians get bribed."

Out of the corner of my eye I could see the air force sergeant encoding the message smile as he typed it into the coding machine.

******

Brigadiers Goldman of the Air Force and Woods of the Army, were both waiting at the foot of the stairs as I walked down the steps from the plane with three of my aides, Colonel Peterson, Captain Solomon and Sergeant Willow. Waiting with them was one of Sholakov's translators, Lieutenant Basilov and the ever jovial Colonel Miskin.

Basilof is the slender young guy with short hair and bad teeth who was Shokalov's translator when I was here the first time. After I left, Basilov was assigned to Woods and Goldman as their interpreter "in case your Colonel Miskin is not available." Basilof is apparently the one of the few officers at Sholakov's headquarters who is fluent in English; he is also almost certainly an intelligence officer.

Come to think of it, I need to send a message to Shelton and Spelling reminding them that any people we send out should be accompanied by Russian speaking translators whenever possible.

"I think I secrets no betray, General Roberts, when I say General Sholakov is anxious very much for talk. He has sent me and your generals in personal car to carry you to him directly." Woods and Goldman nod. *Grimly I note. Wonder what's up.*

On the drive in from the airfield Miskin softly said, "something's up and we do not know what it is."

Sholakov's anxiety was quite apparent as the eight of us bounded up the concrete stairs to his headquarters. The place was a beehive of activity and we could hear him bellowing into the phone as we briskly walked down the corridor and into to his office.

Sholakov nodded as we entered. Then he put his hand over the phone and said something to Basilov, with an ordering nod towards me for him to translate

"There has been a contact report from a platoon of village reservists. This morning a large Chinese unit, maybe as many as a battalion the local officers think, crossed the border about two hundred kilometers south of here."

Sholakov was continuing to shout into the phone. *I cannot understand a word of what he is saying but it is obvious from the tone of his voice that he is giving very pointed orders to someone.*

A few moments later Sholakov put the phone down and welcomed me with a big Russian bear hug.

"It is good to see you, Christopher Ivanovich. The Chinese are crossing the border and we have taken several prisoners. But we do not know how many have crossed or their purpose or if more are coming. We are trying to find translators so we can question them."

That is surprising. I would have thought he would have lots of them. I will have to ask Dick Spelling to get more

Chinese and Russian translators out here as soon as possible. Also, if it has not been done already, maybe he can arrange for increased satellite surveillance of the border.

"I suspect they found out we are moving our troops around and are trying to find out where they are going and how many are left on the border. On the other hand there may be a full scale infiltration going on just like the one you described in Korea."

"Uh..." I ask, "Yuri Andreovich, what exactly is the current situation?"

******

Sholakov's description of what he is doing was quite interesting. He appeared to have taken my experience with choke points to heart. And he thanked me profusely for the food and monetary assistance that was beginning to pour in from the United States. "More than we've been getting from Moscow."

There is nothing like good hot food, green dollars, and officers giving decisive orders to restore the morale of the troops. I just hope the Special Forces guys are actually getting the food and money to the Russian troops and their families. Got to check that with the colonel Dick put in charge of the program out here. His name is Bowie. I have not met him yet.

The bottom line was that Sholokov had been pulling some of his troops and engineers away from their units and using them to build three choke points—two where the railroad goes through a couple of particularly mountainous areas that would be hard to bypass and a third on the relatively short Trans-Siberian branch line running south to the Amur River border and over it on a bridge to the Chinese city of Heihe.

At least, in the past the railroad ran over a bridge to Heihe. The Chinese closed the border during the Usurri River war in 1969 and never reopened it. And Sholakov certainly does not want them to start now—the bridge is high on the list of those that need to be knocked out when the war starts.

Sholakov's troops and their equipment were mostly moving to the choke points by train. Also moving by train are the troops assigned to guard the key bridges. The trains that do not stop at the choke points and key bridges keep going until they reach the rail junction at Podovsk, about six hundred and fifty miles to the east. That is where the branch line of the Trans-Siberian cuts away towards Heihe. There is a good airfield and a lot of fuel reserves in storage just beyond the Podovsk junction.

Many civilian refugees were also moving westward to Podovsk to escape the coming fighting and avoid the Chinese troops. What they did not know is that, when the Chinese actually invade, Shokalov plans to declare the cities and villages he cannot defend to be "open cities" and not even try to defend them; most of the refugees would probably be safer if they remain at home.

Shokalov's plan is simple. Try to hold the Chinese at the border. If that fails, which he and everyone else including me expects, he'll try to hold them at Khabarovsk and at choke points in the mountains along the railroad right of way. If the main body of invading Chinese is able to push westward and reach the choke points, he plans to cut them off from their supplies and reinforcements by using "left behind" partisan units to destroy the bridges behind them and attack their rear areas.

He also intends to cut up their rear with armor raids. "Just the way they tell me you did to us a couple of months ago."

But how and where will the Chinese attack and does he have enough time to get ready and will he have enough forces to drive them out of Russia without using his nukes? There are a lot of unanswered questions. There always are.

******

Total chaos is the best way to describe the situation we saw when we visited the bedraggled and rundown train station at Khabarovsk. Around the clock all the available trains, including those normally based further inland and at Vladivostok, were constantly loading military and construction equipment and supplies and pulling out for the choke points under construction and to the rail junction where the line that used to run down to the Chinese city of Heihe.

The trains coming in from Vladivostok and going out from Khabarovsk are an impressive sight to see with the troops packed around their tanks, armored vehicles, and construction equipment. Some of the troops were even riding on the roofs of the passenger and freight cars. Civilian passengers are allowed to take any remaining space with whatever household items they can carry aboard. At least that is supposed to be the plan. In reality the troops and civilians are riding everywhere they can squeeze in including on the train roofs and the equipment-carrying flat cars.

As we drove away from the station I noticed an old coal burning switch engine that has been pressed into service. It was puffing little black smoke rings into the air as it moves down the line pulling flat cars loaded with bulldozers and troops.

Military trucks, military dependents, and civilian vehicles are not going on the trains. The dependents are going out in the planes that bring in supplies; the military trucks and civilian vehicles are required to drive on the two lane east-west dirt highway that doubles as the service road that runs along the Trans-Siberian Railroad's tracks in this part of Russia.

Both lanes of the road have been converted to one-way traffic for most of the day. And civilian vehicles are not allowed past the checkpoint at the edge of the city unless they are carrying enough fuel to make the entire six hundred and fifty mile trip to Podovsk. Many are being turned back.

For some strange reason the Trans-Siberian Highway is complete, albeit mostly just graded dirt, all along the railroad from Lake Baikal to Khabarovsk and Vladivostok. It is in the middle of Russia, west of Lake Baikal where the Germans destroyed the railroad bridges, that the highway to Moscow was never completed. In the past cars and trucks driving on it have been loaded on railroad flat cars and carried around the missing sections to where the road begins again. That eliminates the need to build road bridges.

We used to do the same thing in Alaska to get cars and trucks from Anchorage to the Port of Whittier and it works pretty well. Sholakov's problem, of course, is that now the railroad cannot be used to fill the gaps in the road system because the Germans destroyed so many of the railroad's key bridges.

Things are equally chaotic about three hundred miles west of Kharbarovsk at Arkhara, according to Brigadier Woods. He flew out with General Turpin for a visit yesterday. Arkhara is important because it has an air force base and will be Sholakov's supply base and rally point if he gets forced out of Kharbarovsk. At the moment its two relatively small sidings are jammed with unloading trains and construction crews working to expand them and build a third.

Arkhara was either a very small city or a very large village depending on how you look measure such things. Military dependents that somehow ended up in Arkhara by train were being bussed by road to the military air field. From there they were being evacuated by air on a space available basis.

Civilians arriving in Arkhara by train, on the other hand, are being trucked to a haphazard tent camp a few miles beyond the village. They are being held there until space can be found for them on the American and Russian planes that periodically bring supplies into Arkhara. So far very few civilians have gotten out unless they have had enough money to bribe their way on board one of the departing planes.

Jack Peterson went out to Arkhara for a look while I was in the States. He describes the civilian tent camp as a barely livable open sewer with more people arriving every day than the supply flights can possibly carry out; I can only wonder what it will be like in the Siberian winter. *If we stick with the Russians we will probably end up having to run a humanitarian relief project until the refugees can get out on the empty supply planes.*

* * * * * *

Television coverage of the unexpected arrival in the United States of forlorn and destitute Russian refugees coming in on the returning supply planes has awakened Americans to the possibility that the Secretary of State's treaty has gotten us enmeshed in another war. Some of the politicians and media are beginning to blame her for involving us while others, mostly the knee jerk media supporters of her party, are defending her "for doing the right thing." *Whatever the hell that is.*

Whatever the pros and cons of the treaty, the Secretary's position as a potential candidate for the Presidency seems to have suffered a setback and Khabarovsk and Podovsk are being flooded with American television crews sending back stories of the Russian "retreat" and trying to find Americans to interview.

Fortunately, their search for Americans has not been very successful; there are very few Americans on the ground other than our Special Forces guys at the off-limits Podovsk air base, and they are hard to spot because they all wear Russian fatigues and caps, even me. Our Special Forces troops make really good Russians with their beards and their inability to speak English when questioned by reporters.

Chapter Six

Moscow's distress.

Moscow is furious about the refugee and "retreat" stories saturating the international media and even more furious that the money going to Sholakov's troops is not being routed through Moscow so they can get their hands on it. Sure enough, while we were visiting Sholakov they ordered him to immediately report to Moscow "for consultations and to explain his strategy."

Sholakov was not without friends. He immediately received several back channel messages telling him he was about to be replaced by his senior political officer and would be arrested as soon as his plane landed in Moscow.

Instead of climbing on a plane and going to Moscow, Sholakov sent an apology and explained that he could not come to Moscow immediately because he was too busy getting his troops ready to fight the Chinese. He has instead, he informs Moscow, dispatched a senior Russian officer, his Deputy Chief of Staff, Major General Vasily Kafanov, to "explain his strategy." Then he added that I would be accompanying Kafanov to discuss the plans for America's assistance.

I am going to tag along with Kafanov to present the American perspective. What we will not in any way mention is the plan to use partisan teams and frogmen to blow the bridges in China and behind the Chinese army if it reaches the choke points. *I won't because I do not want the Chinese to find out and Kafanov cannot—because he does not even know about it.*

The good news is that several weeks ago Sholakov put together a very carefully selected personal guard of airborne enlisted men and junior officers. Their job is to protect him from anyone who tries to arrest him or replace him.

It's a good thing he has a protection detail. The last thing the Russians need in command out here is another politically correct oaf like the political officer Moscow sent to Magdeburg a couple of months ago to command the Warsaw Pact armies.

******

Sholakov pretended he does not know about his pending replacement and arrest. Instead he alerted his guards and waited. Sure enough, the next day some of his senior political officer's subordinates walked into Sholakov's outer office and arrogantly demanded to see him immediately "on a matter of great importance."

They were politely shown into a conference room and informed that Sholakov would be right with them. Unfortunately for them, about a dozen heavily armed and carefully selected airborne troops arrived instead of Sholakov.

"Follow me, Comrades," ordered the Lieutenant leading them. He ignored their commands, and then their offers, and took them to an abandoned basement room. It had once been used to store coal for a nearby furnace.

"Now," said the lieutenant, a pug-faced young officer who'd been born in Siberia to political prisoners and absolutely hates the party, "let's talk about why you are here. Unfortunately for you, we received word that the Chinese have bribed some Moscow officials and army political officers to assassinate General Sholakov and surrender to the Chinese.

"And here you are," he says menacingly as he cocked his head with a questioning look.

"Oh no, comrade lieutenant, you are wrong. We are here on official business." That from the Lieutenant Colonel who had arrogantly demanded to see Sholakov.

"Oh, and what exactly, very exactly, is that official business, Comrade Colonel."

"We are not allowed to say. Orders you understand."

"Oh yes, well that is a pity."… "And do you know what you are supposed to do but are not allowed to say, Captain?" He said mildly to the officer standing next to the colonel.

"Of course I know," he said irately, "and if you know what's good for"…

The shot reverberated in the room and a plume of the luckless captain's blood and brain matter splattered the dirty concrete wall and the lieutenant colonel standing next to him."

"Perhaps you know, Major?" the airborne lieutenant inquired mildly of the officer standing on the other side of the lieutenant colonel.

"Yes, of course. I will tell you," said the wide-eyed and trembling political major as he stared in horror at the body slumped against the wall with its legs still spasming and the rapidly spreading pool of the blood its heart is still pumping.

According to the suddenly talkative major, they had been ordered to arrest Sholakov, Turpin, and three other officers; then take them to the Khabarovsk prison and shoot them. Orders from Moscow.

"And who told you to do this?"

"General Tretyak. About an hour ago. He and his deputy commissar, General Tolovko, are to replace Generals Sholakov and Turpin."

"And who told General Tretyak to arrest him and who else knows of the order besides those two and the officer who decoded the message?"

"Well, General Tretyak said it was ordered by Marshall Petrov. But I am not sure of that. Colonel Kaletski was there when he told us. I think there is no one else."

We were in Sholakov's conference room and could hear the faint sound of gunshots coming from somewhere in the building.

******

"Generals Tretyak and Tolovko, and Colonel Kaletski," the breathless airborne lieutenant told the stocky woman serving as General Tretyak's receptionist, "are needed at army headquarters as soon as possible. General Sholakov has been arrested and there are reports of a major Chinese incursion."

If anyone had asked who sent him the lieutenant would have said that it was a lieutenant colonel commissar he did not know. Neither the receptionist nor Tretyak asked.

An hour later a flash message informs Moscow that Generals Tretyak and Tolovko have been revealed as being in the pay of the Chinese and, quite unfortunately, have been killed along with some of their staff while trying to escape to China.

******

We landed in a rainstorm and Moscow was as bleak and unpleasant as always. But the Military Committee knew that General Kafanov had hitched a ride with us and sent a car to meet him at the airport. To my surprise, and without even asking, I was invited to accompany General Kafanov and join him when he makes his report. Arnie Miskin came with me to be my interpreter.

I nodded my head in agreement as Kafanov concludes his report:

... "accordingly, we have been ordered to dig in and every unit is expected to stand firm and fight. The reality, of course, is that the Chinese will concentrate their forces and may be able to break through because our troops are strung out in a thin line all along the four thousand kilometers of border."

Then, perhaps making a career and life-threatening mistake and not knowing it, Kafanov associated himself from Sholakov.

"General Sholakov, wisely in my opinion, is erecting additional defensive positions at Khabarovsk and at several locations along the Trans-Siberian Railroad in case such a breakthrough occurs."

Kafanov obviously does not know that these guys have a contract out on Sholakov. He probably would have been more circumspect about his support if he had known.

A stocky 60ish civilian in the rumpled and ill-fitting brown suit sitting next to Marshall Petrov grunted audibly at Kafanov's conclusion and then turned to me and asks, rather nastily, "and you, General Roberts, why are you here?"

"I am here to provide you with your ally's analysis of the situation and to tell you what we *are* willing to do to help—and what we are *not* willing to do."

Brown suit grunted his acknowledgement so I continued with my translator chattering away as I spoke.

"It is my professional opinion that General Sholakov is taking exactly the right steps if Russia is to have any hope of defeating the Chinese. The fact that a professional soldier like Sholakov is in command, instead of one of your political generals, is the only reason that I have recommended that the United States continue to provide food, supplies, and money for your troops."

Then I got a bit pissed and more than a bit insulting, though I think only a few of them realized it.

"Frankly, meeting all of you here, instead of at the front, helps me to understand the reasons why you lost the last war so quickly. One of the reasons is that you appointed political officers to commands they were not qualified to hold; another is that you tried to run the war from a great distance. And another is that you ignored the interests and concerns of your allies."

Then I issued a warning though once again I am not sure they all understood it. "All and all, it sounds to me, from the orders you have been issuing from thousands of kilometers away from the front, that Russia is about to again make the same stupid mistakes and lose another war."

"You speak very bluntly, General Roberts, but why should we listen to you? The United States broke our agreement."

"No we did not. The United States agreed to come to Russia's aid if the Chinese attack. And that is exactly what we are doing. Who the hell do you think is feeding and paying your men out there? You sure as hell are not."

Then, after a pause while the translator caught up, I continued.

"Personally, I do not give a rat's ass who wins the coming war. Both your countries keep your people in poverty by restricting their freedom and not applying your laws equally. But I am a loyal soldier and my Commander in Chief has ordered me to help you. So, despite my personal loathing for your miserable system of government and how you mistreat your people, I shall do so to the best of my ability."

Some of the men sitting around the room were clearly seething and outraged by the time Arnie finished translating what I say; others, however, were leaning forward with great interest and studying me intently. One of the more fit-looking and younger civilians in the room, a short little guy with a ferret face, silently nodded in agreement.

******

My flight from Moscow to Reims was uneventful. We were on the Starlifter, we were going home empty, and I was exhausted. So I put a rubber air mattress and sleeping bag on the floor and slept most of the way using my rolled up Russian field jacket for a pillow. So did Peterson, Solomon and Willow. Kafanov will catch a Russian flight from Moscow back to Khabarovsk.

Someone obviously radioed ahead because there was a car and a protection squad of the Detachment's Marines waiting when we land at Riems. Thirty minutes and an extended family hug later and I was sitting in my overstuffed easy chair with a big smile reading a new *Doctor Seuss* to my son and daughter. Then I told Dorothy all about the trip and took a long hot shower.

I just do not quite get it about the appeal of Dr. Seuss. But Susan and John Christopher love his books and that is all that counts.

Tomorrow I am going to visit the Detachment and then head to Brussels to get an update on how NATO is doing in terms of getting our troops back to their homes. And sometime during the next few days I would like to once again check out the repairs underway in Heidelberg at Campbell Barracks, the headquarters of the United States European Command. *I have also developed a periodic toothache and need to visit the army dental clinic there.*

Campbell Barracks' repairs are being done by a German contractor because the headquarters building was heavily damaged by a Russian Spetsnaz attack at the beginning of the recent war. In the past it was the *de facto* NATO headquarters. Now, and until we move back in, both the American and NATO headquarters will in Brussels in fact as well as in name.

Hopefully the Chinese have not yet penetrated Moscow to the extent the Russians penetrated Brussels. On the other hand, it did not work for the Russians so maybe we can pull a similar fake on the Chinese by feeding them plans the Russians won't be following. But how?

Chapter Seven

Another trip to the Russian East.

When I got to the Detachment the next morning, Dave Shelton introduced me to his new aides, Captain Evans and Master Sergeant Duffy, "Special Forces guys who did real good in Hungary." Then he had Captain Evans pin up the latest satellite photos of the Russian choke points and the defensive positions being constructed at Khabarovsk and north of Vladivostok.

Sholakov had obviously lit a fire under someone. Two of the choke points seemed to be making real progress. *Let's hope they never have to be used. I wonder where in the mountains they are going to hide the fire control observers?*

Then we went over the Detachment's shipment schedule for the penetration teams' pallets and explosive packs. They have begun piling up unshipped because of delivery delays for certain crucial items. They could be delayed for as long as three weeks if we wait for everything to arrive. *Do we have that much time?*

Captain Evans made everyone ham and cheese sandwiches for lunch and we ate them while we studied the maps of the areas between the choke points and the border. *Got to remind myself to bring some mustard and lettuce for next time.*

After lunch the Detachment's analysis team headed by Jack Riley and his new deputy, Terry Adams, briefed us on the targets in China, mostly bridges, that they think will need to be knocked out to stop the Chinese from bringing up supplies and reinforcements.

Riley's photo analysis guys have also begun looking for the Russian bridges that might need to be cut if the Chinese reach the choke points and where small teams of Russian partisan infantry and swimmers might be able to hole up while they wait for orders to hit the Chinese-controlled bridges and transportation.

Then our two new armor experts, Lieutenant Colonels Jack Marshall and Dave Rutherford, suggested locations where Sholakov might be able to stash "partisan armor units" to fall upon the Chinese rear and the routes their raids might take. They cautioned us that before the Russians use a location they should have someone on the ground check it out, as well as the routes in and out, to see if the ground is strong enough to handle armor. *They did not say it, but they obviously do not trust the Russian maps. Neither do I. Tanks and APCs do not do well in swamps.*

Sholakov's basic plan, if the Chinese break though his border defenses, is to hold out at Khabarovsk and Vladivostok, and let the Chinese push the main force of

Russians several hundred kilometers westward along the railroad to the most distant choke points in front of Arkhara.

When the Chinese get deep enough into Russia, he'll cut them off from their supplies and reinforcements and let them wither and die, just as the Germans recently did to the Russians and the Russians did long ago to Napoleon. *His partisan infantry attacks and armored raids behind the Chinese lines will speed up the process.*

But there are major differences. Some good; some bad. The West Germans fighting the Warsaw Pact armies retreated slowly and deliberately without actually losing control. And the retreating units and our skirmishers took a tremendous toll of the advancing enemy while they were doing it.

Can the Russian do that? Not likely. What is more likely in the current situation is that the Russian retreat will be disorganized and chaotic just as ours was in face of the Chinese invasion during the Korean War and Napoleon's was in Russia.

Perhaps the only good news for the Russians, besides the fact that the United States, the UK and Australia are helping them, is that cutting the Chinese invaders off from their supplies and reinforcements will not require as many air drops as the Germans needed earlier this year to cut off the Russians. The Russian East is so rough and undeveloped that most of the partisan teams working the

Chinese supply lines can be stashed away in isolated locations near their targets instead of having to parachute in or arrive by helicopter.

Similarly stashed away can be small Russian armored forces to provide the equivalent of our ferry-borne and forest redoubt forces in the recent war and the armored raid I ran into the Chinese rear in the Korean War. Sholakov and his officers have begun referring to them as their "partisan armor units." According to Dave and Mike, the Russians plan to add a number of small units of infantry and Spetsnaz volunteers to the partisan armor mix.

Russia's demolition swimmers, on the other hand, will all have to come in by helicopter. The good news for them, such as it is, is that the border bridges over the Ussari and Amur rivers and, most important of all, those within China which the Chinese Army must use to bring its supplies and reinforcements to the front, are all fairly close to the border and within the roundtrip range of Russian helicopters if they refuel from fuel bladders on the Russian side of the border.

Significantly, and the best news of all according to the Detachment's analysts, is that five of the Chinese bridges, including three over the Amur, are of particular importance because there are no alternative routes for the Chinese troops and supplies to take. If those bridges go down the Chinese will have to replace them with pontoon bridges that cannot handle rail traffic.

******

"Okay," I say to Dave when we finished two hours later, "I am pretty sure Sholakov's officers will *try* to do the right thing with the equipment and supplies we are sending out to them. But I am not at all sure they know how. So you and me and our aides, and Colonels Marshall and Rutherford, are going to have to join Mike out there to monitor the situation and provide low key guidance when the Russians ask for it."

Then I added the bad news.

"I will probably have to come back to NATO sooner or later. So you and some of our guys will have to stay out there for a while, with you in command, to be our on-site link with Sholakov and his men—particularly you so that someone from the Detachment has more rank than the two brigadiers Dick Spelling sent out. They are good guys but they do not have the experience we have and I do not want them calling the shots.

"We also better take Bobby Geither with us so we can get a good handle on the signals situation and someone to handle photo interpretation. We will also need some of our Marines as drivers and guards; maybe Gunny Robinson, the new gunnery sergeant with all the tattoos, and half a dozen of the other single Marines. Same as before, we will leave the married Marines like Corporal Afoa to guard this place so they can spend some time with their families." *and not leave widows and orphans with measly pensions if we run into trouble.*

"Everyone is to travel light. Tell them to bring only what they can get into one duffle bag and that includes one personal weapon and one clip of ammunition. And as soon as possible put them away and start carrying Russian weapons. But absolutely no grenades and grenade launchers. None. And make sure the Starlifter is carrying ninety days of rations and winter sleeping bags and air mattresses for everyone including the crew. Some extra jars of instant coffee and water purification pills would be helpful if you can get them.

"Oh, I almost forgot. Get a lot of tea bags too. A lot of Russians drink tea and you'll want to be able to offer it to visitors – and me," I say with a smile. "I am thinking about permanently switching over to drinking tea instead of coffee; it seems easier on the stomach.

"Also, if there's time, you might want to send Captain Evans or someone to hit the Metz Base Exchange this afternoon or tomorrow morning for lots of Tootsie Rolls, dry noodles, and energy bars; the Russian field rations are apparently even worse than ours. We will leave from Reims on the Starlifter tomorrow at 1100. First stop Khabarovsk.

"Oh yeah, one more thing. Please remind me to tell everybody to take their rank, their names, their insignia, and everything else off their fatigues and jackets that would make them out to be Americans. We will want to get everyone into Russian battledress and weapons as soon as possible. They can leave their American uniforms and weapons in the Starlifter when we get the Russian gear.

"Let's see. What else? Oh yeah. Please do not let me forget to tell the men, order them, never to talk to any media and to never, absolutely never, admit to anyone that they are Americans or military. They are to walk away without speaking a single word if a civilian approaches them."

I am going to remind everyone of that order and the need to get into Russian battledress once again after we take off. If we wear the Russian stuff and let our beards grow we may be able to get away with pretending not to speak English, particularly if the guys with weapons are carrying Russian AK-47s.

Finally, before I took off, Dave and I have a private talk in my old office, Dave's now, about the implications of Vladivostok being cut off and desirability of adding one or more naval officers to the team to work with us on its resupply and support.

We have Mike Morton, of course, but Mike's always been a SEAL and demolitions guy, never a supply officer or deck officer.

What we finally decided, two cups of coffee and a couple of donuts later, was that we probably need a couple of navy guys and that, if we get them, we'd better make damn sure they do not outrank Mike and start giving orders instead of advice.

Jeez this coffee is really getting to me. Maybe the Russians are on to something. I think I will switch to tea starting now

.

******

Terry Martin, the Starlifter pilot, and his crew had to hustle to get the plane ready by painting out its U.S. insignia and lining up the aerial refueling. But they did it and we were on our way.

There were about twenty of us from the Detachment on board in addition to the crew and a couple of warrant officers I grabbed from the Eleventh Airborne to join the commo team already out there, the one headed up by John Liska. Since we are carrying so few people some of the seats in the rear have been removed and we are also carrying explosive packs for the swimmers and the initial part of a big shipment of Israeli anti-tank missiles for the Russian motorcycle troops I hope to encourage Sholakov to implement.

Our young Marines were quite excited and trying not show it. Most of them spent the war as headquarters guards so they ended up never getting even close to combat. *Hopefully they won't see any this time either.*

In the back of the plane, in between the cargo nets the plane's loadmaster was using to hold the cargo boxes tight against the fuselage, Dave Shelton had set up a row of four folding card tables, tied their legs together so they would not slide apart, and covered them with maps. Presently, we were standing around the maps and going over everything once again.

There was a real sense of urgency; it was beginning to sink in to our troops that we were about to be involved in another war and they would be right in the middle of it.

After a long and scrambled talk on the satellite phone with Dick Spelling and his intelligence chief, General Arpasso, to get updated on the latest news and intelligence from Washington and Russia, I suddenly felt very tired and decide to take a nap. I do not know what it is but these long trips are really starting to get to me.

I woke with a start. Something Arpasso said suddenly jumped out at me - that the elderly Russian Orthodox Patriarch was apparently trying to mediate between the old-line Russian communists who hold the top positions and a somewhat younger group of reformers who hold many of the important positions just below them. "It appears to be some of the younger reformists who tried to remove Sholakov."

I would have thought it would have been the old guard who wanted him removed. Why would the up and comers want to do that?

******

Khabarovsk was covered with fog and clouds and its radar was out this morning. Major Nelson twice aborted his approach and poured on the power to get us up and around the nearby mountains. He looked cool as a cucumber sitting up there and I would not have worried about the missed approaches except I could see extremely nervous looks on the faces of the reserve crew sitting across the aisle.

By the time we finish making our second failed approach everyone in the plane, including me, had picked up on increasing nervousness of the reserve crew. But the third time was the charm and there was a collective sigh of relief, and more than a few clapping and cheering Marines, when we finally came through the clouds and the tires squealed as we settled onto the wet and foggy runway. *I had to stifle my urge to join them.*

Generals Woods and Goldman along with Colonel Miskin and the ever present Lieutenant Basilof were waiting on tarmac as the portable stairs were pushed into place so we could get off. So was someone important I had not met before, Colonel "Jim" Bowie, the commander of the Special Forces troops Spelling sent over to pass out the food and payroll money. Mike Morton was not with them; he and his guys were already in Arkhara training Sholakov's Spetsnaz teams and swimmers.

My plan at the moment was to meet with Sholakov this morning to make our manners and exchange briefings, then go on to Arkhara to see how Mike was doing. Our schedule thereafter would depend on how things developed.

A briefing from the Americans on the scene was what I needed before we go off for our scheduled meeting with Sholakov. So I asked Dave Shelton and his aides to remain on the plane while everyone else including the Marines goes down the portable stairs to stretch their legs and have a smoke if they so desire. Captain Solomon went down with them to get Woods, Goldman, and Bowie so we could talk in private.

If Basilof tried to board with them, Captain Solomon, who knows him from our last visit, was to tell him politely, very politely, that I was not ready to get off the plane yet and wanted to talk with my senior staff privately before I did.

Woods, Goldman, and Bowie came up immediately and welcomed Dave and me back to Kharbarovsk. Colonel Bowie has been staying with Woods and Goldman and sharing the information he has been getting from his teams in the field. Each of the three was fully informed as to what the others know and think.

And Bowie got real comfortable real fast when he came into the plane saw Dave Shelton standing next to me at our makeshift map table. Randall "Jim" Bowie, it turns out, had been a captain at Bad Tolz and deep dipped at Shelton's recommendation for an early promotion to major when Dave commanded the Special Forces group.

Basically all the reports I heard were positive. Both Woods and Goldman think the Russians, both army and air force, are going all out to try to do what they told us they would try to do. Bowie agreed. According to him, the Russian troops have been ordered to cooperate with us and were doing so. There was a lot of curiosity but no overt hostility; perhaps, he suggested, because the local Russian troops were stranded here and missed the recent war with NATO. *And besides, it's just plain stupid to bite the hand that feeds you food and money.*

Bowie, however, was concerned about two of his Special Forces teams who had not reported in yet. He had heard from the other teams, however, and they reported that the food we were providing was getting to the troops and the Russian soldiers were getting paid.

"Apparently, General Sholakov made it quite clear what will happen if anyone interferes with them or tried to steal or divert the food and money. The word is that they will be shot on the spot by the nearest political officer. The troops believe it because it's true."

They know the political officers will do it and the other troops will applaud; it's their food and their money.

******

Sholakov was his usual warm and welcoming self. Even Turpin smiled at me. I got the impression their confidence in us was growing. After the traditional welcoming bear hugs, I introduced everyone and we got down to business in front of the three huge wall maps in Sholakov's conference room even before the arrival of the traditional tea and cookies.

Pacing up and down as he talked, and with Miskin and Basilof constantly translating, Sholakov pointed to the maps on his briefing room wall and gave us an update. He beamed agreement when I asked if we could record the briefing in case the translators missed a point.

Most of his staff, Sholakov tells us, were already at Arkhara getting things organized and checking the various communications links to make sure they are up. In the morning, if his signal guys confirm all the links are up, he himself intended to fly there and Arkhara will become the new headquarters of the Far Eastern Military District.

I immediately introduce Bobby Geither and suggest that Bobby and Mister Liska's commo team might be useful to have around if there are any gaps in his communications that we might be able to help his signal staff fill. Sholakov said that it sounded like a great idea and immediately agreed when I suggested they stay at Arkhara for as long as he needs them.

His choke points were coming along nicely, Sholakov reported, even though he had to remove one of the division commanders "who slept too long and drank too much." His biggest current problem, Sholakov said, was that the movement of so many men and so much equipment up the rail line was taking much longer than he and his staff expected.

"We will never be able to get all our troops and equipment evacuated into fighting positions if we wait for the war to start before we begin to pull them out of their current positions," he admitted. "So I am trying to get as many as possible of my men out into better positions." *Very smart.*

Accordingly, Sholakov said he was pulling even more units back while he still has time, particularly those still north of Khabarovsk or in the more isolated areas that the Chinese are likely to bypass. He is also relocating some of his other units so they can more easily fall back on the railroad right of way and two potential lines of communication that presently only have pioneer roads.

That is actually quite smart and I tell him so. And it really is—he can retake the secondary territory he abandons after he defeats the main Chinese effort.

Sholakov also reported that the food and money we have been providing seems to be reaching his troops. "But, of course, you know more about it than I do, but everything I hear is good and on behalf of my men I thank you."

After a brief moment of meaningless pleasantries while the inevitable tea and coffee was brought in and savored, I re-introduced Lieutenant Colonels Marshall and Rutherford with a bit of detail about their recent combat experience as tank battalion commanders, and told Sholakov about the plans and maps they have developing for the possible use of armored raiding units to cut up the Chinese rear. *This Russian tea isn't half bad.*

Jack used the big wall map to briefly explain the concept and point out some example locations and force compositions for some small independent armored formations that Sholokov might put together as his forces fall back—and then use them to tear up the Chinese rear once the mainforce units have gone past.

Sholakov liked the idea. He promised to immediately appoint an overall commander to head up the project "to make sure it actually happens." We said we'd provide him with maps and more details when we meet again tomorrow morning in Arkhara.

After a moments of reflection, Sholakov said he will have a General Rutman, who is "good with armor," head up the organization and placement of the independent armor formations and asked if Colonels Marshal and Rutherford could be attached to Rutman's office for a few weeks to act as his advisors. I agreed instantly.

"Rutman will be with me at Arkhara; and so will you and your men, I hope." I agreed to that also and we decided to meet again tomorrow morning in Arkhara with Rutman present.

Then Dave Shelton and I discussed the bridge blowing and swimming teams, and where they might be stashed and used both in Russia and in China, and how they might be activated once enough Chinese had passed through to justify cutting them off. The teams going after targets in China, the ones Dave is training up in Arkhara, would have to be flown in after the war starts, preferably on the first night of the war. And that means a sufficient number of Russian helicopters need to be standing by and ready to go.

Dave did not give Sholakov the specific locations the helicopter borne swimmers would hit, he just described them generally and the progress that has been made on implementing the operation. Sholakov seemed especially pleased when Dave told him the required supplies and equipment have already begun arriving at the Arkhara airfield and that our man there, Admiral Mike Morton, reported that he was working well with your Spetsnaz Commander, Colonel Krutchovy.

I chimed in that we would know more in a couple of hours when we get to Arkhara ourselves and have a chance to meet with Mike and Krutchovy.

Sholakov took me aside and quietly thanked me as we got up to leave.

"Vasily Kafanov told me what you said in Moscow and I appreciate it. I also heard from some friends who were present. You impressed them with your honesty and your message."

And then, with a deep sigh of obvious sadness as he walked with me to the door, he told me about the "unfortunate loss" of General Tretyak and some of his political officers before they could be questioned about their dealings with the Chinese.

"We are investigating the matter, of course. A report will be sent to Moscow as soon as I can free up someone to work on it," he said, "perhaps after the war is over."

******

Late that afternoon the Starlifter landed at the airbase near Arkhara and we piled into Russian-style military Jeeps driven by Mike Morton and his four NCOs, the guys who are working with the Russian swimmers and the Spetsnaz troops who are learning how to blow bridges. They will make a second run to get the Marines; and a third to get the duffle bags and food crates that are being unloaded as we drive away.

Most of the plane's crew would sleep in one of the plywood shacks that function as the base's transit facilities, except for the signal corps warrant officers and a couple of the Marines. They will stay on the Starlifter as guards and to operate its twenty four hour message center with its nifty little antennae aimed at a satellite.

Tomorrow morning we will meet Sholakov along with General Rutman and Colonel Krutchovy, the commander of Sholakov's Spetsnaz troops, and talk about the bridge blowing teams and their use of partisan infantry and armor units behind the lines; tonight we Americans will have a working dinner at the Russian squadron leader's residence assigned to Mike Morton and his instructors.

Mike's residence used to belong to one of the Russian Air Force squadron leaders. It was a square log hut with a crude sink for kitchen and bathing purposes, a wood burning stove for warmth and cooking, and two bedrooms. The outhouse was out back and smelled horrible.

Rank has its privileges so Mike was in the small bedroom and the four veteran enlisted swimmers and demolition experts he brought as instructors were in the other. They were all using the sleeping bags and fold up cots they had brought with them. The cots literally filled the room so that the guys have to crawl over each other to get to their sleeping bags.

It was an interesting and revealing quarters for a Russian field grade officer. There was a wooden table and four chairs, cold running water of dubious quality from a tap in the kitchen, and each room has a light hanging down from the middle of its ceiling. The latrine was accessed by going out the front door and following the path around the north side of the house to the outhouse in the backyard.

I can only imagine what the quarters for the families of junior officers and enlisted men look like.

Five identical log residences on the dirt street have also been assigned to us. I will share one with Peterson, Solomon, and Willow. *I gave myself the smaller bedroom. They can share the big one. Presumably the squadron leaders' families have been evacuated; wonder where the officers are? I don't think I will ask.*

Mike quickly showed everyone where to throw their gear and how to find their outhouse. "Then come on back to my place and bring back your mess kits if you want to eat."

After a few minutes everyone except the Marines and Mike's instructors was jammed into Mike's hut with the mess kits we'd quickly dug out of our duffle bags. Our enlisted aides and the Marines are eating with Mike's instructors at another hut across the way.

Then Mike surprised us. He brought in some steaks from our daily meat shipments to the Russians and announce, to enthusiastic whistles and applause, that we are to grill our own meat on the jerry rigged barbeque he has set up outside his front door. And that is what we had for supper—steaks and lukewarm coffee from the pot on the wood burning kitchen stove. *Thank God the steaks are large. I am starved.*

Our enlisted aides and the Marines, Mike assured us, were getting the same menu served up by his instructors. Actually that was not the case. It seems Mike's instructors "happened to find" some canned vegetables, fresh bread, and ice cream to go with their steaks and coffee. They also heard Willow's significantly expanded tale of the battle of the staircase and were greatly impressed.

* * * * * *

It was getting chilly as we stood around outside grilling our steaks and eating while we talked informally and watched the Russian and American cargo planes coming and going from the nearby runway. Then we all jammed into Mike's hut and stood around the walls to get ourselves updated. It was time hear about any problems related to the Russian special operations teams and swimmers, and once again discuss what else we might suggest about the armor and partisan raids when we see Sholakov, Rutman, and Krutchovy in the morning.

Mike began by telling us about the special tent encampment the Russians have set up at the edge of the airport for the swimmers and bridge-blowing teams. The Russian guys are outfitted okay, even if the war continues on into the winter, he reported. But the dozen or so swimmers who have arrived so far, and that is nowhere near enough, were not allowed to bring their wetsuits and did not bring any winter gear. And none of them really knows much about explosives and blowing bridges.

"Anyhow, when the Spetsnaz guys found out what the swimmers were there to do, they took to them like brothers and found winter gear for them. More importantly, they found an English-speaking translator somewhere and we've started running a bridge blowing course for everyone.

"But we have to get survival suits for the swimmers. The water out here comes off of glaciers and is just too damn cold to even try to work in it without them. Some of the Spetsnaz on the partisan teams will also need them if they have to go in the water to set their charges."

"Okay," I said. "Make me a list of the wetsuit sizes you think we will need if we get enough swimmers and how many you want of each size. You better double the numbers so that everyone gets a wetsuit that fits."

"We will send the list tonight," I told Eddie Rasmusson, one of Liska's Signal Corps warrants. I will give you the message after we wrap things up here. *I have got to remember to ask Sholakov to light a fire under his navy to send more swimmers.*

"Another problem," Mike said, "and it's a big one, is letting the teams know when to make their move." *What?*

I looked at him quizzically and he explained.

"We do not have enough portable radios and the ones we have do not always pick up the local Arkhara radio station even though it's right next door. Its signal is too weak. And the station's too shaky. It's using an AM broadcast transmitter that is got to be at least sixty or seventy years old and periodically has technical problems and goes off the air. It still uses tubes for God's sake."

I had to smile. Years ago, when I was a kid in Cordova, I used to work sometimes at the little AM station there, KLAM. Its 1950s-era transmitter used tubes and the only ones the station manager could find to buy were imported from Russia which was the only place where tubes are still being manufactured.

"If that station goes off the air or gets hit, the Russians are screwed. We need a backup transmitter and more of those cheap little battery powered boom box radios. We have to get them or our teams won't know when to launch their strikes."

Boy, that got Dave's attention. He never thought of that. Neither had I.

The good news, Mike told us, is that there is a much bigger station at Chita further to the west, a real boomer, which can be heard all over eastern Russia at night and much of the east during the day. We can use it as a backup—unless the Chinese hit it.

"Okay," I said. "I will try to get a portable transmitter, and it and the notification problem goes on the list of things we will take up with General Sholakov in the morning. I will ask him to arrange a link to Chita and ask him to have a reliable officer there to broadcast the message when he wants his counter attack to begin."

Our discussions lasted so late into the evening that it was almost midnight and the sun was finally going down when I walked out back to pee one last time and crawled into my sleeping bag. I was really pooped. But at least I have a list of things to talk about when we meet with the Russian brass tomorrow.

The last thing I remember seeing in the dimming twilight was two patrolling Marines standing outside the window of my hut carrying what look like AK-47s.

******

After all our efforts to get ready, it turned out that Krutchovy was weathered in somewhere and Sholakov and Rutman were delayed and would not even be in Arkhara until late in the afternoon at the earliest. So the meeting was postponed and we spent the morning once again going over the maps and planning nasty surprises the Chinese won't expect; things we think the Russians can implement with what they have or we might be able to get to them.

One suggestion we will for sure put forward is that the Russians set up skirmisher outfits recruited from their bike-riding Spetsnaz and airborne troops. I am going to advise Sholakov to grab up every motorcycle he can get his hands, even civilian bikes. According to Colonel Marshall, whose tank battalion worked with some of the bike-riding German skirmishers, they really worked against the Russians and it looks like they might work out here too against the Chinese, at least until it snows. *I did not discuss this in Khabarovsk because I wanted Sholakov's head Special Forces guy, Colonel Krutchovy, to hear about it first and become an advocate.*

"Hell Dave, if Krutchovy's got enough really aggressive riders we could use the C-130s to bring in some of the dirt bikes that the German skirmishers returned to the Detachment's warehouses. I am sure a lot of Russians know how to ride bikes because I saw them zipping around everywhere both on our trips to Moscow and in Khabarovsk."

"Dave, do you have any idea as to how many of the dirt bikes the Germans have returned?"

"About seven hundred so far, General. But some of them are really fucked up."

"Okay, I am going to send a message to Terry Ann to get the good ones on the next available C-130s along with the all the little battery powered AM radios and batteries she can find that can pick up 1080 and 520 on the AM dial."

I am also going to ask Dick Spelling to send some portable AM radios in case Terry Ann cannot find enough. They can clean out the retailers if necessary. I am also going to ask Klausen to get as many more of the skirmishers' motorcycles back to us as he possibly can in the next ten days."

We once again kicked around the idea of setting up small units of volunteer partisans from the Russian Spetsnaz and airborne troops. Even if they do not have dirt bikes they could still come out of the vast forest tracks between border and Podovsk as additional raiders. *I am pretty sure Sholakov already has this in mind. But I am going to ask.*

Then I suddenly feel like kicking myself. Something I'd seen parked in the mud next to a building as we drove over to our log cabins finally rang a bell. A big tracked bus-like vehicle waiting for the snow to arrive. *Of course, you fool, snow machines. Not bikes.*

"Mike," I said. "Did you ever use a snow machine?"

"No boss. I am a California guy."

"Well I have. When I was growing up in Alaska. They totally replaced dog sleds for getting around out in the bush. And that is what the Russians need more than the bikes, snow marchines. Hell, there is going to be a lot of snow soon and even dirt bikes do not work all that well in the snow."

Damn I feel stupid. I should have thought of this a long time ago.

******

We finally got in to see Sholakov after supper. Krutchovy and Rutman were with him along with Kafanov and half a dozen Russian generals I did not recognize. I made it a point to be deferential to them.

"Alexander Ivanovich, I know you and your staff and commanders have been planning for a long time to fight the Chinese so will you all please pardon me if I bore you with silly questions and suggestions about things you and your officers already know. But please indulge me and let me have a few minutes of your time."

I start by telling the Russians about our skirmishers and their use of motorcycles called "dirt bikes" which are designed for off road use.

"We found them to be quite useful in the hands of experienced riders taken from our Special Forces and airborne troops," I told the Russians.

"They can carry handheld missiles in their saddlebags and be rapidly ridden long distances to wherever they are needed to fill gaps and cover troop withdrawals; and they really work well in rough and wooded terrain where big tracked vehicles such as tanks and BMPs cannot go."

"If you think they would be helpful and want them, Yuri Andreovich, I may be able to fly in as many as five or six hundred dirt bikes for your motorcycle riding Spetsnaz and airborne troops to use; you could do what we did, find out who among your elite troops knows how to ride a motorcycle and divide them among your divisions and perhaps hold some as a strategic reserve."

"On the other hand, it is going to be cold soon and motorcycles, even dirt bikes, do not work all that well on snow. There is something even better that your troops can use." Then I told Yuri and his officers about our little two-man snow machines and explained how they have changed the way people get around in Alaska when snow is on the ground.

More and more I am beginning to think that snow machines might be the tool that will defeat the Chinese if the war drags on into the winter—if we can get enough of them.

Sholakov and his men really liked the idea of using snow machines. One of his colonels got really excited about the idea and his enthusiasm quickly convinced the others. He apparently had actually ridden on one when he'd been posted to Finland a couple of years ago.

"Da. Da. Exactly." He said loudly with real enthusiasm as he stood up and waved his arms around. He talked so fast that Miskin missed some of what he said as he explained to the other Russians how snow machines work and how they could be used.

There were a lot of back and forth questions and the Russians get more and more excited as they increasingly realized the edge they would have if their men had snow machines and the Chinese did not.

After things settle down and the colonel lit up a cigarette and sat down with a look of accomplishment and satisfaction on his face, I assured Sholakov that we would try to get some dirt bikes and as many snow machines as possible for his troops. Then I brought up a variation of the idea of stashing armored units in the bush to raid into the Chinese rear.

"You mean partisans, Christopher Ivanovich? We know about partisans. You are suggesting partisan armor?" *Sholakov's a sharp guy. We had already discussed this a bit yesterday. His comment was to inform his officers what we were going to be talking about and his demeanor was to convey his interest*

"Yes, I am General," I said very respectfully as I held up a folder. "Here are some suggestions and possible plans for you and your officers to consider. I hope you will find some of them useful. They will, of course, have to be improved and modified by your own planners.

"Basically, what we are suggesting is that you consider leaving some small armored raiding formations behind if you are forced to pull back, maybe just a single tank or BMD in a few places; maybe more other places. Hide them off the probable Chinese main lines of advance as you pull back, and then use the Chita radio station's regular programming when you want to order them to attack into the Chinese rear when you want to wreak havoc and confusion."

What I handed to Sholakov and Rutman are map sets for the possible initial locations and attack routes for a dozen or so armored raiding formations, each with about one or two tanks or BMD infantry fighting vehicles, and a host of start points and targets for small platoon and squad size partisan units of men with dirt bikes and snow machines.

"Where you would actually put them, of course, would depend on where you are and what armor you have available at the time."

I also very respectfully pointed out where our analysts think the Russians might find it profitable send their construction equipment and engineers to build new choke points when the Russian finish building the first batch.

Rutman and Krutchovy seemed quite pleased. So did the head of his engineers, a tall string bean of a guy whose name I did not catch. They should be. What I was suggesting meant their commands and responsibilities would substantially expand.

Then I got to what really bothered me. There are two land routes with pioneer roads that the Trans-Siberian could have followed but did not because they are farther from the border and zig and zag as they move from east to west. I strongly urged him to put some kind of mobile blocking force on each of them with rally points all the way back.

Sholakov smiled and we absolutely beamed at each other, and I gave him and his staff a little bow of acknowledgement, when he told me his staff had already identified them and blocking forces were already moving into place.

His officers are obviously quite pleased by my acknowledgement of their readiness. I have got to remember to stay super respectful and keep giving them compliments.

I also respectfully suggested that, in the case of a withdrawal, he require all his division commanders to assign a specific engineer officer the responsibility to pre-mine the key bridges and blow them after his troops get past.

"I hate to admit it," I said with a deliberately wry smile and embarrassed shrug to help make the point, "but you can learn from my mistakes in the recent war." Then I explained both verbally and with appropriate hand gestures.

"We found the destruction of bridges and the roads to be a problem in Germany," I explain. "The division commanders gave the proper orders. But sometimes in the confusion of pulling back the orders did not get to the engineers in time or the engineers who received the orders did not have enough explosives or expertise."

Actually, we left the bridges up deliberately but the Russians do not need to know that.

"It was my mistake," I admitted. "I should have required the division commanders to assign the responsibility for having the appropriate men and explosives on hand at each bridge to a specific officer instead of to their engineers in general."

I was watching the Russian officers as the translator repeated my words. I think from the expressions on their faces and the understanding nods that they got it.

Finally, I expressed concern that there was only one choke point being constructed on the Trans-Siberian branch line that used to go across the Amur to the Chinese city of Heihe. Perhaps, I suggested, it might be useful to put a battalion size unit with armor and mobile artillery in the mountains in front of the choke point or in the mountain pass behind it and for the commander of the choke point to identify some rally points behind it.

Our suggestions were well received, perhaps because moving troops into these positions before the Chinese attack fits in with the Russian observation that it is going to take longer to move their troops about than they initially anticipated. Sholakov admitted as much to me yesterday in Khabarovsk. *Apparently the chaos and delays at the train station had been a real eye opener for everyone.*

Then we all settled in for a banquet of epic proportions and a night of heavy drinking and informal discussions in a smoke filled room. Despite my "medical problem" I drank a couple of bottles of Russian beer and ate a lot of cheese and pretzels. *Really good beer and I especially like the pretzels.*

Chapter Eight

We find our missing men.

Special Forces Colonel Randall "Jim" Bowie was waiting for me the next morning when I came out of the commo hut after getting a message off to General Spelling. In it I asked Dick to corner the market on snow machines by buying every single one that can be found and shipped within the week.

Bowie is really worried. One of his missing two-man teams of special operators showed up. They'd been tied up and robbed. They are pissed and embarrassed but otherwise okay. The other team is still missing and so are the eight Russian Spetsnaz troops assigned to accompany them as they made their rounds paying the Russian troops and making sure the food deliveries were reaching them .

He also let me know that in a few weeks many of the Russian units were going to start running out of flour and whatever else you need to make bread.

"Bread's real important to the Russian troops, General. It's the most important part of their rations. Christ, they even have bread baking ovens mounted on some of their Jeeps." *Damn, I did not know that.*

"I did not know that, Jim."... "Well, I will get a message off to the States. What do you think – split the food cargos fifty - fifty between flour and meat?"

The Colonel did not know the answer and got red faced with embarrassment. "I do not know, Sir. But I will find out immediately."

******

I was busy stuffing my dirty clothes in a duffle bag about an hour before my flight back to the States when Mr. Simmons, one of the Signal Corps warrant officers, jogged up to my hut and barged in the door.

"Priority call for you General. We have the Vice President on the scrambler phone." *The Vice President. What the hell is he doing calling me out here?*

I trotted two huts down and motioned for the troops inside to step outside as I picked up the phone.

"General Roberts here."

"General, it's Bernie Carey."

"Hello Mr. Vice President. What can I do for you, Sir?"

"Ah...General, I apologize for bothering you but I wonder if we might be able to get together, privately that is, the next time you get back to the States."

"Your timing is pretty good, Mr. Vice President. I am leaving for the States in a couple of hours. I will be staying at my father-in-laws' house tomorrow night and maybe the next night too. Would you like me to call on you at your office Tuesday afternoon?"

"No General, please let me visit you at the Senator's place; tomorrow evening. About eight if that is alright?"

"Yes sir, that would be fine." *Wonder what this is all about.*

"Thank you, General. I look forward to speaking with you."

******

"You really do not know why he wants to talk to you," asks my father-in-law, the Senator, with a little grin.

"No Pops, I do not. What do you think it is?

"Well hell, Chris, he wants to know if you are going to run for President." *He is pulling my leg.*

"You are kidding me, right?

"Nope. We won the war and that means you are a hot political property. Both parties see you as another Eisenhower. Meaning you could win and leave the governing and patronage to them. You did not know that?" he asks looking at me rather shrewdly.

"No. But so what? I am not sure I could handle the endless bullshit and indecision you guys have to endure and I have got to see this Chinese thing through." *But it sure is flattering.*

******

"Hello, Mr. Vice President. Come on in... You know the Senator I am sure?"

"Sure do. Hello Jim. How ya doing?

"Hey Bernie, good to see you again. Come on in. I will rustle up some coffee and make myself scarce so you two can talk. Come on in the kitchen. Best place to talk."

"Well General, I am sure you know why I am here?"

"No sir, actually I do not".... "Oh, here's some sugar. Or would you prefer some sweetener?" So what's up, Mr. Vice President? I admit I am curious; what brings you out here tonight?"

"Well damn it, Barbara's putting it about that you are thinking about running in the next election. She is got her staff passing the word that, if you decide not to run, you'll agree to serve as the vice-presidential candidate if she gets the nomination. Any truth in that?"

"Jesus Christ!" I exploded. "She is a goddamn liar. First saying I supported her stupid treaty and now this. I have never even had a conversation with her or anyone associated with her. Not one. She is the last person in the world I would ever want to see in the White House. You are the one who ought to run, not her."

The Vice President looked at me very intently and quietly asked, "Well how about you? Are you going to run?"

"Me? Hell no. I don't think I could put up with the endless indecision and bullshit that goes with the job; and I could not even if I wanted to because I have got this Russian and Chinese mess on my plate. Christ, if we are not careful we are gonna end in the middle of a goddamn nuclear war."

After a pause, I added "thanks to that stupid woman and her goddamn stupid treaty."

Well, he is smiling. Pops nailed it; that is what he wanted to hear.

****** *China*

An obscure four story red stucco office building inside a compound on Red Banner Street is where the Military Committee of the Chinese Communist Party meets. The Chinese army, unlike all the other armies in the world, is under the direct control of a political party, the communists. It does not in any way answer to the Chinese government even though they are basically one and the same - the Party Chairman is also the President of the county.

Today's meeting of the party's Military Committee that morning was to consider a very important question: Should or should not the Party direct the Red Army to proceed with military action to reclaim some of the lands that were stolen by the Russians years ago? And, if so, when should the attack begin and which war plan should be used?

The answers are preordained, of course, but the formalities required by the Party's traditions have to be observed.

Li Ping, the Chairman of the Party's military commission, was, quite conveniently, also the Party Chairman and China's president. He and the committee's other members listen intently as General Wu, the defense minister, presented the army's recommendation.

When General Wu finished, and reasonable answers were provided for the few perfunctory questions that were raised, the seven members of the Party's military committee nodded their heads and in so doing voted unanimously to order the Red Army to regain the stolen lands according to the proposed plans and schedules.

Small advance units of Chinese troops will begin infiltrating over the border immediately. The initial attacks will begin at dawn on August twenty eighth. Forty four divisions of the Red Army will begin crossing the border at 0614. More than eighteen hundred Chinese planes and helicopters will provide around the clock air support until the Russians are defeated and the lands not claimed by Russia are restored to China's rightful ownership. Nuclear weapons will not be used. A quick victory before winter sets in is the Red Army's goal.

China is on the move after centuries of decline; and its objectives are much more than just the return of the disputed Ussuri River lands to Chinese control.

******

I was in Brussels when Jack Peterson rushed into my NATO office and rescue me from an unimportant staff meeting to discuss the planning for a larger and equally unimportant meeting. He was carrying a flash message from Dick Spelling—NSA intercepts have confirmed that the Chinese will launch a non-nuclear invasion of Russia on the morning of August twenty eighth. *I almost wish he had not rescued me.*

Almost immediately the phone began to ring. A White House aide. There will be a meeting of the National Security Council within the hour. The President wants me to call in and attend via teleconference. I told the President's aide I would be present. But before I started down to our secure conference room I placed a satellite call on the scrambler phone to Dave Shelton at Arkhara.

"Dave, it's on," I said without preamble. "The Chinese will launch their invasion at dawn on the morning of August twenty eighth. I want you to take Arnie to translate and meet with Sholakov. Right now. Barge in if you have to. But get to him immediately and tell him the Chinese are coming sometime in the middle of August." *I emphasized the word 'middle.'*

"Do not tell anyone else, not even our guys and certainly no other Russians. Just him. And, whatever you do, do not tell Sholakov or anyone else the precise date. Just that it will be some time around the middle of August or a little after. We will give everyone the precise time and date later."

I do not want the Chinese to know how seriously we have compromised their communications. And I still do not know who Arnie really works for.

"Here's the thing," I told Dave. "We do not want the Chinese or Moscow to know we have penetrated their communications. So I want you to tell Sholakov that I most strongly suggest he call Moscow immediately, preferably before you leave his office, and merely say that his Chinese sources confirm that the Chinese will launch a non-nuclear invasion sometime around the middle of August or a little thereafter.

"And Dave, ask him to please be sure not mention or even hint to anyone that it was the United States who warned him. Tell him to say that one of his own highly reliable agents in the Chinese army is his source."

As soon as I hung up I called Dick Spelling.

"Yeah, I know. I just heard about the meeting and why," Dick told me.

I informed Dick that I had ordered Dave Shelton to immediately alert Sholakov about the invasion but not to give him the precise date. I also told him that Dave is going to suggest to Sholakov that he immediately inform Moscow that one of his Chinese sources confirms that there will be a non-nuclear invasion of Eastern Russia sometime around the middle of August.

"It's my hope," I explained to Dick, "that if everyone can keep their mouths shut long enough, the Chinese will think it was a Chinese agent of Russia's military intelligence who revealed the invasion, not NSA."

"Fat chance of that," was Dick's the cynical reply.

******

The National Security Council meeting went about as well as could be expected under the circumstances. Everyone expressed concern that we could be pulled into a nuclear war and suggested a course of action:

The President's Chief of Staff wants to take a poll to see how people want the President to respond; the Secretary of State wants to commence "shuttle diplomacy" by hustling between the Chinese and Russian capitols with a large contingent of press from all over the world "to show their leaders how much the world is concerned;" and, the Secretary of Defense reported wryly, the Navy wants to a carrier to sail up and down the Chinese coast "to intimidate those people" into stopping the invasion.

I do not know whether to laugh or cry at the various proposals. But I did speak in support of the NSA request that we neither issue orders nor take action of any kind for at least forty eight hours. NSA is right. We want to keep the Chinese from knowing the extent of our intelligence capacities. Best to let them think we got it from the Russians. The President agreed.

And the odds are better than even money that one or more of them, probably the Secretary of State, will leak the news to their staff who will then, in turn, leak it to New York Times or Washington Post within the next three or four hours.

About the only other thing everyone could agree on is that we have to step up our supply and equipment deliveries so the Russian forces in the east have a better chance of driving off the Chinese without using their nukes.

After I hung up I decided to call it a day and go home. But before I did, I called Terry Ann Androtti, the Detachment's administrative officer. I told Terry Ann to accelerate the shipments to Russia to the highest possible levels, particularly the snow machines and handheld missiles—even if it means shipping them in partially full planes without all the other stuff. I did not tell her why, but she is not dumb; she probably figured it out before I hung up. *The Russians have their own combat rations and winter gear; we've already got the little AM civilian radios going out separately.*

I also told TerryAnn to find out how many snow machines are immediately available for a cash sale and use our black funds to buy every one she can locate that is available for delivery now and all those that can be produced and shipped in the next thirty days. Not just in the States, I told her. Also check with the Swedes and the Canadians and everyone else, even the big retailers. Bombardier in Montreal makes a full line of them, I suggested. Buy them all. *Terry Ann is a Department of the Army civilian employee and a real go-getter. Probably why she makes a lot more money than I do.*

The Chinese soldiers crept out of the trees and moved down to the river bank in the moonlight. They were carrying full packs and would be paddling across in rubber boats as they have been practicing to do for years; then the paddlers will bring the boats back so there will be no evidence of their infiltration. There were not supposed to be Russian soldiers anywhere near this isolated stretch of river but the Chinese were not taking any chances. Not a word was spoken.

There were quiet splashes as the Chinese waded ashore on the other side. They quickly climbed the muddy river bank and then silently melted into the trees and began climbing the tree covered hillside that ran up from the river. There were one hundred and twenty two of them, all carrying Chinese-made AK47s, under the command of twenty nine year old Senior Lieutenant Bao Wei.

Lieutenant Bao's men formed a long line as they walked further and further up the hill with the lieutenant leading the way. Five hours later, long before dawn, they hid under the leaves of a heavy grove of trees and ate a cold meal. They would not eat or talk or move about until darkness returned. It came easy to them; they'd been practicing for years.

Tonight, and in the nights that follow, Bao would lead his men deeper and deeper into the mountains of Eastern

Russia. Their target is an old stone railroad bridge about a hundred miles north of the Amur River. When they reach it they will fade back into the trees and wait.

Only Bao Wei and his second in command, a squat and powerful mean-looking senior sergeant named Shen Ji, know the target and which songs on the radio will tell them to proceed or quietly return to China. The Chinese are carrying enough rice balls and dry noodles to last for quite some time. If they stay longer they will have to rely on whatever they can take from the Russians.

****** *Senior Lieutenant Bao*

In the middle of the night four days later, as my men and I were moving down a hill in the dark, there was a click and pop and we instinctively froze as a flare streaked upwards towards the sky and then popped to brightly light the night. Then the shooting started; we had walked right into the middle of some kind of Russian troop encampment.

I shouted out for my men not to fire, but it was too late. Everyone began shooting at everyone else and kept on shooting until the light of the flare faded out. It was a shouting and screaming scene of chaos. Then the shooting stopped and no one dared move for almost an hour in the moonlit darkness despite the pitiful cries from the wounded.

Dawn's early light resulted in another burst of firing as the men began to be able to see other men near them. But that soon die away in response to my bellowed commands and those of my sergeant, Shen Jie. Within minutes everyone can see everyone else and all the casualties.

The Russians are dead, all ten of them. They are literally, in some cases shot to pieces. But there are many more Chinese on the ground than Russians; mostly the result of friendly fire.

We quickly pulled our wounded men and the bodies of the dead from the open area on the hill and into the nearby trees. I ordered my men to move fast so we would be less likely to be spotted from the air if the Russians were able to get a message off and someone came looking. *I do not think they had time to send a message but there is no sense taking chances.*

Our losses are substantial; there are seventeen dead Chinese and thirty two wounded of whom at least four are almost certain to die and the prospects of two or three more look bleak. All we can do is fill the most seriously wounded with morphine from our limited supply and wait to see who among our wounded can recover enough to be useful.

While we waited we dug holes and buried both our own dead and the dead Russians. Normally we would leave the Russians to rot, but our orders are to keep our existence a secret; so I decided to bury them so they would be less likely to be seen or smelled. When we searched the packs the Russians were carrying we found what appeared to be large amounts of some kind of foreign money.

What really surprised us, however, was that the Russians were all carrying Chinese assault rifles with strange lettering. We already have more than enough extra weapons from their own casualties so we threw the Russians' weapons and the extras from our own casualties into the shallow grave with them. We will keep the Russians' ammunition, however, to replace what we used to kill them.

Two nights later we again began moving slowly north as fast as our surviving wounded can travel. Four of our most seriously wounded were left behind with one of our medics who had himself been wounded very slightly to tend them. I also left enough food and morphine for another week. *I bet Ma volunteered to stay with the wounded so he could get some the painkiller for himself.*

Sergeant Shen wanted to mercifully end the suffering of the four men. But in the end I finally decided against it because leaving the seriously wounded behind would not compromise the mission; they do not know where our company is headed or what our job will be when we get there.

So far as the seriously wounded men and everyone else in the company knows, we are a company of scouts and will be back to pick up our wounded and return to China—when our "reconnaissance mission" is finished.

Indeed, we may be able to come back this way and rescue them if they are still alive. If we can, we will. There is also the fact, as I explain to Shen, that no matter how mercifully we end their suffering it will distress the other men and may encourage desertions and bad behavior. And that I cannot have; we are already short of men. Besides, my mother would not approve.

******

The headquarters of the 112th Guards Division was located about two hundred miles north of Khabarovsk. Its approximately ten thousand men and reservists, however, were scattered over more than a hundreds of miles of frontier along the Amur River and at bridges and other key points and villages behind it. It was arguably the most isolated division in the Russian army.

The 112th is an infantry division and far from being a formidable fighting force. There are nineteen small villages and no paved roads in the twenty thousand square miles of Russia it is supposed to defend. Even so, the division itself was beginning to stir.

Three weeks ago all of its engineers and construction equipment bounced their way slowly south on the rough dirt road that runs along the river towards Khabarovsk. From there they were to go inland to help build defenses along the railroad right of way. Then, last week, part of its battalion-sized tank regiment and all of its tanks and tracked vehicles were detached to follow them.

Rumors flew among the troops of the 112th's tank battalion, not a one of them over five feet five inches tall so they can fit into their tanks, as to where they were headed. But no one, not even the bald headed little lieutenant colonel commanding them, Ivan Stransky, seemed to know.

Initially Colonel Stransky had merely been ordered to load his tanks and personnel carriers on tank carriers that would be coming as soon as they finished delivering construction equipment. When he reported that they were loaded, he was told to take his tanks and APCs, and just the men needed to operate them in combat, south to Khabarovsk and wait for new orders. The rest of his men, the truck drivers, clerks, and cooks, were to be left under the command of one of the battalion's officers to form a provisional infantry company. *The least useful officer: he'd make sure of that.*

One of the more interesting things about the movement of Stransky's armor was that the battalion's trucks and jeeps were to be left behind with the newly formed infantry company and the BMP infantry fighting vehicles were to be loaded to the gills with all the extra supplies and ammunition they can carry. Even the tanks were to pile on all the extra supplies and ammunition they can carry even if it meant they could not swing their tubes and rotate their turrets.

Obviously we are going to operate in rough terrain for an extended period of time without access to supplies. But where and doing what?

Then yesterday an order had come down that all the men in the division with heavy weapons training, such as its mortar men, SAM operators, and machine gunners, were to be trucked down the dirt road to the railroad. They are to bring with them all their weapons and all their ammunition, including the "war reserves" that had not been out of the ammunition bunkers since the Ussuri River War with the Chinese in 1969.

What this left the 112th division and its unhappy commander, Major General Ivan Bulganin, was about five thousand infantrymen, if one included all the clerks, truck drivers, and cooks, to protect almost two hundred kilometers of border. And then today, to Bulganin's dismay, he was ordered to organize and thoroughly arm and provision one hundred enlisted volunteers and ten senior sergeants for long-term hazardous duty assignments behind the lines as partisans.

Every man who volunteered to serve as a partisan, including the NCOs, was to be immediately promoted two ranks and paid his next six months pay in advance, three thousand American dollars and a lot of useless Soviet rubles.

Two hours later the General was ordered to immediately report to Khabarovsk to receive further instructions and to bring with him all his remaining supplies and equipment, his air support company with its four light observation aircraft and six Mi-8 helicopters, and all his men except the one hundred and ten volunteers. *This is too much. What have I done wrong?*

Bulganin's distress ended abruptly when he reached Khabarovsk. His efficiency and honesty in getting the food and money to his men, and his rapid dispatch of the troops and armor detached from his division had been recognized and appreciated. He was additionally given the command of the 83rd Guards Division based south of Khabarovsk.

The luckless commander of the 83rd, Bulganin was informed, has been relieved because he diddled and dawdled and hoped that no one would notice he did not send his engineers and tried to get his hands on the money and food the Spetsnaz brought to pay his troops.

His first job, an elated Bulganin is told by the frontal commander, General Sholakov, is to move the 83rd and what was left of the 112th into a blocking position where the Trans-Siberian Railroad begins to go through the mountains about one hundred kilometers west of Khabarovsk.

When he gets there, Sholakov tells him, he is to dig in and be ready to give the Chinese a bloody nose; and then, if the Chinese break through his lines, lead his men in a fighting withdrawal down the railroad line by leapfrogging from one pre-selected rally point to the next. He is to inspect the withdrawal route and select the rally points in person.

Getting all that done, General Sholakov told him, "will undoubtedly require that you and your political officers immediately take a hard line, a very hard line, with the slackers and defeatists you find."

Bulganin took on his new assignment with the enthusiasm and determination of a man reborn—his lack of a "patron" that resulted in his being given the most isolated division in the army has generated an opportunity for him to shine—and he is determined to do so.

Chapter Nine

Two divisions.

An elated Bulganin immediately ordered one of the young majors accompanying him to return to the 112th to organize the partisan units and make sure his deputy commander immediately starts moving what's left of the division to Kharbarovsk and then down the rail line into the interior. Then he helicoptered south to the 83rd with three of his officers.

He also ordered his two most dependable men, a lieutenant colonel and a major to Khabarovsk. They are to wait there, he tells them, for the rest of the division's Mi-8s helicopters to arrive carrying certain men and supplies.

As soon as the helicopters arrive and refuel, the two officers and the men on the helicopters are to fly west along the railroad and set up a preliminary base camp at the rail spur nearest to where the two divisions are to dig in and establish their initial defenses.

******

Bulganin found the 83rd every bit as bad as Sholakov had described it. Maybe even worse. But then he brightened considerably when he realized that it was a great opportunity for him to make his mark because the 83rd could only get better.

The disgraced general of the 83rd had already departed in one of the division's three operational Mi-8 helicopters by the time Bulganin arrived. The division's chief of staff, a rather untidy colonel with a sandwich in one hand and a cigarette in his other, explained that the departing general mentioned something about sending it back after it had dropped him off the Khabarovsk airfield.

"But it never came back," the colonel reported with a shrug of his shoulders.

Bulganin had landed his helicopter next to the 83rd's division headquarters, and caught the staff sitting around smoking and playing cards. They thought it was the general's helicopter returning and ignored it.

Bulganin's face got red and he went ballistic; he was shouting and the staff were standing stiffly at attention as he told them they were one inch away from being stripped of their ranks and sent to a penal battalion for gross dereliction of duty.

"And you," he screamed at the division's political officer. "You knew about the orders to send the construction equipment and armor; and you knew the men did not initially get the money sent to pay them and the food to feed them. You were supposed to prevent such disobedience from happening and report it if you could not."

"Did you report them to General Sholakov or to the office of the military district's political commissar or any other authority? No. You did not. I know you did not. I checked."

"Get rid of him," he snapped at one of the officers who'd accompanied him from the 112th. "The rest of you come over here," he orders as he points to the map one of the officers who had accompanied him is busy tacking up on the plywood wall.

He was in the midst of giving orders as to where and how the 83rd's units are to be relocated, and the order in which they are to move, when he was interrupted by a brief rattle of gunfire.

Then there was a single shot. The already highly attentive officers became even more attentive. The 83rd just suffered its first casualty of the coming war.

I am still uneasy about shooting the political officer. I probably would not have done it but Sholakov said it would be necessary to encourage the others.

******

Five days later Bulganin's men began arriving at their new position. It was spread out on the hills on both sides of the railroad line at kilometer post one thirty seven. There was a small rail spur three miles further on and Bulganin was there watching as his self-propelled artillery, and what was left of the armor of his two divisions, was unloaded from a long line of flatcars using a makeshift ramp. The ramp was, and rightly so, the first thing Sholakov's engineers constructed when they arrived eight days ago.

Bulganin was not the only one watching. A small party of Russian officers and a couple of men, obviously military, in unmarked fatigues landed in a Mi-8 and were looking at the unloading as they walk over to him. None of them know it, of course, but an even smaller party of Chinese was also watching through powerful binoculars from a hill several miles away.

A few moments later the new arrivals walked up and saluted. A young lieutenant, Borisov according to the name on his fatigues, introduced them as "foreign friends here to observe your progress."

Several of the foreigners asked very pointed questions as to his plans and the progress he was making. They wanted to know what forces and equipment he already had in place and about the men and equipment en route. Then one of the foreigners, the older tough-looking one with the close cropped white hair, whose name is apparently something like "Schell tin," asked him if it is true he had a firing squad shoot one of the officers responsible for delaying his men's pay.

There was no use denying it. So, very defensively, Bulganin admitted it.

"Yes. I had him shot. It had to be done; and it was not just the men's food and pay. He was the division's political officer and he said nothing and alerted no one when the division commander, the man I had shot, tried to steal the men's money and then ignored the orders he received to send his armor and engineers to Khabarovsk."

Bulganin is relieved by the interpreter's translation of the response of the tall gray-haired foreigner.

"Good man. You did the right thing." *Thank God. I thought I was in real trouble.*

Then one of the aides of the foreign officer spread a big map on the ground. They stood in a semi-circle around it and spent more than an hour discussing where various kinds of Chinese attacks might come from and how he and his men would respond to them. The foreigners had several helpful suggestions and observations.

All and all, it was a very helpful discussion, he later decided. That evening, he used some of the foreigners' ideas to impress his senior staff as they stood in front of a similar map in his command tent.

The old man is tough and he really knows his stuff became the generally accepted view of the 83rd's officers about their new commander. *They liked the idea that he cares about his men and was thinking ahead as to how the Chinese might attack and where rally points might be established if they were pushed out of their assigned position.*

What Bulganin was not told was that the foreigners came to see him primarily because the payroll and food distribution team assigned to the 83rd was still missing and two of its ten men are Americans. He also did not know that they'd be back in a few days when the 83rd's infantry arrives. They had already checked out the division's armor and engineers; they were all paid last week. So were all the units in and around its headquarters.

Only some of the infantry, those who had been scattered in isolated posts along the border and in the villages, remained to be questioned. They were still inbound on trucks somewhere on the service road; they would be questioned about when and how they received their pay when they arrive.

******

Bulganin surveyed his first four days in his new command with satisfaction. Most of his vehicles and artillery from the 83rd and the 112th were still on the road; but his officers and men, with their wives and children safely evacuated, and eating better food and being promptly paid, were responding even better than he had thought possible. *We just might pull this off, he told himself.*

Even so, everything was certainly not going as smoothly as he had hoped. For one thing, it had been impossible to get all the men and weapons and supplies of the two divisions into the available trucks. He'd actually flown back to both of the divisions' original headquarters to see for himself before he finally accepted the reality that his trucks would have to go back for a second load, and maybe even a third and fourth.

Having to wait for the arrival or his infantry and supplies was a serious problem; the terrible state of the dirt service road running along the railroad made for very slow travel even though it had been closed to civilian vehicles. But it had to be used; it was the only road running east and west in this part of Russia.

A big problem was that no one had any idea when the two divisions' towed artillery would arrive. The somewhat garbled radio message he'd received yesterday seemed to suggest it would start arriving tomorrow. Then it will take at least a week for the trucks pulling the artillery to turn around and go back to get the infantry and their weapons and supplies. And even then they may not be able to carry everything and have to make yet another trip.

Will I have enough time? That is what worried Bulganin more than anything else. Sholakov himself helicoptered in this morning and complimented him on the work in progress. And then ruined his day by saying that the Chinese invasion might reach his position as early as in the next two or three weeks.

Well, he would do his best. If it does not work it won't be for want of trying or driving his men. Then he decided to take another look at his second artillery fire base, the one to the southwest. It was in a good position to support his main line of resistance, he thought. But the foreign officer was right, he admitted to himself; the way I initially planned to deploy my artillery makes my guns too vulnerable to an infantry attack if the Chinese get around my main force by walking over the mountains and attacking my rear.

Should I relocate the firebase or just reconfigure it to be more easily defended? Damn. Most of the gun pits and fighting positions are already dug. Time is running out so better to stay where we are and improve our defenses.

******

Bao Wei, Shen Ji, and what's left of their Chinese infantry company moved slowly, very slowly, every night. Even so, three or four of the recovering wounded could not keep up and several of them had developed serious infections. But he could not abandon them for fear of further damaging his men's sagging morale. So the able bodied men were carrying the gear and weapons of the wounded men and doing their best to help them along, even carrying them at times.

Periodically the Chinese could hear planes overhead and once they heard the sound of a distant helicopter. But it was otherwise quite peaceful, like taking a long holiday hike through the woods, except, of course, that they were in rough mountains and can only walk at night with one man and a shielded flashlight leading the way. On several particularly dark and rainy nights they did not even try to walk at all.

It was also quite different from their training in China. There were actually wild animals in the forest. Most of the men had never even heard of moose and elk, let alone actually seen one. So they became quite excited, and some even worried and loaded their weapons when a moose wandered into their camp while they were quietly resting and sleeping under the trees.

The men watched in utter fascination as the moose stripped twigs and leaves off the trees and shrubs around them without even apparently knowing they were quietly sitting and standing all around it.

Bao watched the moose for a moment and then made up his mind when Sergeant Shen raised a questioning eyebrow and made a shooting gesture with his hands. The men were all watching as Bao nodded and held up a finger—one careful shot. They will have meat with their noodles tonight.

More and more moose and other wild animals are seen as the Chinese walk deeper and deeper into the mountains. One night as they walked they heard the mournful howls and yips of what could only be wolves. Not a single one of the Chinese soldiers had ever seen or heard wolves before, but they all knew instinctively what it was they were hearing.

Somehow the possibility that they might see and hear more wild animals when they go to ground each morning caused their spirits to rise as their "reconnaissance patrol" continued. Within days the memories of the disastrous confrontation with the Russians receded into the past along with the wounded they had been forced to leave behind.

Lieutenant Bao himself became increasingly upbeat and so did his men. Despite the slow pace it increasingly looked as though he and his men would reach their intended destination with time to spare. It was an isolated spot on a forested mountainside from which they can sally forth when their radio broadcasts the song that is the Bao's signal to proceed.

Exactly forty-eight hours after he heard it he was to destroy a certain railroad bridge and begin attacking the railroad and everything associated with it.

What Bao knows, and his men and Shen Ji do not, is what they are supposed to do and where; they are supposed to cut the first bridge where the railroad enters the mountains, about one hundred kilometers west of Khabarovsk. What he does not know is when.

******

Bao only realized that they had found the railroad when word was passed back from the scouts leading the Chinese column that they can see vehicle lights flickering below them about ten kilometers away. He immediately turned the company around and withdrew to a densely wooded forest ravine they had struggled through an hour earlier. Then they went to ground.

When morning arrived Bao Wei took one man with him and cautiously moved forward to check things out and plan his attack. He was surprised to see a lot of military traffic on both the railroad bridge and on the dirt service road running along side the tracks; and most of the traffic seems to be flowing westward. *Has the invasion started— are the Russians retreating?*

It was not until the next day when he walked further west into the mountains on a similar two-man reconnaissance that Bao realized that a major Russian military strong point was under construction. With his binoculars he could see it on both sides of the railroad about ten kilometers to the west.

What Bao did not know was that that particular spot was picked for the blocking position because the small stream running off the northerly side and running under the railroad could provide its defenders with water. The water runs under the railroad tracks in a culvert that will be destroyed or blocked when the bridge falls on it.

Raw and recently denuded mountain slopes now existed on either side of the tracks where the railroad passes into the mountain range. The angry slash of red dirt contrasted greatly to the rest of the heavily forested lower slopes of the mountain range that was visible to the men working on the position and the Chinese watching them. Where there had once been trees along the railroad tracks and service road there were now rough patches of bare reddish earth torn with numerous trenches, holes, and sand bagged positions.

The source of the destruction was obvious: Twenty or more huge bulldozers and other types of heavy construction equipment were working all over the site and the adjacent hills and mountain sides; the troops walking and working around the equipment looked like an army of ants. There were obviously many thousands of them. Their tents and equipment were everywhere.

This is a major construction project, was Bao's first thought as he adjusted the focus on his binoculars and settled in to watch. Both civilian and military vehicles were constantly moving westward on the railroad and the road running along it. It was instantly obvious from the armor, artillery, and military vehicles parked everywhere that this is a military project. *And it's new; it is not shown on the map Colonel Ma gave me.*

Unfortunately for Bao, his company's "radio man" is only carrying a bulky older battery powered portable radio good only for listening; he cannot report that the Russians are here in force instead of along the border as he and his men had been led to believe. *Oh well, he thought. Sooner or later someone will report it.*

Also, but not unfortunately for Bao, is the fact that at least one of his men is an informer planted by his regiment's political officer. Having such an informer in every company is party policy. It means that if Bao does not attack as ordered he will be denounced and severely disciplined if and when he returns to China. *It really makes no difference even if the informer becomes a casualty; if I go back to China without attacking someone will report me if he does not. I have to either lead the attack or defect and try to surrender.*

Then he brightened as he recalled an earlier thought.

"I do not have to attack a bridge where the Russians are strong and get us all killed. I can hit another bridge either above or below this place. No one will know whether it is the right one."

****** *General Roberts*

We flew into naval airfield at Vladivostok in the Starlifter. It was instantly obvious that the Russians on the Vladivostok airfield had never seen a plane like it before— it immediately attracted a small crowd of curious personnel. They disappeared as if by magic, however, when the door opened and General Sholakov began walking down the portable stairs that were hurriedly pushed into place.

A small group of officers was waiting at the bottom of the stairs to welcome Sholakov and they too are plainly curious about the plane. The cars and Jeeps they came in are parked to the side. As they saluted and greeted the General, a car and a bus pulled up to take us to the local military headquarters. Sholakov did not introduce me or anyone else in his entourage. He just crisply saluted the assembled officers and headed for the transportation.

Sholakov and I rode in the spacious back seat of an old black Zil limousine with a dirty interior along with Colonel Miskin and Lieutenant Borisov; everyone else rides in the bus. *I do not know what kind of a car we are in so I asked. It's an old Zil. It reminds me of an old American model that had long ago gone out of business. A Packard or Nash I think they were called.*

As we pulled away from the Starlifter I could see one of the Russian naval officers hurry to a jeep and speak into a handheld radio microphone. He seemed a bit excited and was obviously reporting that someone important has unexpectedly arrived in addition to General Sholakov, a man wearing a Russian officer's fatigues without any rank or insignia.

What made my arrival so unique and obviously caused the officer's hurried report was that I was riding with Sholakov in the limo while several Russian generals and a number of colonels and other officers were riding on the bus. *Who is that masked man? That is my irreverent thought as we drove away and I saw the naval officer's gestures as he spoke excitedly into the phone.*

******

Vladivostok is a godawful place. The only thing more dingy and run down than the airfield and the military headquarters is the city itself. All we saw was row after row of ugly concrete apartments as we drove in on the pot holed concrete road from the airfield to the Naval Headquarters.

It really was a mess. Laundry was flapping out of the windows and cars are haphazardly parked around them, many of them obviously rusty derelicts in various stages of decay. A handful of pre-teens and teenagers were clustered at some of the building entrances smoking.

All in all, it looks like a damn depressing place to live. It reminds me of the housing projects I saw in Chicago.

Vladivostok itself is a port city located at the very end of the Far Eastern Military District which Sholakov commands. It is important to Russia because it is Russia's only all-weather port with access to the Pacific.

It is particularly important at the moment because, in addition to its regiments of naval infantry, it is also the home of one of Sholakov's armies, the Fourteenth, consisting of six under strength army divisions and a number of navy and air force fighter and reconnaissance squadrons. The Fourteenth Army is one of the four new armies that were brought into the Russian East some years ago when the Chinese attacked in 1969 in what turned out to be a futile effort to take back some disputed territory around the Ussuri River. They have been here ever since.

During the past ten days, four of the six army divisions began moving north to Khabarovsk and most of the aircraft, at least those that could still fly, left for Podovsk. The Fourteenth Army's other two divisions will begin moving as soon as rail space is available.

Their repositioning, Sholakov confided on the flight, was occurring despite serious naval opposition which resulted in orders from Moscow that seemed to suggest that he should leave the six divisions and the planes in Vladivostok.

"Unfortunately," he explained with a smile, "we are having communications outages so I won't get the definitive orders to do nothing until it is too late to stop the planes and troops from redeploying."

There will be, he admitted when I asked, quite a row at the Defense Ministry about his orders relocating the divisions. But the defense minister is a former general and the army has more political power than navy—so at some point the order will be quietly rescinded and forgotten.

What I know from the NSA intercepts, and Sholakov may not, is that the Vladivostok-based general in overall command of the Fourteenth Army and its six army divisions and planes chose to obey Sholakov's orders and pretend he had not received those from Moscow ordering him to stay in Vladivostok. He'd heard about the fate of the political officers.

And Sholakov is doing the right thing by redeploying the six army divisions and Vladivostok's air force squadrons to the interior. Taking Vladivostok and denying Russia a port with access to the Sea of Japan and the Pacific may be one of China's goals. But Sholakov's reality is that he needs to concentrate his forces to win the war, not split them up to win a battle to hold a port and the lands around it that will almost certainly be lost if the war is lost.

Russia faces same choice in Vladivostok that it faced in Berlin a few months ago—and the answer is the same as well: Do not keep troops away from the main battle to protect something that will surely be lost if the main battle is lost.

Whether the Russian admirals like it or not, the Russian navy will have to dig in and fight on its own to defend the port if the Chinese attack. And they will have to do so without some of the naval infantry regiments, the Russian Marines, stationed here. Sholakov wants to take at least half of them as well, maybe more.

He nodded when I told him I thought he should take them all while he can and replace them with the reinforcements that land at Vladivostok after the railroad line running out of Vladivostok is cut.

But will the Chinese even attack in an effort to take Vladivostok and, if so, when and how? And how long can it hold out? Those are significant questions because Vladivostok could possibly be significant for the Russians as a staging area for a second front. For example, enough Russian forces might be shipped here after the war starts to support an attack up the rail line towards Khabarovsk in an effort to draw Chinese troops and equipment away from the main conflict.

Alternately, the Russian forces at Vladivostok could attack directly over the border into China itself in an effort to draw Chinese troops away from the main conflict. In any event, so long as the port holds out and the rail line and the road running north remain open between Vladivostok and Khabarovsk, the Russians can bring troops and supplies from Vladivostok and use them to reinforce Khabarovsk and the interior where the crucial battles for the Russian East are likely to be fought.

Obviously the Chinese know all this so they are likely to cut the Vladivostok railroad line and road to Khabarovsk as soon as the war starts. Or they might launch a serious effort to try to take the port to prevent its use as a staging area for a counterattack. Or the Chinese might let a Russian build up occur and move north, and then come out of China and cut it off and destroy it.

It's like a big chess game with the lives of many thousands of men on every square.

Chapter Ten

Vladivostok.

I was the one who wanted to visit the big naval base, not Sholakov. So far as he and Turpin and his other generals are concerned the Russian navy is on its own and won't cooperate. They see Vladivostok and the Russian Navy as being of no further use once the Chinese cross the border and cut the final leg of the rail line running north along the border from Vladivostok to Khabarovsk, *I was not so sure about that but I did not try to reason with him. At least not yet.*

In any event, if I had to bet, and in a sense I am, I would bet that the Chinese will launch an attack on Vladivostok but that it will be a diversion, not the major attack that decides the war. What is much more likely is an attack designed to pin the Russian forces here so they cannot be used wherever the decisive battles are actually fought. I agree with Sholakov about that.

What we both think is that there will be a vicious battle for Vladivostok, but it will only be a bloody feint. We expect the Chinese to concentrate their forces further to the west for the main battle and merely cut the rail line and the road running along the border so that supplies and reinforcements cannot be landed at Vladivostok and shipped north to wherever the Chinese main thrust occurs.

Why do we think this? Because that is what we would do; concentrate our forces for use in the main battle which is likely to be fought somewhere else.

Convincing Admiral Krusak, the Russian commander of the Pacific Fleet based in Vladivostok was another matter. He is a tall, lean, gray haired man and absolutely furious at Sholakov for withdrawing his planes and army troops. He was so anxious to tell Sholakov that he did not even wait for us to sit down, let alone offer us the customary tea and cookies.

"Do not you understand how important this naval base and port is?" he shouted as he waved his arms about. "For God's sake it's the only year-round port we have in this part of the world. It must be defended."

"If that is the case," I snapped back via Basilof before Sholakov even has a chance to reply, "you need to move fast to get as many of your naval infantry regiments up north so they can participate in the key battles to save Vladivostok for Russia. And you've got to hurry before the rail line to Khabarovsk and the road running along it are cut."

He looked at me accusingly. "You are an American. An enemy. You want Russia to lose this port."

"Frankly," I responded, "I personally do not give a shit whether you lose it or not. But my Commander in Chief is the President and he ordered me to help Russia keep it. Otherwise I'd just stand off and laugh at how your stupid thinking is going to cause Russia to lose it." *I am glad looks do not kill. If they did I'd be dead by now.*

"Look Admiral," I said, poking a finger at his chest for emphasis, *I bet it's been a long time since he got that treatment* "there is going to be a war with China and it is going to be a land and air war that is won, or lost, by Russia's army and air force. If China wins, the Chinese will take this port and its naval base despite the fact that you were able to hold on to it while the war was being lost."

"Nonsense. I do not even believe there will be a war."

"If there is no war you can order your naval infantry to turn around and come back. But if there is a war, and Russia loses it because you sat on your hands and would not let your naval infantry join the fight, what do you think is going to happen to you. Hmm? *They are going to shoot your ass, you fool. You really want to risk that?*

An orderly brought in the tea and smoked herring and we talked and talked and talked. And the Russians smoked and smoked and smoked. *And no one touched the fish.*

The more we talked about a Chinese invasion and the more the room filled up with cigarette smoke, the more obvious it became that serious tensions exist between the Russian army and the Russian navy.

On paper the naval forces, including naval infantry regiments in Vladivostok, the Russian Pacific Fleet's Marines, all belong to Sholakov's Far Eastern Military District. In reality, as Sholakov explained to me on the flight coming here, they are totally independent. The Russian navy and the Russian army do not get along and rarely cooperate on anything. *Sounds like the Pentagon.*

"Russia's bottom line," I told Admiral Krusak as I pointed to the map Sholakov had unrolled on the Admiral's table, "is that Vladivostok can be resupplied and reinforced by sea; and it can get its artillery support and air support from Russia's naval forces; Khabarovsk and the interior cannot, and that is where the war will be won or lost."

"That, Comrade Admiral, is exactly why everything that Russia can get to the interior has to be sent there immediately. Once the war starts it will be very difficult to get significant amounts of supplies and reinforcements to where the main battles will be fought and the war won or lost."

Krusak finally began to see things in a new light when I told him that I was going to recommend to Washington and Moscow that, as a condition of continuing United States assistance, that Russia immediately deliver, 'deliver,' I repeated to Krusak with emphasis, not just assign or promise, every single ship and naval infantry regiment in its inventory to his Pacific Fleet for use against China.

"Even if they arrive after the war has already begun you can use them to close down the Chinese ports and launch a counter invasion into the very heart of China."

Admiral Krusak was obviously not much of a poker player; the idea that he might command a much bigger fleet and more Russian Marines obviously held great appeal. I could see it on his face. So did the idea that he would be able to direct a campaign of unrestricted naval warfare against China from the relative safety of Vladivostok.

What I did not tell Krusak is that our analysts think China has so many Pacific ports available for use as alternatives to Vladivostok that Vladivostok is a likely candidate for China's first tactical nuclear strike if it decides to make one.

Krusak's antagonism really began to turn around when I pointed out that some of the replacements for the Russian Marines he sends north can be flown in to replace those that get away before the line between Vladivostok and Khabarovsk is cut. The planes bringing them in, I point out, can also carry his dependents back to Russia.

I knew things were starting to go our way when Krusak began talking about the problems he would have evacuating his dependents.

"Most won't go," he tells us. "They have heard how bad things are in Russia now that the Soviet Union has collapsed. At least here they have apartments and beds."

Four hours later, over dinner and the vodka I did not drink "because of my medical condition," Krusak left the room for about twenty minutes. When he returned he announce, with slurring words and a lot of satisfaction, that he has just ordered his Marine regiments to move north and place themselves directly under Sholakov's command.

We all touched glasses. *My canned orange juice was nothing to write home about.* Then Krusak showed his big tobacco stained yellow teeth with a smile and asked how soon we think "the first of my additional ships will start arriving."

******

Immediately after the banquet broke up I got a ride back to the Starlifter and send a long scrambled satellite message to Dick Spelling explaining the situation and strongly suggesting that he ask the President to call Moscow and strongly suggest, *read require if they want our assistance to continue*, that the Russians immediately assign every ship and Marine regiment in their inventory to Admiral Krusak's Red Banner Pacific Fleet.

"It's absolutely imperative," I wrote on the message pad, "that every Russian naval ship that floats get underway at flank speed with every Russian Marine, helicopter, and winter-equipped soldier the Russians can quickly cram on board. If they do not do that, Russia will almost certainly lose the war and we need to seriously reconsider continuing to provide assistance if it's all going to be for nothing." *We sure as hell do not want to keep helping these fuckers if they won't help themselves.*

Then I chatted with Dorothy and the kids for a while and got some sleep in a sleeping bag in the Starlifter. *My ability to speak with Dorothy from Vladivostok amazes me; apparently there is some kind of a telephone connection on one of our new satellites.*

******

I am not sure where the Russians spent the night but the next morning they were all on the plane eating breakfast when I woke up as the Starlifter's engines started and we began taxiing for takeoff. Some of the Russian officers look like they have serious hangovers. The only ones missing were a Russian general and three colonels. Sholakov left them behind with instructions to work with Admiral Krusak to accelerate the move of the naval infantry and the remaining army troops and equipment out of Vladivostok.

As I understand it, the ranks and defensive positions of the Russian troops and naval infantry who move north will be refilled by the cooks and clerks of the Russian navy and a couple of regiments of reservists drawn from the civilians in Vladivostok and the local villages. The executive officers of each of the naval infantry regiments, battalions, and companies will remain behind and be their commanders. The executive officers will be elated; the Russian promotion system results in an automatic promotion if an officer has enough time in grade and is placed in a position that rates a higher rank. It's an interesting system. I wonder if it works.

******

All twenty-seven members of the Chinese Communist Party's all powerful Politburo were unusually tense as the Chairman sat down and called the Politburo meeting back to order after lunch. Up until now, for security reasons, only the eleven Politburo members on the party's Central Military Committee knew the full scope of the plan to invade Russia. Everyone else had been led to believe our efforts would be aimed at recovering the Ussuri lands and isolating the port of Vladivostok.

General Wu's report changed everything and caused everyone to get even tenser.

"Those are not probes designed to confuse the Russians," exclaimed a surprised Wang Jiang, the vice premier in charge of transportation, as the senior colonel conducting the briefing pointed to a list of units assigned to the Chita front. "This is a major invasion into the very heart of Russia."

"Into the heart of the Chinese lands that the Russians stole from us over the years, Comrade Wang," General Wu gently corrected him.

"We all know the territory on both sides of the Amur has historically belonged to China; now is the time to reclaim it...when Russia is weak and the Americans are leaderless."

"I am not opposing the army's plan, Comrade General; I am only asking questions because I am truly concerned that our railroads and road system in the north are not yet strong enough to support the plans." *And I do not want to be blamed if they prove to be inadequate.*

"Of course your concerns are understandable, Comrade Wang. But the army's experts have looked at the situation very carefully. Their conclusion is that our roads and railroads have been sufficiently improved for what we need to do, particularly since we have already positioned so many troops and so many supplies close to the border." *And infiltrated many thousands of them over the border already, he thought but did not say.*

"We may never have another chance like this," Chairman Li interjected to help guide the discussion so the desired consensus will be reached. "It is our duty to reclaim our stolen lands before Russia regains its strength and completes its road and railroad lines into the stolen lands."

"But," Wang persisted, "we just heard a report from our intelligence departments saying the Russians are mobilizing men and equipment to finally begin filling the gaps in their Trans-Siberian highway and complete the construction of the Baikal-Amur Railroad."

"The Russians' plan," interjects General Wu with a collegial nod of agreement towards the Chairman, "is to deploy huge numbers of troops and construction crews to repair the bridges the Germans destroyed and then keep them moving eastward to fill the gaps in the highway and finish the Baikal-Amur railroad that will run north of the Tran Siberian. But that will take them many years. Indeed, it will take them several year just to rebuild all the bridges that the Germans destroyed and at least ten years to complete the rest, maybe more.

"It's now or never," Chairman Li said to the emphatic nods of the members of the military commission. "Presently the Russians are vulnerable because their military is in shambles and their transportation corridors to the east have been severed, totally severed."

"Once they rebuild the railroad and their military forces, and certainly when they complete the highway and finish the Baikal-Amur rail line, Comrade Wang, they will be able to greatly expand their population in the stolen territories and quickly bring in military forces to oppose us. Then it will be very difficult, perhaps impossible, to ever get them out."

"But what about the Americans and Japanese; what will they do?" inquired the Vice-Premier for Industry who, like Wang, was not a member of the Central Military Committee

"Bah. The Japanese are nothing militarily and the American government is weak and indecisive and really does not care who wins," explained Yang Jei, the Deputy Party Chairman who was also a member of the Military Committee.

"That is why the Americans repudiated the treaty last week. Let's face it, the Americans cannot do much to help the Russians even if they wanted to, which they obviously do not."

Then General Wu summarized the situation once again,

"Today's reality is that the Red Army can get troops and supplies to the battlefields where the war will be won or lost because we have railroads and roads running north to the border where the fighting will occur; the Russians cannot get troops and supplies to the battlefields because the war with NATO caused the Russians to temporarily lose their ability to use the roads and railroads running east from Moscow to the battle area. It is really as simple as that.

"As for the Japanese," Wu added disdainfully as he wrinkled up his nose and took a puff on his cigarette, "they have no reason to help the Russians. They do not like them—and one reason they do not is because the Russians occupied Sakhalin and those four little Japanese islands the day before Japan surrendered—and refused to give them back after the war."

Then, with a modest and knowing smile and another puff on his cigarette, the Chairman added, "anyhow, it does not matter; we have been talking with the Japanese and assured them that we would have no problem if Japan lands its troops and takes back the islands. Indeed we said we would help them if they need help. They are very receptive to the idea and are quite agreeable to our reclaiming the lands the Russians stole from us."

"Do the Japanese know how soon we plan to act, Comrade?" Deputy Premier Wen Hijian asks anxiously and a little breathlessly as he sucked on a long cigarette holder with an unlit cigarette in it.

He is short of breath because he has lung cancer. He thinks the others do not know. Most of them do and several of them are already positioning their supporters and sons to take his place. .

"Of course not, Comrade Wen. I am sorry. I should have made that clear."

"Will the Russians use their nuclear weapons?" asked a hunched over little man at the end of the table.

"We do not think so, Comrade Bo, the Chairman replied as he turned to face him.

"They may be weak militarily at the moment but they are not stupid; they know we will retaliate if they do. All they can accomplish by using their nuclear bombs to destroy our big cities is to cause Russia's big cities to be destroyed by our nuclear bombs. And even if they do use them and destroy our cities, China will still exist and we will still have regained all of our stolen lands."

"Even so," General Wu carefully pointed out, "we will, of course, take the necessary precautions and move all important political cadres and their families out of potential nuclear target zones before the war begins." *I should have mentioned this earlier. The relief on the faces of some of the members is obvious.*

Everyone around the big table nodded. The required consensus had been achieved.

There was no actual vote by the Politburo members, there never is. But it was clear to everyone in the room that the required consensus was in place; the military operations to recapture the stolen lands would proceed as planned.

Now it is certain history will remember me, Li mused as he watched the smoke curl up from the cigarette he was holding. Russia is about to lose a lot of territory and its access to the eastern seas and China is about to begin using its huge and hungry population to fill the lands east of Lake Baikal with Chinese. Yes, in a few months the Alaskans will see Chinese instead of Russians when they look across the few miles of water that separate Alaska from what is now Russia.

******

"It will be a major invasion to take all the Amur River lands, even those north of the river," the daughter of the Vice Premier breathed very softly into the ear of the girl who worked in the office of the Japanese trading company. They were smoking cigarettes and languishing naked on a very rumpled bed. "We are going to one of the Party's vacation villages before it starts."

"According to what my father told my mother last night, the main attack will involve many divisions of troops and large amounts of armor and artillery. The army is going to throw pontoon bridges across the Amur near Manzhouli and proceed down the railroad branch line to take Chita and the land east and north of Lake Baikal.

"My father says China is certain to win and regain its stolen lands because this time Russia cannot use its roads and railroads to supply and reinforce the troops it has in the lands they stole from us.

"He told my mother all about it," she whispered. "There will be initial attacks in the vicinity of Khabarovsk and Vladivostok, many small units will infiltrate all along the border, and the divisions of our parachute troops will drop on their airfields including the big field that protects the entrance to the eastern territories on the other side of the big mountains. Then the big attack will come further to the west at Manzhouli.

"He also told her many thousands of troops have already infiltrated over the border and into the vast empty spaces on the other side of the river; they will become active when they get the signal."

Then the girls snuggled together and talked in very low whispers into each other's ears about how wonderful and understanding Mai's mother is and how it will be when they are rich and free in America.

Mai did not know it, and never would, but tomorrow her girlfriend will literally whisper into the ear of one of the Japanese middle managers in her office and he will quickly make a business trip to Tokyo.

Nothing will ever be written down or transmitted by phone or radio; it won't even be spoken in a normal voice for fear of being picked up by a hidden microphone. The Americans will have it by tomorrow night.

Chapter Eleven

I am surprised.

A long coded message began coming in on the scrambler as we lifted off from Vladivostok to return to Kharbarovsk. It was from Dick Spelling. The intelligence analysts have revised their conclusions based on new information coming out of Japan. The situation can be summarized, Dick wrote, as "the Chinese goals and the military assets they are committing appear to be significantly greater than we initially imagined."

According to Dick, our intelligence confirms there will be a massive Chinese ground and air attack designed to occupy the entire Amur River drainage east of Lake Baikal and perhaps even all of the Russian territory east and north of Lake Baikal. *My god, this thing really might go nuclear. Sholakov and the Russians will never give up all that without using everything they have.*

My face must have shown my shock as I make my way back towards Sholakov and Shelton. They stood up with concern on their faces as I lurched down the aisle past them with the message in my hand.

"The maps," I snapped to Solomon and Evans as I jerked my head to indicate they should follow me, "Get the big map showing China and Eastern Russia."

"We've been had," I said to no one in particular as Sergeant Willow began setting up the folding tables and Solomon leafed through our map case and then began unfolding the map he'd selected.

Sholakov's face turned white, and so did Miskin's, as Miskin read the message to him. I passed it to Shelton and Peterson to read together and signaled them with a jerk of my head to share with the others when they were finished.

"Jesus Christ." …. "My God." ….. "How many divisions?"

"Okay people, we have a new and bigger ball game."

Or could it be a Chinese trick to draw Russian resources away from the Ussuri, Khabarovsk, and Vladivostok?

******

Thirty minutes later our destination has changed, we were functioning as Sholakov's staff. Within an hour he had the beginnings of a new defensive plan and was already beginning to implement it. The priorities had changed and time was running out. Now the main Russian defenses would have to be concentrated in front of Chita.

Sholakov had no choice. The Chinese plan sounded all too real. We should have anticipated it from the beginning.

There are good reasons for Sholakov to change the Russian troop dispositions: losing Chita means losing the entire Russian East; losing Khabarovsk and Vladivostok means losing only that part of the Russian East south of the Amur.

Sholakov moved quickly and began making calls using our in-flight phone system that bounces calls off one of our satellites.

"It is safe, Yuri Andreovich," I told him, "at least at this end; it is a deeply scrambled line of sight transmission and it is being bounced off a satellite."

"Alexi Gregorovich," Sholakov said to the commander of his airmobile troops who was listening at his headquarters in Arkhara, "I am at this very moment sending you a message. It will be delivered to you by hand from an unexpected source. You are to instantly act on the orders in it but you are not to discuss them with anyone, not even your deputy."

"Yes, that is correct. You are to begin executing them immediately. I am diverting to Podovsk and will arrive in about two hours. We will talk when I get there. Please meet my plane."

What Sholakov was sending was an order to the general commanding the 73rd Guards Airmobile division to immediately move his division from Podovsk to the airfield at Chita. There he is to dig in and prepare to repel an expected attack by at least two, and possibly three, Chinese airborne divisions, an attack that is expected to occur as early as the middle of August.

Although Sholakov does not know it, a copy of his message will also be sent as a flash message to Dick Spelling with a request from me that the Detachment and I receive, at least every three or four hours until further notice, satellite photos and intelligence updates regarding everything that might be related to a Chinese attack towards Chita or anywhere else.

Sholakov's next call was to Turpin. "Andrei Ivanovich, I am at this moment sending you an important message with new orders and information. It will be delivered to you from an unexpected source. You are to act on it instantly and discuss it with no one. I will be in Arkhara in about two hours and then return to Khabarovsk this evening. We will talk about it and I will explain my orders this evening when I arrive in Khabarovsk. Please meet my plane."

What General Turpin would receive in a few minutes was an order to instantly begin an around the clock effort to move armor and troops to positions between Chita and the Chinese border, including some of the armor units that had previously been sent to the choke points and detached to be behind-the-lines raiders.

Turpin will also receive an edited version of the warning message Spelling sent to me and an order to instantly and personally burn both messages as soon as he reads them, and not discuss them with anyone.

We spent all of the rest of the flight gathered around the maps and reading the intelligence updates that began flooding in. They all confirmed the initial warning.

How could we have been so blind? Russia may damn well lose this war. And what will it mean for the U. if it does lose?

******

Sholakov radioed in a request for no honors before we arrived so the only senior officers present when he trotted hurriedly down the steps at Arkhara were the very concerned Commanding General of the 73rd Air Assault Division and its attached independent airborne battalions and his equally concerned deputy—who was concerned because his commander was so obviously upset about the message he had just received. *What did it say? What is happening?*

The 73rd was the only intact Russian airborne division. All four of the other Russian airborne divisions were decimated at Reykjavik and their survivors have only recently begun to be repatriated. Their repatriation had been delayed because all the available planes were being used to return American troops from Germany and the occupied countries to the United States.

The Russian airborne general, a big mean looking guy named Karatonov, was obviously surprised, and then tried to hide it, when he realized that many of the officers accompanying Sholakov were Americans. So I mischievously had the ever present Basilof lean over and tell him that we are as surprised to be here as he was to see us.

Basilof must have mentioned my name when he told Karatonov because the good general responded with such an incredulous double take that it would have won an award in a Hollywood comedy. I smiled at him encouragingly. *Damn, I'd like to get this guy into a poker game.*

Within minutes things got deadly serious as the visibly shocked airborne general and his now equally shocked deputy stood in front of the map as Sholakov explained what he and his men are to do in Chita and why. Then Sholakov gestured towards us and said something that was not translated.

I do not know what he said, but Karatonov and his chief of staff, a colonel whose name I never did get, turned towards me, came rigidly to attention and saluted, and then turn back to Sholakov.

Constantly clenching and unclenching his fists the now grimly determined Russian paratrooper general and his equally grim and determined deputy stood with us around a map table and listened intently as Sholakov discussed how Chita might be attacked by the Chinese and defended by their men.

It was unspoken but everyone in the room understood that the future of Russia's eastern territories, the entire eastern half of Russia, may well hinge on how well their men fight. Chita and its airfield must be held at all costs. It not only sat astride the Trans-Siberian Railroad but also the road system along the border and the only road through the mountains and into the north towards Tynda, Magadan, the Bering Sea, and Alaska.

Sholakov and the two Russians listened even more intently when I introduced Captain Solomon as a Marine officer "who had been in the middle of the fight and wounded when your paratroopers dropped on the Reykjavik airport." Solomon described the battle from the American perspective, including the initial failure of the American fighter planes to defend the airport.

"The two important things," Solomon told them, "are to make sure your men have more than enough ammunition to kill the people coming down in parachutes before they have a chance to get organized, and that your men not get caught out in the open, particularly on the runway and the flat areas around it. It is a death trap from small arms fire with no place to hide."

Then he explained.

"Our perimeter circled the Reykjavik runways about two hundred yards out. And our little two man holes with the shoulder level sandbags around each of them and lots and lots of ammunition made all the difference in the world; we could fire up at the men in the air and through gaps in the sandbags when they were on the ground with nowhere to hide."

The Russians listen intently as Basilof simultaneously translated what Solomon was saying. They paid particular attention to what Solomon described as "our big mistake:" locating the Marines with hand held SAMs too close to the ring of troops around the airport and the airport not having any vehicle mounted missile defense systems on the approaches to it.

"The transports were already dropping their paratroopers by the time they were in range of our handheld SAMs," Solomon tells the Russians. "We should have located the SAM teams much further out to hit them before they jumped."

Hmm. I wonder if the Chinese know what went wrong for the Russians at Reykjavik and will learn from it. I had better ask Dick Spelling to have NSA run a search of their Chinese tapes to see if anyone mentions Reykjavik or Iceland. And I must remember to talk to General Goldman about the Russian air defenses and strategy; we have not looked into that enough.

Miskin pulled me aside while we were waiting for our ride back to the airplane. He told me he had just listened to Moscow Radio explaining the Chinese threat and America's assistance. And he is really pissed.

It seems Radio Moscow is reporting that the Russians were winning the war against the fascist Germans when the every watchful KGB discovered the Chinese were planning a sneak attack on Russia. So, desperate for peace because the Russian troops were winning, America agreed to stop fighting and to pay reparations and help Russia fight the Chinese.

"What these cocksuckers are doing is using you and me and the aid we are sending them as living proof that they won the goddamned war."

"Yeah, you are right," I said. "It is a really stupid thing for Moscow to say and it is a great excuse for us to tell the Russians to go fuck themselves and go home. On the other hand, it might be that the Chinese are doing to the Russians the same thing we did to them when we published the articles with the fake research results. Eh?"

Miskin's eyes got wider and wider as I told him how we had gotten articles published in Russia that conned the Russians into not using their hand held SAMs and not firing at our motorcycle skirmishers. What I did not tell him was how we worked with the British Intelligence to con the Russians into starting their attack early so we could destroy their air force and get our special operations teams and swimmers inserted before they had a chance to stop them. The fewer people who know about that, the better.

I could see from the expression on Miskin's face that the idea this might be a Chinese deception operation really got to him. What I did not mention, but think is equally possible, is that it might be an American or British operation designed to make it politically impossible for the United States to continue helping the Russians.

Then I send an encrypted message to Dick Spelling asking if there is any chance that the Russian television broadcast was a Chinese or American disinformation operation designed to make us stop helping the Russians. I am pretty sure Miskin will be sending a similar message to the CIA. Also, please ask NSA for all transcripts of any Chinese discussions about the Russian attack on Reykjavik and Iceland.

******

Everyone was exhausted by the time the Starlifter took off to carry us back to Khabarovsk. I could not help it; I fell asleep as soon as I sent the message to Spelling inquiring about a possible Chinese disinformation operation via Russian radio. Sergeant Willow nudged me awake when we were about to land in Kharbarovsk several hours later. "Here's some coffee, Sir. We are about to land." *I really had a strange dream. But, as usual, I could not remember it.*

The Starlifter's tires squealed as we touched down and I suddenly became wide awake and anxious to get off the plane—I could see a lot of Jeeps and cars through the porthole windows as the portable stairs are being pushed into place so we can deplane. Turpin himself was waiting at the foot of the ladder with a lot of armed soldiers. *Something's up.*

Sholakov deplaned first and was instantly surrounded by armed guards and hustled to a waiting car with Turpin waving his arms and talking to him. It roared away as soon as he and Turpin got in. *Oh oh.*

We waited anxiously on the tarmac while Miskin trotted over to the airfield offices to find out what the hell was going on. He came back empty handed—no one knew anything. Even so, I decided to keep everyone together and wait in the plane.

Two hours later and we were still inside the Starlifter and killing time by brainstorming possible Russian responses to the Chinese invasion. That was when Basilof drove up and leaped out of the Jeep he was driving and ran up the stairs three steps at a time. He moved so fast that the Marine guards at the door started to raise their weapons. Basilof saw their alarm and came through the door with hands held shoulder high and obviously excited.

"General," he began...

******

A couple of minutes later the situation became much clearer. There was some kind of a coup underway in Moscow and another attempt to replace Sholakov with a political officer was expected.

Most amazing of all, according to Basilof, is that the coup is actually being covered live by Russian television. It was a first. So Dave, Miskin, and I piled into Basilof's Jeep and headed off with him to the rooms that have been permanently assigned to us in the best of Kharbarovsk's rundown hotels.

We never have been able to get the 1950s style TV set in my room to work so we went next door and barged in on Woods and Goldman. Their set works and there it was live in flickering black and white.

It seems a group of hard line communists have arrested the relatively new Russian Party Chairman at his seaside vacation home and their leaders are now barricaded in the Russian parliament building which is surrounded by tanks manned by troops loyal to the Chairman.

If I understand Basilof correctly, troops in units whose officers are loyal to the hardliners in the Russian parliament have the Chairman's vacation home surrounded and troops loyal to the Chairman's supporters in the army have the coup leaders surrounded in the Russian parliament building. *Damn, it's a Mexican standoff if there ever was one. I wonder what it will mean for the war effort.*

"Chairman Gorbachev made a big mistake," Basilof explains. "He called for loosening the party's control over the economy and negotiations with the Chinese. The leaders of the coup are afraid they will lose their privileges and the Chinese will get some of our land."

What surprised me was that Basilof seemed to be more surprised and excited by the TV coverage than he was that there was a coup attempt underway and that General Sholakov and the war effort might be in danger.

Coverage about the coup on Russian television seemed pretty mundane with a well dressed pretty young woman talking with great excitement into a microphone and periodically gesturing towards the building across the way and the tanks that are surrounding it—while everyone else stood around with blank looks on their bored faces. It could have been a CNN broadcast.

Then everything changed. All of a sudden the tank crews disappeared into their tanks and closed their hatches. A few seconds later one of the tanks rocked back on its springs and its gun puffed a perfect smoke ring as it fired. *Jesus Christ.* Basilof gasped out loud.

A corner of Russian Parliament building suddenly exploded and fell away. Then two more tanks fired almost simultaneously. There was much running around in the open area in front of the building as pedestrians and onlookers began running for safety. I did not see any return fire, but there may be some since some of the onlookers suddenly dashed to get behind the tanks.

"What does this mean for General Sholakov?" I asked a shaken Basilof a few minutes later in the relative privacy of my own almost certainly bugged room. I was there with Shelton and a couple of our aides, Captains Solomon and Evans.

"Those people in the building think General Sholakov supports the Chairman, so they will try to replace him if they win. I think, perhaps, it will depend on who the KGB supports. We have our own troops, you know." Then he realized what he just said and shrugged his shoulders.

"I think we need to talk to General Sholakov," I said to Dave. *Or maybe we should head to the airport and get the hell out of Dodge.*

Basilof nodded and we started towards the door. But after a few steps, I turned around and rustled through the little gym bag carrying my toilet kit and clean underwear. Then I stuck the little pistol I'd grabbed in my belt behind my back and tug my Russian windbreaker down over it.

Dave Shelton saw what I am doing and raised his eyebrows in a question. I shrugged and gave a little nod.

******

All of us crowded into Basilof's Jeep, even Dave who had to run to his own room to get a jacket. Rank has its privileges so I sat in front with Basilof and the other two sat in the back. The streets did not seem as busy as usual but nothing seemed out of order as we pulled up to the front of the headquarters and parked.

General Sholakov was in a meeting and we were not expected. So we pulled up chairs in the lobby of his office and waited along with two quietly talking groups of officers who have obviously arrived for Sholakov's next appointments.

I recognized several of them and nodded and they nodded back. Basilof said something genial to two of the senior colonels who were chatting together in low voices and they smiled in agreement as they replied. Everything felt normal.

Then it dawned on me. These guys have been waiting here for Sholakov and do not know about the coup. Does he? He must. That is undoubtedly why Sholakov rushed off when we landed.

We waited about half an hour and everything continued to seem as relaxed and normal as things might be at a headquarters preparing for an imminent war. Sholakov even came out when his visitors left and shook hands with everyone even though we'd just been with him on the Starlifter. He had obviously been informed by his receptionist that we were waiting

Sholakov said he would like to talk to us, but first he needed to talk to the people who had come in from the field to see him so they could go back out and get to work. He smiled at them as he said it and they smiled back. *Is there really a coup?*

"Yes, I know about the coup," he volunteered a few minutes later when we were admitted to his office, even before I have a chance to ask.

Then he really surprised me. "The Patriarch is acting as an intermediary. He is the only one both sides trust."

"The word I just received from a friend in Moscow is that the conspirators are about to surrender. If the Chairman is smart he will shoot them immediately. But he probably won't if Patriarch Alexi is involved."

"Patriarch Alexi?" *Who the hell is the Patriarch Alexi?*

"Patriarch Alexi of the Russian Orthodox Church," Shokalov explained. "He was apparently out of the country making his first visit to the United States, your Alaska of all places. Aeroflot is sending a plane to Anchorage to fly him back according to the reports I received."

Basilof saw the questioning and uncertainty in everyone's eyes and explained further. "Many Russian

Orthodox people live in Alaska, you know—from the days when we owned Alaska."

Of course. There is a Russian Orthodox seminary in Kodiak training priests. Hell, I commercial fished with several of them in the summer when I was in high school . Good people. They do not get paid for being priests; they and their wives have to find jobs or fish commercially when they need cash. In the villages they live in the same native housing as everyone else and subsist on whatever food and clothing their parishioners bring them as gifts. Even the bishop in Sitka lives in an old mobile home someone donated. They are honest to a fault. People trust them.

"Of course. You are right; he is believable and his involvement may save the rebels." *And I wonder if the Chinese have anything to do with the coup.*

"Yuri Andreovich, do you think the Chinese might somehow be behind the coup?"

******

I quickly sent a message to Spelling informing him that, despite the distractions of the coup in Moscow and the possible threat to his personal safety, General Sholakov was continuing to respond very appropriately to the new intelligence we have been providing. For example, some of the armor initially assigned to the stay-behind armor raids has already been reassigned to Chita and General

Rutman has been given command of all the forces on the Chita Front.

One of Rutman's deputies, a general whose name I do not recognize, has been assigned to run the partisan armor and the partisan troops.

And Sholakov was moving fast: Rutman and Karatonov were already in the air flying to Chita and Turpin himself was at the Khabarovsk train station with some of Rutman's officers to help speed up the movement of their armor units and the other units that were rushing to join them.

Some of the armor that had been deployed for behind-the-line raids was being recalled; but a good part of it was being left in place. Also being redeployed was a substantial portion of the armor and artillery at the chokepoints; they too were being reassigned to the Chita front.

First to arrive of the additional units being sent to the Chita front will be the naval infantry regiments presently coming north out of Vladisvostok, the Russian Marines. According to Sholakov, the trains and trucks carrying them will just roll right on through Khabarovsk and Podovsk and keep going until they reach the positions Rutman is setting up in across the river from the Chinese city of Manzhouli.

Because of the mountain range separating China and Russia, the Manzhouli area is where the Chinese will have to cross the Amur if they are going for Chita - unless, of course, the Chinese have done a deal with Mongolia and can move their troops further west and come through Mongolia to hit the Russians even closer to Chita and Lake Baikal.

Sholakov will return to Podovsk by himself sometime this evening or tomorrow morning. I won't be with going him. I have just been handed a message ordering me to immediately return to the States for "consultations."

"Will they shoot you?" Sholakov inquired with a grin.

* * * * * *

Major Martin's Starlifter was almost empty. Shelton and everyone else, including the Gunny and his Marines to guard and assist them, were staying to work with the Russians. Even John Liska and his signal warrant officers were staying.

The only passengers were me and my three aides and one of our grimy and bearded Special Forces sergeants who somehow broke his leg while carrying twenty dollar bills and food out to the Russian troops in the bush. The Russian medics put a splint on his leg and his buddies obviously held a farewell party for him and fixed him up with a bottle of vodka to keep it going.

Sergeant First Class Tookens sang quite loudly during the takeoff but fell asleep almost immediately. *He has a lousy singing voice like me; but what the hell, I like "You*

Are My Sunshine" so I sang along with him. *It reminded me of the Legion.*

As soon as we got airborne I sent off an encrypted message off to Dick Spelling telling him I was en route to Washington in the Starlifter and asking him about my recall.

I also requested, just in case, that he have the satellites and NSA continually check out the Mongolian railroad and roads for any indications of troop movements towards the Russian border. I did not call Dick directly because it was the middle of the night in Washington. But sure enough, he called back within a few minutes of my message going out.

"Working late?" I inquired

"Christ, I am sleeping in the office again. How ya doin?"

"Coming home as ordered. I just left Russia so I will be at Andrews about the time the sun comes up in the morning. What's up?"

"Congressional hearing. Some special subcommittee wants you to testify."
Say what?

"About what?"

"About the hotel shootout. Story in the *Washington Post* this morning says you may have deliberately killed an unarmed man."

"You've got to be kidding me."

"Nope. The word on the street is that someone's trying to smear you in case you decide to run for President." The interesting thing is that the subcommittee was set up and the hearings scheduled before the story appeared. It's an ambush aimed straight at you."

"Well the *Post* and the politicians certainly could have saved themselves the trouble if they'd bothered to ask. I am not running. In case no one's noticed, I have got this Russian problem to handle."

"Yeah, I know. But this is Washington and everyone's paranoid. Sometimes reality does not run very deep after you've been in Congress or a political appointee for a couple of years."

"When is the dog and pony show scheduled?"

"Anytime you want in the next couple of days. They have got me scheduled for ten o'clock this morning. You want to come with me? I could yield to you so you can speak before I do."

******

"Oh... Uh.. I apologize, Mr. Chairman. I was daydreaming during your speech. What was the question again?"

"I asked, General Roberts, what you were thinking about?"

"What was I was thinking about while you were making your speech, Mr. Chairman? If that is the question, I'd rather not say. It's rather embarrassing and would serve no useful purpose."

"That is for this committee to decide. You have to answer the question, General, you are under oath." *He is very smug and talking to the television cameras lined up along the side of the room instead of to me.*

"Well Sir, I'd rather not say what I was thinking as you spoke... But if you absolutely insist, I ...." ...

"Oh I do insist, General, yes I do," Jackson interjecte self-righteously as he continued to beam at the cameras instead of looking at me.

"Well Sir, while you were making your speech I was wondering to myself how a grandstanding lightweight like you ever got elected." I shrugged. "Sorry Congressman. You insisted on the truth and I am under oath."

There was a brief moment of stunned silence and then the hearing room broke into an absolute uproar of laughter and clapping. Some of the crowd actually cheered. Even Spelling grinned though he desperately tried to hide it. It was contagious.

Congressman Jackson was beyond furious when the room finally quieted down. "You Sir, are in contempt of Congress. Do you realize that?"

"No Sir, that is not true. I in no way hold the Congress in contempt. To the contrary, I can tell you, under oath, that I hold our political system and our Congress in the very highest esteem and consider myself totally bound by the laws it passes and the decisions of our President and Courts.

"We really do have the finest system of government in the world, you know, and Congress is a very important part of it... It's only you personally, and whoever is pulling your strings, that I hold in contempt."

There was another brief silence and then the hearing room broke into an even greater uproar of laughter and clapping and many of the people in the audience stood up to get a better view. Some of the crowd sitting in the back actually climbed up on their chairs so they could see Congressman Jackson's response as they cheered and clapped.

But the now irate congressman was not to be denied. After much pounding of his gavel Congressman Jackson pointed his finger at the TV camera instead of me and self-righteously demanded that I answer a question.

"Isn't it true that you deliberately tried to kill an unarmed man on the exit stairs of the Excelsior Hotel in Bonn, Germany?"

"No Sir, that is not true. I did not deliberately *'try'* to kill anyone. I absolutely succeeded. I either killed or helped kill at least one, and probably two, armed terrorists on the exit stairs of the Excelsior Hotel." *I emphasized the word 'try.'*

"But one of them was unarmed, was not he?"

"No Sir, that is not true either. Both of them were wearing ski masks and carrying UZI machine guns. Perhaps you might find it helpful to read the police and intelligence reports."

"But after you shot them did not you deliberately kill one of them by breaking his neck?"

"It is absolutely true that I shot the first attacker with a pistol provided by one of our Marines and then stepped on him as I was picking up his machine gun, which I then used to shoot the second attacker coming up behind him. A very fine young Marine captain then picked up the second attacker's machine gun and used it to shoot the third attacker a few seconds later."

Then I continued.

"As you well know from the various official reports, Mr. Chairman, if you have read them that is, the emergency exit staircase is very narrow and dozens of people, including my wife and a number of the Americans, were following me down and had to step on or over the attackers. So did many firemen and policemen who were coming up the stairs in the other direction. So I am not absolutely sure I am the one who stepped on him and broke his neck. But if it got broken I certainly hope I am the one who did."

"You hope you are the one who killed him?" *He emphasized the 'you hope' with an incredulous look to the left towards the TV cameras instead of towards me.*

"Yes sir. Absolutely. I have a moral and legal duty to protect my wife and my fellow Americans and everyone else our Congress and the President says should be protected. No decent man, and certainly no one serving in our military, would run out of a building to save himself and leave vicious attackers, men carrying machine guns and wearing ski masks, behind to kill his wife and other civilians."

And then leaning forward and pointing my finger at the Chairman as the flashbulbs flashed and the television cameras roll, I added "and no decent man would expect him to abandon his wife and fellow Americans to such people. You should be ashamed of yourself. Have you no decency, Sir?" *It was a famous concluding question from an earlier age.*

The audience roared and the outraged Chairman started to sputter and say something. But then, after several members of his hovering staff began urgently whispering in his ear, he adjourned the hearing for lunch. It never restarted. And many tens of thousands of supportive letters and telegrams began to pour into the White House and Pentagon. *And, so I was told, many tens of thousands more poured into Congressman Jackson's office suggesting he resign and worse.*

Pops was elated and I was besieged with requests for interviews and talk show appearances as I left the hearing. Three hours later I was on the Starlifter and bound for Riems with a cargo of explosives and snow machines that would continue on to Arkhara after it dropped me off at Riems.

Chapter Twelve
The Chinese are coming.

There was no question about it. Our various intelligence agencies continued to agree that there would be preliminary attacks elsewhere to draw off the Russian reserves, but that the jumping off place for the main Chinese invasion of Russia would be the Chinese city of Manzhouli which is south of the Russian district capitol of Chita. It is the most westerly of the Chinese cities on the Russian border that is fully integrated into the Northern Chinese system of railroads and roads.

Manzhouli is where the Chinese railroad system used to cross the Amur River border with Russia and connect to the Trans-Siberian railroad which runs east and west across Russia on the other side of the Amur River.

With twenty-twenty hindsight the analysts of our intelligence agencies looking at the latest satellite photos agreed that it was significant that the Chinese highway system leading up to Manzhouli had been greatly improved in the last couple of years and so had the rail line leading up to the Russian border. Not only had the rail line been double tracked and upgraded to carry significantly heavier loads, but a large number of new sidings and unloading docks had been constructed, many in the past few months.

Perhaps the only surprising thing about discovering that the main thrust of the Chinese invasion was likely to come at Chita through Manzhouli was that we did not realize it before now and understand what the improved infrastructure meant.

What made the recent Chinese construction so significant was that in 1969, during the Ussuri War, the Chinese closed the border and the rail line coming through Manzhouli to connect China to the Trans-Siberian—and never reopened it. The rail and road bridges over the Amur River are still there but have not been used for years. In other words, the new construction has no civilian purpose, just military.

Probably the reason we did not initially understand what the Chinese were going to do is because Manzhouli is on the same rail and road system as the Chinese cities south and west of Khabarovsk. We along with everyone else thought the military supplies and equipment being stockpiled along the rail line there is so they can be moved eastward to support a Chinese invasion aimed at taking Kharbarovsk or Vladivostok or the Usurri lands south of the Amur. In fact, if our intelligence is right, they are there so they can be moved westward to support an invasion aimed at cutting Russia in half and annexing the entire eastern half of Russia.

What really ruined my day when I got back from the "hearing" in Washington was Jack Riley pointing to a couple of satellite photos pinned up on the conference room wall and giving me the bad news—the Chinese started moving their invasion supplies yesterday. Most of them are headed west so they can be used in an invasion aimed at Chita and Lake Baikal.

Then I broke Jack Riley's heart by telling him that he and Jim Adams and their three senior sergeants would have to continue working at the Detachment instead of coming with me back out to Russia to join Dave Shelton and the rest of the guys.

Long ago I learned the importance of have a continuing independent analysis of the intelligence information we receive. We also need someone who is instantly available to handle special requests. The Pentagon and our intelligence agencies are good but sometimes they are slow and, even worse, sometimes they "refine" the results to adjust the facts to support the prevailing views of the politicians and military bureaucrats—and that inevitably leads to mistakes, bad mistakes.

******

It was over. The revolution, that is. One of the ringleaders committed suicide and a couple of others fled to Finland. The rest, it seems, have surrendered and are under house arrest. On the other hand, the threat of losing a large part of Russia to the Chinese has suddenly galvanized the surviving Party hierarchy; it's given them something they can use to rally the Russian people to the government and the party leaders despite the corruption and the sad state of the Russian economy.

Russia was finally starting to get its act together. The sudden realization that China was actually going to attack and might well win probably explains why the satellite photos of the Russian naval base at Kalingrad showed the nuclear powered attack submarine *Admiral Potkin* and its sister ship, the *Lira,* to be beehives of activity as they lay along the dock. Crewmen and spare parts, torpedoes, and rations were being taken from a third sub to provide the necessary supplies and spares for one of the longest combat deployments ever taken by the Russian navy. *At least that is how Jack and his people interpret the photos.*

Two Russian attack subs will be ready to sail for the Chinese coast within the next twenty four hours and, if the latest CIA report is accurate, and it should be since the CIA rates its source of Russian naval information as highly reliable, one of the subs will lie off Shanghai and the other off Canton. *Highly reliable means the CIA either has someone important in their pocket or NSA has been listening to such a person without them knowing it.*

What was surprising was that the *Potkin* and the *Lira* were the only seaworthy attack subs left in Russian hands of the eighteen Kaliningrad-based submarines of the Baltic Fleet that put to sea a few months ago to fight in the recent war. NATO sinkings and the Ukraine took the rest.

According to the CIA, four other attack subs and three boomers capable of launching nuclear tipped and conventional cruise missiles were already en route to China from the Northern Fleet at Murmansk. There were also reports of a suddenly increased level of activity at all of Russia's naval installations with what appears to be military vehicles and supplies being loaded on some of Russia's remaining operational ships.

That is it. Nine subs are all the Russian portion of the once great Soviet submarine service can contribute to a war with China—until the Turks agree to let the ships of its Black Sea fleet pass through the Bosporus and Dardanelles. If the Turks cooperate there will be two more subs for a total of eleven. So far the Turkish government has refused.

Hopefully the Turks will change their minds. The Russian-based portion of the Soviet Black Sea fleet came through the Spring War relatively unscathed except for a destroyer the Turkish air force picked off in the Mediterranean and a submarine that made the mistake of trying to get through the Dardanelles without the permission of the Turks.

About a mile away, at two other Kaliningrad docks, the Kotlin class destroyer *Bravy* and the six of the other surviving destroyers and frigates of Russia's similarly reduced Baltic Surface Fleet also appeared to be undergoing the same around the clock refitting and resupply. They too were being prepared for a high-speed dash around the world to Vladivostok.

This morning's CIA and NSA reports confirmed each of the destroyers has been ordered, in addition to its crew, to additionally squeeze aboard two or more companies of naval infantry, as Russia's Marines are called, and carry a deck cargo of whatever light tanks and other tracked vehicles they can stuff aboard. Some of the tanks are visible on the decks and others on the docks alongside.

One thing is for sure: It's going to be a long and unpleasant experience for everyone in the ships. I get seasick every time I set foot on a ship—standing there listening to Riley and Adams talk about how the Russian troops were being crowded into the Russian ships made me feel a bit queasy just thinking about being on one of those destroyers. *It probably all goes back to the troopship I was sent to Korea on when I first joined the army—I got so seasick I barfed thirty three times in eleven days.*

What was surprising, according to Adams, was that so many of the Russian surface ships were *not* being prepared to sail, not one of the three Russian carriers, none of its cruisers and missile ships and tank-carrying landing ships, none of its civilian ferries and container ships, and, of course, none of the Russian ships that are permanently bottled up in the Black Sea by Turkey's control of the Dardanelles.

After listening to Major Adams, I sent a message to Dick Spelling with a long list of intelligence questions starting with what the Russian navy is doing and its immediately available carrying capacity. He'll forward them on to the appropriate agencies. I also decided to send some of the same questions to Sholakov, to NATO intelligence, and to Boots, my Sandhurst friend in British intelligence.

I also suggested to General Spelling that he hold his nose and ask the Secretary of State to impress upon the Turks our desire for the Russian fleet to be allowed to pass through the Turkish waters.

"Try to be friendly when you ask her, Dick," I suggested when I called him to follow up. "If we want to help the Russians, we need her to really try to get Turkey's cooperation." *Dick does not like her at all. I wonder why?*

Then I sent Mike and Dave a flash request for an update on the Russian swimmers and acknowledged Mike's earlier message confirming he had passed on to Krutchovy some additions to the list of crucial bridges and an operational plan for each of them. They were all in China.

Mike and Dave were out in the field and out of contact, but Shelton's aide, Captain Evans, replied within minutes. He reported that he had been left behind to mind the store. According to Captain Evans, Colonel Krutchovy is fully aware of the new revelations regarding the Chinese objectives and has already reoriented his plans to a revised list of bridges and partisan targets so that more of his assets are concentrated on bridges related to Chita. *Evans must be a bright kid if Dave and Mike are willing to count on him to mind the store.*

Captain Evans also confirmed that the swimmers themselves still do not know their targets; only that they involve bridges somewhere. He reiterated what I already knew—for security purposes each team will only get its specific assignment an hour or so before its members board their helicopters and head into China. *That is a damn smart move. Sholakov is going to be in deep shit if the Chinese find out about the swimmers in time to intercept them.*

According to Captain Evans, the most important news he has to report is that no additional Russian frogmen have shown up; the only ones who have arrived so far are the dozen or so that came from Vladivostok. It means Krutchovy, if he sends a full complement of swimmers to each bridge, only has enough swimmers to take out three or four of the most important bridges of the twenty or more in China that should be blown. *Well we cannot send swimmers; who can? The Taiwanese? Nah, it would leak for sure. Better some than none.*

If no more swimmers arrive the Russians will be forced to choose between leaving most of the Chinese bridges intact or sending fewer swimmers to each of the most important bridges or making costly air attacks that may leave the ground troops without air support by using up the available Russian planes and pilots. *That is the same choice we faced when the Russians attacked NATO; we got more swimmers and sent them all.*

Sholakov's only other alternative is to use airborne assaults in an effort to put engineers and assault troops on the ground to attempt to destroy the key Chinese bridges. Either way, direct air or ground attacks will be costly and likely to fail because the satellite photos show the Chinese have placed serious amounts of anti-aircraft and other forces around almost every one of the bridges we think are important.

But there was some good news I cannot share with Captain Evans—the Chinese seem to be expecting any attacks on their bridges to come from the air just as the Russians did in Germany. It meant the swimmers that do get into China will probably have a fairly high success ratio.

There is absolutely no getting around it. Russia is going to need more swimmers if it is to prevent the Chinese from bringing more troops and equipment into the battle for

Chita than the Russians can handle. Maybe I ought to go to Moscow and try to shake some loose.

******

Russia's buildup was proceeding but, unfortunately for the Russians in the Russian East, everything was happening slowly, too slowly. The Russians were using Il-76 and AN-12 cargo planes to bring tanks, armored personnel carriers, and missile firing anti-aircraft vehicles to Chita. The planes and armor were survivors of the recent war with NATO and some of them are pretty beat up due to years of inadequate maintenance.

Worse, the Russian cargo planes were built as tactical planes capable of carrying small loads the relatively short distances that the Soviets thought would exist in a war with NATO. *In other words, they can only carry a single tank or vehicle and they have such short legs they have to stop at least once along the way to refuel.*

The only transport planes in the Russian inventory with sufficient range and carrying capacity to go non-stop to Chita are the surviving Russian AN-22s. They are a bigger version of the AN-12s and can carry up to four armored vehicles. Unfortunately for Russia, there are only eleven of them left and the majority of them are not operational due to a lack of spare parts and maintenance.

There are not many AN-22s because of losses in the recent war and because not many were ever built in the first place. They were not developed until the Ussuri River war woke Russia up to the fact that it had no way to quickly bring armor and heavy equipment to the Chinese border.

Russia's problem is quite simple—only four of the surviving AN-22s are available; all the others are out for repairs due to years of shoddy maintenance and a lack of replacement parts.

I have always wondered why in 1969 the Chinese repeated the World War Two German mistake of not cutting the Trans-Siberian railroad. It would have been relatively easy to accomplish because the railroad runs so close to the Chinese border. The only explanation I can come up with is that the Chinese did not want a bigger war, just to send a message that they would not any longer be bullied or allow more Russian land grabs. This war is sure going to be different.

******

Snow machines are beginning to arrive at the Detachment. The first batch from Canada landed in Riems three days ago. But should we send them fully assembled or semi-assembled in their shipping boxes from the factories?

We tried packing a C-130 both ways—and quickly decided to leave them in their boxes because it is so much easier and faster. The boxes are okay because the snow machines are basically ready to go when they come out of the box—just add the skis, engine oil, and handle bars. Simple enough so that even untrained users can do it in isolated Arctic villages.

Actually, according to a message that came in yesterday from Dave, he and Mike want the snow machines shipped in their original boxes because it's a good way to screen potential riders. The Russian troops who cannot even figure out how to bolt on the skis, attach the battery, and add oil are probably such klutzes that they will wreck their rides before they can reach the Chinese and begin shooting.

In any event, Dave Shelton and Mike Morton called in this morning and reported the training of the initial batch of snow machine drivers was going quite well even if there isn't any snow on the ground. The Russian troops think it is fun to roar around on the snow machines and the Russians running the operation are being overwhelmed with volunteers from Karatonov's airborne companies. It is so easy that most of the training time is spent learning how to use the Israeli sub machine guns and, particularly, the great Israeli hand-held missiles.

We need to get the snow machines into service as soon as possible. They can replace the remaining partisan armor and infantry units and free them up for use in front of Chita.

Then I called Arkhara and again spoke with Captain Evans. A couple of additional frogmen showed up yesterday afternoon and that is it. The Russian navy supposedly has quite a few of them scattered around but the base and fleet commanders were apparently not willing to release them to Admiral Krusak. It is obviously time for another visit to Moscow.

I went home at noon to tell Dorothy and the kids I would be gone for a few days. I forgot it was a school and pre-school day and the kids would not be home for hours. I decided to wait because I wanted to see them before I left. Then Dorothy, little baby bump and all, looked at me with a twinkle in her eyes; so I gave the au pairs the rest of the day off and told them to take the train to Paris to "air out the apartment" and spend the evening in Paris. It took them about three minutes to get ready and rush merrily out the door. We spent a wonderful afternoon.

The kids came home on the school bus that serves the village and drops them at the end of the lane. They were fine with my trip, particularly after I promised I would try to be back in time for John Christopher's next soccer game and that we would all go to the game to cheer him on and then take the whole team and all the parents out for pizza. John and his friends love pizza and there is a new pizza restaurant in the next village. Dorothy's going to call the coach and extend the pizza invitation to everyone including the parents.

Pops called with some interesting news as I was leaving for the airport. He just learned a recently retired General named Pettyjohn, now Hoffman's deputy assistant secretary for military affairs, was the source of the effort to smear me. Pettyjohn apparently read the official reports on the hotel incident and reached out to the Secretary of State's campaign manager with the suggestion I had done something they could use to discredit me.

Pettyjohn and the congressman, according to Pops, have visions of big political appointments when the Secretary is elected President. *When? Does Pops really think she will be elected?*

"Pops, do you really think she might be elected?"

"Well, she is got a good chance because she is got good name recognition because of her husband and the media. It will depend on what Bernie does and who the President decides to support."

******

The Starlifter crew, Miskin, and my aides Peterson, Solomon, and Willow, were waiting and ready to go when I finally got to the Riems airport as the sun was going down.

About an hour after we took off I finished reading the latest intelligence reports and make a scrambled satellite call to Boots, my Sandhurst friend in British military intelligence.

"Any chance we can repeat our 'special projects' with the Chinese?" I ask him.

Boots said he did not know but promised to do some checking. Then I had Sergeant Willow get out my sleeping bag and blow up a rubber air mattress for me. I needed to get some sleep or I was going to have a really bad case of jet lag when we reached Moscow.

Sleeping seems to be the only way I can reduce my inevitable jet lag when I travel more than a couple of hours. For some reason I no longer seem to be able to sleep sitting in airline seat. That is always sort of a surprise; years ago when I was a young soldier it seemed I could sleep anywhere at anytime. Now I need a sleeping bag, an air mattress, and a place to sack out on the floor. Sheesh.

******

Moscow's military airfield was its usual dingy and drab self. But this time the welcome was somewhat friendlier, for whatever that might signify. We were met by an English-speaking colonel with a smile and a military limo, the usual big black Zil. There were also a couple of vans for the rest of the guys and our luggage.

The colonel wanted to take us straight to the Russian military headquarters but did not object when I told him to first take us to the American embassy. That is where we will be staying this evening before we head out to Podovsk tomorrow morning.

We were expected at the embassy and a line of immaculate Marines in dress uniforms jumped to attention when I got out of the limo and hustled myself into the building. Then they rushed to help unload the luggage from the van that pulled in behind us while Colonel Miskin and I had a brief meeting the ambassador and some of the embassy's political and intelligence staff. We needed an update on the local situation.

The accuracy of the intelligence materials I had read on the plane was confirmed by the CIA station chief— Cherenko has apparently survived the coup attempt and is apparently even stronger than before since it disposed of a couple of his enemies. The good news is that the army's stock is particularly high because it actively sided with the ultimate winner, the party chairman. The KGB, it seems, backed the wrong side and is being reorganized under new leadership. *Good. Sholakov seems safe.*

Then it was back into the Zil and we once again zipped through the packed streets in the empty center lane until we reached the Russian Military Headquarters on the outskirts of Moscow. Miskin and Peterson were with me and once again we started with a visit to Marshal Petrov's office for the ritual cup of coffee and a briefing.

A slightly different bunch of people, all uniformed military this time, were in the briefing room as we walked in; I recognized some of the faces but not all of them.

This time the Russian briefers, again there are two, and again both are colonels, ignored the political and theoretical differences between China and Russia. Instead, they concentrated on the Russian and Chinese orders of battle and the supply and equipment situation in the east.

What was so interesting about their information was that it was not accurate. *Either that or, God forbid, ours is not.* In any event, a number of the "facts" we were told did not jibe with what we ourselves saw on the ground and heard from the Russian officers on the scene. The only thing that rang true was that the Russians were doing their best to airlift in key supplies and reinforcements. Unfortunately their best was not very good—there is not much they can do with the resources they have.

Then it dawned on me. Sholakov has not informed Moscow about the changes he made in the disposition of his troops or where he thinks the Chinese will attack or what he thinks are the Chinese objectives. Moscow only knows the Chinese are coming; but they do not know where and they do not know how Sholakov intends to fight them.

Of course Moscow does not know. Sholakov is a smart guy. If Moscow does not know his plans and preparations, they cannot be leaked to the Chinese.

In response to the information we received, I briefed the Russians as to part, but only part, of what we understood to be the size of the Chinese forces and their objectives. There were obvious expressions of dismay and rejection when they heard our conclusions as to the possible Chinese objectives. A couple of them, one in particular, a general I have never seen before, repeatedly pressed me for information as to how Sholakov was going to respond if the Chinese attack and where Sholakov thinks they will attack.

Moscow, as we did us initially, apparently still thinks the Chinese will be making another effort to retake the disputed territory around the Ussuri River. They all stared at me with appalled looks on their faces when I disagreed.

"According to our latest intelligence, what appears to be shaping up is a huge Chinese military effort to take Khabarovsk and Vladivostok and cut Russia off from its only warm water port in the Pacific."

I am not about to tell them we think the Chinese are going after the whole of Russia east and north of Lake Baikal. The President ordered me not to; he is afraid that Moscow will decide to use nukes if they find out about the

Chinese intentions before Sholakov gets enough reinforcements in place so that he has a chance to win without them. I fear the President may be right.

There are sharp intakes of breath and expressions of disgust and disbelief as I spoke. To a man they were aghast. Many obviously did not believe it.

I do not speak Russian but the men sitting around the room puffing on their cigarettes and drinking coffee responded to their translator's words with looks of incredulous dismay on their faces. Their thoughts are obviously along the lines of "it cannot be"….. "impossible"….. "American trick."

Things warmed up slightly when I passed around copies of the satellite photos showing the new rail and road construction all along China's northern border and pointed out the troop concentrations, supply dumps, and tank parks. No one disagreed, at least not out loud, when I informed them that it appears as if the Chinese are preparing for a major military action aimed at Russia and that their goal might be to try to take more than just the disputed Usurri lands.

What I do not tell them is that the main Chinese attack will probably be against Chita in an effort to cut off the Russian forces further to the east and that Sholakov is relocating his forces to confront them. Sholakov obviously does not trust Moscow not to leak his plans to the Chinese. And he is right. There is no sense letting someone tip off the Chinese that he knows where they will attack and is reorganizing his defenses to meet them.

By the time we returned to the embassy the Russian military leadership had enough additional information about the situation in the east to be even more worried than ever about the outcome of the coming war.

I am more worried too – because after we get past heated demands for an explanation about our rejection of the treaty, the questions and discussion soon turned to the possible use of nuclear weapons and how Sholakov was going to deploy his forces to fight the Chinese. I said not a word about Sholakov's troop deployments but I did hasten to assure the Russians, quite emphatically as a matter of fact, that we have neither seen nor heard anything about the Chinese using of nukes. I told them neither Sholakov nor The United States thinks the Chinese will use nukes unless Russia uses them first.

"We have heard nothing about nukes from the Chinese except that they are afraid *you* will use them. We are concerned about a nuclear war ourselves. In fact, the only reason the United States is helping you with money and food supplies is so you will not have to use your nukes and subject us and our allies to the resulting fallout."

As the meeting drew to a close Marshal Petrov looked pointedly at the men sitting around the room as he assured me Sholakov has been ordered not to use nukes and that Moscow was more determined than ever to get additional reinforcements and resources to him so he would not have to use them. Everyone nodded in agreement. No one smiled.

The only problem, and it was not a small one, was that no one representing Sholakov was among those nodding their heads and doing the agreeing.

What Moscow still did not realize as the meeting breaks up was that the Chinese attacks on Vladivostok and Khabarovsk would probably be diversions—the big attack, with thirty or more divisions and large amounts of armor and artillery, increasingly looks to be aimed at Chita with the goal of taking over all of Russia north and east of Lake Baikal. *I will leave it to Sholakov to tell them.*

******

I had just gotten back at the embassy and was on the phone getting new orders from the President, via Dick Spelling, when Marshal Petrov called. Could I please come right now and meet with some important officials? He was sending a car.

According to the President, it's now okay to tell the Russians that the Chinese are likely to be going after more than just Khabarovsk and Vladivostok. But only, he orders, tell them about the land south of Amur; do not tell them the Chinese invasion may be aimed at taking over all of Russia east of Lake Baikal; it might trigger Moscow to order a nuclear attack even if Sholakov and his generals do not.

Once again Miskin, Peterson, and I were driven down the center of the road and the traffic lights automatically turned green to pass us through. There was a big difference however—this time the meeting was at the Kremlin. *Very impressive skyline. It was the first time I have seen it.*

We arrived at the door of a very imposing stone building with lots of officials and guards clustered around the entrance. The Russian colonel who picked us up at the embassy delivered us to the building and turned us over to another colonel in a resplendent dress uniform. He was waiting as we pull up. The three of us were in battle dress as usual.

"Please follow me, General."

We climbed up the long stone steps, went upward in an ornate elevator, and got off at the entrance to a very impressive room. *Dark wooden paneling, a high painted ceiling, and old master paintings on the wall.* There was a huge ornate desk at one end and a very large conference table between the entrance door and the huge desk. Several dozen men, mostly stocky older men in civilian clothes, stood in a group near the entrance and eyed us with obvious curiosity as we entered. *It looks like a meeting of retired Teamster organizers.*

An older man stepped forward to greet us. "Welcome to Moscow, General Roberts, I am Konstantin Chernenko. Thank you for joining us on such short notice. Marshal Petrov told us about your meeting this afternoon at military headquarters." A middle aged woman with her gray hair in an austere bun translated my words into his ear as the Chairman and I shook hands; Miskin translated his for me.

Chernenko was quite affable. He took me by the elbow and guided me to a chair. Then he sat down at the head of the table next to me and the others hurriedly seated themselves to join us. Jack was guided to a chair in the corner and Colonel Miskin stood behind me ready to interpret if the Russian woman falters. The table was covered with papers and coffee cups. We have obviously interrupted a meeting in progress.

Chairman Chernenko got right to the point after a few words of pleasantries and an offer of coffee which I declined with an appreciative smile.

"As you might imagine, Comrade General, we are more than a little taken aback by your news. Can it really be true that in a few days the Chinese will attempt to take Vladivostok and Kharbaovsk?"

"I regret, I deeply regret, Mr. Secretary, that the reports of a Chinese attack appear to be true. We have reason to believe they will launch a major military assault in the east in the days immediately ahead."

Then I went on. "But it now seems there is much more to it than we initially thought. As you may know, I was at my embassy and in contact with Washington an hour ago, just before coming to meet with you. While there I received a very distressing intelligence update from the President himself. He has authorized me to share it with you. In a word, the situation is much more difficult and dangerous than I reported to Marshal Petrov this afternoon."

Then I describe part of the "intelligence update" I have just received, at least that part of it I was told I could share—that America's intelligence agencies now conclude from their various sources that Harbin will be the main Chinese staging area and that the region around the Chinese city of Heihe looks to be a major launching site for the Chinese attack—with the occupation of the entire Amur River drainage as the goal including Khabarovsk and Vladivostok.

Yes, we know the Chinese objectives are even greater and that the attack coming out of Heihe will be a diversion with the subsequent main attack coming through Manzhouli towards Chita. But the President wants Moscow to only know enough to motivate them to increase their efforts to support Sholakov and leave the nuclear and war fighting decisions to Sholakov; not so much that they throw up their hands and go nuclear. Makes sense to me.

To a man the Russians jerked forward and opened their mouths in shock as the gray-haired lady translated my words. Even she seems taken aback.

"The only good news," I said, "is that there are absolutely no indications that the Chinese intend to use nuclear weapons."

"Are you sure of all this Comrade American General?'

"No Sir. I am not. I am not sure of any of it. And I certainly hope our intelligence is entirely wrong." *Boy do I ever.*

"So do I... So do I," the Chairman repeated slowly. "Unfortunately our intelligence organs are telling us the same thing."

They have not yet according to the CIA and NSA. I wonder why the Russians have not been able to do a better job of monitoring China. Do their much-touted satellites and KGB operations actually work? Or are we penetrating the Russian communications less than we believe?

We look at each other in silence and then he asks me a question. "Does America have any ideas as to how we might prevent this crisis...or survive it?"

"Unfortunately we do not have any idea how the Chinese might be deterred from commencing their invasion. On the other hand, there is, of course, still a possibility that you can adequately reinforce General Sholakov and his men in time to defeat the Chinese."

Chernenko looked around the room before he responded. "We are doing all we can. But you of, all people, know our problems."

Then, after another pause, he continues: "You have had recent experience and I am told you yourself fought the Chinese, rather successfully I hear. What do *you* suggest we do to assist General Sholakov?

This is going to be tricky. "Um...Mr. Chairman, I would strongly suggest that General Sholakov is likely to know better than anyone else what he needs to defeat the Chinese. So it is important to get him whatever he asks for rather than ignoring his requests because they do not seem important to people who are not out there with him."

When, after a brief pause while his translator finishes speaking, I continued. "Under the circumstances it might be appropriate to send an order to every military commander in every one of your services that filling General Sholakov's requests, even those that seem small and unimportant, is their highest priority—and letting it be known that even the slightest delay in filling a doable request from the Far East will be considered a very serious failure and immediately dealt with." *I emphasize 'and immediately dealt with.'*

The Secretary General and the men around the table listened intently as the translator repeated my words in Russian. Then the Chernenko leaned forward and spoke rather sternly.

"You have visited with General Sholakov several times, Comrade American General. Do you know of such problems?"

"Every commander has such problems, Mr. Chairman. Human nature is such that sometimes officials far away from the battlefield try to maintain their empires by holding on to people and assets that could be better employed on the battlefield. But I know of no problem that would not be immediately fixed if such an order is given and enforced." *I emphasize 'and enforced.'*

Chernenko looked around the table slowly and grimly nodded his head in understanding. *Maybe Sholakov will get some additional swimmers after all.*

Then Chernenko gave me the opening I have been hoping for. "Do you have any questions for us, Comrade American General?" *I certainly do.*

"Yes Mr. Chairman, I certainly do. We would like to know why so many of your navy and civilian ships are neither en route to the Pacific nor loading men and equipment in preparation to sail; why Aeroflot's planes are not being taken out of civilian service and used to carry troops and cargo to your forces in the east; why an effort was made to replace a fighting General like Sholakov who knows the territory with a political general who does not; and why certain people in Moscow keep asking for the details about how General Sholakov plans to fight the Chinese?"

The men sitting around the table were obviously surprised at my audacity and the implications of my questions. There were a couple of audible gasps and a lot of muttering around the table as the white-faced translator gave them my questions while I continued talking.

"In other words, Mr. Chairman, we want to know if Russia is serious about trying to stop the Chinese without using nuclear weapons and why some of your officials appear to be trying to get information *for* the Chinese?" *I emphasized the word 'for.'*

I did not stop. "On the other hand," I said thoughtfully after a brief pause, "perhaps such problems are inherent in your system because you—*I gestured around the table as I spoke to indicate I meant everyone present*—just cannot bring yourselves to allow your people to make the many millions of individual decisions necessary to win wars and have a strong economy."

Chernenko opens his mouth and starts to speak as the obviously appalled translator finished repeating my words. Then he stopped and looked around the table at his equally stunned colleagues. *People do not usually talk to you like that, do they comrades?*

After prolonged pause while he and the others digest my message with a good deal of stress and anger, Chernenko finally dismissed me. "Thank you for meeting with us Comrade General. We appreciate your candor. Answers will be provided to your questions."

So I stood up and, with a wry smile and a little nod of my head, waved a casual farewell hand at the table as Peterson, Miskin, and I were led out of the chamber.

"Jesus Christ," exclaimed Miskin after the door was shut behind us. "That was priceless."

******

Late that evening, after I returned from my meeting with the Chairman and the military committee of the Politburo, my Sandhurst friend, Boots, returned my earlier call and was patched through to me on a secure line in the embassy. Boots said he'd made some inquiries and could not help with the "interesting new project" but that one of his good friends suggested I might find it profitable talk to a John Jay Masters at the NSA. They have some "interesting new capacities."

Two minutes later, and with a half-eaten ham and cheese sandwich still in my hand—*no lettuce and not enough mustard*—I was patched through to Masters. This was no time to beat around the bush so I told him who I am and where I am and why I am calling. To my surprise, he knew all about our war-time efforts to mislead and misdirect the Russians; and, to my disappointment, he did not think the NSA could help even though "we are working on it." *Damn.*

"Billy," I yelled as I put down the phone. "Call the plane and tell Major Martin we want to leave for Riems as soon as we can get to the airport." *I have got an important soccer game to attend.*

Chapter Thirteen

Unexpected players.

It was a bombshell and no one saw it coming. Yesterday afternoon the Chinese Party Chairman, who is also China's President and the head of the Party's military commission, Li Ping, made a surprise visit to Tokyo and this morning he signed a treaty to settle various territorial and other disputes between China and Japan.

Our intelligence agencies obviously blew it—the United States did not learn about the treaty until the story appeared in the Japanese media. Dick Spelling called me immediately to tell me about it.

Interestingly enough, according to the CIA, not a word about the treaty has yet appeared the Chinese media. *I wonder how the CIA and NSA missed finding out about the negotiations. Or did they?*

In any event, it seems the Chinese made the Japanese an offer they could not refuse—the Chinese will immediately return the Kuril Islands to Japan, recognize Japan's claim to the uninhabited Senkaku Islands, and recognize Japan's claim to the southern part of Sakhalin

Island which Russia seized from Japan at the end of World War Two.

In exchange for the return of the islands, Japan will reaffirm its neutrality and announce that it will remain neutral and allow neither China nor Russia and its allies, meaning the United States, to use its ports and airfields in the event of a conflict between China and Russia.

Japan also agreed that the East China Sea and the waters beyond the returned islands' three mile limit belong to China along with the waters around the Senkaku Islands even though they are also claimed by Viet Nam and the Philippines. The parties also agreed to recognize China's claim to the Spratly Islands and Japan's claim to the Paracels.

It was an easy Japanese decision and an immense Chinese coup. In effect, Japan regained the territory it lost in World War Two by recognizing China's territorial claims in Russia and declaring itself neutral in the event of any conflict involving China.

Moreover, the CIA now reports it is likely Japan also agreed that in the event of a Sino-Russian conflict it will immediately send troops to Sakhalin Island to "protect" its citizens. Such a Japanese movement of troops to recover Sakhalin would be significant because there is a Russian garrison on the island. If the Russian garrison resists the Japanese landing there could be fighting that would have the effect of bringing Japan into the war on the side of the

Chinese. *And where does that leave us and our military treaty with Japan?*

There was jubilation in the streets and office corridors of China and Japan; dismay and foreboding in Moscow, Washington, and Taiwan.

Dorothy and I were eating breakfast at home when Dick Spelling called with more news. He had just gotten the word about the new Sino-Japanese treaty and wanted to talk to me about it. He was worried about a possible Japanese move against Sakhalin Island and seriously pissed that our intelligence people did not find out about the treaty until it was too late to try to stop it.

Two hours later he called me at the Detachment with more news.

"I just saw a transcript of the Secretary of States call to the Japanese foreign Minister, Guns, and I do not know whether to laugh or cry. Listen to this."

"I am very surprised at your concerns Madam Secretary. I would have thought you would be very pleased. After all, it was your country that insisted our constitution should require us to be neutral and it was you yourself who told me just a few weeks ago that we should try to work out our differences with China"

"....ah, here it is..."

"All it means, Madam Secretary, is that the United States' military cannot use ports and airfields in Japan to support Russia if there is a war. And that should not concern you since the United States has already renounced its military assistance treaty with Russia."

"Goddamnit," was my response. "We have been using the airbase on Okinawa as a trans-shipment point to get supplies and equipment to Sholakov."

"I know. That's why I called."

Then I had a worrisome thought. "Dick, what does the restoration of Sakhalin and the other islands mean for us? I mean, are we obliged under our defense treaty to help Japan if it begins fighting with Russia over Sakhalin?" *That is all we need—fight the Russians in one place and help them in another.*

******

An hour later I was at the Detachment drinking tea and eating stale donuts for lunch and waiting for a call from the President. *Yeah. I'm still drinking tea. Decided it is easier on my stomach than coffee.* I was still waiting two hours later when a White House aide finally called and asked me to standby to be conferenced into a National Security Council meeting.

Five minutes later there was "bing" on the line and I could hear talking in the background, so I chirped "Roberts here."

"Ah, General Roberts. Glad you could join us," said a familiar friendly voice. *He sounds very weary.*

"Thank you, Mr. President."

"Ah, General, the Security Council has been meeting for several hours regarding this new development. The Japanese treaty, I mean."

"Yes Sir."

"Ah, General, how do you think it will affect your program to help the Russians?" *My program?*

"Actually Sir, not all that much. We can route any supplies and equipment we want to send to the Russians through South Korea, Taiwan, and the Philippines."

"Ah, that is good to know. It confirms what we've been hearing here in Washington. We will let you know what our decision is as soon as possible, hopefully later today. Thank you." Then there was a click and I was cut off. *Decision?*

******

Dick Spelling called a couple of hours later. The National Security Council just adjourned, he said, and the President has made a decision.

"We are gonna stick with quietly providing help to the Russians, at least for now, and we are going to pull a Kennedy and keep using the airbase on Okinawa even if the Japanese tell us not to."

"That is a bit surprising and pretty smart," I respond. "I keep expecting to hear that we are gonna back off and wash our hands of the whole thing, let'em fight it out without us."

"Yeah, me too. But now there's something else."

"Jesus, now what?"

"We have picked up more intel about China's intentios. Serious stuff. The CIA and NSA now believe that the Chinese are going after a lot more than Vladivostok, Khabarovsk, and the Amur River drainage; they are going for the whole enchilada, everything, and I mean everything, east of Lake Baikal. If they win they will be our new neighbors up in Alaska."

"Holy shit."

"You got that right. If they win, Russia gonna be just another marginal country on the fringe of Europe; Japan's going to be significantly larger, and China will be the biggest country in the world and a major threat to us with all that new territory and all its new resources and allies.

* * * * * *

Two days later I was back in Arkhara getting updated by Dave Shelton in the little hut that passes as his home and office when he got a call from someone at Sholakov's headquarters about our missing Special Forces team.

"Captain Evans," Dave shouted. "Evans, get in here pronto."

"Sorry Sir, I was out back using the latrine."

"A call just came in from the Russians. The guy who called did not speak very good English but I think he was saying they may have found something about the whereabouts of Williams and Kramer. It sounds like they are sending some troops to check it out."

"That is good news, Sir; really good news."

"Yeah, it is. So I want you to get down to the Russian helicopter detachment on the south side of the strip and go with them if they will let you on board. Take Harry, Sergeant Duffy, with you and ask for Colonel Naumenko. ... Yeah, Naumenko, and take whatshisname the new interpreter with you. You know, the Russian guy who showed up this morning.

"General Sholakov is sending a couple of infantry companies out to the site to act as security. You and Harry are to accompany them. But watch yourself, Dick. You and Duffy are not to take any unnecessary risks and that is an order. It's little worrisome that they think they need to send so many men... Come to think of it, I think I will ride down there with you and see what's going on. You want to come with us, Chris?" I nodded.

"Corporal Miller," Dave boomed.

"Yes Sir," came an answer from from one of the men who had been standing just outside Dave's hut while we talked.

"Dusty, General Roberts and I are going down to the airstrip with Captain Evans and Sergeant Duffy. If anyone calls, tell'em we will be back in about an hour.

"Yes Sir."

******

There were at least a couple of dozen helicopters sitting on the wet grass when we arrived. They looked run down and abandoned except for a couple of Russians who seemed to be working on one of them. The Russians glanced at us as we drove up, and then went back to work doing whatever they are doing.

A few minutes later a bunch of Russian trucks drove up; they were loaded with heavily armed troops. With a lot of shouting and arm waving, the men jumped down from the trucks and began lining up next to some of the helicopters. We just stood there and watched.

After a while a really tall Russian officer walked over, saluted, and said something in Russian to our new interpreter, Ivan something. Ivan stood at attention and kept nodding and saying "da, Comrade." Then the big officer saluted again and walked away.

"Officer is Ukrainian," Ivan told us. "Maybe no go home when Ukraine go away. Maybe born Russia I think. Is Colonel. Name Naumenko. Mens tell is okay guy. He tell some mens tell they see things on ground. Mens are having big search. Maybe is helicopters. Tell okay Americanski come."

General Roberts liked the idea.

"Okay Captain. You and Sergeant Duffy can go with them. Take your interpreter with you and report to General Shelton when you get back if I am not around."

****** *Dick Evans*

A few minutes later a stocky Russian sergeant came over to us, saluted the generals as he walked up, and motioned for Harry and me to follow him. He led us to

one of the helicopters and motioned for us to get aboard.
I climbed in and sat next to Duffy and Ivan, the new
interpreter. None of us were armed.

A few minutes late half a dozen Russian troops also
climbed in and settled themselves on the bench across
from us. They were obviously more than a little curious
about seeing unarmed foreigners wearing Russian
uniforms with officer epaulettes. They all looked to be
teenagers. Conscripts for sure.

Ivan chattered away and pointed and they all gave us
very surprised looks. "Amerikanski?" one finally asked.
Harry nodded and Ivan said "Da. Amerikanski."

They chattered briefly among themselves—and then
all of them simultaneously offered us cigarettes, and then
light up themselves along with Duffy and Ivan. I declined
with a smile and a nod of thanks.

*Duffy is something else. He is a master sergeant who
looks like a bearded old hippy with all those tattoos and his
long hair in a bun with a rubber band. More Hells Angel
than parade ground material—but he is a Special Forces
operator from the Fort Benning cadre with three tours in
Vietnam. General Shelton says he is one of the best
soldiers he is ever known. The Russian grunts sure seem to
like him. Wonder what they think of Americans. Grandpa
would have a fit about his hair and beard.*

"First time I ever seen troops allowed to smoke on a
chopper," Duffy said with a shake of his head. "These guys

must have never seen a chopper burn. I seen a couple go up in Vietnam. Not good."

The Russian kids did not put out their cigarettes when Colonel Naumenko climbed in and, a few seconds later, the rotors began to turn. I winced. Duffy saw me wince and shrugged, and Ivan tried to blow smoke rings despite the drafty air.

****** *Dick Evans*

Our helicopter hovered over the landing zone while the others landed one by one and unloaded their troops. Then it was our turn and we settled into the somewhat grassy open area at the foot of a hill. We all remained seated until the tall colonel with the Ukrainian name jumped down. We watched as he bent his head as he strode under the blades and then as he straightened up and began to walk toward the Russian troops and the equipment and supplies being unloaded on the other side of the open area.

Harry and I jumped down behind him and tagged along as he walked up to a couple of smartly saluting young officers. The troops who had flown with us jumped off behind us and promptly disappeared into a large group of men who were forming up in the trees on the other side of the helicopter.

"Saluting in the field," muttered Duffy to me under his breath. "Guess they do not think they have got any snipers to worry about."

Next to the waiting officers a group of Russian soldiers were busy setting up a tent and unpacking a field radio under the direction of an older enlisted man with graying hair. They even had a fold up card table and four collapsible chairs like the ones you might find at a Walmart.

We hung back until Naumenko wave us over and began saying something to the two officers standing with him. They were obviously surprised at what he was telling them and looked us over with a great deal of curiosity while he was speaking. Then he said something else and both smiled and nodded at us.

"What did he say?" I asked Ivan.

"Nothing Comrade Captain. Only tell Americanski comrades is okay."

There was a lot of talking and gesturing going on among the three officers. Then one of the officers yelled something over his shoulder and a Russian grunt waiting nearby ran over and saluted. His fatigues were wet and really dirty and he needed a shave. He kept pointing up the hill as he talked, and got more and more excited as he went along. Then he pointed into the sun towards another little hill about a mile or two away to the west.

"What's happening? What did he say?" I asked Ivan

Ivan pointed to the hill and then swept his hand towards it as he explained what he had heard.

"He tell many mens here. He tell Russian cigarette paper. Is possible maybe yes many mens is here."

Whatever the man said, it was enough for the Colonel. A minute or so later whistles and shouting begin and the Russians spread out in a long skirmish line that looked to be at least a mile long, maybe more. Then more whistles blew and everyone began walking east into the heavy growth of trees between us and the distant hill.

We followed behind Colonel Naumenko in roughly the center of the Russian line. Behind us we could see the men who had been setting the tent up hurriedly begin taking it down.

A few minutes later and a couple of the Russian helicopters began flying very low about a mile ahead of the slowly walking line of Russians. The sky was dark and cloudy as it has been every day for almost a week. It looked like rain.

****

After about an hour of walking there is a lot of shouting from over on the left and the forward movement of the Russian line slowed to a stop. Then I could see a man, obviously a runner, trotting towards the colonel. He did not have to run far because Naumenko was already walking rapidly towards the shouts. We followed. *Wonder what's up?*

Empty cartridges covered the ground in the open area we reach. And they were still shiny. There were also a lot of pieces of wax paper with strange markings scattered about. And as we walked up, one of the Russians began shouting and waving a bloody bandage. It had obviously been recently used and discarded.

"Chinese," Naumenko said as he looked over at me. "It is Chinese." *Damn, he speaks English. Well that figures.*

Almost immediately there were more shouts. This time from a couple of Russians who have ventured beyond the open space and into the woods to relieve themselves. We walked toward the shouting and immediately saw two recently dug parcels of ground that were mounded up a bit. Every one of us instantly knew what we were looking at.

"I sure wish to hell I had a weapon." I said.

"You got that right, Boss. I do not like the looks of this shit at all."

Naumenko obvious did not like it either. There was a bit shouting and those of the Russians who had not already done so began chambering rounds in their AK-47s.

Then there was more shouting and some of the Russian troops began moving cautiously into the trees ahead of us to set up a perimeter; the rest of the Russians got out their entrenching tool shovels and began digging into the dirt mounds.

It did not take long.

There were shouts and loud and obvious curses from the men digging in the little pile as they moved back away from it. Almost immediately the men working on bigger dirt pile had pretty much the same reaction. One of them gagged and threw up his breakfast.

We followed behind Naumenko as he and one of his captains went forward to look while their men resumed digging and the first bodies were dragged out. Uniformed bodies.

"Chinese," Naumenko hissed at me through clenched teeth. "Those are Chinese uniforms."

I am pretty sure I know who was in the other grave but I had to be sure. So did Duffy and the Russians. And we were right. The dead men were in Russian uniforms and their weapons and gear have been tossed in with them.

"Motherfuckers, son of a bitch cock sucking mother fuckers," Duffy wailed as he pointed. "That's Willy Williams, I am sure of it." I knew him at Benning."

I did not know what else to do so I put my arm around Harry's shoulders for a moment and give him a consoling hug. Some of the Russians had tears in their eyes.

******

"Yes Sir, I am positive. We found Williams and Kramer and the missing Russians".... "Yes Sir, buried with their weapons and gear. The missing money too... "Cannot tell, Sir, but they obviously went down fighting. There are a shit pot full of dead Chinese buried nearby, looks to be twenty or thirty of them"... "Yes Sir, I will.

"Harry, I am supposed to stay with Colonel Naumenko and his men while they try to find the Chinese. You can go back to escort Williams and Kramer to the States or go along with us. General Shelton says it's up to you."

"Shit man, they're dead. Nothing I can do for Willy and Jack now. I'm coming with you. Maybe we can get those motherfuckers."

******

Colonel Naumenko's troops were really spooked. It was not surprising; they were all barely trained teenage conscripts. In any event, despite the efforts of the officers to hurry them along, they were moving very slowly, afraid there were Chinese around every corner.

I was not exactly rushing forward myself and neither was Duffy. We each picked up one the AK-47s the diggers pulled out of the grave. We were cleaning them as best we could while we walked. The Russian grunts walking near us shared some of their rations and ammunition with us as we moved slowly through the trees all day long.

They'd seen our reactions as their men and ours were pulled out of the ground and we'd seen theirs; we were all comrades now. My God, the Russian field rations are terrible.

We followed the Chinese for hours and it was easy to do. There were a lot them; they left their footprints all over the place as they moved through the increasingly dense forest. I was not sure, but it looked like they were heading east towards the railroad.

One of the Russian officers must have said something because pretty soon it became obvious that a couple of squads of the young Russians were sticking particularly close to us. Almost too close; they had not been trained enough to know that it is not a good idea for soldiers to bunch up when they were on a patrol.

It turned out that having the Russians stay with us was Colonel Naumenko's idea. We were walking behind him when he stopped for a second after the first hour or so of walking. When we caught up to him, he explained.

"You and your sergeant are experienced soldiers and my men are not. They are just boys and need someone to tell them what to you. Try to keep them alive when we find the Chinese, eh?"

I immediately nodded my head and agreed, and so did Duffy; we'd both been on Special Forces A-teams and had experience leading foreign troops in battle in the mountains of Iraq. I had there at the very end of the war and had very little experience; Harry had done three tours and had a lot.

That night we made a dry and hungry camp and slept out in open. It seems the Russians had never slept out in the open before, not even the officers. But they all had cigarette lighters and the forest was full of dead wood. Soon we were all huddling around little fires with growling stomachs from the field rations that the Russian troops were carrying. Their campfires were burning everywhere and obviously could be seen for miles. *Christ, I hope the Chinese are not close and hostile.*

Harry and I took pity on the Russians; we began showing some of them how to dig out a little hole in the ground for their hips. Pretty soon the others caught on to what they were doing and began copying them.

It got surprisingly chilly as the night progressed. The Russians were wearing the hooded field jackets they had been carrying. They put them on as soon as the sun went down and then talked softly and tried to sleep all scrunched up in front of their fires.

We, on the other hand, did not expect to stay out all night and have nothing to wear to keep out the cold. All Harry and I could do was sit huddled and shivering near a fire with our arms wrapped around our knees. *Damn, we should have taken a couple of jackets off the dead Chinese or Russians.*

Our distress at the cold was obvious and must have been discussed by the Russian troops because a few minutes later a couple of Russians going on guard duty brought us their jackets and motioned that we should put them on. They pantomimed that they would trade out with the next two guys who stand guard and stay warm by jumping up and down and moving around a lot.

Harry and I were effusively grateful and everyone smiled at everyone by the light of the fires.

Early the next morning at daybreak, after a cold night of constantly waking up and doing jumping jacks in a futile effort to warm again, we got up and gave the jackets back to their young owners with sincere professions of thanks. They did not speak English but our gratitude was obvious.

We joined the Russians as they began moving at first light without waiting to eat. A couple of hours later a shot was fired and there was a lot of shouting. The troops on our far right have come across some Chinese, five of them.

A sorrier bunch you'll never see. One was obviously dead with his jacket pulled over his head; all the rest were wounded and starving. One of them looked to be a goner for sure.

Out came the canteens and what was left of the field rations and the Russian medics got to work. Naumenko was puffing on a cigarette and waving it around with his hand as he talked on the field radio his radioman was carrying. *No matter what they have done it's hard to be pissed at people when they are in this kind of shape and totally harmless.*

And we had a problem. The surviving Chinese were effusively grateful and talking and gesturing between gulps of water and bites of the food some of the Russians dug out of their pockets. But none of us spoke Chinese, and not a one of them spoke anything else. So we were not exactly sure what the wounded Chinese were trying to tell us.

After a lot of gestures and pointing we got the picture, or at least we think so; there are about a hundred Chinese troops somewhere ahead of us. At least that was what the Chinese seemed to be saying with their pointing gestures and counting on their fingers.

It turned out they were really pissed at being abandoned and know they will never be able to go back to China and their families. More citizens for Taiwan, Duffy suggested with cynical smile. He'd spent time there and likes the place.

While the talking and gesturing was going on, one of the two old Mi-8 helicopters that had been scouting ahead for us landed and quickly loaded the three most seriously wounded Chinese and five or six of the Russian troops including one of the medics. The rest of the Chinese will be evacuated when more helicopters arrive.

****** *Dick Evans*

Things really began to pop about thirty minutes later. Three Russian gunships flashed over the tops of the trees and began systematically patrolling in a great circle around us while a stream of troop carriers coming in behind them landed and began disgorging troops. They were also unloading ration boxes and mounds of canvas that turned out to be tents. *Looks like we are going to be here a while.*

And then things got even more interesting. "Heads up, boss," said Harry. "Here comes a shitload of brass."

Roberts, Shelton, and a couple of Russian generals were climbing out of a Russian chopper that had just settled onto the landing zone in a cloud of dust. We trotted towards them and saluted as they came out from under the turning blades and approached us.

All the brass looked grim as they walked with us to see the remaining prisoners. They had already stopped to see the graves and the dead men.

"How are you two doing," Roberts asked.

"Good as could be expected, Sir" I reported. "We are freezing our asses off but getting along fine with the Russians."

"Yeah, and you are carrying weapons, which is what you are not supposed to do."

"Sorry Sir, it's my fault, not Harry's. It started feeling a bit hairy out here by ourselves so I told him to grab a couple of the weapons we found in the grave along with Williams and Kramer. Sergeant Duffy was obeying my orders, sir."

"Yeah, and it was a good decision under the circumstances. I should have known better than to send you two out unarmed. Okay, you can carry weapons so long as you are out here in the bush with the Russians. But do not carry weapons when you are in a camp where media types might see you. And do not you dare even think about going into China armed or unarmed."

"Yes Sir, Thank you, Sir."

******

Corporal Ma came into the camp with a stitch in his side from running so hard. "Lieutenant Bao," he gasps as he holds his side. "Troops are coming this way. Lots of them."

I was not surprised. We'd been sitting here watching the Russian helicopters fly around on the other side of the valley since about noon yesterday. They overflew us a couple of times but they could not see us because we set up our camp under the trees where there was a lot of cover.

Damn. We have to move but if we move now the enemy helicopters will see movement and find us. We will have to wait until dark.

"Sergeant Shen, order the men to remain absolutely motionless. Remind them that it is movement that attracts the eye. We will break camp and move deeper into the mountains as soon as it gets dark."

It was not to be.

****** *Dick Evans*

Late in the afternoon our happy little band of hungry Russians and Americans crossed the valley. At the moment, Harry and I are following the long Russian skirmish line of searchers into a particularly heavy stand of trees. Harry and I were wearing the field jackets Generals Roberts and Shelton took off and handed us when they went back to headquarters.

Suddenly there was a brief rattle of gunfire and one of the Russian kids walking off to the right of us flopped over backwards without saying a word.

I hit the ground along with everyone else. There was a very brief silence followed by heavy firing all up and down the Russian line. It was the knee jerk reaction of green troops; the two or three I could see looked to be aiming at the tops of the trees instead of into them. Then there was lots of shouting and swearing, obviously "cease fire" orders, from the Russian officers and NCOs.

I watched as one of the Russian officers who had greeted Naumenko when we landed yesterday, the young one, comes running along the line to my right yelling at his men. He was obviously telling them to stop firing when there was another burst of firing and he cartwheeled down right in front of us. I could hear rounds whooshing overhead as I crawled forward to check him out. *Nope. No hope. He's gone.*

"You okay, boss?"

"Yeah," I called back to Duffy. "You?"

"I am okay. What ya think?"

"I think we found the Chinese and need to keep our asses down." *Jeez. This is exciting.*

"You got that right."

******

"Well that is that, thought Lieutenant Bao. *They know where we are.*

"Sergeant Shen. Order the men to pull back about three hundred meters and take defensive positions behind the bigger trees. We will break contact and pull back to our base camp as soon as it gets dark and their helicopters cannot see which way we are heading.

"And bring me the anti-aircraft missile Private Hong is carrying as soon as it gets dark. I will carry it from now on."

******

Our three helicopter gunships repeatedly raked the area in front of the Russian line until the sun went down and for some time thereafter until they ran out of fuel or ammo. It was a very impressive show—and totally useless because they could not see the Chinese and neither could we. They were probably long gone.

Harry and I and all the Russians spent the entire cold night shivering flat on the ground and worrying that the gunships will shoot us up in the dark. It was worrisome because we had no flares to mark our positions and we did not know if the Chinese were coming at us in the dark or not. The Russians did not have night sights on their weapons.

Several times during the night a nervous Russian began firing and everyone else got spooked and joined in until the sergeants and officers could stop them. Towards morning a helicopter arrived and began dropping flares over what its crew thought might be the Chinese position. But we still could not see anything and neither did the helicopter crew.

There was a lot of shouting and blowing of whistles as the first light of dawn came up and a long line Russians once again began to slowly and carefully move forward. I motioned emphatically for Harry and our Russians to stay down and we all did.

Duffy and I finally stood up when the Russian line got far enough ahead of us; I was stiff as a board and my teeth were chattering. *The field jacket General Shelton took off and gave me before he left helped but it sure was not enough.*

Ivan the interpreter was nowhere to be found. Then a runner came up and motioned for us to follow him. He led us to Naumenko who was walking with one of the Russian captains about fifty yards behind the slowly advancing line.

Naumenko shook his head in disgust as we walked up.

"Gone. The Chinese are gone. The pulled out in the night. So far we've found a couple of very dead Chinese and one very seriously wounded man who must have been lost in the darkness and abandoned. They were probably hit yesterday afternoon when the gunships raked the area to our front."

"Now what, Colonel," I asked.

"We are going to go forward and try to make contact, of course." *Sounds like the right move to me. Harry agreed.*

* * * * * *

The Russians moved very slowly and very carefully throughout the morning as we followed the tracks of the Chinese and the terrain got rougher and rougher. Nothing. The ever-present helicopters searching in front of us could not find anything either.

Everything changed about mid-day as the line of Russians swept across an open meadow area towards another big stand of trees. There was a bang as a shot was fired somewhere off to our left, and then two more shots.

Duffy and I hit the ground and looked at each other. So did our little band of troopers even though most of the Russians just stood there and watched; our guys had been told to follow our lead and do whatever we do. We went down so they did too.

"Was that one of ours or one of theirs?" I ask.

The answer came in an instant as the Russians on the left opened a ragged volley of return fire.

"Well the Russians seem to think it was one of theirs," Duffy replied with a bit of irony in his voice. A few seconds later the two helicopters patrolling over the forest three or four miles in front of us suddenly swing around and come back towards us. The other one seems to have disappeared. Probably went back to refuel again.

We are up on our elbows watching the two choppers come towards us when two thin streaks of smoke flash out of the trees behind them and rise towards the helicopters. They did not have a chance. One exploded in a great ball of fire and the other staggered drunkenly towards the ground in ever widening circles.

"Oh shit," grunted Duffy as we put our heads back tight against the ground and looked at each other.

Sporadic firing started up all along the Russian line and some of the Russian troops instinctively stood up and started to run towards the crash sites. This time there was a Chinese response, a big response; I could see the flash and flames of small arms fire coming from the tree line ahead of us and to our left.

******

"We are too exposed here," I shouted to Harry. "We have to get into the tree line." He nodded and began crawling.

I began crawling forward and to the right. After I'd gone about thirty yards, and scrapped up my knees and elbows pretty good, I looked back and could see Duffy and most of our little band of Russians crawling along behind me. I could not see many of the other Russians but those few I could see do not seem to be moving, although some are firing back—mostly into the air from the way they are holding their weapons.

We need to run some weapons training for these guys when we get back to base. Aim the fucking things.

A couple of minutes later I crawled into the trees and lay flat on the ground behind a tree trunk while I tried to catch my breath. Duffy was about twenty yards away and a half dozen or more wide-eyed Russian teenagers were on the ground between us. The young Russian closest to me had clearly pissed his pants and lost his rifle. *But at least he had the good sense to follow me as he'd been ordered instead of staying out in the open to get shot. Okay now what*?

"If we stay close to the tree line we are likely to get shot by the Russians," I shouted to Duffy. "So we have to move into the trees a bit more." He gave me a thumbs up and began crawling forward and to his right. I motioned for the Russians to follow him and began crawling deeper into the woods myself.

After a bit I got off my belly and began to move slowly forward in a very low crouch. I was about twenty yards to the left of Harry. The Russians repeatedly bunched together behind us despite my periodic pointing at guys and waving for them to spread out. *Christ, I am more like to get shot by one of these guys than the Chinese.* So I waved them forward until we were more or less in a line.

The sound of the firing got softer and softer and more and more to our left as we moved deeper into the trees. Finally, I waved to Duffy and the Russians and indicate we should make a sweeping turn to the left. *It's time to go hunting.*

After a few yards I stopped everyone and went from man to man spacing out the Russians and checking the readiness of their weapons. Six of them were hurriedly grouped into two man teams between me and Duffy; one is at each end of the line teamed with me and Harry; and the one guy with no weapon is to follow about ten yards directly behind me.

We start moving cautiously through the trees after Harry and I finish checking everyone's assault rifle to make sure it was loaded and ready to go with the safety off. *Damn this really is exciting.*

Chapter Fourteen

The Russians increase their efforts.

According to the satellite photos Russia's run-down naval base on the Black Sea at Krasnodar Krai was humming with activity for the first time in years. To everyone's surprise, Turkey responded to America's pleas and promises by unexpectedly giving permission for the Russian remnants of the once mighty Soviet Black Sea Fleet to transit the Bosphorus and Dardanelles. It was the first time Russian warships have been allowed passage in many years. *Maybe it's General Bezman's way of thanking us for saving his ass at the hotel. Or maybe it's just that the Turkish generals like the idea of communists killing each other.*

The Russians did not have many functioning ships in the Black Sea, just three obsolete guided missile frigates, a couple of big landing ships, a couple of attack subs, and some smaller surface vessels. According to the photos, they were also loading a couple of sea-going civilian ferries that have been pressed into service. The Soviet Black Sea fleet had been significantly larger but much of the fleet had been based at Sevastopol and had been claimed by the newly independent countries of Ukraine and Georgia.

The activity around the two landing ships, the *Saratov* and *Orsk*, appeared to be particularly intense. Both were loading armored vehicles and troops bound for Vladivostok half the world away. They will be escorted by the three missile frigates and, although their captains do not know it yet, they will also be escorted by several American attack subs and refueled at sea by one of our navy's fleet oilers based in Osaka, the *Sacramento*, before they enter the Sea of Japan.

Thirty-six hours later the Russian crews and the troops they are carrying marveled at the lights of Istanbul as the little convoy passed in the night through the Bosphorus and into the Aegean Sea.

For some reason we heard about the civilian ferries being allowed to pass through the Bosphorus with troops and equipment but neither Sholakov nor I found out about the equipment and troops on the Black Sea frigates and landing ships until they were halfway to China. Everyone assumed we had been told by someone else. But every little bit helps and maybe the troops and equipment they are carrying will ended up playing an important role.

******

I looked up from trying to help Susan put a "yucky" worm on her hook when I heard the splash and little John's shout as a fish broke the surface of the pond.

"Wow... I think you've got a big one, John Christopher...Do not jerk...Reel him in... very slow. ..Good boy... You've got him."

Little Chris's eyes were as big as saucers as his fish flopped around on the grass. "Can I show it to Mom?" He asks.

"Sure. And tell her that Dad said you'd caught a nice fish for our dinner. She'll be really proud of you....And tell your mom that I said that if you ask her real nice she'll show you how to clean it... Whoa. Wait a minute. Let's get him off the hook first."

Twenty minutes later a laughing Dorothy asks "Did you tell John Christopher I was supposed to show him how to clean that thing?"

"Yes," I confess with a guilty smile. *Caught.*

"Well," she smiled back with a wicked grin, "I told him that the rule in this family is that whoever catches the fish has to clean them and that *you* would show him how. He is waiting in the kitchen, sweetie. And then two light bulbs need to be changed in the hallway ceiling."

It is so good to be home.

******

A helicopter picked me up in the pasture in front of the house and flew me through the rain to Brussels in the morning. Tony Perelli and I are going to spend much of the day going over the decisions needed to conduct the almost normal business of a newly peaceful NATO. Tony is the American deputy commander. He stands in for me when I am in Russia or otherwise not available.

Our big effort of the moment is to see that all the NATO troops, and particularly everyone's dead and the wounded still in the military hospitals, are transported back home as quickly as possible. As far as I am concerned it's happening too slowly for the American troops, but there is nothing much that can be done to speed up the process since the White House released the civilian airliners back to the airlines.

Another big problem we are working is getting food and supplies to the NATO troops who replaced the retreating Russians in Hungary and Czechoslovakia. Otherwise, knock on wood, things are going unexpectedly well, particularly for the Germans.

Germany seems to be doing okay. The German refugees have pretty much already gotten back to their abandoned homes and businesses and the reunification of the two Germanys seems to be going more smoothly than expected—helped perhaps by the pensions of the East German retirees and the salaries of their military personnel and public employees immediately being increased to West Germany's much higher levels and paid in West German deutschmarks. The additional money flowing into the economy pulled everyone up.

Winning the war together has certainly brought our allies closer. According to this morning's Le Monde newspaper there is even talk among the bureaucrats of France and Germany about giving up their deutschemarks and francs and adopting a common currency. *Does not seem like a very good idea to me. What will they do if Germany needs tight money to fight inflation and the French need a monetary expansion to encourage more spending and production?*

Where there is real unity is in the determination of Germany and France not to provide assistance to the Russians. There is no way they are going to get involved in the fight between the Russians and the Chinese. Even the Brits abandoned the idea; they joined the United States in repudiating the treaty but did not step back in unofficially the way we are.

On a somewhat brighter side, the Germans are continuing to return their unused Israeli missiles even though they know we intend to send them on to the Russians.

Otto and I talk about the German returns as we walk into our two o'clock NATO briefing. I admit to him that it would not have surprised me at all if the Germans had dragged their heels about returning them in order to hurt Russia. And he admits he was not happy about doing it—

but says he understands and agrees with our concern about letting the dictators of lawless China get more powerful.

******

Lieutenant Bao was scratching the lice in his shirt with his left hand and watching his front with binoculars held in his right when heavy firing suddenly broke out on his left.

"We are being flanked," he instantly shouted. "Fall back to the rally point."

It's in an isolated location about ten kilometers to the rear on the right side of the mountain behind us. None of us had ever been there but I pointed it out to my men this morning.

The Chinese troops immediately picked up their packs, at least some of them did, and started desperately running to the rear. They poured through the heavy trees in front of us—and those coming from the left side of the Chinese line became vulnerable and easy to hit as they ran right along the front of the little skirmish line of Russians which suddenly materialized on their right.

Thirty or so of the Chinese closest to us, the ones we could see as they came across our front, were easy pickings. Duffy rarely missed and the Russians and I did almost as well—most of the nearest Chinese did not make it through our fire. The remaining seventy or so Chinese farther out ran like hell and quickly disappeared into the distant trees. Suddenly it became very quiet; not a sound in the forest except the distinctive metallic clicks as new magazines are inserted into some of the Russian AK-47s.

I was smiling as I turned around to check out the teams between me and Duffy. And that lasted until I saw the unarmed Russian kid who had been dutifully following along behind me. He was flat on his back in a pile of pine needles staring at the sky with unblinking eyes. *Shit.*

After a long pause while we carefully searched the forest in front of us and listened to the running footsteps of the last of the Chinese, we began moving slowly and carefully forward.

Almost immediately there was a burst of fire from Duffy and a brief scream. Everyone froze and I quickly dove behind a tree trunk—and and land on a root sticking out of the ground and damn near let go of my weapon as I fell on it and smacked my face into the ground. I desperately scurried backwards on my hands and knees to get behind the tree. *Whoa that hurts. Breathe deeply. Get a hold of yourself.*

******

It was not until almost two hours later that Naumenko and the main force of Russians finally reached us. There was almost a friendly fire exchange as they approached. After more than a little shouting back and forth, the first of Naumenko's nervously advancing main force came into the clearing where we were gathering the dead and wounded Chinese and their weapons. Our guys were more than a little puffed up about their success and there was a lot of loud hand waving explanations and pointing at the dead and wounded Chinese.

The happy chatter slowly tailed to a halt and turned into curses as Duffy walked into the clearing with our dead Russian teenager slung over his shoulder. Willing hands reach to out to lower him to the ground amidst the muttered curses of the new arrivals.

Colonel Naumenko was pleased; what had been shaping up to be a slaughter of his men caught out in the open had turned into a minor victory and a pell-mell Chinese retreat.

"Thank you, my friends, thank you," he said to me and Duffy as he saluted and reached out to shake our hands. And then he said something that surprised me. "Are you wounded, Captain?" And then he barked something in Russian and a couple of the Russian medics left off tending the wounded Chinese and ran over to us.

I must have looked surprised because Duffy explains, "Your nose, Boss. You are all bloody. Looks like it's broken. Don't you feel it?" I put my hand up to my nose and it came away bloody. *Shit. That is tender. I must have landed on it when I tripped.*

I waved off the medics and shooed them back towards the Chinese. "It's nothing. I'm good." But I did accept a Russian wound dressing of white cloth and tried to use it to clean my face. It did not work. A few minutes later I wet the dressing with canteen water offered by one of my Russian kids and blotted off as much of the dirt and blood as I can. *Now the damn thing really hurts.*

While I was blotting away at my face Naumenko did something I thought was really smart. Right there in the field, with the rest of his troops still arriving, he lined up our eight surviving Russians and said something in Russian that obviously pleased them immensely. Then he saluted and walked down the line shaking each man's hand and kissing him on both cheeks. The men beamed proudly while the gathering crowd of other Russians watched enviously. Then he comes over and saluted and shook our hands again.

A few minutes later whistles blew, officers and sergeants shouted, and we once again begin walking through the trees to find the Chinese. This time was very different and everyone was super cautious—there were no helicopters in the air ahead of us; or behind us for that matter.

It seems the commanders of the Russian helicopter companies are well and truly spooked by the loss of their two birds. It would be hours before they are even willing to let their medevac choppers land to pick up the Russian wounded.

I heard about the argument between the Russian air commanders from Ivan as Duffy and I walked along behind Naumenko. We were once again moving slowly through the woods – some of the Russians, including me and Duffy, were going with the Colonel in pursuit of the fleeing Chinese; others peeled off to try to find the two choppers the Chinese shot down.

Naumenko has been on the radio for quite a while and was quite obviously extremely pissed about something. Just from the tone of his voice I could tell it was serious.

"What's up," I asked Ivan.

"Colonel is angry helicopters no come for wounded. Tell big general pilots are cowards. Tell big general shoot coward pilots."

****** *Lieutenant Bao*

I picked up my pack and ran like the devil himself was after me, and angled off to the left to get away from the Russians coming in on our right. "Fall back," I screamed at my men. "Fall back."

Sounds of small arms fire began coming closer as I ran. I could see my men desperately scrambling through the trees on either side of me; and I could see other men off to the right in the distance, Russians for sure, coming through the trees towards us.

"Go to the rally point"... "Go to the rally point." I shouted it over and over again as I ran.

It seems like ages but it was less than a minute later that the sound of firing began to fall off behind me. I could see a couple of my fleeing men running ahead of me as I stopped for a second to try to get some idea of what was happening. I could hear the sounds of running but the only person I could clearly see was Corporal Su Chou. He was laboring through the trees behind me carrying our last remaining missile. *Good man.*

I waved Chou past me with a thumbs up gesture of approval and motioned for him to keep going. Then I waited while the firing died away and the forest again became deathly silent. It took longer than I expected before figures began to appear among the trees in front of me. The Russians were coming slowly, but they were coming.

It's time to slow them down even more. So I raised my assault rifle and waited for one of the Russians to step between the trees and into my sights.

******

Harry and I were moving with Naumenko just behind the slowly advancing Russian line when there is the familiar double tap sound of an AK-47 being fired twice by an expert—and the little Russian teenager walking in the line in front of us throws up his hands and tumbles over on his back as if he had walked to the end of a rope and been jerked over backwards.

We instantly dove to the ground; and I banged my nose again.

"Well we found them," Duffy said laconically from the mud puddle in which he landed with a splash.

"I am getting seriously tired of this shit," I said.

"Maybe it would be easier if you did not keep diving on your nose."

"Beats getting your dick wet without enjoying it."

Duffy laughed. And I could not help it; I started laughing too. The Russians on the ground around us were shocked. Even Naumenko looked back incredulously as he lay flat on the ground trying to reach for the mike his radio man was pushing towards him. Then he looks back and saw, and realized what we said—and he started laughing too. *He really does speak English.*

A minute later Naumenko, shook his head in disgust and tossed the mike back to his radio man. Then he began shouting orders. To my surprise, and relief, the Russians on either side of us began slowly crawling backward.

Harry and I waited while one of the Russians slithered on his belly over towards the kid who'd been shot in front of us. He stopped when he got about five yards away, shouted something, and began backing up.

"Shit, we cannot leave him," I said to no one in particular. So I crawled over to the kid on my belly, grabbed him by his shirt collar, and began pulling him backwards along the ground. Duffy took over after a while and then some of the Russians.

* * * * * *

There was a shout and we wait with our Russians until Naumenko and his radio man crawl back to us. "What's up?" I ask as Naumenko looked at the dead boy and shook his head.

"We are ordered to wait for air support and all American observers are to go back to base on the next available helicopter. That is the good news. The bad news is there will be no air support—because we have no smoke to mark our positions and there will be no helicopters because helicopter colonel is a coward."

"Oh well," I said. "The sun is coming out. Maybe we can have a picnic while we wait." There is no response.

Duffy just shakes his head. *What. Now no one appreciates my humor?*

"Oh yes," says Naumenko as he backs past us on his stomach, "and your General Roberts says you are to leave your weapons here."

Hours later, with a new and even bigger bandage over my nose and several fewer buttons on my ripped and filthy field jacket from constantly crawling around on my stomach, helicopters finally began coming in to evacuate the wounded and we were able to get a ride back to base. The big boss himself was sitting in a Russian Jeep waiting for us when we landed.

He took one look at the bandage and asked both Harry and me if I needed to go to the hospital. After I assured him that it had been taken care of, he said, "I hear you both did real good. Have a sense of humor too, according to Colonel Numenko." *Uh oh.*

"Sorry Sir."

"Nothing to be sorry about. The Russian commander said it helped steady the men when you laughed and made fun of each other while everyone around you was panicking. He also said he was going to get medals for both of you for going forward under fire and turning the Chinese flank. Killed a bunch of the Chinese, he said. That true?"

"The Russian grunts did a lot of it, Sir. Good kids."

Then we climbed in the back of his Russian Jeep and began telling him what happened as he drove us back to the American headquarters huts. *God I am starved and thirsty. And why is an American general driving himself around a Russian military base without a protection detail?*

* * * * * *

Colonel Bowie walked in while we are eating in the boss's hut and, between mouthfuls, we told the story all over again. He was visibly upset about Williams and Kramer and questioned us very closely about how we found them and what happened after that.

We were surprised not to see General Shelton, so while we were still eating I asked the big boss where he is so we can report to him.

"Oh yeah," was the answer. "General Shelton is at Arkhara visiting Chief Matthews and his swimmers. The plan is for you two to work for me until he gets back. But that has just changed."

"It seems we have a problem," General Roberts explained. "Apparently there is a leak in Moscow. As a result of the casualty reports, the media has somehow picked up a story about Americans being involved in fighting with the Chinese. A CBS television new team somehow got to Arkhara and is trying to find Americans.

The last thing we want them to do is come here and find you two.

"The bottom line is," the big boss said with a wry smile, "The President has ordered us out and you two have got to get out of here and back to Riems, right now, without waiting to for General Shelton to get back. There's a MATS flight coming in from Kadena that should be landing in about thirty minutes. It'll be turning around and heading right back to Okinawa to pick up another cargo as soon as it unloads. I want you two on it and heading back to Reims. Report to my senior aide, Colonel Jack Peterson, at my office in Brussels. He'll arrange transportation for you back to the Detachment."

****** *Harry Duffy*

It was such a bumpy flight from Arkhara to Kadena that Captain Evans and I could not sleep even though we were absolutely exhausted. Worse for him, his heavily bandaged nose was really sore. In any event, the Kadena transit lounge was a welcome relief even though it only had a little stand selling cokes, stale sandwiches, and shit like that. *But that is all we need so what the hell.*

Both of us walked next door to the transit office and signed up for the next flight heading towards the States or Europe. Then we walked back to the terminal waiting room and instantly sacked out on the floor. We were scruffy, dirty, and in ripped up and unmarked Russian fatigues. And Dick was still wearing the bloody white bandage the Russian medic stuck on his twice-broken nose.

I was sound asleep and dreaming about something when someone kicked me in the ribs. Hard. I opened my eyes in time to see a foot winding up to kick me again. So I instinctively pushed my hand forward and grab the kicker's leg and jerked it, hard, as I opened my eyes. *What the fuck.*

It was like watching a movie in slow motion as a big MP with a shiny helmet went over backwards and hit his head of linoleum floor. Captain Evans woke up and came off the floor like big cat as another MP stepped forward and at the same time began reaching for his pistol. It never cleared the holster; Dick lurched up off the floor, grabbed him by the back of his neck, and smashed him face down on to one of the chrome arm rests on the line of connected airport chairs next to where we'd been sleeping.

Then we look at each other and, almost in unison, both of us say "what the fuck" as the second MP slid off the chair and hit the floor. When he landed his pistol slid out of his holster and went under one of the chairs.

"Well hell, Boss," I suggested a few seconds later as I slowly sat down in one of the chairs and surveyed the scene. "Maybe we should pick up that guy's teeth, he may need them."

"Yeah, you are right," Dick agrees as he sat down next to me and groggily rubbed his eyes. "You okay? What the hell was that all about?"

"Damned if I know. One moment I am sleeping and then that fucker is kicking me." I say as I pointed to the MP who was still flat on his back.

Then Evans' guy staggered to his feet and said something like "arggh" as he touched his bloody mouth and staggered backwards looking at the blood on his hand. He was obviously disoriented and seemed to be trying to find his pistol. *Christ they are MPs. I think we are in deep shit.*

Dick made sort of a shooing wave to send him away and we just sit there until a bunch of MPs, or whatever they are, showed up and arrested us.

******

Colonel Miskin and Dave Shelton and I are looking at the big wall map with Sholakov and Turpin when an aide came in, handed Sholakov a message, and said a few words.

"Um, Christopher Ivanovich," Sholakov said through Miskin as he handed the message to me. "One of the men of your plane's crewmen just brought this for you. There apparently was an incident yesterday afternoon in Japan at the Okinawa airfield. It seems to involve those two men of yours who did so much to help Colonel Naumenko."

Dave and I look at each other. "What?"

It did not take Dave and I long to say goodbye to Sholakov and get to the plane. We were leaving anyway except now we will go through Okinawa instead of direct to Brussels. Miskin will stay with Sholakov and so will Mr. Liska and three of his signals team. Only those four and a handful of Mike Morton's instructors will be in Russia for the media to try to find. The American air crews bringing in supplies won't be found because they are not allowed to get off their planes while they are being unloaded and refueled.

******

After a flight that was bumpy all the way we landed at Kadena in driving rain. I had been on the satellite phone getting information about Evans and Duffy—and something did not seem right. I'd had Major Martin call in with the usual signal that there is an O-10 general on board and request no honors—but I wanted the base commander and the base's senior Military Police officer to be on hand when I landed along with Captain Evans and Master Sergeant Duffy who are presently, or so it would seem, in a cell at the base police station.

There was quite a crowd of uniforms waiting under umbrellas as we taxied up to the terminal. Through the cabin window I could see Evans and Duffy in handcuffs waiting under the overhang by the terminal door.

Major Martin and Dave surprised me by zipping out the door and saluting as I stomped past them and hurried down the steps in the pouring rain. They trotted along behind me as I hustled into the terminal as some air force colonel tried to run alongside me with a big umbrella.

The umbrella crowd followed me in. I had't had a chance to change so I was still in my unmarked Russian fatigues. *Dave is in his American uniform with his rank showing and I know exactly what he is doing—he just sent a message to the officers down waiting down below that they better not be fooled by my unmarked fatigues.*

"You two," I say as I crooked my finger to Evans and Duffy who were standing at attention as I walk past them and into the terminal. "Come."

I led them into a waiting area and then hold up my hand to stop the crowd following us through the door from approaching.

"Okay. What happened?"

The story I got was quite different from the various charges of disorderly conduct, assault, willful disobedience, improper uniform, drunkenness, resisting arrest, and improper travel orders.

"Okay." I say rather loudly, "Where's the arresting officer and air police commander?" A worried looking air force colonel and air police major came forward and saluted.

An equally worried looking Air Force brigadier starts forward with them. "No," I say pointing at him, "You wait over there while I talk to these officers.

"Okay. Now you tell me what happened. You first major. Are you the arresting officer?"

"Uh. Well no. One of them is off duty and the other is in the base hospital. I am the commander of the Air Police. But the story I heard."

"The story you heard? *I emphasized 'story.'*

"Sorry Sir, all I have to go by is the charge sheet." I made a 'gimme' motion with my hand and he took a piece of paper out of a file folder and handed it to me.

I read it. And then I read it again. It says two drunken men wearing improper uniforms and claiming to be military personnel had refused to identify themselves and assaulted AP Airman Arnold Johnson and AP Airman Jason Pierre, causing them serious injuries.

Then I an idea struck me. I walked over to the two Japanese ladies working at the transit lounge's snack counter on the other side of the room and politely asked them if they had been on duty yesterday and seen the incident. They had and they told me what they saw. Then I returned to the two anxious officers.

"The Japanese ladies over there saw everything and are quite clear about what happened," I told them rather loudly and angrily. "They say your APs saw the two men sleeping on the floor and walked over and kicked one of them in the chest, really hard, without saying a word. Then there was a very brief fight; and then the two men sat on the bench and waited for the police."

I motioned for the Air Force brigadier, the base commander it seems, to come over and icily repeated what the ladies had just told me. I pointed out that the ladies' story was exactly what Evans and Duffy said, and very different from what is on the charge sheet.

"What happened here," I said with a great deal of menace in my voice, "is that a couple of your APs walked in here and saw those two men sleeping on the floor, and kicked one of them because he did not like how they looked."

"It's lucky for them, and for you assholes too," I hissed as I tore up the charge sheet and threw it at them, "that your boy did not kick the wounded officer or I'd have you three join your two stooges in front of the court martial they deserve and better get."

I do not know why but I was furious I was almost trembling. So I leaned forward and put my face about three inches from the shocked brigadier's and gave him hell.

"Captain Evans and Master Sergeant Duffy are in the uniforms they were issued, just like mine you might want to notice, and they have had no access to booze for weeks. They were on your terminal floor scruffy and sleeping and covered with mud and blood stains because they'd just been evacuated from a battle zone after they spent the last seventy two hours without sleep desperately fighting for their lives and killing a bunch of people up close and personal."

"So you miserable shitheads better listen up real good. I am going to keep checking on you three and this fucked up base. I hear one peep about any more false reports being filed, or another man being hassled or delayed when he comes through here, and I am going to see all three of you up on gross dereliction of duty charges—because your men are not properly trained and supervised."

"Now get the cuffs off those two men and get the fuck out of my sight before I change my mind."

"And you two get on the plane and get something to eat and some sleep. We are going to Brussels." *And then home.*

Then I stomped through the rain back to the plane feeling both self-righteous and foolish. *Now I will probably catch a goddamn cold.*

******

It was a long flight from Okinawa to Europe and everyone but me caught up on their sleep while I read through a bunch of NATO and Detachment reports. It was not until we were coming into Brussels that Captain Evans and Sergeant Duffy finally woke up and I finally had a chance to ask how they were feeling.

"Good Sir, thank you….Uh, Well Sir, Sergeant Duffy and I want to thank you, for standing up for us I mean… By the way, Sir, my grandpa said to say hello and give you his best regards. He says he met you in Korea when you were sitting on a wooden ammo case getting your back sewed up."

"Really? Who is your grandpa?"

"Clyde Evans, Sir. He was the commander of the 22nd Division when he met you."

"My God, General Evans. I sure do remember the first time I met him. Very vividly, in fact. He was one hell of a soldier just as you are. Must run in the family. You may not know it, but we might well have lost the war if your grandfather had not kept his wits about him. Well give him my very warmest and most respectful regards. "

"And please give me his address; I'd like to write to him myself."

Chapter Fifteen

Reinforcements.

The seriously overloaded missile cruiser *Admiral Markov* finished loading everything it could squeeze on to its deck and into its holds just before 2200 on Thursday. It immediately cast off and moved into the rainy darkness for a high speed run to Vladivostok.

Russia's new plan is simple and probably the best Moscow is likely to come up with under the circumstances: Get every ship they can get their hands on crammed with all the immediately available troops and equipment it can carry and on its way towards Vladivostok and the East China Sea at its highest sustainable speed.

Markov and the other ships Russia is sending to the Russian East will stop at Vladivostok to drop off the troops and supplies they are carrying. Then they will either return to pick up more troops and equipment or join Russia's subs in positioning themselves outside Chinese waters so they can attack Chinese ports and shipping if there is a war.

The only exceptions will be a few destroyers and frigates. They will continue on to patrol off Sakhalin Island in an effort to discourage a Japanese landing—and oppose it if the Japanese attempt to land.

If there is any good news, it is that Moscow finally seems to understand the urgent need for the Russian Navy to get as many reinforcements as possible into Vladivostok. They need to be offloaded and moving north before the war starts and the Chinese cut the rail and road links. What Moscow still does not know is where the Chinese attacks will be concentrated and how Sholakov intends to respond.

To the absolute fury of Admiral Krusak, Sholakov told me with a smile in his voice, the ships Krusak had expected to command were being controlled directly from Moscow. More importantly, Krusak has been ordered to immediately send all of Vladivostok's remaining naval infantry north to Khabarovsk for redeployment into the interior where the main battles of the war will be waged. The Admiral's only consolation is that, once the railroad to Khabarovsk is cut, the ground forces available to defend the port will be restored and built up as more and more ships arrive with reinforcements from Russia.

It was increasingly obvious that Sholakov and his officers were beginning to see their situation as comparable to what Russia faced in World War Two at Leningrad and Stalingrad: They are fully on board with the idea that Vladivostok and Khabarovsk are to be held at all costs with minimal numbers of sailors and troops while the main battle is fought elsewhere by the bulk of the Russian forces. *I doubt Moscow even knows how the naval infantry and reinforcements Sholakov is getting will be used.*

Making a stand in a city to fight off invaders is something every Russian understands—only this time the invaders are coming from the east and the reinforcements everyone hopes will turn the tide of the battle are coming from the west.

******

Russia's huge Baltic naval base at Kalingrad was the main staging area for the troops and equipment Moscow is sending by sea to reinforce the Far Eastern Military District. The railroad line and roads from Moscow and the Russian interior to Kalingrad are available. They are available because NATO did not waste resources destroying them during the war—because they do not run towards Germany.

Even better, the Russian units in the area are largely intact and immediately available to head towards Kalingrad naval base and embark for the east—because we ignored them during the war once we destroyed the bridges so they could not get to Germany and join the battle.

Russia's problem, of course, is that time is running out to get its troops and their equipment to Kalingrad and loaded on the ships that are available.

Railroads and roads are bringing the Russian troops and equipment to Kalingrad. But once they arrive at the port they cannot be loaded on the available ships fast enough. The men can march aboard the hastily readied ships but there are not enough cranes and cargo helicopters to quickly load their equipment and supplies. The result is a railhead and naval base that are increasingly paralyzed with a military traffic jam approaching epic proportions; equipment and supplies are arriving faster than they can be loaded.

Holding up one of the aerial photos of the Kalingrad naval base for me to see, Jack Riley said "this has got to be one of the largest and most fucked up concentrations of troops and military equipment in the history of the world. The Russians better hope the Chinese do not have some missile subs hanging about offshore to hit it when the war starts." *Jeez, he is right.*

"Mort, Chris Roberts here," I said to Morton Stanfield, the commander of our Atlantic Fleet. "Mort, the Russians have a problem at their Kalingrad naval base. They have got a huge and growing traffic jam of the armor and vehicles being brought in to load for Vladivostok. It's about the juiciest target I have ever seen."

"Yeah, really."… "Well the thing is this. We need you to get some attack subs and surface vessels up there to help the Russians keep an eye out for Chinese subs with cruise missile capacities?" *Mort's going to jump on this; it's an excuse to keep some of his ships and subs here instead of sending them to the Pacific Fleet.*

******

Initially, the Russian troops and equipment were loaded at Kalingrad on the relatively few surface vessels which the Russian naval commander at Kalingrad grudgingly released for reassignment to Admiral Krusak's Far Eastern Fleet. That changed in a hurry when Moscow replaced him and the new admiral emphatically ordered all seaworthy Russian ships to load everything they can cram on board and get underway for Vladivostok and the east. And do it fast.

According to the NSA report I read the next day, Moscow made it crystal clear that any bureaucratic delays and red tape is to result in immediate and very severe disciplinary consequences for everyone involved. Maybe my little "come to Jesus" speech helped.

Good. Russian officials are finally beginning to respond to the growing chaos at Kalingrad and Sholakov's increasingly desperate calls for reinforcements and supplies. To Sholakov's surprise, the new port commander at Kalingrad called him to ask what he needs most and then ordered that the priority use of the loading cranes and port equipment was to be the loading of helicopters and helicopter-related supplies on Russia's three aircraft carriers.

Russia's carriers sat out the recent war tied up to the Kalingrad carrier dock with skeleton crews. The Russian admirals apparently considered them too valuable to risk losing in a war. *But then why the fuck did they build them? I wonder if there is something missing in the selection process for admirals; ours acted the same way until we lit a fire under them.*

In any event, all three of the functioning Russian carriers have been ordered to load and head to Vladivostok—the helicopter carriers *Moska* and *Leningrad* which normally carry 14 helicopters each, and the *Kiev*, Russia's only real carrier, which normally carries twelve planes and sixteen helicopters. At least our surface navy and carriers finally joined the fight in the last war; the Soviet surface navy, including all of their carriers and carrier planes, basically stayed in port and sat it out.

The Russians have a fourth carrier, the Kiev Class *Minsk*. But sometime just before the recent war the *Minsk* had a major problem that rendered it unseaworthy. According to the CIA, its officers, at the order of the head of the Soviet Navy, sabotaged the *Minsk*'s power plants when the Soviet military command ordered the *Minsk* to sortie and support the attack on Iceland.

Allegedly some or all of the carrier's big turbines have been repaired and the *Minsk* will soon be loaded and join the long string of Russian ships slated to carry reinforcements to the Russian East.

Each of the Russian carriers and its escorts will immediately leave for Vladivostok and soon as they finish stuffing aboard all the helicopters they can carry and as much armor and other tracked equipment as they can load. The Russian navy's planes will fly out on their own.

In the end, loading the troops turned out not to be the least of the Russians' problems; they all got on board before the carriers finished loading the equipment. The carriers were packed like cans of sardines. *I would not be surprised if the Kiev does not set a record for the most people ever on a single ship. It sailed carrying an entire Russian armored division, its navy crew, and the overflow from the divisions assigned to the two smaller carriers— and not enough food* to feed them all.

What would happen when they arrived was equally problematical. They were supposed to be unloaded and move east to Podovsk and Chita. There was, unfortunately, a very real question as to to whether that would actually occur—because both the railroad and the deteriorating and heavily potholed two lane concrete highway from Vladivostok to Khabarovsk were jammed with men and equipment moving north.

As Spelling and I explained to the President and the National Security Council over and over again—how many of the potential reinforcements leaving Vladivostok will actually reach Chita will depend on how soon the Chinese attack begins, and how soon thereafter and where the railroad and road running from Vladivostok to Khabarovsk to Chita are cut.

* * * * * *

Oh Shit. Dick Spelling just called to tell me that the NSA and the CIA are both confirming that the Russian navy has received an order to fight if the Japanese try to land troops at Sakhalin. He also reported that negotiations are underway between Russia and Taiwan for Russian ships to use Taiwanese ports, and that Moscow is actively negotiating, using its natural gas supplies as bait, to regain some of the Soviet ships that were taken over by the Ukraine and Georgia when the Soviet Union collapsed.

Getting some of the Soviet ships back from the Ukraine and the other former Soviet countries really does not mean much at the moment; there is little chance any of those ships can be crewed up and sufficiently serviced and loaded in time to get them to Vladivostok before the war starts and the railroad is cut. But it's the right thing to do; they will be needed if the war lasts very long.

Washington's reaction to the unfolding situation was chaotic and confused.

On one hand Secretary Hoffman was reassuring the Japanese that we will honor our defense treaty even it means helping them fight the Russians. On the other hand, we are moving ships, particularly fleet oilers and supply ships, to Okinawa, Taiwan, and the Philippines so we can, if the President so orders, refuel and resupply the Russian ships.

We were also returning the Pacific fleet, which had come to Europe to help fight the recently concluded war, back to the Pacific. Some of the ships of the European Fleet were going with them as part of foreign policy "pivot to the east." *Whatever the hell that means.*

Secretary Hoffman and the Pentagon admirals are sure that returning so many of the American Navy's ships to the Pacific this will somehow "send an important message" to the Chinese—even though they cannot quite explain exactly what the message might be, particularly since they are simultaneously promising not to use the fleet.

Even I was confused. On one hand, we were sending ships to the Pacific from Europe and the Mediterranean to support the Russians and discourage the Chinese; on the other hand, Hoffman and the admirals are simultaneously telling Congress and an increasingly nervous American public that the ships being sent to Pearl Harbor and Taiwan will "under no circumstances" be involved in any hostilities that might break out between China and Russia or between Russia and Japan.

What's the message—if we change our minds we will be ready?

******

Day was passing into a rainy night as the missile cruiser *Admiral Markov* slowly pulled away from its Kalingrad dock—and then revved up its two steam turbine engines and rushed into the stormy Baltic to start a high speed run to Vladivostok. The *Markov* was among the first of the many Russian ships that will be carrying Russian reinforcements half way around the world to the Russian East.

Things went wrong from the start. The *Markov* was top heavy and rolling badly in the heavy seas of the Baltic. It had always been top heavy, but it was even more so now that it had been overloaded with tanks and armored personnel carriers be carried on its deck and helicopter pad.

On the *Markov*'s helicopter landing pad alone are nine PT-76 light tanks and five BMD infantry fighting vehicles. Three more BMDs were lifted by shipyard cranes into place in the bow even though they block the *Markov*'s missile launchers and anti-aircraft guns. Pallets of artillery ammunition are piled everywhere and four containers of tank ammunition and spare parts are stacked on top of each other and lashed down on the helicopter pad next to the armor.

Down below wedged into the *Markov*'s little two helicopter hangar are four assault helicopters. They were carried down by the helicopter elevator and jammed into the mechanics work space next to the missile cruiser's one and only anti-submarine helicopter. The elevator itself then went back up to be part of the deck. At the moment, it has three BMD infantry fighting vehicles parked on it with cases of ammunition and spare parts stacked on top of them.

The lieutenant colonel commanding the Russian naval infantry battalion on the Markov, Russian Marines, decided to keep the carrier's anti-submarine helicopter aboard instead of replacing it with another assault helicopter—because it can be quickly configured to carry ten passengers instead of anti-submarine torpedoes. *Maybe I will need it to move my men around.*

It would be a gross understatement to say that the men on the ship were in for an unpleasant voyage as the top heavy ship rolled and shuddered as it forced its way through the stormy Baltic and Atlantic Oceans.

One of the *Markov*'s big problems was the number of men on the ship. It was sailing with more than triple the number of men it was designed to carry. The ship itself is operating with a skeleton crew of 261 men instead of its regular complement of 380—so that it can squeeze aboard an entire 920 man battalion of naval infantry and all of its weapons and equipment.

And squeeze is the right word. The *Markov*'s enlisted crewmen are hot bunking to free up space for the Russian Marines—they are allowed an eight hour sleep shift and then must turn their bunk over to someone else. This freed up more than two hundred bunks for use by double bunking the Marine officers and triple bunking battalion's NCOs.

The enlisted sailors, at least, have bunks to sleep in— most of the enlisted Russian Marines do not. They are sleeping and throwing up on the floors of the passage ways, under the bunks and in the corridors of the sickbay and common areas, and anywhere else they can find space including in and under the helicopters and on top of the stacked supplies of ammunition and equipment.

That things are not going well aboard the heavily loaded and top heavy missile cruiser is an understatement. Three days into the voyage and the crowded conditions and sixteen hour work days for the crew and boredom for the seasick Marines was already beginning to take their toll. Worse, one of the ship's two steam turbine engines overheats and had to be shut down only six hours after the *Markov* cast off and began its long trek around the world to Vladivostok.

Captain Apraksin reported the turbine's failure and requested permission to return to port for engine repairs. Permission was denied. Make the repairs while you are underway was the response. The Russian Admiralty message did promise to sortie an ocean-going tug to follow the *Markov* in case the second turbine fails—as soon as they can load the tug with Marines.

Morale was in the pits. The sea was too rough for anyone to be on deck and the stench below where the Marines and the crew were sleeping and throwing up in the passageways, messes, and common areas was beyond belief. Even worse, the *Markov*'s speed dropped from its thirty four knots per hour maximum to twenty three when it lost the turbine.

Unless the damaged turbine can be repaired at sea, it will take the *Markov* almost a week longer to reach Vladivostok, perhaps not until late in the month if it encounters more bad weather.

Markov's understaffed and overworked crew was furious and Captain Apraksin was happy to be on the enclosed bridge. One brief trip into foul smelling chaos below was enough for him to decide to eat and sleep on the bridge for the entire voyage. The only other relatively unaffected areas are the ship's combat operations center and the cabins of the ship's double bunking officers; they merely smell bad as the Markov's ventilation system constantly recirculated foul air throughout the ship.

Senior seaman Gennady Ushakov, one of the *Markov*'s eight remaining cooks, was particularly upset. When the ship's complement had to be reduced, he turned down a discharge and a chance to stay ashore because he had nowhere to go. Anything was better than going back to the communal farm from which he had escaped almost five years earlier by joining the navy. Now he is cooking and washing dishes sixteen hour per day and sharing a filthy bunk with two other sailors.

It was not the work and hours that pissed him off, Gennady decided as he cracked open eggs to fry two at a time, it was the Russian naval infantry, the Marines. Their officers keep lining them up for meals, and then they cannot keep the food down in the heavily rolling ship long enough to even make it to the passageways outside the mess area. The floor in front of food tables was awash with vomit that rippled in little waves across the mess deck each time the ship rolled. Already, or so rumor had it, one of the Naval Infantrymen has thrown himself overboard to escape the agony. *I believe it, Gennady thinks grimly.*

Chapter Sixteen

Uncertainty reigns.

I was reading reports at the Detachment this morning when I received a flash intelligence update from Washington. NSA and the CIA now say they have solid information confirming their earlier intelligence estimates about the Chinese intentions. *Is this print getting blurred or do I need glasses?*

There is now no doubt, they both report—the Chinese are going for a lot more than just the territory China claims Russia stole from them. Their objective is the entire eastern part of Russia including its access to the Pacific Ocean; they are going after much more than just the lands China was forced to surrender to Russia in a series of one-sided nineteenth century treaties. Their objective is everything north and east of Lake Baikal.

In effect, according to a source the CIA rates as a five on a scale of one to five, the Chinese are going after all the land east of Lake Baikal including land the Chinese never owned or previously claimed. Moreover, they also intend to go north to Yakutsk and cut the Lena River corridor so the Russians cannot go around the top of Lake Baikal and get to the Pacific by going across Siberia further to the north and east. *The entire eastern half of Russia is the Chinese objective.*

There is no question about it—the Chinese intend to do a lot more than just cut off Russia from its only year round Pacific port. They intend to relegate Russia to a medium sized power on the fringes of Europe and make China the biggest country in the world. That is why it was not nearly enough to deprive Russia of its only warm water port in the east. They also intend to deny it access to saltwater anywhere in the east and to the great reserves of minerals and energy thought to be in Siberia and in the Russian Arctic and in their oceans.

Chairman Li's quote to the Military Committee said it all.

"There is much open land up there for our people to settle. Our population is not too large, it is merely too concentrated. Restoring the lands the Russians stole will remedy that."

My immediate feeling after reading the new intelligence estimate was that I should go to Moscow and Arkhara to see how the Russians were going to respond when they find out their worst fears have been confirmed. I need get an update on the Russian preparations and intentions. Dave Shelton can remain in Germany to help accelerate the flow of aid coming out through the Detachment. But I need to make sure it getting to where it is needed most.

That, at least, was my thinking as I picked up the phone and called Dick Spelling. Then everything changes.

"No, you cannot go back out to Sholakov's headquarters and Mike Morton and Woods and Goldman have to return immediately. And so does Bobby Geither and Bowie and his paymasters. President's orders." *What the hell.*

"What the hell, Dick. What's that all about?"

"What it's all about, buddy boy, is that you and your senior guys have been grounded. The President is afraid the inevitable media reports about high ranking American officers working with the Russians will tie us too tightly to the Russians—and cause the Chinese to see us as the belligerents we are instead of the neutrals the President wants us to pretend to be."

"A handful of low ranking observers and food and payroll assistance is one thing,"Dick says, "particularly if the observers dress like Russians and do not get spotted by the media; but recognizable flag officers, especially someone like you, are something else." *Shit, he is right.*

"Shit Dick, I hate to say it but the President's right."

"Yeah, he is. You can go to Moscow and Beijing for talks to help end the war; but you cannot be seen as helping the Russians fight. All you can do is keep a few junior officers out there as observers and have them report in constantly. And that might be a good idea—so we know for sure that our food aid and special supplies are actually getting through to the troops."

Special supplies meaning stuff like the Canadian snow machines and Israeli SAMs and anti-tank missiles.

That evening after the kids had gone off to bed I broke the news of my "grounding" to Dorothy—and my big strong wonderful and very pregnant wife jumps into my arms and begins sobbing. "Finally," was all she managed to get out. *Oh Jeez.*

******

Dave Shelton and I met with our aides the next morning to give them the news—they will have to go out to Arkhara without us and act as our personal observers. Then we spent most of the day giving them lots of instructions and advice as to what they are to do and not do when they get there. Much of it has to do with how they are to relate to John Liska's signals team, the two lieutenant colonels serving as armor advisors, and the jovial Colonel Miskin.

They are obviously tremendously pleased and trying hard not to show it. They will go out tomorrow on an American C-130 with Russian markings. It will be carrying food and more snow machines for the partisan companies Sholakov is forming. The only one dejected by the announcement was Jack Peterson. I told him he could not go because his rank is too high.

Jack's wife, I suspect, will be as elated as mine that he has to stay home, particularly when she finds out next week that the real reason he cannot go is that he is on the promotion list for brigadier.

Any questions I have had as to who to put in charge of our newly formed "observer team" was answered a couple of days ago when Dick Evans' name appeared on the promotion list as a deep dipped selection for major. Ari Solomon will be his number two. There were even bigger smiles all around when Dave and I informed Andy Willow and Harry Duffy that, like it or not, they will be going out as warrant officers so they can attend officer-only events and meetings.

A few minutes later I laugh out loud when I overheard the four of them, all bachelors, planning a big night at a restaurant and bar in Riems to celebrate their collective misfortunes.

I could only shake my head and sigh when I heard their plans for the evening. Then I called Sholakov on the secure line and, with the ever present Lieutenant Basilof translating, explained why my "personal observers" are coming and why Dave Shelton and I cannot. *And for some reason I felt a little sad.*

******

This morning the President once again called Chernenko on the hot line at behest of Secretary Hoffman. She and his Chief of Staff were in the oval office with the President when Chernenko came on the line.

"Yes, Mr. Chairman, I understand the Chinese are likely to attack.".... "But please do not risk a nuclear war, Mr. Chairman." ... "It's important to avoid nuclear hostilities at all cost."

Chernenko is not just disagreeable, he is rather insulting. "So how would you have us respond if they attack us, Mr. President? Do you really think we should surrender instead of using all our weapons? Is that what you would do if America is attacked?"

"Of course, you have to defend yourselves and so do we. But if you use your weapons of mass destruction on them they are likely to use theirs on you—and you will still lose. Is that not so?"

"Perhaps there will be no tit for tat, Mister President," the Chairman replied. "Our intelligence and military organs believe there will not be a Chinese nuclear response if our nuclear and gas weapons are used on the Chinese troops who are on Russian territory along the border, not on Beijing and the other Chinese cities."

"Bombing your own country? Uh, well, uh. I guess I see your point. I certainly hope you are right."

******

Dick Spelling just called with a heads up. Congress is becoming increasingly concerned, and rightly so, about the United States getting sucked into a war between Russia and China. The result is a Joint Intelligence Committee closed door hearing and they want us both to testify along with the Secretary of Defense. *I wonder if that fool Congressman Jackson will be there. Probably not, I heard he'd been arrested for fiddling his expense account. Besides, according to Pops, the Joint Intelligence Committee is one of the few committees whose members are vetted for brains and integrity before they are appointed.*

My Starlifter is permanently gone. Dick Evans and his team flew out this morning on a C-130 from Riems carrying the latest shipment of Canadian snow machines. So I am going to Washington tomorrow on one of the extended range Gulfstreams based at Rhine-Main. It will pick me up at Riems at 1030 and drop me at Andrews. I will spend tomorrow night at Dorothy's mother and father's home in Georgetown.

I feel really sad about not being on the C-130 with my guys.

****** *Washington*

"Hi Pops. I got a ride from Andrews and the door was open so I just walked in. Where's Grammie?" *Yeah, I know. Baby talk. But that is how the kids began calling them and it stuck.*

"Hey, Chris. Good to see you. Heard about the intelligence committee hearing. What's the good word?

"Well Pops, as the saying goes there ain't no good word. As you may have read in the *Washington Post*, there's gonna be a war. Unfortunately they are probably right for a change. It looks bad."

"Anything we can do?"

"Not much more than we are already doing. At least I cannot think of anything."

"Well then, let's have a beer and you can tell me all about the kids."

****** *Chris Roberts*

It's an unbearable time of the year in Washington. The temperature outside was pushing 100 and I wass already getting hot and sweaty when I paid off the Georgetown taxi on Constitution Avenue in front of the Dirksen Building. The committee room was a standard congressional hearing room, except that there are Capitol police at the door and it has, so I have been assured, been swept for bugs. *And, thank God, the air conditioning is working.*

Dick Spelling and a bunch of his uniformed aides walked in as just as I sat down in front of my name card on the witness table. So I stood back up so we can shake hands and huddle for a few private words. Nothing important. Just ask about each other's families. Then, for some reason, I told him I was really down about being here instead of flying out to the war with my guys.

"I know how you feel, Guns. This is probably my last congressional hearing. Tommy Talbot is going to take over the middle of next month, you know. It's just beginning to sink in. I think I am going to miss it. But I gotta ask you. Are you going to run? If you do I'd like to help."

I started to say "thank you and hell no I am not going to run" just as several of the committee members came over to chat the meaningless talk that always seems to accompany such occasions; then the rest of the members filed in and the chairman banged the gavel and ordered the room cleared.

"Think of the coming war between China and Russia in American terms," I suggested an hour later to make the point to the members of the committee.

"It's the equivalent of a newly powerful and highly motivated Mexican army going to war with a suddenly smaller and recently defeated American army to take back California, Arizona, Texas, and New Mexico. And if we win, say the Mexicans, what the hell lets take Utah and Oregon too."

The point I was trying to make is that Russia and China have a lot of history and there is not a damn thing we can do to change it. I do not think I made it very well.

After the closed meeting adjourned, Bill Kretzner of the *Washington Post* buttonholed me on the building steps. He asked if I can tell him anything that would help people better understand what is going on.

Bill had been fair to me in the past when Pettyjohn and Congressman White tried to get me so I gave him a quote "off the record." The only change I made was changing 'coming war' to 'possible war.'

Then it is off to the White House with Dick for a National Security Council meeting. Secretary Hoffman wants to cut off the food and money we are sending to the Russians unless Russia agrees not to use nukes. I disagreed rather strongly.

"Madam Secretary, with all due respect, I think that would be a terrible mistake that is quite likely to *cause* the very nuclear war you rightly want to prevent.

"The reality we face is that the current Russian government you are trying to deal with is a kleptocracy whose head thieves are desperately trying to cling to their power and wealth despite losing the war in Afghanistan and then the recent war with us. They will almost certainly fall if Russia loses yet another war and a good part of Russia along with it. So, if you insist on a commitment, Moscow will certainly agree that they will not use nukes in order keep our aid coming. *She raises both hands in a touchdown gesture of triumph.*

"But, no matter what they promise you, when the choice comes down to keeping their word or losing their power and their heads and going down in history as the men who lost half of Russia, they are going to forget their promises to you and use their nukes. Sorry," I shrugged.

After a pause, I continued because I can sense the President's interest.

"Once again, let me remind everyone of the two things we must keep in mind at all times. One is that Moscow does *not* control all of Russia's nukes; Sholakov controls those in the Far Eastern Military District and he has more than enough of them. The other thing to keep in mind is that it is Moscow jumping the gun and using its nukes prematurely that we have to worry about, *not* Sholakov jumping the gun and using his nukes."

"The danger as I see it," I explain, "is that the party bosses in Moscow are so desperate to hold power for a while longer, and so out of touch with what is happening on the ground, that they may prematurely use some of their nukes in an effort to hold on to power."

"For example, Sholakov may do something such as a strategic withdrawal to set the stage to win, which is then seen in Moscow as proof that he is losing and that it's time for them to use their nukes.

"Our basic problem," I explained once again, "is that Sholakov believes he cannot take the chance of a leak by keeping Moscow informed. He thinks, rightly in my opinion, that Moscow is so corrupt that it has undoubtedly been penetrated by Chinese intelligence. As a result, he does not dare share his plans and troop dispositions for fear the Chinese will know what he is doing and take steps to counter it.

"In other words," I explained yet again with a different set of words because I can still see some incomprehension in the eyes around the table, "in its ignorance of what is actually happening on the battlefront, Moscow might panic and order its nuclear weapons to be used; Sholakov, on the other hand, is much more likely to know what is actually going on and not use his nukes until he is absolutely certain there is no alternative."

"You are saying," suggested a suddenly pensive Hoffman, "that we must share our intelligence takings to keep Moscow fully informed as to what is actually happening so they do not overreact?"

"Absolutely not. Keeping Moscow informed would be disastrous and is likely to cause Moscow to overreact and cause Moscow to use the nukes it controls. Any details we give them about what is actually happening in the east will almost certainly leak back to the Chinese and cause the war to go badly for the Russians—and that will almost certainly result in Moscow and Sholakov using their nukes."

I put both my hands on the table and stare hard at the Secretary as I very emphatically state my position:

"You cannot, you must not, Madam Secretary, give Moscow any of the details we uncover about Sholakov's plans and strategies and troop dispositions. Whatever you tell Moscow will quickly reach the Chinese and almost certainly make *you personally* responsible for causing the very nuclear war we are trying to avoid and kill your political career." *I emphasized the words 'you personally' and said them very slowly. I can see from the look on her face that she took it as a threat instead of an explanation. Actually it was not threat—it was a goddamn promise.*

"But what can we do," the President asked, emphasizing 'can.'

"One thing that can be done, an important one, Mr. President, is for you and Secretary Hoffman to do everything possible to get Moscow to agree to leave the nuclear decisions to Sholakov.

"Your best argument is that Sholakov is on the scene and will always know the situation on the ground much better than they ever will and, thus, he is less likely to jump the gun." I emphasized the 'less likely to jump the gun' and said it slowly.

Then I continued.

"The best thing we can do now to avoid a nuclear conflict is keep sending Sholakov supplies and money to pay his troops so he has a chance of winning without using his nukes. And we particularly need to get our satellite and other intelligence to him to him as quickly as it comes in. That way he may be able to counter China's moves with his conventional forces instead of being forced to use his nukes.

"The bottom line," I concluded, "is that we want Sholakov making the decisions because he is more rational than the crooks and thieves in Moscow—and because we may be able to influence him because we are sending a lot of aid and information directly to him." *Does she get it? Does the President? Christ, I hope so.*

****** *China*

All of the Central Military Commission offices between Red Banner Street and Red Swallow Street in Beijing were bustling with activity. Both the Second and Third Departments reported extensive Russian troop movements both in the occupied territories and in Russia proper.

"They know we are coming. That is to be expected. But do they know where and when?" That was the question Party Chairman Li Ping addressed to General Wu

Fengqui, the Minister of National Defense. *He had summoned Wu and General Xu Wanquan, the Chief of the General Staff, to his office because this morning's intelligence reports suggested a faster and larger Russian buildup than had been thought possible.*

"Things are going exactly as we planned, Comrade Chairman. We do not believe they know either our plans or our objectives or even if we will attack. All they know is that we have begun rapidly moving men and equipment into positions on the railroad line that runs along the border."

"But they are moving in reinforcements far faster than we anticipated," Li Ping exclaimed as he held up a sheaf of papers from his desk.

"Not exactly, Sir," said Xu. "It would be more accurate to say that they are trying to move in reinforcements." He emphasized the word *'trying.'*

"Please look at this satellite photo, Comrade Li Ping" said Wu as he handed it to him.

"We were able to get it from one of our Washington sources. It shows the Russian naval base at Kalingrad yesterday morning. They are moving the army units that survived the recent war to Kalingrad for shipment to Vladivostok. But they are short of ships and cannot send them all."

"We have already dispatched two of our long range city-class missile boats, the *Canton* and *Sian,* to the Baltic. They will be on station long before the war begins. As soon as the war begins they will destroy that equipment and the ships in the harbor in a rain of cruise missiles. Our diesel powered attack subs will also do their part. Every attack sub we can get to sea, more than fifty of them, is being placed along the sea lanes the Russians must use, and particularly in the waters off Vladivostok where all the Russian ships must go to unload."

"Comrade Chairman," explained Xu, "much of that equipment will not sail and much of what does sail will never reach Vladivostok and much of what reaches Vladivostok will never reach the front because we will cut the Russian rail and road lines."

The head of military intelligence agreed,

"General Wu is correct, Comrade Party Chairman, for all practical purposes only the Russian men and equipment that have already sailed have any chance at all of getting to the front. And that is not anywhere near enough to keep us from victory."

"But what of their other deliveries, their air deliveries and the Americans?"

"According the Third Department's contacts in the Pentagon, Comrade Li, the Americans are limiting their assistance to food and the Russian airlift is inconsequential—because they lost so many planes in the recent war. Sholakov is getting no more than we expected he would get, perhaps even less."

"We are going to win and that is why the Americans, British, and Japanese changed their positions," Said Wu. *But not everyone, the Chairman knew; the Taiwanese, South Koreans and Philippines were being obstinate. Even the Japanese were asking for Kamchatka.*

* * * * * *

Colonel Bo Huwang and his 114th Infantry Division were in a dither. They were in Jiamusi and, with much shouting and whistle blowing, were in the process of climbing off the flat cars of the Northern Railroad and forming up on the service road next to it. Being unloaded with them were their supplies and equipment, including the inflatable rubber boats with which they had been practicing for the past sixteen months. It was a madhouse of noise and whistles blowing and messengers running to and fro with the owl-faced Wang Yon, the very young general commanding the 114th, standing around and giving foolish orders.

When the sun goes down so they cannot be seen by Russian and American satellites, the men of the 114th would be boarding trucks that will drop them off as close as possible to their secret jump off starting point near the Russian border. They will walk the rest of the way and paddle across the Ussuri River border above Bikin in a few days—before the war even starts.

After Bo and his men climb on the trucks, General Wang will return to Bejing and travel with his father and other senior party members to a place of safety from which he will issue orders for the 114th. The officers of the 114th refer to General Wang as "our prince" and, truth be told, are glad he is not going with them to fuck things up.

Colonel Bo and the men of 114th have an important job even though they do not know why they have it. They are to cross the river border a little north of the little Russian town of Bikin and prepare to capture it as soon as they are ordered to do so. That will cut the rail and road connections between Khabarovsk and Vladivostok and stop the flow of Russian supplies and reinforcements to the main front.

North of Bikin is such a logical place for an attack that, unknown to the Chinese, the Russians have just this morning decided to leave the first of their newly arriving battalions of armored naval infantry, including its tank company and reconnaissance platoon, to defend it.

Russia's orders to its troops are to hold Bikin and keep the railroad line open as long as possible; China's orders to its troops are to take Bikin and be prepared to cut the rail line and the road running next to it when they get the word.

******

The American C-130 painted with Russian insignia touched down at Arkhara just as the early morning sun broke through the clouds and blinded the pilot just long enough to cause him to land about twenty feet off the center of the runway—and put his nose wheel right into the deep pothole that tore it off and dumped the plane's nose onto the runway.

The hole had developed in the winter during the freeze and thaw cycle and been periodically filled with earth and gravel. The Russian ground crews had been so busy unloading planes for the past ten days that they had ignored it.

Evans and his men had been belted into seats on the left side of the plane immediately behind the pilot. That was fortunate for them because the snow machine crates that broke lose as the plane partially spun out and came to a nose-down screeching halt were on the right side behind the co-pilot

The co-pilot and the two crewmen belted into the seats behind him did not even have a chance to scream. The plane's sudden stop caused the massive bulk of the snow machine boxes to be pushed forward so fast and hard that it pushed what was left of the two crewman and the co-pilot and his half of the plane's instrument panel past the pilot's seat and ten feet out in front of the cockpit windshield.

"Get out. Get out." The pilot began shouting even before the plane finished skidding to a stop with its tail facing down the runway.

Getting out turned out to be surprisingly easy.

The passenger door and the left side of the plane were totally intact. In an instant, one that seemed like slow motion minutes to everyone still alive in the plane, the exit door handles were raised by the crewman sitting behind the pilot. The observer team, along with the pilot and two crew members who had been sitting on the left side with them, vaulted out the door of the nose down plane and jumped down to the ground—and began running.

Andy Willow was the last one out. He landed on the pilot who had jumped after Evans and Solomon and could not get up because he had broken both his ankles; and then Andy tripped over Harry Duffy who'd gone out the door just before him and stumbled. Even so, he instinctively reached out and grabbed the pilot by his belt as he landed and pulled him about ten feet.

In an instant Duffy regained his feet and caught up with Willow to help drag the gasping pilot to safety even faster.

"Run. Run." Willow was shouting at the pilot as Evans and Solomon turn back to help. *Why isn't this asshole running?*

Then there was a loud "crump" and the fuel sloshing out of the C-130's wings exploded into flames and a towering plume of black smoke.

******

"I heard about your plane, Major Evans," Miskin translated for Sholakov when Ari Solomon and I reported to him a couple of hours later to make our manners. "I am sorry for your losses."

Thank you," I said as I nodded. "We will be evacuating the survivors of the plane'screw on the C-130 due in at 1645." Then I followed General Roberts' orders and briefly, with Colonel Miskin translating, explained why we were here and what General Roberts has ordered us to do. There were no questions, just nods of agreement; he had obviously heard it before.

Later that evening we gathered in Colonel Miskin's hooch, at his insistence, to bring each other up to date while we ate. Almost all the Americans left in eastern Russia were there except for the few Special Forces guys still embedded with the Russians to distribute food and payrolls—the four of us along with Colonel Miskin, the armor officers Marshal and Rutherford, Sean Mathews the wiry Navy Master Chief heading up the Swimmers' instructors now that Admiral Morton is gone and his four instructors, and the three Signal Corps warrant officers.

All the signal warrants are old soldiers who served in Viet Nam in the 101st Airborne. Their senior guy, John Liska, is a stringy, slow talking old warrant officer who looks like he might be real steady in a serious fight. So do the four SEALs who are helping Matthews' with the Russian swimmers.

"I am getting tired of these here steaks and C-rations," Liska says. "Any chance one of you bosses can get us some hamburger meat or pizzas?"

"How about sausages, John?" asks Sean, the Master Chief who heads up Mike Morton's instructors. "My Russian swimmers have a sausage source in the city; they have been trading steaks and bread for them."

"Christ, I'd hate to think what's in those sausages," exclaimed Harry. "But for God's sake do not tell me. I don't want to know." We all laughed. *God, I do not want to know either.*

Colonel Miskin is the intermediary between us and General Sholakov now that the big bosses are not here anymore. So after we drank a couple of Russian beers, Ari Solomon and I got him off in a corner and asked him how he thinks we should proceed.

It was an important question. As it stands, Ari and Andy Willow are supposed to report on the state of the airfield defenses; Harry and I are to hang around with Colonel Miskin and be available for whatever special assignments he or General Roberts give us.

Actually, though no one has said it out loud, it looks like a lot of what Harry and I are going to be doing will duplicate some of what Colonel Bowie's Special Forces payroll teams had been doing before they started being pulled out last week—checking out the combat readiness of the Russian units and looking for gaps that need to be filled and problems that are being ignored.

I bet that is it. The big boss is gonna use us to cross check the reports he is getting from our guys and the Russians. Our cover is going to be that we are checking up on our guys to make sure they are getting enough food and money to the Russians.

****** *Andy Willow*

Ari and I were watching Evans and Duffy board a Russian transport at Chita while we waited for Colonel Miskin and Generals Sholakov and Karatonov. Ari and I are going to accompany Karatonov and his entourage on an inspection tour of the Russian airfields. According to Colonel Miskin we are to act as Karatonov's "experienced foreign airfield defense experts."

As Colonel Miskin explained it to me last night, at each field Karatonov will evaluate its defenses against Chinese air and airborne attacks and Sholakov will meet with the local commanders to discuss their troop dispositions.

According to Colonel Miskin, we will be traveling by helicopter with Karatonov, five or six of his officers, an interpreter, and his personal protection squad of four airborne troops under a Lieutenant Alexander Vasilevich Pylcyn.

We met General Karatonov on our last trip when we briefed him and his deputy on our experiences at Reykjavik. He is the commander of the Russian airmobile division that was rushed to some place called Chita. That is where the Chinese are expected to hit with an airborne attack similar to the one the Russians hit us with on Reykjavik. *Apparently Karatonov has been promoted and is now responsible for the defenses of all the airfields* out here.

Lieutenant Pylcyn is a piece of work. He is very standoffish to say the least. He is a stocky guy with crew cut and a funny shaped head, really flat on the back. According to Piotra, our interpreter, Pylcyn is an Afghanistan veteran who hates Americans because they helped the Afghan rebels drive the Soviets out. Piotra did not say it, but I suspect Pylcyn also hates hippies and thinks anyone with long hair like Harry's is a hippie. *Fuck him.*

Why do I think Pylcyn hates hippies? Because he nodded toward Harry as he and Evans started walking over to the Russian plane and said something under his breath to the Russians officers waiting with us for General Karatonov to arrive.

But then it was all I could do from laughing out loud when Ari turned to Pylcyn and, with the most innocent of expressions on his face, asked, "Lieutenant, when you were in Afghanistan did your very best men, your really serious killers, ever dress and grow beards and long hair to try to blend in with the local people, at least at a distance, so they could get close enough to kill them?"

"Yes, of course."

"Ah, then your very best men are like Mister Duffy, eh?" Pylcyn's eyes widened in surprise as the general's interpreter repeated the words. Even a couple of the Russians smiled. *That shook the asshole.*

Chapter Seventeen

Vladivostok and Bikin.

Some of the Russian naval infantrymen were so anxious to get off the foul smelling and filthy *Markov* that they literally tried to run as they staggered down the gangplank carrying their weapons and duffle bags. Then they waited in ranks in the rain for hours because it took most of the afternoon before the cranes at Berth 31 were manned and began to lift their tanks and armored personnel carriers off the ship.

Finally, as the last of the tanks was lifted down to the dock, the word was given and the soaking wet men of the naval battalion began marching through the rain towards the Vladivostok train station. There, they were told, they would find a train waiting to carry them and their armor north.

There was a notable exception to the enthusiasm of the troops who are desperate to get off the ship and put the horrible voyage behind them.

One look at the map and orders he was handed when the *Markov* docks and the appalled Lieutenant Colonel commanding the six hundred and ten men of Second

Battalion of the Thirty Eighth Naval Infantry Regiment made a fateful decision. *They want us to keep the line open as long as possible at Bikin with no line of retreat. We will be isolated and cut off. It's a death trap.*

Increasingly distressed as he thinks about his orders, the Colonel waited on board the ship with the captain commanding his tank company until the last of his armor was being swung down to the dock and the crew of the *Markov* prepared to cast off and sail back to Russia to pick up more troops. As the two officers walked together down the gangplank, the colonel suddenly announced that he had an immediate dental problem, a toothache, and would be temporarily re-boarding the ship in search of medical assistance.

"Take your tanks and BMDs to the train station and begin loading them for Bikin. I will be along in a few minutes," he ordered the captain.

A few minutes later the colonel was on board and hiding in a cabin below deck when the *Markov* slowly backed away from the pier and swung its bow around so it could sail back to Russia for another load of troops. The captain commanding the battalion's company of light tanks stood on the dock with his mouth open as he watched the *Markov*'s gangplank being raised and the ship's mooring lines cast off—then he rushed to his tank and hurried to catch up with the battalion.

At that moment, though he did not know it yet, the command of the Second Battalion of the Thirty Eighth passed to a thirty-three year old major, Konstantine Tulun, the battalion's executive officer. Major Tulun was more than a little surprised an hour later when the excited captain gave him the news.

More unexpected trouble came when Major Tulun's rain soaked Russian Marines reach the railroad station and started to form up in ranks under the tin roof that covers the station's four tracks. The last of the tanks and BMDs of the battalion's tank company were rumbling onto the station platform for loading on the waiting flat cars when an absolutely spotless Zil limousine drove up and an admiral jumped out and demanded to speak to the battalion commander.

Upon learning that Major Tulun had just assumed command as a result of the battalion's colonel somehow sailing with the *Markov* back to Russia, Admiral Krusak immediately countermanded the battalion's orders to move north to a blocking position at Bikin.

"Wait here." He ordered the confused major who was just beginning to realize that he was in command of the battalion. An hour later Russian navy buses begin arriving.

* * * * * *

NSA was seriously monitoring communications coming in and out of Vladivostok. So it was not surprising that the NSA listeners picked up the order to send the buses to the train station and take the troops of the Second Battalion to positions on the Vladivostok defense line, positions vacated earlier by one of the naval infantry battalions General Sholakov ordered north.

Diverting troops scheduled to take up blocking positions in the Bikin area in order to reinforce Vladivostok was a major change of plans. An alert NSA duty officer caught it and quickly informed the Pentagon. I got the call in the middle of the night and immediately called Sholakov to find out why his dispositions were changing. *Does he know something we do not?*

It took me a while to get through to Sholakov. Apparently he and an entourage including Arnie Miskin, Ari Solomon, and Andy Willow were getting ready to go on an inspection tour of his air bases and troop dispositions.

When I finally reached him Sholakov was more than a little pissed when I gave him the news and asked why he was changing his plans.

"It's that goddamn Krusak. Not me. He does not want the railroad line to stay open; he wants it closed as soon as possible so the troops and equipment that offload in Vladivostok will remain there and to be available to defend the port."

"What will you do?' I asked.

Two hours later I was again awakened by a call. Dorothy sat up and listened as two calls arrived for me almost at the same moment—one from Arnie Miskin calling from Chita where he was traveling with Sholakov and one from Dick Spelling. They both told me the same thing; Admiral Krusak is being recalled to Moscow and General Turpin is being sent to assume temporary command of Vladivostok. Turpin will arrive tomorrow and be accompanied by a small but lethal "support force" of military police from the airborne division to ensure the transition to army control occurs smoothly.

"That is good news, Arnie," I said. "The reinforcements and equipment coming through Vladivostok are really important. It's something we really need to keep on top of. If it's not too late, see if you can get Sholakov to let Evans and Duffy ride on Turpin's plane so they can get off at Vladivostok and go up there as observers. We need to know how long they think that part of the rail line can be held."

The sun was coming up and Dorothy had already handed me a cup of hot tea and the morning paper by the time Dick and I finished talking. After I hung up the phone I just stood in the window with a cup in my hand and watched the sunrise reflect off the pond. *Damn I like this place.*

******

Things had gone off track in a good way at Sholakov's headquarters this morning when Miskin started to introduce Harry and me to Colonel Naumenko. Both General Sholakov and Colonel Miskin were more than a little surprised when Naumenko greeted us with a big smile and friendly bear hugs and cheek kisses.

Colonel Naumenko, Miskin explained to us after everything settled down, has just been ordered to build a scratch Russian brigade around an armored infantry battalion of Russian Marines that has just arrived at Vladivostok. His brigade's assignment is to protect the rail line and road from Khabarovsk to Vladivostok and keep them open as long as possible.

It took a while for things to settle down because Naumenko immediately leaned out the window of the headquarters building and called in two of the men who had gone forward with us last week for more salutes and greetings. Then he had them take off the medals on their fatigues and pin them on ours. He would replace them, he assured everyone with a smile, as Sholakov and Turpin beamed their approval. *Nice looking red medals with big red stars. Wonder what they mean.*

According to Colonel Miskin, General Roberts thinks that how long the railroad running north from Vladivostok is kept open will be one of the keys to whether Russia wins or loses the war. Even one or two additional trainloads of troops and armor getting through to Chita could be the difference between winning and losing.

At General Roberts' request, Miskin explains, with Sholakov and Turpin listening carefully, Harry and I are to fly with Naumenko to Vladivostok. Then we will go north with him to some place called Bikin by either helicopter or train.

Bikin is apparently a mostly abandoned village, a whistle-stop on the railroad in the middle of nowhere. But it is important because the geography where it is located makes it the logical place for the Chinese to try to cut the rail line and highway between Vladivostok and Kharbarovsk. We are supposed to evaluate Naumenko's ability to hold Bikin and keep the railroad and the highway running next to it open.

The troops who will be the core of Naumenko's brigade are four companies of Russian infantry who apparently had staggered off a Russian destroyer yesterday and a bedraggled reinforced battalion of Russian naval infantry who just arrived by in Vladivostok on a missile cruiser. The Russian Marines, according to Naumenko, who was consulting a piece of paper he was holding while periodically puffing on a cigarette drooping from the corner of his mouth, have nine light tanks and eight BMD infantry fighting vehicles. "They have probably got some mortars also," he added.

Naumenko's brigade will also include three additional companies of army troops and a forty man Spetsnaz company, all veterans of Russia's lost war in Afghanistan. The army and Spetsnaz guys have already been flown into

Khabarovsk from Moscow and are, supposedly, in the process of being trucked down to Bikin. The four companies of infantry that came off the destroyer are either already there or will be shortly.

If all goes well, Miskin informed us, the Russians plan to add more and more troops and equipment to Naumenko's brigade as they become available.

"You two are to leave before the shooting starts. I will send a helicopter for you." *I should hope so. If the Chinese overrun Bikin, the Russians who survive, if any, will have to walk out. It will be a very long walk.*

******

Four helicopters carrying Generals Sholakov, Rutman and Karatonov and their entourages from Chita to the field at Darasun raised great clouds of dust as they settled to the ground. They landed in an open area next to long lines of tanks and other vehicles all neatly lined up for inspection.

Captain Solomon and I were on the number four bird with our interpreter and a bunch of Russian colonels. As jumped down from the doorway I could see the generals ducking their heads under the blades as they made their way through the billowing dust to a number of waiting Jeeps and officers.

Almost immediately we can see that there is some kind of trouble. Rutman was pointing and waving at the lines of tanks and vehicles; and it does not take a rocket scientist to pick up the anger in his gestures and the frightened postures of the officers in front of him. They are standing at rigid attention and he was screaming into their faces from about three inches away. Even with the helicopter engines still winding down I can hear him.

Karatonov was standing belligerently with his hands on his hips staring at the assembled officers and Sholakov was talking intensely to a couple of colonels who had flown in with him. *I do not know what Rutman is saying but Karatonov and Sholakov are obviously as pissed as Rutman about something.*

Then Rutman turned and said something to Karatonov which caused him to turn and look over towards me and Solomon. Then Karatonov said something to Pylcyn who was standing behind him and motions, I think, for us to join them. Almost immediately one of Pylcyn's Spetsnaz troopers dashed over to us in an all-out run and confirmed Karatonov's summons with some gasped Russian and "come" gestures with his hands.

Ari and I double timed over to the generals with Piotr hurrying along behind us. An officer we had never seen before shouts "American officers here please" as we jogged up.

"General Karatonov tell you please with him to headquarters."

The local Russian officers who had greeted the generals literally run to their Jeeps. Sholakov and Rutman stomped after them with Karatonov and the officers who had flown in with them hurrying along right behind them.

Karatonov, with us following, reached a Jeep and barked an order that has the officers in it hastily get out as he climbed in the front with the driver. Then he waved me and Ari into the rear seats along with Piotra, our interpreter and said something to the driver in Russian, obviously an order to 'step on it.'

"Big Generals," Piotra reports as he settles into a corner seat and grasps the sides to steady himself for the bumpy ride ahead, "are no happy tanks and personnel carriers are in inspection ready instead of in fight ready."

* * * * * *

Russian military headquarters at Darasun is on the military side of the airfield's relatively short concrete runway. It was a shabby square three story concrete building with a muddy parking lot and dirty gray concrete stairs running up to front door. About forty years ago it might have been painted white.

We parked next to Rutman's Jeep and got out on to the muddy gravel in time to watch Sholakov and Rutman, and then Karatonov who rushed to join them, bound two or three stairs at a time up the stairs and into the building. We followed and tried to keep up.

Several dozen or more anxious looking Russian officers, both army and air force, copied the generals rapid entrance and so do we and so does Colonel Miskin who is now, interestingly enough, wearing a Russian uniform with colonel's epaulets. *I am going to ask Ari to ask someone about that; I thought we are not supposed to wear Russian ranks.*

Our three generals and several of the senior officers who met them went straight into an office and closed the door; the rest of us were ushered into what was obviously a briefing room with a table at one end and five or six rows of chairs in front of it. There are maps on all the walls. Ari and I sat in the corner on a couple of rickety wooden chairs with Piotra standing behind us.

The officers who did not go behind the closed doors with the generals quickly filed into the room behind us and began talking nervously and quietly among themselves. They obviously do not know what's going on and appear to be more than a little apprehensive.

We quickly became the objects of interest even though we are wearing Russian officer uniforms without insignia or rank. One of the officers said something to Ari.

He just shrugs—but Piotra, our interpreter, spoke up and whatever he said obviously surprised the hell out of the Russians. Their jaws literally dropped and they all stared at us in total disbelief, every single one of them.

"What did you tell them?" Ari asked Piotra.

"Officers tell me to tell who is you. I tell you American airfield defend experts. Tell you American Marine officers fight at Reykjavik."

Ari started to say something but stopped as the door opened and generals came in. Everyone including me and Ari jumped to attention. The three officers who met with the generals privately, an air force general and two army colonels, followed our three generals up to the front of the room. All six of them look grim and determined.

Sholakov said something and everyone sat down. So did we. Then he launches into a flood of Russian. I do not know what he was telling them but the officers suddenly sit up even straighter and I hear several of them sitting around us literally gasped out loud in surprise. *What the hell is he telling them?*

"What is he telling them," I ask our equally stunned interpreter who was sitting between me and Ari.

"He tell big Chinese attack come Chita and Darasun. Tell China want all of Russia east of Lake Baikal."… "Is true?" Piotra asked.

Then Rutman said something else and gestures towards Karatonov, and then towards one of the colonels who accompanied us to Chita, and then towards us. There are more surprised faces and everyone turns and looks at us incredulously.

"He tell Chinese come big parachute attack on airbases. Tell Darasun for sure. Tell Colonel Altaysk is command Russian forces for airfield war here. Tell you are American airfield defend experts and all officers who do not immediate Colonel Altaysk obey is political officers being shoot. No time for court martial." he translated it to us with a shrug of his shoulders.

Things began to move faster and faster. We and the other aides and assistants just sat there and looked on as the generals and colonels gathered around a big map on the table. Every so often an order was barked and an anxious officer or two hurried to the front of the room, received orders, saluted, and rushed out.

I was just coming back from taking a piss in the smelly latrine down the hall, and starting to get hungry, when the meeting finally broke up and Karatonov brought Colonel Altaysk over to us. We jumped to attention and saluted as we are introduced.

It seems the two of us, or three if Piotra is included, are going to spend the rest of the afternoon helping Altaysk prepare the Darasun airbase defenses for a Chinese airborne or airmobile assault. Tomorrow we will fly with the Generals to another Russian base and repeat the process with another colonel. Altaysk will stay here with the local division commander and be responsible for the defense of the Darasun field.

What we want at each air base, Karatonov says with Piotra constantly translating, is to make the defenses so strong that either the Chinese won't even try to take them, or, if they do, they will suffer huge casualties and fail.

It quickly became apparent that, at least initially, the defense of Darasun was going to be very different from that of Reykjavik. Rutman and Sholakov have obviously decided to kill two birds with one stone. They are going to initially hold some of the local division's armor around the airport as reserves so they can be rushed to reinforce whatever Russian troops bear the initial burden of the main Chinese attack.

The decision to hold the local commander's armor reserves around the airbase was both significant and smart. It meant an airborne assault by lightly armed Chinese paratroopers and air assault helicopters was going to face a storm of fire from both its infantry defenders and from the tanks and armored vehicles that would be concentrated around it.

Even so, the airbase would have to be ready to repel an airborne or helicopter assault if it occurs after the armor moves out. That meant Colonel Altaysk, the man who will remain and command the infantry left to defend the Darasun base, must establish fighting positions and policies as if there is no supporting armor. *That, apparently, is where Ari and I come in.*

China

Not all is going well for Chairman Li and China. The Chinese negotiations with Japanese are still not finalized. Japan has agreed to use its troops to take Sakhalin Island and to coordinate their attack with the Chinese—if Japan gets to keep all of Sakhalin and can permanently take possession of Kamchatka at the same time.

After a lot of talking and messages back and forth to Beijing, the Chinese negotiators agree that the Japanese can have Kamchatka—on the condition that the Japanese government simultaneously orders various Japanese companies to build factories in China and share their technologies with the Chinese.

According the CIA, the Chinese negotiators even gave the Japanese a list of the factories and technologies they want. The problem, of course, is that the Chinese cannot get their arms around the reality that Japanese manufacturers are only influenced, not controlled, by the Japanese government.

Japan's manufacturers must have been consulted, said the NSA, because many of them quickly made it clear to the Japanese negotiators that they will never agree to give away the technologies of their production processes to potential competitors. "Only short-sighted corporate fools would do such a thing," one said. According to the NSA, the talks then adjourned so the Chinese negotiators can consult with Beijing.

A somewhat similar, and far less important, Chinese outreach intended to deny the Russian navy access to South Korean ports and supplies is going even worse - absolutely nowhere. Vague Chinese promises regarding the reunification of North Korea with South Korea have not been greeted with enthusiasm. To the surprise of the Chinese, South Korea did not see much value in merging with North Korea and "sharing power" with the Kim family who control the north.

"We are finally beginning to enjoy real economic progress. Bringing in all those poor people and foolish economic policies from the North would, at the very least, cause real damage to our economy and our people. Even worse, reunification might end up resulting in a bloody fight even if you provide the help you are promising." *And if there is a fight you will undoubtedly help North Korea, not us. That is what everyone around the table was thinking but was too diplomatic to say.*

What was going well were the Chinese preparations for the war. The Chinese were aware that the Russians have begun a desperate eleventh hour buildup, but they are confident they have sufficiently large numbers of troops ready to overwhelm them.

Russia's buildup, according to Chairman Li, is "too little, too late."

******

According to the latest satellite photos the continuing Chinese buildup of military supplies and troops is occurring all along the recently upgraded railroads and roads that run east and west along the northern Chinese border with Russia. The supplies are safe so long as they are there because most of them are beyond the operational range of the Russian Air Force unless it uses aerial refueling tankers. And the Russian only have a few left.

Both the NSA and the CIA now report the Chinese plan is to initially attack over the border towards Khabarovsk and Vladivostok. The Chinese expect their initial attacks will cause the Russians to rush reinforcements eastward from Chita and their other positions along the Trans-Siberian. The main attack will not begin, however, until the Russian reinforcements stop moving eastward. *How the hell will the Chinese know that? They do not have operational satellites according to the CIA and NSA. Or do they? Nah. It's got to be observers reporting in by radio.*

According to the CIA, only when the Russians stop moving their troops eastward towards Kharbarovsk will the Chinese launch their main attack over the Amur—far to the west and aimed at Chita. They will not try to cut the Trans-Siberian anywhere so long as the Russian reinforcements are moving eastward away from Chita.

That is because, as we now already know from our intelligence sources, the main Chinese attack will fall on the Russian territory far to the west near where the Chinese, Mongolian, and Russian borders meet. That is where the Chinese intend to launch their major attack and attempt to win the war. They are going to wait to launch their main attack so long as Russia's reinforcements are moving east after the initial attacks start because they want the Russian forces in the Chita area as weak as possible when they attack.

Only when the Russians stop weakening their defenses at Chita by moving their troops and armor eastward will the Chinese launch their main attack—against Chita. They will not even try to cut the Trans-Siberian Railroad so long as the Russians are using it to move their forces eastward away from Chita.

****** *Chairman Li*

Our plan of attack is a sound one. But an unexpected problem is developing that is encouraging—the Russians are so confused that they are not behaving as we expected. Instead of reinforcing Kharbarovsk and their far eastern cities, the Russians are frenziedly moving armor and troops in the other direction. Some of it is going west to the key road junction at Borzya across the Amur from the Chinese city of Heihe and, in even larger amounts, into the invasion corridor to Chita that begins immediately opposite the Chinese city of Manzhouli.

Indeed, the Russians are using the Trans-Siberian Railroad to bring troops and equipment to Borzya and the Manzhouli invasion corridor from both the Russian cities in the east such as Khabarovsk and from the reinforcements that are being airlifted into Chita at an ever increasing rate.

What's obviously happening is that Moscow has finally figured out that we are coming—but their intelligence is so poor that they neither know where we intend to hit them nor our objectives. So they are accumulating reinforcements outside of what they expect to be the war zone; troops and equipment which can be rushed on the Trans-Siberian Railroad to wherever we attack.

That is why we must initially attack elsewhere and leave the railroad intact—so it can be used to move the Russian troops and armor away from where our main attack will ultimately occur.

The Red Army agreed.

"Of course the Russians are locating some of their troops along the Trans-Siberian east of Lake Baikal, Comrades," explained Marshal Wu.

"Their intelligence as to our intentions is so lacking that they do not know where else to put them. That will change when we make our initial attacks towards Khabarovsk and Vladivostok and leave the Trans-Siberian rail line open. Then they will use the railroad to rush their troops to the front – and clear the way for us to take Chita and all the lands east of Lake Baikal." *At least that is what better happen. If I am wrong I will be reeducated or worse.*

"Once Chita is taken the rest of the Russian cities and forces in our stolen lands will be totally cut off and fall into our hands as ripe apples fall from a tree," said Chairman Li Ping as General Wu smiled and nodded in agreement.

******

Vladivostok's harbor was jammed with arriving ships and more were on the way, including the first of Russia's three operational carriers and their escorts. The first carrier that would arrive, the *Moskva,* was still six days out. The *Moskova* and its escorts are carrying with elements of the two armored infantry divisions. The two other Russian carriers and their escorts are a couple of days behind it with the rest of the divisions' men and equipment. The *Minsk's* engines are still being repaired.

Russian naval ships were not the only ships in the Vladiostok harbor. The Taiwanese tanker *Soft Wind* slipped in last night and began discharging ninety five thousand tons of bunker fuel to top up the port's storage tanks. When it finished delivering its oil, the *Soft Wind* would go back for another load; this time it will pick up diesel fuel in Pusan. Two other chartered tankers flying Liberian flags and an American navy fleet replenishment oiler, the *Sacramento*, are also inbound with bunker fuel for the navy, gasoline and diesel for the army, and JP-4 for the air force.

Chapter Eighteen

Bikin.

Harry and I flew into Vladivostok with Naumenko and some of his officers in a Russian crewed C-130 Hercules. The weather was nice and we landed without incident. Even so, I found the flight a bit nerve racking, particularly since our last C-130 flight did not end up so well and the plane we are on has Russian pilots.

I know damn well that the Russian pilots only receive a few hours of training to transition from the somewhat similar Russian planes they are used to flying—and that is not enough no matter how many hours a pilot has in a similar type of plane.

Vladivostok was a madhouse. Our plane was absolutely swarmed by soldiers and civilians acting as cargo handlers as soon as the pilot lowered the cargo door– which took a while because he had to talk to the pilot of another plane before he could figure out how to work the door switch. When we finally got off the plane we could see large numbers of civilians and military dependent evacuees lining up next to the runway to board it for the return flight to Moscow or wherever the plane is headed next.

Fortunately we are expected. There are trucks to take the cargo to the train station and Jeeps to take Naumenko and his officers, including me and Harry, to the three helicopters assigned to Naumenko for the trip to Bikin. It'll be an IFR trip—which in Russia seems to mean "I follow roads" or, in this case, "I follow railroads."

We got an inauspicious late start because our pilot happened to look at the fuel gauge after Naumenko's chopper had already taken off and the engine of ours had already begun spinning up to follow him. Sure enough, we needed fuel. So we sat there in the cigarette smoke of our fellow passengers while the copilot went off to find a fuel truck. *I wonder what else they missed. All the pilots did when the fuel truck finally disconnected its hose was flick their cigarettes out the side window before they started the engine.*

I held my breath, the helicopter's engine spooled up, and we were airborne and on our way to Bikin. We seemed to be running flat out in an effort to catch up with Naumenko as we flew along the railroad tracks and passed low over two long and heavily loaded troop trains moving north. At least I assume the sight of men standing around their guns and vehicles on the flat cars and sitting on the roofs of the passenger and freight cars means the trains were heavily loaded.

The men on the trains seemed pleased to see us; absolutely everyone waved as we passed over them. Poor sods, they probably think they have been abandoned. *Jeez, I wonder how they take a dump or pee if they have to ride up there all day.*

******

Bikin is nothing, just a couple of dozen rundown log homes clustered along a rutted dirt track running up from the railroad and the dirt "highway" that runs along it. The yards around the log homes are filled with abandoned refrigerators and beaten up old trucks and Jeeps with flat tires. One look at the "highway" that runs through it and its crystal clear why the Russians are moving everything out of Vladivostok on the railroad.

Our helicopter was just settling down when we watched the major commanding the four infantry companies already at Bikin and his officers greet Naumenko with great formality. Then we followed them to the log house the colonel will be using for his headquarters and watched as maps began to be tacked up on its walls. *It looks to me like it might have once been used as a one room school or maybe a little store.*

Major Vorshilov and his men only arrived by truck a couple of hours before us but already the village's log cabins were a beehive of activity; trash and broken furniture was being hauled out, doors and windows unboarded, and radio equipment installed. A portable generator was already up and running even though a big power line follows the tracks and there are several smaller lines running into the village.

"At least this time we were smart enough to bring our own clothes, tent, and sleeping bags." That had been my only comment as we walked from the helicopter to the log house that seemed to be getting everyone's attention.

"Should'a brought our own rations," was Harry's response.

* * * * * *

Three hours and two passing northbound troop trains later, there was a lot of loud locomotive horn blowing and we watched as a bearded civilian in ragged clothes materialized out of nowhere to lift a huge lever to switch a northbound train on to the rusty rail siding that ran along next to the double tracked mainline.

The train very slowly chugged and rattled through the switch until it came to a stop and troops begin pouring off with lots of shouts and officer whistle blowing. The first thing almost everyone did was pee and poop next to the track. It's a reinforced battalion of naval infantry under a Major Talun. They arrived yesterday in Vladivostok after a terrible voyage all the way from Kalingrad.

Only then does the first of Naumenko's many problems become obvious—there is no station platform to use to unload the battalion's tanks and military vehicles from the flat cars. Whistles blow and the digging started immediately.

******

It was after dark and candles were flickering in the Russian tents when a sentry ran into the command post to report headlights, lots of headlights, slowly coming down the dirt highway.

Thirty minutes later Duffy and I watched quietly from a corner of the room as half a dozen army and Spetsnaz officers clumped up the wooden steps and reported in to Naumenko. He took them to a map tacked up on one of the walls and began pointing and giving orders.

It may be my imagination but I get the impression that the new arrivals like what they are hearing.

It soon became obvious why the new officers seem to like what they are hearing. They should. According to what Piotra is whispering in my ear as Naumenko gives his orders, they are getting independent commands and responsibilities.

Each of the three newly arrived army companies is to dig in to guard the tracks around one of the three key bridges over the Bikin River and the swampy area on its southern side. Once they have finished digging in they are to aggressively push out patrols and establish listening posts in an effort to intercept the Chinese before they can reach the bridges.

Colonel Naumenko told the major commanding the three companies to get back on the trucks and take his men further south to the bridges and defend them for as long as possible. He is to locate his command post on the dirt service road between the bridges and establish a mobile reserve that can be an instantly available relief column.

In contrast to the three companies charged with defending the bridges, the Spetsnaz were ordered to operate independently. They are to locate themselves and patrol as their captain sees fit with the goal of ambushing the Chinese long before they have a chance to get close to the railroad and bridges.

Harry and I both think that is a very smart decision on Naumenko's part.

And the army and Spetsnaz troops are getting some unexpected reinforcements: three of the Russian Marines' light tanks and three of their tracked BMD infantry fighting vehicles will drive down the road with them and be stationed at the bridges.

The armor will give the major commanding the bridge defenders his own little armored response team. He will also get a couple of the Marines' mortar squads. The mortar men will set up their heavy mortars in the beds of a couple of the trucks carrying the men to the bridges so they can quickly move from one place to another. *I can see what Naumenko is doing and I like it. Very smart. Harry agrees.*

"Colonel is telling the bridges must be held as long as possible so reinforcements can get to comrades in interior," whispered our new interpreter whose name is Eugene. "He is telling, how you tell it, track is fast repair; bridge no fast repair."

What Naumenko was ordering the new arrivals to do really does make sense. Before we left Podovsk Colonel Miskin explained to us that everything north of Vladivostok up to ten kilometers south of the bridges is the responsibility of the regional headquarters at the port; the tracks immediately south of Khabarovsk are the responsibility of its regional headquarters.

"All Naumenko has to worry about," he had said cynically, "is the middle one-tenth of the transportation corridor—the bridges and tracks where the Chinese attacks are almost certain to occur because it's the only place where the Chinese won't have to cross any streams and rivers except the Ussuri to get to them."

After the airborne and Spetsnaz officers left Harry and I agreed that Naumenko has again impressed us; he hit the ground running and, even before he got here, he'd already decided where he would locate his initial forces. Then we set up our little tent and got some sleep. *So far so good was my last thought as I drifted off to the sound of Harry's snoring.*

Sunrise woke us up to a scene of military bliss so far as I am concerned— whistles tweeted and someone blew a bugle to greet the day and wake the men. The Russian Marines poured out of their little tents and began eating field rations and making hurried trips into the woods to pee and poop. So did we. It was a glorious sunny day. *One thing about Russian troops, they rarely waste time digging latrines or covering what they leave behind. It means you've always got to watch where you are walking or sitting.*

About an hour after sunrise there are more whistles and shouting and the Marines and the men of the army companies begin hurriedly striking their tents in preparation to move out to their various newly assigned positions around Bikin. When they reach them they will dig in to fight off attacks and prepare themselves to move out instantly if an attempt on the railroad is made elsewhere.

For a while we just stood around and watched the Russian troops strike their temporary camp. Then, as another heavily loaded troop train chugged its way north past our camp, we wandered over to the headquarters house to get the latest news. *Where is the damn interpreter?*

Chapter Nineteen

Defending the airfields

If I do say so myself, Dave Shelton, Mike Morton and I and the rest of the guys at the Detachment are a damn good team of military planners and doers. We ought to be after all those years of trying to get the biggest bang for the relatively small amount of bucks we had available to spend.

Our edge, I decided long ago, was our experience in the real world of combat while most of our peers were playing musical chairs at the Pentagon. It's probably why it took us so long to get promoted.

Being grounded by the President has its benefits. Those of us with a lot of years at the Detachment will once again be able to keep in close contact with each other. And that includes me because I intend to continue to live right where I have always lived and spend a lot of time at the Detachment. I will commute to Brussels and Campbell Barracks by helicopter or teleconference whenever the headquarters bureaucracy actually needs me. *Infrequently is my best guess.*

I can commute because rank has its privileges and we have a shit pot full of newly arrived helicopters and pilots as a result of the recent war. And I want to do it because I want stay close to the thinkers and doers I trust even if it means spending time away from NATO's Brussels headquarters with its great food and the paper pushers being groomed for promotion.

And yes, the food at NATO headquarters is really good. It should be; it's prepared by Belgian draftees who, in the interest of defending Europe and the free world, are deferred from being called up until they complete their Cordon Bleu training and apprenticeships.

******

Russian pilots do not like to fly at night and neither does anyone who knows their safety record and has a choice. Russian generals have both knowledge and choices—so Ari and I spent the night at Darasun and left with them at sunrise to fly to Borzya. It was our second stop on the big bosses' whirlwind tour to check out and improve the Russian defenses at the various airfields the Chinese are expected to hit.

Borzya is much closer to the Chinese border than Chita and Darasun. It sits astride one of the main corridors into the Chita district. Without a doubt its airfield will be a prime target for the Chinese. But will they hit it with paratroopers or just try to bomb and shell the living shit out of it?

Each arrival at an airfield proceeds in the same way starting with the local army and air force commanders waiting to meet us as we land. Borzya is different in that many more officers were waiting when we land. Little wonder in that. There are three Russian armies headquartered here, each the equivalent of an American corps. According to Colonel Miskin, each of the Russian armies has two infantry divisions in hand and at least one more in the process of arriving. They report directly to Sholakov—who will be located here during the war and personally command the Chita Front. *At least that is the plan as we understand it.*

Borzya's air force general has a number of squadrons of MiGs under his command, the survivors of those that had been flown west to fight in the NATO war—they were not worth squat against the NATO planes and pilots, at least that is what we'd heard, but they might do okay against the Chinese who are reported to be flying Chinese-made MiG-21 knockoffs and even a few earlier knockoffs of the older MiG-17s.

There were a lot of tanks, infantry fighting vehicles, and artillery in sight as we landed at Borzya. They were scattered around the field, but not in prepared positions or at carefully selected locations. In other words, they look like they'd just arrived and been parked. The local generals probably heard about the furor at Darasun when the bosses found the armor and equipment all lined up for inspection instead of in their fighting positions.

Most of our day was spent driving around the airfield and clustering around maps spread out on the hoods of Jeeps and on tables in the local district office or at the various army and divisional headquarters. By the time we left the airfield defense was beginning to take shape and one of the newly arriving infantry divisions, including its armor, was on the base's long rail spur and beginning to unload. Its troops immediately began to dig in around the runway. They seem to be in a hurry. *I do not know what the officers told their troops but some of them seem quite frightened; they were constantly looking up to search the sky.*

Activity around the field became even more intense as the helicopters and planes based on the field began dispersing. The helicopters and their support troops were already beginning to move to the surrounding villages as the helicopter carrying Ari and me lifted off for Areda. The fighters were apparently being dispersed to auxiliary fields around Chita and to bases further to the west on the other side of Lake Baikal.

******

Areda is a very isolated village whose only source of jobs seems to be the little Russian air base located next to it. What the airbase has is a long and barely usable concrete runway which does not even have a taxiway, just a concrete apron in front of the two log cabins that serve as its terminal and control tower. It was light years away from the busy field at Borzya.

The base itself is nestled in the foothills behind the great range of mountains about 150 miles east of Chita. The village and the airbase are at the end of a fifty mile long dirt road running south from the Trans-Siberian mainline and the access road running along side of it.

All Areda has to defend it is a forgotten squadron of older MiG-21 fighters and its only facilities are three rundown hangars and a bunch of log cabins scattered about. There isn't even a control tower, just a radio in one of the two "headquarters" cabins. The base is so isolated and forgotten that its dependents have not yet been evacuated.

Everyone at the field was clearly quite astonished to see us. They were even more astonished when they learned that the base was about to receive a defensive force and some of the fighter squadrons being dispersed from Chita and Borzya.

Indeed, the first of the hurriedly relocated fighters began landing soon after we arrived, including one that ran off the end of the runway and sunk up to its wings in a marsh. The planes' support troops and supplies will drive in on the Trans-Siberian access road and begin arriving as early as tomorrow afternoon.

Colonel Miskin says the Russians think Areda will be a really important base if the fields at Chita, Darasun, and Borzya are hit. That is probably why Karatonov assigned one of his colonels to command the Areda ground forces and organize its resistance in case the Chinese decide to hit it with an airborne attack.

Karatonov's colonel was with us at the bases we already visited. So at least he knows the airfield defense drill against paratroopers. But he was obviously going to have a very big problem carrying out his duties—there were no Russian armor or infantry units in the vicinity for him to use to defend the field.

According to Colonel Miskin, General Sholakov was beginning to recognize Areda's significance and has decided not to take a chance on losing it; he is going to divert the next few troop carrying transport planes inbound from Moscow to Areda. They will be the field's defense force.

Ari and I spent most of the day driving around field with its newly appointed commander in a Russian air force Jeep marking infantry positions. Somewhere along the line Ari asked the newly appointed defense colonel an important question—does the base have food and ammunition for the men who are going to dig the new positions and fight in them? No.

Supplies and conditions at Areda were apparently so sparse, other than the usual surplus of fuel resulting from decades of five year plans calling for the construction of ever more fuel storage tanks, that Ari decided to request a big food shipment be flown in. He also, at the request of Sholakov, fired off a request to Roberts and Moscow for intelligence updates. General Sholakov particularly wanted to know if Areda has been mentioned in any of the Chinese intelligence reports. *I know that is what he asked about because Colonel Miskin wrote up his request and asked me to carry it over to the signal corps warrant, Jimmy Nelson. Jimmy is temporarily attached to the plane's crew to handle Miskin's communications.*

According to Jimmy, Sholakov wants the latest intelligence as to how many paratroopers and air assault troops the Chinese have available and where they are expected to hit. He also asked if the United States can fly some food and payroll deliveries directly into Areda and carry out civilians.

I sure hope he sent a message to someone asking them to quickly send small arms ammunition, SAMs, and tents. This place is going to be up shit creek if they do not get them. I am going to suggest to Ari that he mention it the next time he talks privately with the colonel.

Everyone was boarding the helicopters by the time Jimmy finished sending the message. Then we lifted off and flew west to Ulan-Ude to repeat the process.

******

Ari and I stay in hastily organized quarters at Ulan-Ude that evening, a plywood shack next to the officers' mess. It had an unusually smelly outside latrine. Late the next morning, after a look at the defenses around the local airfield, we flew east with Miskin and the Generals to Belogorsk.

As usual, when we got to Belogorsk we inspect the defenses of the air field and made some recommendations. Then we reboarded helicopters to visit the district's other two military airfields and repeat the process.

At the moment our traveling road show is in the air with three rundown MI-4 helicopters—each carrying officers, communications equipment that does not seem to work very well, and a couple of Pylcyn's troopers as a protection squad in case it goes down.

When we finish inspecting and organizing the fields around Ulan-Ude we will apparently fly along the railroad to visit the air fields around Khabarovsk, and then on to those around Vladivostok. *What the hell do I know?*

If the past couple of days are any guide, at each air base Sholakov and the local corps commander will meet with the officers commanding the local troops and go over their troop dispositions and preparations. While he is doing that Ari and I will ride along while General Karatonov drives around the airfield in a borrowed Jeep and give instructions and suggestions for its defense.

When we finish each inspection, If General Karatonov thinks none of the officers available locally are up to organizing and commanding the field's defenses, one of the Russian officers traveling with us will be assigned to take command.

We find the same problems at every base—and inevitably the base officers are surprised to learn they are not in any way ready for either the coming war or an attack on their airfields. Many of them obviously do not believe a war is imminent, at least they do not until Sholakov and Karatonov and our traveling road show rush down the boarding stairs and start "counseling" them.

So far, the same things have happened at every field we visit. An airfield defense commander is appointed and Sholakov orders the commander of the local ground troops to position some or all of his armor reserves, if he has any, around the airfield; Ari and I suggest to the newly appointed airfield defense commander where he might position his armor and the infantry fighting positions and how the positions should be built and supplied; and then everyone commiserates with everyone else about the shortage of anti-aircraft missile batteries and handheld SAMs.

The Russians are supposed to have a lot of mobile batteries left over from those that guarded the various bridges our swimmers blew from air attacks. Karatonov said something about having them being shipped in but so far we have not seen any at any of the fields we have visited.

What there is at each field is a lot of anxiety about the arrival of the Generals. But at many of them there is no real sense of urgency about an imminent war—until Sholokov and Karatonov light a fire under them. Will it stay lit? Will the local ground and air commanders cooperate? *Do I give a shit?*

Ari told me he has already decided that when he gets access to a secure radio he is going to send a report to General Roberts telling him that at the moment only the Chita air field is well defended and ready to fight off a major airborne attack; the others are not ready, but most of them will probably be ready in the next few days. A few will never be ready.

Ari says he is also going to tell Roberts that all the Russian fields appear to be short of anti-aircraft missile batteries and that Areda needs food, gear, and ammunition for the troops that are being diverted to it.

There is no question about it—the Russians are going to be well and truly fucked if the Chinese take out the

Russian airfields and establish air supremacy. Shit, even I know that.

******

General Bulganin became increasingly concerned as he and his two aides boarded the helicopter that has been sent for him. Something's up. He is been ordered to turn command of the 83rd and 112th divisions over to his deputy and report immediately to General Sholakov at the Khabarovsk airfield.

Now what have I done. Am I being relieved because I shot that political officer? Maybe it's because I did not relocate the artillery where that foreign officer suggested?

Bulganin knows the Khabarovsk airfield. He had flown in and out of it just two days ago. It's about eighty miles from the Chinese border and the closest airfield to the mountain pass where his two seriously under strength divisions have just finished building a choke point along the railroad.

He was astonished by the change in the airfield in the seventy two hours since he last passed through it. Tanks and infantry fighting vehicles are everywhere and thousands of troops are beavering away filling sandbags and creating fighting positions. *What is happening here?*

The major and the jeep full of MPs who met Bulganin took him directly to the military district's two story concrete headquarters.

"What's up?" he asks the major, but he does not get much of an answer.

He was still searching his mind for what he might say in defense of where he located his artillery as he followed the hurrying major up the steps and into the building.

At least they did not take me to the military police headquarters. At least I do not think it's in this building.

******

"You may go in now, General."

Sholakov smiled as I marched into the office and saluted. *He is smiling. Sholakov is smiling.*

"Major General Bulganin reporting to Colonel General Sholokov as ordered," I said as I stood rigidly to attention.

Sholakov returned my salute and came around his desk and held out his hand. "Thank you for coming so promptly, Ivan Ivanovich. I need your help again." *He needs my help again? Thank God!*

"I want you to take over as the frontal commander here," said Sholakov. "It won't be easy," he said. Then he explained why. *The Chinese are going to do what?* It was breath-taking and I would have thought it unbelievable if it had not been General Sholakov himself telling me.

"You will command the new army I am forming here with the rank of Colonel General, Ivan Ivanovich. And you and your men must, at all costs, keep the Chinese out of Khabarovsk and prevent them from cutting the Trans-Siberian main line for as long as possible."

Then Sholakov went on to explain to me that one of my divisions was already digging in south of the Amur and another en route from Vladivostok that will be arriving shortly. Those two plus another division now being unloaded in Vladivostok will give me an army of three divisions. *A three division army and a promotion! I must be dreaming.*

"But here's the thing, Ivan Ivanovich: The Chinese attack here will undoubtedly be very strong since it is intended to draw troops away from Chita to reinforce you. But the reinforcements won't come; you must stop the Chinese yourself without them. And once you stop them, you must be prepared to quickly load a good part of what is left of your army on the railroad and bring them to the Chita front to join the main effort under General Rutman.

"I will hold them Comrade General; I will hold them." *That is all I could get out. I almost got emotional about it.*

Then, while we ate sausage sandwiches and drank tea, we spent several hours in front of the maps discussing the disposition of my three divisions, the artillery and air support I might or might not receive, the smallest possible skeleton force that is to be left at the choke point so it can be reoccupied and used if necessary, and the need to immediately move the troops and equipment of the 83rd and 112th at the choke point to Chita before the railroad line is cut.

One of the things that surprised me was the need to guard the airfield from an air assault. Then he really surprised me by introducing me to General Karatonov, whom I'd previously met, and a couple of American Marine officers who are "airfield defense experts." *They had been at Reykjavik? Impossible.*

"You must hold them off as long as possible, Ivan Ivanovich," General Sholakov said once again as he started to climb the stairs to board his plane.

Then he stopped and turned around and looked at me again after he'd gone up only a couple of steps on the stairway.

"Remember, Ivan Ivanovich. The main battle will sooner or later switch to Chita. When that happens, you must be prepared to leave a small screening force here and quickly move almost all of whatever is left of your armor and artillery, and their munitions, to Chita on the railroad."

"At your orders, Comrade General. I will hold here and then move quickly to Chita as you require. You can count on it, Comrade General. I will hold here and then be in Chita with my men."

Who is to tell Colonel Evensy to move the 83rd and the 112th to Chita? Am I supposed to tell him? And I better get some makeshift loading docks built in a hurry west of the city so we can leave in a hurry. And do I have enough docks here in the rail yards for the divisions that are arriving? My head is spinning with so many things to do.

"General Sholakov, Sir." I shouted after him as he turned and and again began walking up the stairs. "Do you want me to order the 83rd and the 112th to move to Chita or will your headquarters send the order?"

* * * * * *

Things are really heating up as the invasion approaches. The Russians in Moscow have become increasingly anxious. The flash message I received an hour ago from Dick Spelling reports that Chernenko is in Tokyo or soon will be.

Bob Gates at the CIA says Cherenko intends to offer Japan a deal to immediately restore Sakhalin Island to Japan and recognize Japan's claim to the Kuril and Senkaku islands—in exchange for peace. It's an unofficial trip. According the CIA report, he will meet the Japanese Prime Minister at the Tokyo airport.

Chapter Twenty

The plot thickens.

"I will come right to the point," Chernenko tells the Japanese Prime Minister at the Tokyo airport. "There is no need for you to risk a nuclear attack on Japan to get your islands back."

"It seems there is to be a war between Russia and the Chinese. But if it goes nuclear, and there is a good chance it will, all of Russia's attackers and their supporters will suffer terribly."

"All of them," he repeated ominously looking straight at the Prime Minister and emphasizing the word 'all.'

"Russia does not want to use nuclear weapons, Prime Minister," he said sadly. "But the reality is that General Sholakov has taken control of all our nuclear weapons in the east. He has informed Moscow that he intends to use them if that is what it takes to stop the Chinese."

Then he leaned toward the shaken Prime Minister and displayed the toughness that had taken him to the top of the Soviet hierarchy and was keeping him there in the new Russian Republic.

"If Sholakov uses his nuclear weapons, the Chinese will use undoubtedly theirs; and then Moscow will have to use ours—to insure that none of our enemies are left who can rebuild faster than we can. *None*." He leaned forward and emphasized the word 'none.'

"So here's our offer. You immediately take islands. All of them. Every single one. We know you have ships out there already and more ships loading. So order your ships to head for Sakhalin Island and land your troops and Marines. Land them right now. Today.

Then, while your men are unloading, you simultaneously load our troops and their equipment and their supplies on your ships and take them straight to Vladivostok. You can fly out our dependents and any of our citizens who want to leave after the war."

"It is your choice, Mr. Prime Minister. Peace, the islands, and a prosperous Japan; or war, no islands, and more than likely, a nuclear devastated Japan consisting of many Hiroshimas.

******

It was a political masterstroke. Chernenko made the Japanese Prime Minister an offer he could not refuse. In just a few minutes the Chairman separated Japan from China and freed up a few more immediately available Russian troops and ships for the war. The only problem was that not everyone in Russia appreciated what he had accomplished.

Moscow was in turmoil about surrendering the islands Russia took from Japan in the closing hours of World War Two. Some of the senior military officers were furious about the surrendering of any part of Russia no matter how insignificant. The result was another mutiny.

Tanks and BMDs from the Moscow garrison surrounded Chernenko's plane and would not let him disembark when he returned to Moscow from Japan. The mutineer's tanks, in turn, were promptly surrounded by tanks and BMDs of the Moscow regiment of MVD troops under the control of the Ministry of Internal Affairs.

The standoff at the airport continued for hours until Marshal Petrov, in a room jammed full of senior officers glaring at each other, was able to get Sholakov on a speaker phone. *The officers in the room did not know it but Petrov spoke to him earlier and alerted him to the situation.*

Sholakov was emphatic.

"We need the Sakhalin troops and the navy ships around the island for the fight with China. Those islands are going to be lost for sure if we do not win; we can take them back if we do."

Senior officers of every persuasion were crowded into the conference room and listened intently as Sholakov continued.

"Do you remember the huge battle between the French and the Germans early in World War One, Comrades? The battle on the outskirts of Paris that we all studied at our military schools? Well, then you remember the French won when the very last French battalion to arrive at the front made the difference between winning and losing the crucial battle—the battalion whose men were brought straight from the train station to the front line in Paris taxicabs?"

"Well, goddamnit, here at the front we see the troops the Japanese navy will bring in from Sakhalin as coming to us on Japanese taxicabs. We need them here to fight the Chinese, not sitting on their arses on some useless island for a couple of extra weeks until the war is lost and Sakhalin Island with it."

******

To say the Chinese were furious about Tokyo's abrupt about face would be a massive understatement.

"They are treacherous liars." Those are the first words the Party Chairman Li said to the hastily assembled meeting of the party's Central Committee. "And it does not matter; Japan's participation isn't important; we never counted on it in the first place."

No one said a word. Finally the elderly little man at the end of the table spoke up.

"If Japan is not important to us, Comrade Chairman, then it is curious that the Russians are willing to give up so much to separate them from us. Would you not agree?"

"Yes, Yee Shin, it is indeed curious. But it is also very encouraging. It means the Russians are so desperate that they gave up all that territory just to get the insignificant handful of troops on Sakhalin over to Valdivostok to help fight us."

"And the ships. We must not forget the Russian ships," said someone else.

"What ships?" Li demanded.

"Last week you said it was important that the Russians had moved ships to Sakhalin to stop the Japanese, ships they could not bring into the battle against us."

"Perhaps I was too enthusiastic about the importance of the ships. If so, I apologize to everyone. This will be land war, not a sea war; isn't that so comrade Defense Minister?" *I will remember you, Yee Shin.*

But before Wu could answer, there was another question.

"Isn't it time for another review of our preparations before we proceed," asked the portly head of the security services. After all, did not you and General Wu say we could pull back if victory was not guaranteed?" *They are getting cold feet.*

"Unfortunately Comrades," General Wu piped up before Chairman Li could answer, "the time has passed for that. We have already infiltrated more than twenty thousand men over the Amur and Ussuri Rivers and into the mountains. The Russians have already made contact with some of them. For all practical purposes the war has started."

There were gasps and scrapping sounds as chairs were pushed back. Then everyone started talking at once.

****** *Ari Solomon*

Our helicopter went down about an hour after we left Belogorsk and began following the Trans-Siberian tracks towards Khabarovsk.

We had barely finished passing over a westbound train loaded with troops and vehicles when the engine began sputtering as we passed over a snow covered ridge and the pilots begin cursing and shouting at each other.

When the engine gave one last "pop" and quit completely, we auto rotated down through the trees and hit the hillside with a hard bounce. The blades were still coming apart from hitting the trees as we jumped out and ran to get clear.

But all ended well except for the loss of the helicopter. Everyone got out and we began waving to the helicopters circling overhead above the canopy of trees. *Whew. That was close. Thank God it did not blow.*

We stood around for an hour or so at the edge of the snow line waiting for the rescue helicopters and tending to a couple of men who've been slightly injured in the crash. A couple of men even walked up to the snow and began throwing snowballs at each oher. Then everything changed; there were troops coming out of the trees to our right. Strange uniforms.

At first we just stood there and looked at them. Several of our men even waved. Then there was a shout and shots were fired, and it seems like we all begin running at the same time. Chinese! As I was running I could see Andy and some of the Russians dart off to the left. I took about ten more steps and dived behind a tree when the shooting intensified.

Then there was silence and muffled talking. I could hear the crunches as someone slowly walked through the leaves towards me. Well hell, I have got no weapon and I cannot run. So I stood up and raised my hands as some Chinese soldiers approached. *I sure hope they are taking prisoners.* Then I was somehow on the ground and could

see a big tuft of brown grass right in front of my eyes.
Damn. They are not.

It seemed like only a couple of seconds passed before I heard talking I could not understand and felt the toe of what must be someone's boot trying to turn me over. Then there was nothing.

******

Suddenly I heard myself scream as a terrible spasm of pain woke me up in the moonlit darkness. My god, I am burning all over. The pain is so intense all I can do is scream and scream without even knowing where I am or what I am doing. I have got to get to the snow and put out the burning. I must. Getting to the snow and cooling off is my only thought as I lurched on to my hands and knees and begin crawling in the darkness.

The burning pain kept Ari crazed and semi-conscious for several hours as the sun came up and he desperately crawled over the rocky scree until he came out of the brush and finally reached the snow.

Bones were showing through what was left of Ari's mangled hands as he feverishly tried to burrow himself into the mound of snow that was packed up under a rocky overhang. It was a desperate effort to ease his burning pain. And it worked; burrowing into the snow definitely

helped. His pain flowed away.   Then he gasped two or
three times and rested.

* * * * * *

General Roberts arranged for me and Duffy to fly in
from Bikin to meet with Andy Willow at the Podovsk base
hospital. According to General Roberts, Andy and a
Russian lieutenant had straggled into one of the choke
points on the railroad this morning suffering from a painful
bullet wound to his hand and serious hypothermia from
spending a wet night in the forest. *A bullet wound?*

"Six of our men were found dead of gun shot wounds
at the site of the downed chopper," reported the English
speaking Russian lieutenant colonel waiting for us at the
hospital entrance. "Captain Solomon and one of our
Russians, the helicopter's co-pilot, are still missing."

Colonel Miskin came with us to the hospital to visit
Andy. The Colonel said he'd already spoken to the
Russian survivors and they confirmed that the Chinese
showed up and immediately started shooting. One of the
Russians says he is sure he saw Ari run when the shooting
started.

Andy had just come out of surgery and still a bit groggy
when we visited him. But he was able to talk and said he
was absolutely certain he saw Ari run when the Chinese
started shooting. Andy's left hand was wrapped in a

massive bandage and he knows the Russian docs could not save one of his fingers; the other two will be fine even though another surgery might be needed.

He was adamant about not being evacuated until Captain Solomon was found.

****** *General Roberts*

It's been a day and a half since the helicopter carrying Ari and Andy had an engine problem and went down in the mountains. I was already up toasting a bagel and drinking my morning pot of tea when Major Evans called in with an update.

"No Sir, nothing yet."…. "Yes Sir, He is a tough guy. He'll be fine." … "Yes Sir, we are sure. Colonel Miskin talked to the Russian docs; the only permanent damage is the loss of his finger."…. "Yes Sir, I will ask him again but I am sure the answer will be the same—he wants to stay…."

Okay. It's time to call in and update Dick Spelling.

"Captain Solomon's still missing and it does not look good. The man with him, Mr. Willow, you remember him from the staircase?"… "Yeah, that is him. Well, he had a finger shot off but is otherwise apparently okay; wants to stay out there and I am gonna let him."

"Yeah, it's getting worse. There have been multiple contact reports almost every day and they are increasing.

The Chinese are obviously infiltrating over the border in force. Christ, all they have to do is paddle over the Amur and they are in."

….. "Yeah just like Korea. Except the Russians are not trying to keep their guys from finding out the way MacArthur did to us." *Hmm. That gives me an idea.*

"Dick, do you think anyone would object if I made a brief trip to visit Sholakov with some media people in tow—publically encouraging him to use restraint and not do something stupid like using the nukes he controls would be a great way to send a 'back off' message to the Chinese."

"That is a great idea. It sure could not hurt. I will check on it and get back to you. The President can hold a press conference and announce he is sending you to urge restraint on the general who controls the Russian nuclear weapons in the east."

Then, after a pause, Dick had a thoughtful sound in his voice.

"Yeah, you are right; knowing that Sholakov controls them and might use them might be a good thing for the Chinese to hear. I will get right on it."

Sure enough. Later that afternoon I was asked to standby to be connected to the President. Ten minutes later he came on the line to tell me he thinks such an in-person meeting to call for nuclear restraint in a way that gets in the media and reaches the Chinese is a good idea. He wants the Secretary of State to go with me.

Oh shit.

"I must most respectfully disagree, Mr. President. Arriving with Secretary Hoffman might destroy my credibility with General Sholakov. But Sir, you are absolutely right that someone needs to deliver the message to the Chinese via the media—and I certainly have no problem with the Secretary doing it instead of me."

And Hoffman wants to go. She was insistent on going when I called her thirty minutes later to give her some advice about dealing with Sholakov and try to talk her out of going. *I do not try very hard.*

"Oh no," she said. "My making the trip is very important. I am going to make it quite clear that as the general in charge that he has to be reasonable as to how he responds when the Chinese attack. We absolutely cannot allow him to start a nuclear war." *Allow?*

The bottom line is that within the hour everything was settled. Secretary Hoffman is going to fly to Arkhara with a big press entourage and I am going to stay here. Dorothy is pleased that I am not going. *So am I—but I am not going to admit it to anyone, not even Dick.*

After all, who am I to stop the Secretary if she wants to make a useful fool of herself? General Sholakov will be so afraid she'll leak whatever he tells her that he is unlikely to share anything with her except disinformation to screw up the Chinese." *Actually that is not a bad idea. Hmm.*

******

Moscow quickly approved Secretary Hoffman's trip and the next day she flew into Arkhara with a military attaché from the Russian embassy, a photogenic and racially balanced State Department protection detail wearing vests and carrying automatic weapons, and plane full of her media supporters ready to capture every moment of her triumph.

Unfortunately, it took quite a while for the rusty metal steps to be pushed into place against her plane's door. Then as the Secretary descended the steps she had to stop while her protection detail was disarmed and the military attaché from the Russian embassy arrested. According to all reports, she was clearly not a happy camper by the time she finally set foot on Russian soil.

The small and unpainted plywood box that passes as the airfield's arrival and departure terminal was deserted when the Secretary and her press entourage and weaponless guards finally entered. After some delay while the media crowded into the room and interviewed each other, the cameras rolled as a nice looking General from Sholakov's staff and a young English-speaking lieutenant with bad teeth drove up in a Russian Jeep. The General did the talking and the lieutenant translated. They had both been carefully coached.

"Unfortunately Miss, General Sholakov is much too busy to meet with tourists at this time. We are in a war, you know. Perhaps you could send him a letter or I can give him a message for you.

"Oh. You are not a tourist? You are a secretary? Whose secretary are you?

"Please do not shout, Miss. All I know is that you and your plane should not be here. This is a dangerous war zone. Do not you know we are fighting Chinese here and that Arkara is a military headquarters?

"Of course we are fighting them. The Chinese have been crossing the border everywhere during the past several weeks and attacking us. Big battles are coming to Vladivostok and Khabarovsk and maybe, god forbid, even here. The Chinese are again trying to capture our Russian lands around the Ussuri, you know."

Amidst much confusion and the constant din of planes taking off and landing on the nearby runway, a letter was produced signed by someone in Moscow. It changed everything. Only then does the General reveal that General Sholakov is not in Arkhara and has not been here for several days.

"I am sorry for the confusion, Madam Secretary. Unfortunately General Sholakov is in the field organizing his troops to move to Kharbarovsk so they can help fight off the Chinese attacks."

The English-speaking lieutenant became most solicitous and helpful. "Does your pilot have enough fuel? If you have a credit card I am sure fuel can be arranged."

******

The existence of fighting and the Secretary's explanation as to why she was unable to meet General Sholakov made the news in a big way. And, no surprise, Bill Kretzner of the *Washington Post* called me for a comment.

I proceed to tell Bill there is no way I will talk to him about anything unless it is totally off the record and there is absolutely no way I can possibly be identified as his source. He agreed.

"Yeah Bill, I know about the Secretary's trip into the war zone and I know why she was unable to meet with General Sholakov. It's an interesting story. But all I can confirm to you now is that General Sholakov is getting his troops ready to fight off a Chinese attack and that the shooting actually started some days ago." *All true.*

"Yes, that is right. The fighting started days ago. Apparently, a large number of Chinese troops have already infiltrated over the border and there have been frequent contacts—just as they did to us years ago in Korea. It is apparently a standard tactic of the Red Chinese Army prior to a major invasion."

I was not about to tell Bill or anyone else that at my suggestion Sholakov deliberately gave her false information about moving his troops. Sholakov did so in the hope it would leak to the Chinese. And it did: Word quickly got around at the State Department that the Secretary met with lesser officers because General Sholakov was in the field getting his troops ready to move to Kharbarovsk where an important battle will soon be fought. That is what the Chinese want to hear.

Chapter Twenty-one

New leadership

Chairman Chernenko was sitting in his office reading a report about the coup and who was involved when the pains began. *How many more wars and coups can I survive?* That was what Chairman was thinking when the chest pains knocked him to the floor and his secretary started screaming.

******

I was not invited to the funeral. *No surprise there.* There was a lot of discussion as to whether anyone from the United States should even attend. Finally the State Department decided Chernenko's funeral would be "an opportunity for a new beginning."

In the end, the President asked the Vice President and Secretary of State to attend so we can "start to rebuild normal relations." So they both flew off to Moscow and joined a bunch of African dictators and various and sundry other national leaders who had been receiving Soviet aid and hoped the new Russian leader would keep the spigot open.

Even the Chinese sent their condolences and a fraternal delegation of elderly party leaders. Conspicuously absent were the leaders or representatives of the former Soviet states and the NATO and Warsaw countries. They expressed insincere condolences or ignored it entirely.

Bernie's call from the plane on his way home from Moscow caught me in my Brussels office. "Yeah, you were right Chris. They are thugs. It was like a gathering of Mafia dons."

"But maybe we did a little good. Valerie and I met with this new fellow, Kuznetsov, and encouraged him not to use nukes if there is a war with the Chinese. What do you think?"

"I hope you are right, of course, Mr. Vice President, and you certainly did the right thing by trying. Unfortunately the shooting's already started and Moscow only controls some of Russian nukes. Sholakov controls the rest.

"According to Sholakov and the Russians I have talked to, the big player, the guy who will probably decide on whether the nukes under Moscow's control will be used is probably going to be a real sleaze from the Party's inner circle named Brezhnev. The only question is whether he and his cronies want to continue to pull the strings and money from the shadows or take a more public position and steal it openly."

******

The members of the Central Committee were meeting at Party headquarters on Red Banner Street to get a final briefing. It was positive. According to General Wu, everything related to the invasion of Russia was going better than expected. As soon as the briefing concluded the committee members would leave to join their families. They'd begun quietly moving to safety in the south several days ago.

General Wu's big news for the Central Committee was that the army's plans and timetables have not changed: The first phase of the invasion would begin in the morning at dawn.

"The basic plan remains exactly as we have reported to you over the past few weeks, comrades. There have been no changes of substance. As we reported to you previously, we will start with units of the Red Army attacking towards Vladivostok and Khabarovsk. The main attack towards Chita will commence when the Russians stop moving their troops and armor towards Khabarovsk.

"Our initial diversionary attacks towards Khabarovsk and Vladivostok will be accompanied by the biggest airborne and air mobile assault in history. When the attacks begin, our parachute troops will be simultaneously assault all sixteen of the Russian airfields in the eastern half of Russia. We are using every one of our transport planes and sending all six of our parachute divisions, forty-five thousand men. The goal of our comrade volunteers is simple: to destroy as many as possible of the Russian planes and helicopters so they cannot be used to oppose us."

There were many questions.

"No comrade, there is no indication that they will respond with nuclear weapons. We will be ready, of course, if they do. But both the Second and Third Departments say that the Russians will not do so because they are afraid of our response—as well they should be.

"Yes comrade. You are correct. Our intelligence departments report they are presently moving reinforcements to Khabarovsk from Vladivostok instead of from Chita. That will continue until our invasion begins and we cut the rail line. Then they will have to get their reinforcements from Chita.

"Yes comrade. That will occur quickly. Thousands of our men, over twenty thousand, have already infiltrated over the Usurri and into the mountains overlooking the rail line. They will cut it at the same time we launch our attacks on their air fields and begin our ground attacks towards Khabarovsk and Vladivostok.

"Right here," he said, pointing with his stick to the big map on the wall, "We will cut it first at a place called Bikin. It will be cut elsewhere as soon as the Russians finish moving their reinforcements from the interior to Khabarovsk."

******

Dave and I were sitting in the Detachment's conference room munching donuts with the staff when the flash message came in from the Pentagon communications center. The sun was just coming up on what looked to become another bright and sunny day in the French countryside when we were informed that the Chinese were going to start attacking tomorrow morning at daylight, 0614 Beijing time.

Everyone listened intently as I instantly called Sholakov. It will be our third conversation since about midnight last night. It was already late in the afternoon in Chita.

"Yuri Andreovich, it is confirmed. The Chinese will launch their initial attacks at dawn tomorrow." ...

"Yes, 0614."...

"Yes, my friend, it is time to bring your troops and planes to full readiness. And tonight, as soon as it gets dark, you must send your swimmers to cut the Chinese bridges and your planes and assault helicopters to hit their airfields and depots."

"Yes, I suspect Marshal Petrov is also being informed, but I will call him immediately as I promised him when I visited Moscow. I will also call the Russian Admiralty to warn them."

Over and over Yuri and I have talked about the desirability of a preemptive strike on the Chinese airfields at the same time the swimmers go in. But I still do not know whether he'll actually do it now that push has come to shove. I hope so. It's his best chance to win, maybe his only chance. I am also going to call Miskin, Jim Bowie, Major Evans, and the navy chief, Sean Matthews, who is out there heading up the swimming instructors now that Mike Morton has been pulled out. They will need a heads-up so they can get their men out of the way.

"By the way, Yuri Andreovich, I am not going to mention your swimmers or your preemptive attacks to Moscow or anyone else. I strongly suggest you consider not mentioning them either." *No sense taking chances on a leak.*

Five minutes later I called Marshal Petrov, the Russian defense minister; he and an interpreter came on the line instantly. He'd already gotten the word from Sholakov and from the KGB. *Good.*

Then I brought up the Russian navy.

"I do not know what General Sholakov's plans are, Comrade Marshal. But I do know that he does not control the naval forces in his theatre of operation. So if you have not done so already, might I respectfully suggest it might be time to send war warnings to your ships en route to Vladivostok and to order your navy to immediately, and I mean immediately, begin attacking the Chinese subs in the Russian waters off Vladivostok."

"Yes. Oh, and as we discussed yesterday, you also might want to send any anti-submarine aircraft you still have available to Vladivostok to patrol the sea lanes off the port—before the Chinese subs have a chance to hit your ships that are still en route." *What I do not want is any Russian anti-sub planes searching for the Chinese missile boats off Kalingrad. We have American attack subs up there tailing them and mistakes happen.*

I tried for several hours before I give up trying to reach the Russian Admiralty. No luck. The number I'd used previously was always busy. While I was doing that Mike and Dick reached out to our people in Eastern Russia to warn them to get clear.

Then we spent all day in the Detachment conference room fielding an ever increasing flood of anxious calls and silly suggestions and information requests coming in from Washington.

Chapter Twenty-two

Early days.

Sholakov did exactly as he had planned and promised. A little after it got dark, just before ten in the evening, he gave the order and every available Russian plane and assault helicopter in the Russian East surged southward in the darkness towards all the Chinese airfields and major supply depots they could reach. The goal of the Russian Far Eastern Air force was simple—to destroy as many as possible of the Chinese planes and helicopters before they can begin a massive airlift of airborne troops to the Russian airfields.

Its timing was equally simple: Destroy as many of the Chinese planes and helicopters as possible and still get back to base to refuel and rearm in time to intercept the planes which the Chinese are able to get off the ground to support their scheduled dawn attack.

As you might imagine would be the case on the eve of an invasion, two Chinese AWACS were in the air and the Chinese ground radar installations were turned on and fully staffed. When the Russian preemptive strike began the Chinese controllers saw the mass of Russian planes begin to lift off their airfields and instantly understood that a preemptive attack was underway. They immediately sounded the alarm.

China's fighters and fighter bombers were already fueled and armed and sitting on runways waiting for their scheduled early morning departure to escort the troop transports and provide ground support for the Chinese invasion. When the alarms sounded it was just a matter of quickly recalling sleeping pilots and ground crews from their nearby beds and tents. That turns out to be easier said than done because it had never been practiced. Even so, many of the Chinese fighters were airborne and ready to fight long before the Russian planes could get to the various Chinese airfields.

******

Chinese pilots are not trained for night operations and neither, for that matter, are the Russians. But the fight was not equal because the Chinese air force generals made two bad assumptions: They assumed the Russians would not attack first and they assumed the Russian air force would wait for daylight just as their air force was waiting.

Fighting in the crowded and only partially controlled night skies was vicious and many planes went down on both sides, including quite a number that crashed into mountains in the dark; others crashed as they returned to their bases and attempted to land in the dark, something both sides rarely practiced.

On balance, the Chinese were able to put up more planes up than the Russians expected. Even so, despite the rather heroic efforts on part of some of the Chinese pilots, many of the Russian attackers reached their airfield targets and were able to shoot up some of the waiting Chinese transport planes. A few of the planes the Russians hit were already loaded with troops. Most, however, were not. Then the Russian pilots sped for home to hurriedly rearm and refuel.

Overall, the initial Chinese plane losses were significantly heavier than those of the Russians—but the attacks on the Chinese airfields were not a great success because Russian pilots had trouble identifying specific targets in the dark. Even so, if one was scoring the air war as a prize fight it was obvious to everyone that Russia took round one, but not very decisively.

What did not get particularly noticed by anyone during the initial aerial brawl was the relative handful of individual Russian helicopters that came in low and slow over isolated sections of the border and headed towards certain railroad bridges inside China.

******

China's navy has over fifty operational submarines. All of them were made in China and most of them are very slow and very noisy short range diesel attack subs based on the old 1950s Soviet Romeo class. The Soviet Romeos, in turn, were based on the German U-boat designs of the late 1930s used by the Second World War German submarine wolf packs that ravaged Allied shipping in the Atlantic.

In other words, the Chinese subs were hopelessly obsolete and virtually useless against the significantly faster and relatively advanced technologies employed by the Russian surface ships bringing reinforcements to Vladivostok.

Their subs' shortcomings were well known to the Chinese admirals and planners. They took it into consideration when they began planning for the possibility of today's war. The basic plan of the Chinese Navy was quite simple—since the Chinese subs will have great difficulty intercepting the faster inbound Russian ships on the high seas, they will wait for the Russians to come to them. Accordingly, the Chinese admirals concentrated almost their entire fleet of attack submarines on the approaches to Vladivostok.

Chinese thinking was based on the idea that their subs could wait quietly near Vladivostok and attack the Russian ships as they come in to port to dock. And to some extent it worked. A number of Russian ships still inbound to

Vladivostok were attacked during the last fifty miles of their voyage around half the world.

Unfortunately for the Chinese, concentrating their subs off Vladivostok also meant that the Russian anti-submarine surface ships could be similarly concentrated and easily find them. It also meant Russia's other ships and submarines will be relatively unchallenged if they launch attacks on Chinese shipping and the major Chinese ports.

I'd suggested as much to Chernenko. Attacks on Chinese shipping and the Chinese ports won't do much to directly affect the outcome of the war—but indirectly it will put pressure on the Chinese Communist Party leadership to end the war.

******

Attacks on the inbound Russian ships are scheduled to coincide with the beginning of ground and air war—at dawn on the day of the invasion. Unfortunately for China, by that time a substantial number of the Russian naval ships had already reached Vladivostok and unloaded their precious cargos of troops and equipment.

Also reaching the port with Russian troops prior to China's official invasion start time was a huge troop carrying flotilla of smaller surface ships with various degrees of anti-submarine capability. They had been generally useless against the NATO subs in the Spring War but were more than adequate for use against the technologically obsolete Chinese subs.

Short operational ranges and the technological limitations of the Chinese submarines led the Chinese Navy to schedule the arrival of the Chinese subs in the Vladivostok waters so they would show up just in time for the war to start and, therefore, be able to stay as long as possible. The waters off Vladivostok were packed with them in the hours leading up to the scheduled invasion. More than forty Chinese attack submarines were on station off Vladivostok and scheduled to start operations at dawn on August 29th. 0614 Beijing time.

Circling above them, were more than fifty Russian surface ships ranging from coastal patrol vessels carrying depth charges to relatively sophisticated anti-submarine cruisers and destroyers such as the *Admiral Markov*. The waiting Russian ships had already discharged the troops and equipment and they were carrying and were now patrolling off Vladivostok.

Orders for the Russian Navy to commence hostilities and begin destroying the waiting Chinese subs came at the same time the Chinese AWACs picked up the surprise Russian air attack – about two hours after the sun went down on the evening of the twenty eighth.

And the Chinese subs just sit there and let it happen. They have no inter-sub communications and no way to receive messages from their headquarters without surfacing. Each Chinese captain can hear the steady drumbeat of depth charge explosions but does not know what it means or what he should do other than obey his orders and wait for dawn and the official start of the invasion.

The result is the devastation of most the Chinese submarine fleet before it even becomes operational at dawn on the twenty ninth. Unfortunately for the Russians, not all of the Chinese subs are destroyed.

******

Captain Shi Yunsheng and the crew of the Song class submarine *Swallow* wait anxiously for the 0614 start time specified in their orders. He hears the frequent depth charge explosions and he knows that other Chinese subs are in his patrol area. But he does not know how many of his fellow captains are with him in the waters off Vladivostok or what is happening to them. All Captain Shi and his officers know is that they have specific orders to follow.

Shi's *Swallow* lies silently on the bottom near the entrance to the Vladivostok harbor as it has ever since it crept into position and settled on to the bottom more than twenty hours earlier. Shi and his crew become increasingly anxious as time passes and their air supply continues to diminish. They listen to the sonar operators' continual reports of vessels in the vicinity and can periodically hear for themselves the sound of high speed screws passing overhead and the pinging of searching sonars.

Then something changes. Depth charges begin going off. Lots and lots of depth charges. And they are going off constantly including several times quite near the *Swallow*. Sometimes so close everyone can hear them; sometimes so far in the distance that only the *Swallow*'s two sonar operators hear them.

All night long intensive pinging and the rumbling of depth charge explosions rises and falls but never stops. At times it is almost constant with the sound of pinging and an explosion in one direction often rolling into the sound of pinging and another explosion somewhere else.

Shi and the men of *Swallow*'s crew are understandably worried as they listen to the constant din of depth charge explosions and hear the pings and propeller sounds as numerous surface vessels pass back and forth overhead at high speeds. Despite the reassurances of the officers, it is obvious to everyone that something is happening and not even Captain Shi knows for certain what it is. But they all know what the pinging and depth charge explosions mean and they are greatly concerned.

******

Both the Russian and Chinese air forces have everything they can get into the air before dawn breaks over eastern Russia and northern China on the 29th.

Russia's air force and ground commanders know their fields east of Lake Baikal are going to be hit. They prepare for it as best they can by flying off everything they can get in to the air to alternative strips and manning their ground defense positions.

Their helicopters similarly disperse to the surrounding countryside a safe distance from the air fields. Non-essential staff are pulled off the fields and the cargo planes which have continued to arrive right up until the Russians launch their preemptive attack are hurriedly unloaded and flown off. Similarly, those still inbound that have enough fuel to reach an alternative field west of Lake Baikal are rerouted.

As dawn approaches on September 29th all the Russian airfields east of Lake Baikal are closed to incoming traffic. The few damaged and out-of-fuel fighters still returning from their initial attacks on China are now being routed to nearby unimproved auxiliary and emergency strips.

Then the Russian air response unfolds: The refueled and rearmed Russian fighters, at least those that came back from the preemptive strike and are still airworthy, take off before dawn to intercept the incoming Chinese.

For most of the pilots it is their second flight of the night. And they are controlled by the same four Russian

AWACs which have been guiding them ever since the Russian preemptive strikes began, the sole survivors of the ill-fated Soviet invasion of West Germany.

******

As dawn creeps closer the dark night-time sky is once again filled with hundreds of turning and twisting planes. Casualties are once again high on both sides.

And once again the Russians take a tremendous toll of Chinese planes before they have to break off to head west to safety or attempt to land at their auxiliary fields. Even so, despite their previous losses, the Chinese are approaching the Russian fields with more planes than anyone expected.

It is obvious to the Russian AWACs controllers that the Chinese airborne attacks are going to occur simultaneously at just about every airfield east of Lake Baikal. That is significant. It means the Russian AWACs controllers will have nowhere to send the surviving Russian fighters to refuel and rearm. Both the Russian and the Chinese controllers have anticipated this.

Russian controllers respond to the on-coming Chinese air armada in different ways depending on where their fighters are located. The fighter pilots operating over the Chita front are directed to break off contact when they still have enough fuel to reach the Russian fields west of Lake

Baikal at Irkutsk and Angarsk; the controllers of the Russian fighters operating further to the east guide their pilots to the unlit emergency landing strips and practice fields that tend to be sprinkled around each of the major airfields that is about to be assaulted.

Landing a MiG-21or any other plane in the dark on an unlit and unimproved emergency field is inherently dangerous. That is true even if the Russian pilots are familiar with the fields and know where they are located in relation to their home fields. It's particularly true if the pilots have little or no experience making night landings.

Fortunately, and quite deliberately, the takeoff surge of Russian fighters to intercept the inbound Chinese is timed so the Russian fighters will have enough fuel to stay aloft until the first light of day arrives and they can see to land on their alternative fields. And even the planes that exhaust their fuel or are damaged before the sun comes up have a good chance of landing safely – because their controllers can direct them to auxiliary fields with runway lights provided by the simple kerosene lanterns the local commanders have been ordered to set out to outline their runways.

Then everything changes. The controllers in the Russian AWACS can do little except stare in dismay at their computer screens as a huge second wave of over one hundred Chinese transports and fighters appears on their screens coming north over Mongolia. They are obviously heading for the undefended Irkutsk and Angarsk airfields *west* of Lake Baikal—fields in a military district with a different military leadership that are already packed with Russian planes that have been diverted to them. *They will be sitting ducks is the thought that simultaneously flashes through the minds of both the Russian general commanding the Russian AWACS and the Chinese general commanding the Chinese AWACS.*

Instantly the Russian controllers do everything they can. All available Russian fighters in the Chita area with enough fuel remaining are immediately diverted to intercept the Chinese over Mongolia, all four of them. They are followed a few minutes later by three MiG-21s that returned early from their second flight of the night and just completed refueling and rearming at Chita, and a flight of four Tupolev TU-128s newly arrived and refueling at Angarsk en route further east.

Seven Russian MiGs and four TU-128s are not enough to stop the Chinese air armada rapidly closing on Irkutsk and Angarsk. Not even close.

Everyone on the Russian AWACS and in the air force control centers at the fields instantly understands that the undefended Irkutsk and Angarsk airfields are going to be captured by Chinese airborne troops in the next hour or so. They also understand the significance of losing the fields; it means the Russian fighter squadrons defending the Chita front are going to lose a lot of the planes and pilots that survived their first two sorties. Even more important, much more important, it means the Chinese will have airbases and interceptors astride the Russian air supply route to the east.

Russia is about to lose a lot of planes. The only Russian planes in the eastern squadrons that will still be usable in a few minutes will be those that successfully landed on the unlit auxiliary strips in the dark and those with enough fuel to stay aloft until they can find the auxiliary strips in the early pre-dawn light. And they will only be able to return to their bases and get back into the fight when and if the Chinese paratroopers are defeated and the Russian airfields reopen.

There is no doubt about it. Round two of the air war is going to be won by the Chinese.

* * * * * *

Darkness closes in around Russian Navy Lieutenant Sergey Simanskiy as the helicopter drops him and two fellow swimmers into the cold waters of the Yimin River - and then roars away back north towards the border and safety. Their target is the Chinese railroad bridge at Hailar twelve kilometers downstream.

Sergey and his men expect to swim down river and reach the bridge sometime around one in the morning. An hour later they should be finished mining it and on their way another fifteen kilometers further downstream to a treeless sand bar in the middle of the river.

A second helicopter is scheduled to land on the sand bar at four in the morning to pick them up. Each of the three swimmers has been promised an immediate payment of twenty thousand American dollars if they seriously damage the bridge.

And all three men are fairly certain the helicopter will be there waiting to pick them up when they arrive – they know the pilot has been promised an immediate five thousand dollars for each of the men he brings back, more than three years' pay if he retrieves all three. There is also the not insignificant additional consideration that, if the pilots do not pick them up, the other swimmers with whom Symanskiy and his men have been training will almost certainly kill them.

In fact, though Symanskiy does not know it, their pilot and his copilot are more concerned about being killed by Symanskiy's friends than by the Chinese.
They are so concerned that they will be wrongly blamed if they do not return with the swimmers that they have prevailed upon a swimmer injured in training to ride along as a witness to the good faith of their efforts in exchange for a share of the money they are to receive.

The river water is cold but acceptable as Symanskei and his team move rapidly downstream in their black wetsuits. They are supposed to swim tethered together underwater with each of them towing a floating bag containing ninety kilograms of shaped explosives. But they do not.

It is so dark due to the clouds and waning moon that they can barely see the nearby shore. So Sergey, the team leader, decides they will swim independently on the surface to make better time. It is a good decision. They will never see a light until just before they reach their target bridge and see the headlight of a train crossing it.

Swimming on the surface and not roped together enables the men to reach the bridge almost an hour earlier than they anticipated. They had not known their specific objective until just before they took off, only that it is a rail bridge. But their American instructors had known which bridge they'd be going after and had the three of them practice over and over again on a couple of somewhat similar bridges in Russia.

Once they spot the bridge the three men stop swimming and, without moving at all, let the current slowly carry them down to the bridge and under it. Then they quietly tread water to hold themselves in place against moving current as they watch and listen in the darkness for a good five minutes. Nothing.

They set to work as soon as Sergey gives the signal. Three of the bridge's four big center supports are their primary objectives. Sergey himself is responsible for the initial phase of the operation.

Everyone treads water under the bridge and continues to look and listen while Lieutenant Symanskie unhooks the sixty foot adjustable strap he is carrying in a bag clipped to his swimmers belt. It will go all the way around one of the center support columns. The swimmers will hold on to it while they place their explosives. They practiced with the Americans and know what to do and are prepared to do it despite the almost total darkness.

Mikail, the little Georgian, holds the end in place as Sergey quietly moves around the big support and then cinches the strap tight. He places it about two inches below the water level so it cannot be seen in the dark if anyone should happen to shine a light on it. Then the third member of the team, Andrei from Moscow, begins removing one of their big shaped plastic charges from his floating tow bag. Sergey and Mikail hold it in place while Andrei attaches it to the column with a special form of super glue and activate the timer. Then they move on to another support and repeat the process.

The bridge has four support columns but the men are only carrying three big charges, one each. The American experts said destroying three of the columns would probably be enough to bring the bridge down and, even if it does not, will almost certainly render the bridge unusable and unrepairable.

******

Short and vicious is the only way to describe the air battle that unfolds in the pre-dawn sky over Mongolia. The Russian AWACS gather the eleven Russian planes together into a single force and guide them straight through the Chinese armada of almost a hundred transports and over fifty fighters. The Chinese AWACs see them coming and surge their fighters forward to intercept them.

It is a target rich environment for the eleven Russians and everyone begin firing as soon as they made contact. The Russians fire first because of their superior electronics and missiles. And that may have been a mistake because they knocked down mostly fighters instead of transports.

Three of the MiGs survive their long initial run through the strung out mass of Chinese planes and, with all their missiles and cannon rounds expended, are able to break away and return to emergency fields on the Russian side of the border. Two TU-128s also survive. Unfortunately, both crash while trying to land on an emergency field that turns out to be too short to handle the biggest and heaviest fighter in the Russian inventory.

The Chinese lose more than thirty planes including eleven transports packed with screaming paratroopers who have little or no time to jump.

******

It is late afternoon in the Baltic and eight time zones to the east the Russian pre-emptive strike on the Chinese airfields is underway and various teams of Russian swimmers are moving into China in their helicopters.

Anxiety on the American nuclear attack submarine *Bergall* is high and growing. The *Bergall* has been tailing a noisy Chinese missile boat for almost a week. It is the *Sian* according to its noise signature, and it is thought to be loaded with twenty two cruise missiles including a couple with nuclear warheads.

Bergall's captain, Randy Sheets, is anxious, very anxious. The *Bergall* had been informed almost ten hours ago that in about eight hours, at 0614 local time in the Russian Far East, the Chinese will begin their invasion of Russia. And then, more than an hour ago, a follow up message had been received informing him that the war is already underway.

There is no question in Randy Sheets' mind that the *Sian* will surface sometime in the next eight hours or so, and certainly no later than 0614, and launch its conventionally tipped missiles at Russian targets. The latest intelligence from Washington says that some or all of the missiles of both the Chinese missile subs in the area will be aimed at the Russian army and Marine staging areas of the Kalingrad Naval Base.

"Naval Intelligence does not expect a nuclear strike, but Christ what if they are wrong," Randy has been thinking about it and decides he needs to explain to the crew what the Bergall might be ordered to do and why it will be so important.

"Here's the deal as I know it," he tells them. "The Russian navy has gone east to the Sea of Japan. Every ship that can move. So either we stop the *Sian* or someone's going to take a serious hit. But all Washington has told us so far is to get ready to take it out and to stand by for further orders."

He also repeats what every one of them already knows - the *Sian* is so technologically obsolete that it will have to surface to fire.

"It may give us a leg up," he explains. "At least, we will know in advance if they intend to shoot."

Captain Sheets is anxious, and rightly so. For more than a day the *Bergall* has been standing by waiting for an order to engage the *Sian*. *At least we do not have to worry about the Russian fleet getting in the way or mistaking us for them. The whole damn Russian fleet is on its way to Vladivostok. It's us or nothing."*

******

Russia's attack and missile subs standing off Shanghai and Canton are under no such constraints or uncertainty. The orders to commence unlimited non-nuclear warfare against all tankers and Chinese ships in Chinese waters came through an hour ago as soon as word reached Moscow that Sholakov had launched a massive preemptive strike against the Chinese.

Moscow's Party bosses and the Russian Navy brass grumbled among themselves about Sholakov not telling them in advance about his intention to launch a pre-emptive strike. But the Russian Admirals know the invasion is imminent and are, for the most part, ready when they find out – they immediately order the Russian Navy's attack subs to begin launching attacks against any Chinese naval vessels and all tankers they find inside the Chinese twenty kilometer limit.

"Husband your torpedoes," is the order; "one per tanker"

Similarly, the Russian missile subs are immediately ordered to launch their non-nuclear cruise missiles at various pre-selected petroleum terminal and storage facilities at 0215 local time. They are then to loiter off China and be prepared at to launch their nuclear missiles at pre-selected land targets if the war goes nuclear.

Russia's attack subs have been tailing tankers inbound for China for days and are perched off of China's busiest ports. It's little wonder the Chinese airwaves begin crackling with maritime distress calls long before the official 0614 start of the Chinese invasion.

******

Sergey and his swimmers reach the evacuation sandbar more than an hour early. Then they talk about meaningless things in low voices while they wait anxiously, worried that they have been betrayed and their ride won't appear. Finally, a few minutes before it is scheduled to arrive, they hear the unlit helicopter approaching. Suddenly it comes into view in the moonlight directly over them.

Their ride home is just settling down to pick them up when in the distance they hear their three charges going off almost simultaneously in one long rolling boom. The three men cheer and hug each other.

In the moonlight the swimmers can see the pilots and the unexpected passenger beaming at them as they climb in. Little wonder – they'd seen the swimmers react when the explosions occur and know what it means even if they did not hear them.

"I wonder if we can get another bridge assignment and make more money," is what Sergey is thinking as he gives the pilots and the volunteer observer a big thumbs up and shakes their hands.

Ten minutes later Sergey is shouting something over the engine noise to Mikhail and Andrei about volunteering for another mission when the helicopter plows into the side of a snow capped Chinese mountain.

******

It takes the fifty seven hundred men of the 114th Infantry Division's nine infantry assault battalions almost five hours of walking in the moonlit night to come down the tree covered slopes and reach the edge of the big meadow. The log cabin buildings and a few flickering lights in Bikin are about three kilometers ahead of them. Most of the cabins are on this side of the railroad tracks.

Colonel Bo Huwang, the division's deputy commander in name and actual commander in reality, had watched from the mountain last week as the Russian troops began to garrison the village. It really would have made a lot more sense, he thought with a great deal of twenty twenty hindsight, if we'd gone straight for the bridges.

But orders are orders. No one expected the Russians to be here two weeks ago when the division commander handed him his orders and rushed off to safety just before Colonel Bo and the first of his men began to cross the river. *Maybe we are here because the bridges are too heavily defended.*

******

It is early in the afternoon in the United States and still the middle of the night in the Russian East when reports started coming in to the media about big air battles over China, missile attacks on Chinese ports and ships, and efforts to sink Chinese subs. They are big stories in what is otherwise shaping up to be a slow news day.

True to form, the television networks cancel their morning cooking shows and mobilize their news readers and talk show hosts. Similarly, the world's political leaders immediately began thinking of ways to make political capital out of the war. The news is alarming and photo opportunities abound.

Many world leaders, including the President, quickly call press conferences to lament the fighting and offer solutions. The President, and almost all of the other heads of state, forthrightly calls upon everyone to stop shooting and for the United Nations to hold a peace conference.

The TV Networks are similarly happy; their viewership begins to increase as breathless commentators interrupt their regular programming to discuss the situation with each other. Their conversations are interspersed with "breaking news" which consists of old footage, the arrival of new talking heads, and coverage of the irrelevant press conferences.

In the United States the flash bulbs and TV lights light up as the President strode with determination into the White House Rose Garden and earnestly expresses his concern about the fighting and implores everyone to stop.

Then the Secretary of State, after giving the media enough time to walk over from the White House, earnestly and soberly appears in the State Department's auditorium to announce that she is terribly concerned about world peace and willing to go anywhere at any time in pursuit of it.

At the Detachment all we can do is sit around with our fingers up our asses and wait and worry as an ever increasing number of NSA reports and intelligence updates pour in. One thing we do not even try to do is contact Sholakov and the handful of our men still out there. There is nothing more we can add to what we've already suggested and our own men long ago received their orders and know what to do when the war starts.

Finally, as the afternoon wears on in France and the NSA's first reports came in about the Chinese air armada heading for the Russian airfields west of Lake Baikal, we get out the maps of the area and begin looking for a staging area the Russians might use to recapture the airfields they are virtually certain to lose. At least it will keep us busy.

Damnit, we should have seen that coming. Hmm. Perhaps the Russians could use the airborne troops we are repatriating from Iceland.

With nothing else to do except watch the TV news and read the incoming intelligence reports, I send high priority messages to Dick Spelling, the Marine commander at Reykjavik, and to NATO intelligence. Each message inquires as to the numbers and locations of the Russian survivors of Reykjavik.

Dick calls a few minutes after I get home, mainly I am sure, so we can commiserate with each other about our impotence to affect the unfolding events and enhance the safety of our men who are still in eastern Russia. Dorothy and I are saddened to hear that Marjorie is still being treated for stress related to the terrorist attack on the Excelsior.

It is still light outside so little Chris and I decide to dig some worms out of the worm bucket and go fishing before supper. I take my newfangled portable phone with me.

Chapter Twenty-three

Desperate days.

Everything changed as dawn arrived in Siberia and the surviving Chinese transport planes began dropping paratroopers on every Russian airfield east of Lake Baikal. Each of the fields became a cauldron of intense close quarters fighting as the Chinese paratroopers and, in a couple of cases, helicopter borne assault troops began landing on the airfields. They landed in the face of the ferocious Russian opposition waiting on the ground.

Amazingly, a recently arrived CNN camera crew was still in the Arkhara transit lounge waiting for Russian customs officials to arrive when the Chinese paratroopers began landing. The CNN crew had arrived in the middle of the night on a Malaysian charter out of Seoul and most of them are asleep, or trying to sleep, on the rickety chairs in the little transit lounge when the Chinese paratroopers start landing all around them. They wake up in time to film the assault and beam it back to Atlanta via some kind of satellite hookup.

Dawn was just breaking and the Arkhara runway and the buildings on the air base were just becoming visible when the Chinese paratroopers began landing and the

CNN crew began filming. The Chinese came down everywhere including all around the plywood transit lounge with its potbelly stove in the middle of the room to warm it.

It was quickly clear from the pictures being beamed to the CNN studios in Atlanta that many of the Chinese are being hit either before they reach the ground or as they desperately scramble to get out of their parachutes and try retrieve their weapons from their drop bags. It's fascinating and television networks all over the world pick it up. We watch in our house as we eat dinner.

The Chinese do not instantly start shooting because they drop with their weapons and ammunition in canvas duffle bags attached to each paratrooper by a cord. The bags hang down below each man so they reach the ground just before the men do. It is obvious from the early morning footage that many of the Chinese, but certainly not all of them, are shot in the air or on the ground before they can get to their weapons.

The noise is horrendous, and we can see the transit lounge building shake and most of its windows being blown out. Several times during the almost ten minutes of live filming screams and shouts can be heard.

What CNN is able to broadcast before it suddenly goes off the air is both gruesome and fascinating. The Chinese paratroopers did not have a chance. Neither, in the end, did the CNN crew. The last sound before the broadcast abruptly ended is a screamed cry of "grenade."

******

The Chinese paratroopers are incredibly brave and the fight for the Arkhara field lasts well over an hour. But the Chinese have been dropped on an airfield surrounded by a ring of two-man infantry positions backed up by a second ring of tanks and infantry fighting vehicles. Some of the Chinese land inside the rings and some behind them. But no matter where they land they tend to be in the open and facing Russians who are in protected positions with lots of ammunition. It is a slaughter.

On the other hand, not all of the Chinese are instant casualties and not all of the Russian defenders fully protected. American Marine veterans of Reykjavik watch the coverage with particular fascination; it s the first time they have been able to see what they had experienced first hand.

The battle with the Chinese paratroopers goes through pretty much the same phases at every one of Sholakov's airfields. First the descending paratroopers take heavy casualties as they come down in the face of carefully aimed fire from defenders shooting upwards. On the other hand, they jump at a low altitude, typically two hundred meters, so their period of extreme vulnerability is very brief.

Once on the ground the Chinese paratroopers tend to remain vulnerable, particularly in the first few moments as they scramble to discard their chutes and get their weapons and ammunition out their attached duffle bags. Those who survive long enough to retrieve their weapons then either quickly find some form of cover or die trying.

Everything changes once the surviving paratroopers find cover. Airfields, and certainly their runways and taxiways, appear to a casual observer to be flat and open areas. In fact, there are everywhere slight rises and falls in the ground and numerous buildings and pieces of equipment behind which a trained soldier can take shelter and return fire.

It is amazing how even the slightest rise or depression can provide protection from the bullets whooshing past overhead. It's also a fact that small arms fire from a tank turret or from behind sand bags can travel quite a distance and hit someone across the way. Little wonder that significant numbers of Russian casualties are the result of the intense friendly fire rather than caused by the Chinese.

******

Within a couple of minutes there are Chinese dead and wounded everywhere in the open and the overall battle settled down to numerous individual firefights between Russians in their prepared positions and Chinese who have made it to some kind of shelter.

A number of Chinese, for example, made it to the relatively safe south side of the Podovsk transit lounge where the CNN crew is waiting to clear customs. There the Chinese will be safe, at least temporarily, so long as they stay really low. If they try to rise they are likely to be hit by the small arms fire passing through the transit lounge's windows and thin plywood walls.

Private Bo Shiun heard the sound of moving people and shouting from inside the building where the CNN crew continues to film. He is lying flat on the ground when he overhands two thermite grenades through a broken window and ends CNN's live feed.

An hour later most of the Chinese including Private Bo are down. Then the wary Russian survivors began moving slowly and cautiously as they follow their tanks and BMD's through the hangars and the built up areas around the runways and parking aprons. They do not know it yet but it will take them almost twenty four hours to eliminate all the pockets of Chinese resistance and reopen the field.

******

Things are totally different much further to the west at Angarsk and Irkutsk. The frantic warnings of the Russian AWACS enable a few of the planes on the two fields to be manned and fly off before the Chinese arrive. Very few.

Those that get off in the chaos do so even though many of them are low on fuel or ammunition or both. They will try to make the nearby emergency fields or even, in a couple of cases of planes with some ammunition and missiles left, bravely try to intercept the incoming Chinese before they run out of fuel and crash as their engines flame out.

The second wave of Chinese planes coming out of Mongolia is still being challenged by the remnants of the eleven Russian fighters, and a couple of more that were able to get off in time to join them, as the Chinese planes come in low over the still-packed airfields at about six hundred feet and begin dropping their paratroopers.

On the jammed airfields pilots are still climbing into planes and frantically trying to leave amidst the chaos even as the first Chinese transports roar overhead and parachutes begin to open. Most of the Russian planes do not get off.

One of the Russian fighters trying to escape Irkutsk actually hit a Chinese parachute as it lifts off. It crashes in a ball of flames as its desperate pilot attempts a crash landing in the open area beyond the end of the runway. The fighter behind it somehow succeeds in avoiding the parachutes and dangling men only to flame out and crash a few minutes later as its pilot vainly attempts to reach an auxiliary field before running out of fuel.

Sergeant Chin Haolin of the 1091st Special Company does not know any of this. He and the men of his squad are expecting serious opposition as they pour out of their low flying Chinese-made copy of a Russian AN-12 turboprop and their parachutes jerk open above the Irkutsk airfield. They do not even know the name of the field or even that it is somewhere in Russia.

Sergeant Chin and the men of his company float to ground unopposed in the midst of a target-rich chaos. Russian planes are parked everywhere with men running to and from them and pilots trying to climb or climb out. Others are still attempting to taxi to the end of the runway for takeoff.

Chin and his men are astonished to find that they have landed unopposed. Yes, there is scattered shooting but mostly from nervous Chinese; not a Russian is to be seen except the confused pilots and aircrews, at least no live ones, and there is no return fire, just lots of smoke and noise and confusion.

Each of the Chinese paratroopers has grenades and ammunition in the baggy pockets of his fatigues and he and his comrades know their duties - they begin destroying the Russian planes as fast as they can, even if their pilots and crews are in them. But they do not touch the fuel facilities and airport equipment. Their orders are very clear about leaving them untouched. When they finish they will begin clearing the runways and digging in to hold the field against the inevitable Russian counterattack.

At the crowded Irkutsk airfield the unarmed Russian ground crews and administrative staff received absolutely no warning and are totally surprised and unprepared for the arrival of the Chinese. They flee from the field in every direction. Many of them climb the perimeter fence surrounding the field and head off towards the nearby city of Irkutsk on foot.

******

Things are very different at the airfields east of Lake Baikal, very different. The airfield at Darasun is a good example. Several thousand Chinese paratroopers land on the field at dawn. Colonel Altaysk and his men know they are coming and are ready in their little two man holes. So are the Russian armor units surrounding the field.

Fire from the Russian defenders is intense and many of the Chinese are dead or wounded before they hit the ground. Others are cut down because they are clearly visible in the flat open areas of the airfield's runways, taxiways, and parking areas.

In the end, less than a thousand of the four thousand Chinese paratroopers dropped on Darasun actually get into action. The rest became casualties before they can even retrieve their weapons and find cover. On the other hand, even a few hundred highly trained and motivated paratroopers is more than enough men for an intense firefight no matter how well armed and positioned their opponents might be. The fighting lasts several hours until it peters out as the vulnerable Chinese run out of ammunition and options.

It will take another twelve hours before the last two pockets of Chinese holdouts are finally eliminated. Both consist of about a dozen Chinese who came down off the end of the runway and are holed up with a couple of terrified Russian families in their log homes.

Three hours after the first Chinese touches the ground, and after surveying the field and speaking with the air force base commander, Colonel Altaysk radios to headquarters that by nightfall Darasun will be able to begin recovering the planes that had been dispersed to its emergency fields and handle incoming traffic from the west. There is nothing he can do about the dozens of planes the Chinese destroyed on the ground.

All the rest of the airfields in the east, every single one, are the scenes of similarly vicious battles between their Russian defenders waiting on the ground and the Chinese paratroopers dropping from the sky. And all of them except Irutsk and Angarsk have roughly the same outcome – the waiting Russians destroy the attacking Chinese paratroopers, but not before Chinese paratroopers destroy all the Russian planes on the ground.

Only at Areda is the issue still in doubt. The newly arrived Russians hold one end of the field and the Chinese paratroopers the other. Smoldering and destroyed planes are everywhere. So are bodies.

Russia's basic problem is that the two key airfields west of Lake Baikal and a significant majority of its remaining operational fighters and ground attack aircraft have been lost as a result of the Chinese airborne attacks. The two airfields the Chinese are holding are important because of where they are located. It means Chinese fighters based on them will be perfectly positioned to intercept Russian transports bringing supplies and reinforcements to Chita and the Russian forces further east.

By the time the sun is fully up the Chinese are already beginning to clear the Irutsk and Angarsk runways. Chinese fighters and their supply planes will soon be able to land. The Russian air corridor to the east is about to be severed.

******

Exactly at 0614 Colonel Bo led six of the nine assault battalions of the 114th Infantry out of the spruce forest on the hill and towards Bikin. They surge out of the tree line and into the open meadow with bugles blowing and lots of cheering.

Harry and I are in a slit trench about fifty feet down from Colonel Naumenko when the human wave attack starts rolling towards us and Chinese mortar rounds begin falling all over the place. We are not supposed to be here. But the Russian helicopter sent to pick us up yesterday tipped over on to its side and wiped out its blades as it landed with a mechanical problem.

Bikin's defenders are alert and ready, at least as ready as they can be, as Harry and I watch the Chinese attackers surge out of the trees and begin to move towards us in the early morning haze.

Colonel Naumenko and his Russians are as ready as possible. Yesterday morning they received a war warning and yesterday afternoon a Spetsnaz patrol radioed in to report a large Chinese force moving through the heavy forest towards Bikin. Harry and I know about the Spetznaz report because we came through the door, after watching our ride tip over and seriously ding its rotor blades, just in time to see Colonel Naumenk end a phone conversation with the Spetsnaz commander.

Colonel Naumenko swears as he hangs up the phone. Then he shouts some kind of command to one of the lieutenants in the office, grabs up the AK-47 he always carries, and heads for the door. We turn around and follow with a questioning look on our faces.

"The Chinese are coming," he shouts and motions over his shoulder for us to follow him as he bounds down the stairs and heads for his Jeep. "Okay you come."

It is a wet and bouncy start and stop trip in the cold misting rain. The three of us, plus a lieutenant who apparently is a new aide chosen because he is somewhat able to speak English, drive and walk and sometimes wade from position to position. It's a trip Harry and I have taken with the Colonel several times before.

We spend a wet afternoon with Colonel Naumenko walking and driving the entire Russian defensive line around Bikin. Everywhere men are ignoring the rain and desperately digging their positions deeper and bringing in more ammunition and supplies. Always there are intense conversations with the officers and senior NCOs with lots of pointing and gestures.

This time it's different. Word has gotten out to the troops that the Chinese are really coming. They are all green troops, including most of the officers, and they are all, to put it mildly, either scared shitless or excited about finally seeing combat, or both.

That night we go out again with Colonel Naumenko right after he gets a message informing him that the war has started. This time we walk the entire perimeter in the dark carrying gasoline fueled lanterns. *Which makes us perfect targets, scares me shitless, and has Harry talking to himself.*

Around midnight we reach the three Russian mortar positions, all Russian Naval Infantry, and spend quite a bit of time by lantern light making sure each of the Russian

Marines has enough flares and knows how and when to use them. It's a good thing we do because at one of the positions the men obviously do not have a clue.

Duffy is surprisingly good at spotting such problems. Both the officers and the men, if that is what you can call teenage conscripts, seem particularly grateful and willing to listen - a big change in attitude from "know it all" teenagers we sometimes ran into a couple of days ago. *Duffy thinks the problem is the Russians do not have many experienced sergeants, just conscripts who may or may not be brighter than the others. He is probably right – the conscripts selected to be sergeants are given a couple of extra weeks of basic training and immediately promoted to sergeant.*

When we finish we make our way in the darkness back to the hole we've dug into the wall of a Russian slit trench, readjust the sandbags one more time, and try to catch a few hours of sleep despite the cold. At least the rain stopped while we were out walking around.

******

Naumenko's battle headquarters is a dugout in a slit trench adjacent to his main mortar position. A good part of what's left of the armor he did not send to the bridges, three light tanks and four BMDs, is in hull down positions around him. They are his rapid response force. The rest of his armor, two more tanks and two BMDs, are at another mortar position under the command of the lieutenant colonel who is Naumenko's deputy.

Harry and I are in the slit trench and about sixty feet away from the Colonel as the sun comes up and the Chinese begin charging out of the trees and morning haze. Mortar rounds immediately begin falling on the Russian positions in front of us.

The Russian mortars and armor open up immediately. So, unfortunately, do the Russian Marines—even though the Chinese are hopelessly out of range and they have been ordered to wait.

"Hell Dick, this ain't so bad. We'd be shit out of luck if they had tanks and artillery." *Ever the optimist.*

Then things start to go bad. Almost immediately Chinese mortars begin lobbing smoke rounds into the Russian positions in front of us. The Russian Marines and army infantry can no longer see the mass of approaching Chinese; but they'd seen them start and know they are coming. The army infantry company on the right panics and begins to fall back. That spooks the Russian Marines dug in next to them and some of them also begin to fall back.

A few the retreating men stand erect as they run out of the smoke but most of them keep their heads enough to crawl in an effort to avoid the hail of bullets flying overhead. Naumenko and a couple of his officers then impress the hell out of me – they climb out of their positions and run from one tank or BMD to the next, directing their fire towards the unseen Chinese in the smoke where the Marines and infantry are pulling back.

How the Russian officers make it through the hail of income rounds and mortar explosions I will never know. But they do. About two minutes later one of the officers, and then Naumenko, roll back into the trench in front of us gasping for breath. The other one does not return.

Almost immediately Chinese begin coming out of the smoke behind the retreating men. Duffy is one helluva shot and begins picking off the thrusters in front of us. He is in a half standing crouch in the trench and talking to himself as he fires his AK-47 from the gap between a couple of sandbags. Every time he fired, which is frequently, it seems like another Chinese goes down. I am doing almost as well. It's like shooting ducks in a shooting gallery.

Then the retreating wild-eyed young Russians begin pouring out of the smoke cloud and into our position. Most of them huddle sobbing and breathless on the dirt at the bottom of the trench while we try to pick off the Chinese coming out of the smoke behind them. Even Naumenko is firing. *Christ on a crutch. This is going to be close.*

******

We hold. After a while the smoke rounds stop coming and the smoke drifts away. The battlefield in front of us is littered with Chinese and the small arms fire is intense but noticeably declining. Scattered in among the Chinese on the ground are some of the Russians who ran. Those on both sides who can do so are moving - the Chinese survivors and casualties crawling backwards towards the tree line; the Russians crawling towards us. *We cannot see the casualties in the Russian positions in front of us that got overrun but there is going to be a lot of them.*

Firing tails off even more as more and more of the Russian stragglers and wounded reach the relative safety of our positions in Naumenko's second line of defense. The Russians are still in their original positions to the left of us and in the middle; the Chinese have taken the Russian positions on our right front. It's a horrific mess with the sounds of shouting and what are obviously the screams of the wounded for help increasingly heard as the volume of fire decreases.

Well one thing's for sure. Harry and I are not going anywhere. The helicopter is in flames and, no surprise, the two mechanics who'd spent all night working on it are nowhere to be seen.

So here we are, Harry and I, waiting with Colonel Naumenko in a slit trench as Chinese small arms fire periodically whips by overhead and every so often a mortar round comes down on the Russian positions surrounding the village. *I need to pee.*

******

Fighting at Bikin is intense but nothing compared to the intensity of the Chinese attacks over the Ussuri and Amur Rivers that start at virtually the same moment.

Lieutenant Colonel Stransky, the commander of the 112th infantry's tank battalion on the Kharbarovsk Front, is standing in the gun turret of his hull down T-62 tank as the sun comes up. He is looking at the far side of the river in absolute fascination as a huge mass of running men carrying hundreds of rubber boats suddenly appears out of the morning haze and rushes to the south shore of the Amur and launches them. *It looks like the ground over there is covered with ants heading this way.*

Stransky had been watching the river all night and until now has seen nothing.

"How did they do it?" he asks himself. "Why did not my tank's night vision optics pick them up?"

"Of course," he suddenly realizes just as he gives the order to fire. "They are using rubber rafts and paddles; there are no vehicles or boat engines to radiate heat."

"Go for the rafts. They are rubber. Use shrapnel rounds with proximity fuses," he shouts into the radio mike he is holding. Then a few seconds later he reverses himself and orders his tanks and BMDs to ignore the rubber rafts and concentrate their shrapnel rounds on the masses of Chinese troops and equipment now clearly visible on the other bank. *The infantry can shoot up the rubber boats.*

A few seconds later he closes the hatch as a virtual torrent Chinese artillery fire begins landing around his tanks and BMDs. *Damn it. I fucked up. We shouldn't have given away our position until they started putting their pontoon bridges across.* He isn't alone. The commanders of two of the other three armored battalions in his sector made the same mistake.

"Hold your fire. Wait for their bridging equipment. The infantry can take care of the troops."

But they do not. The Chinese artillery fire and air support savage the Russian infantry despite losing a fair number of planes and helicopters to the Russian infantry's SAMs and ground fire. An hour later and the Chinese infantry are over the river in force and digging in on the north bank.

The Chinese combat engineers and armor do not fare as well as the Chinese infantry.

The engineers' first two efforts at throwing pontoon bridges across the river are shot to shreds by the hull down Russian armor and the Russian artillery dug in at the foot of the valley. But numbers three and four last long enough for a lot of tanks and other tracked vehicles to get across before they too are destroyed. At the moment, the surviving engineers are building three more and the Russians have been pushed back far enough out of range that they may stay up.

In contrast to the initial success of the Russian artillery and armor, the Russian assault helicopters have not been effective anywhere on the battlefield. They are bravely flown but are quickly decimated by hundreds of Chinese handheld SAMs and the Chinese fighter planes that dominate the air and are pounding the Russian ground forces.

Through his binoculars Stransky can see movement on the other side of the river. "Fuck your mother. They are going to bring more troops and armor across."

He is right to be concerned. The Chinese artillery barrage and assault helicopter attacks have been intensive. This time there will be significantly less armor and fewer Russian artillery pieces and assault helicopters to oppose them. *Where is the goddamn air force?*

Although Stransky does not know about it at the time, a very similar attack is being simultaneously launched over the Ussuri River towards Vladivostok. Both attacks have massive artillery and air support as the Chinese assault troops paddle across the rivers in the face of heavy Russian artillery, armor, and mortar fire. The Chinese engineers are right behind the assault troops with mobile pontoon bridges that can carry tanks and heavy equipment.

In each case the Russians are ready and waiting. They know in advance exactly where the Chinese are concentrating their attack forces and mobile pontoon bridges because of the constant stream of satellite photos we are sending them. But knowing where the Chinese are coming is not enough - the Chinese divisions take massive casualties from the waiting Russians and get across.

******

Darkness has barely fallen in the Baltic when, at exactly 0614 eight time zones away in the east, the *Sian* and *Canton* simultaneously surface miles apart and begin firing a full load of their conventional cruise missiles at the packed Russian army staging area at the Port of Kalingrad.

Randy Sheets in the *Bergall* hears the *Sian* begin to move towards the surface and instantly reports it via satellite using a recorded float-up transmitter. A few minutes later his sonar crew hears the Sian begin firing its missiles. He reports that too. There is no response from the Pentagon. None at all. No order comes for the *Bergall* to intervene.

******

Half a world away at 0558, sixteen minutes before the start time in his orders, Captain Shi Leong begins giving orders to the crew of the Chinese attack submarine *Swallow*.

"Blow ballast. One hundred pounds"

Shi gives his orders as he holds on to the periscope handles and continually walks in a circle as the *Swallow* breaks the surface in the pre-dawn moonlight. Two, no three, ships are in sight. Two patrol boats which seem to be moving away and a destroyer with a load of cargo on its deck heading rapidly towards the Vladivostok docks.

"Open air intake vents maximum."

"Open all tube doors."

"Bearing 232. Range two thousand one hundred.

"All ahead very slow. Turn 5 degrees left."

 "Stand by to fire tubes two, four, six, and seven."

Captain Shi waits a full three minutes while cool fresh air pours into the *Swallow*.

Then. "All Stop."... "Bearing 192. Range one thousand three hundred."

At exactly the 0614 start time specified in his orders, Shi shouts. "Fire four"... "Fire six"... "Fire two"..."Fire seven."

"All stop. Close all vents. Maximum ballast. Close all doors. Dive"

The *Swallow* settles slowly back to the ocean floor. It is as silent a torpedo attack as a Romeo-type submarine ever made. Two minutes later the crew of the *Swallow* hears a distinct explosion. Just one.

******

Resolute, a Russian Kashin-class antisubmarine destroyer, maintains its maximum speed of thirty two knots as it approaches the Vladivostok port with its cargo of troops and armored vehicles.

"Really," I say to my executive officer who is standing next to me on the crowded bridge, "this is much too fast for a harbor entry. But that is the order." The exec merely shrugs his shoulders and shakes his head in a gesture of disgust and futility.

Resolute's bridge is crowded. In obedience to the orders I'd received as we entered the Sea of Japan, the *Resolute* is on a high and somewhat unique alert. Our watertight doors are sealed and our lifeboat crews and as many as possible of the more than five hundred army troops we are carrying are on deck and ready to abandon ship.

I have got the men as prepared as I can get them to quickly abandon ship. Even the lifeboats are swung out and partially lowered. They are filled with extremely anxious men, mostly teenage army conscripts wearing backpacks and carrying their weapons.

Why are they so anxious? One reason is because they are in the lifeboats without life jackets. The Resolute does not carry enough additional life jackets to equip all the excess troops we loaded. Unfortunately, by the time I realize it there are none left to be had at Kalingrad. Putting them into the lifeboats is the best I can do.

******

One of my lookouts in the bow spots the torpedo before it hits us. I was looking forward towards the harbor entrance in the distance and could see his face as he realizes what he is seeing. I could not hear him but somehow I instinctively know exactly what he is shouting when he turns and looks at the bridge and points down at the water.

"Torpedo," he screams a few seconds before it hits right under where he is standing, "Torpedo in the water."

I do not have a chance to even begin taking evasive measures before the torpedo blows off the *Resolute*'s bow and knocks almost everyone to the deck including me. It is a massive explosion and it throws some of the men on the crowded main deck into the water. The lookout and the other men who'd been standing on the bow disappear along with the bow itself.

Surprisingly, the *Resolute* does not immediately sink and I am able to get back on my feet even before the ship's forward momentum stops. One look down at the damage and I know what I have to do. *It's strange; somehow I feel very calm.*

"All engines full reverse," I shout. I do not give the order to abandon ship because, more than an hour ago, before we got everyone on deck, we'd shut and tightened all the bulkheads and doors. *Maybe they will hold.*

******

Vehicles and equipment in the army military staging area at the port of Kalingrad explode and catch fire for almost three minutes as Chinese cruise missiles land one after another every four or five seconds. Each lands with a big bright red flash followed by a massive boom and much smoke.

Kalingrad's staging area is a scene of utter devastation as the *Sian* and *Canton* slip back below the surface to start the long trip back to China. The men on the submarines cannot see it, of course, but numerous vehicles are burning or tipped over and just about all the personnel that had been working on them are either dead or injured.

Two hours later the fires are out, the secondary explosions from ammunition cooking off have ended, and the place is swarming with uniformed rescuers and every fireman, fire truck, and ambulance from miles around.

The survivors are already in the local hospital by the time the Russian naval infantry general in charge of the staging area arrives to stand on the hood of his Jeep and survey the destruction.

He is surprised as he realizes what he is seeing and what he will report.

Yes, almost all the men working in the area are casualties. And, yes, a large number of vehicles have been destroyed and damaged. But there were not many men working here in the first place - because all the armor and other high priority vehicles and equipment that could be loaded had already sailed and the men needed to operate them sailed with them. *The Chinese hit a relatively unmanned storage area and destroyed a lot of trucks and low priority supplies.*

"This won't have much effect on the war" will be the essence of his report.

It is late afternoon when the flash message with the NSA transcript of the general's report to Moscow reaches the Detachment. For all their efforts, the Chinese submarines have not accomplished much of anything that will affect the outcome of the war now raging in the east.

Chapter Twenty-four

Early days.

"Yes, Mister President," I agree. "The opening hours of the war appear to have resulted in a number of initial Chinese successes as we all expected."

And that was the truth, but perhaps not the whole truth. China's invasion forces were indeed across the Usurri towards Vladivostok and across the Amur towards Khabarovsk; the Russian air force in the east had been largely destroyed even though most of the Chinese air assaults on the Russian airfields have failed; and, perhaps most important of all, the key airfields at Irkutsk and Angarsk have been captured by the Chinese and are already being cleared for use by the Chinese air force."

I also knew something else which I have not mentioned yet because I was still not sure.

Mike Morton spoke with Chief Matthews this morning to get a report on last night's operation against the Chinese bridges. It took a bit of doing to track him down because the Chief and his four-man team of American instructors unexpectedly found themselves running from some Chinese paratroopers who came down near their camp instead of their intended drop zone.

In any event, Matthews and his men are safe now. Mike finally reached him when he reported in to Colonel Miskin at Sholakov's headquarters. *Matthews downplayed his brush with the Chinese. But I got the impression from Miskin that it had been a damn close call.*

According to Chief Matthews' report to Miskin, some of the helicopters bringing back the Russian swimmers diverted to alternative fields when they found their primary fields under attack. But the swimmers who were able to get back before the attacks begin report success; similarly, the helicopter pilots who radio in to report they are diverting also report their swimmers have been successful.

It's all very encouraging—but not a surprise given the amount of money we promised to pay to each of them if he is part of a successful team. We will know soon enough what really happened - analysts both here and in Washington are already looking at the satellite photos and listening to Chinese radio and telephone intercepts.

Interestingly, the Chinese rail bridges are not mentioned anywhere in the latest NSA intercepts. That may be significant because the NSA communications intercepts are usually accurate. In other words, because it's not there, the report I just read suggests the decision makers at Red Banner Street may not know they have lost a number of crucial bridges.

Hmm. Yes. The Chinese are obviously focused on what they think are more important things. When the teleconference ends I am going to have Mike Morton call Chief Matthews and have him offer another twenty thousand dollars to every swimmer who will go out again, preferably tonight before the Chinese wise up to what's being done to them.

Dick Spelling and I just finished explaining to the President and Security Council that the war is only a few hours old and both sides seem to think it is proceeding as they had hoped and planned. The only unexpected developments from the Russian point of view are serious - the much heavier than expected aircraft losses and the loss of the airfields west of Lake Baikal.

"Dick, can you get one of our satellites refocused away from the river crossings and have them run a scan on the bridges we targeted? We need to know, as soon as possible, which ones are still up and being used."

******

I have been trying for the past hour to get through to General Roberts with a report. No luck. Colonel Naumenko's communications center cabin took a direct hit from a mortar round and the radios in the tanks apparently do not have enough range.

What I want to report to General Roberts is that the railroad from Vladivostok to Kharbarovsk is still open. The Chinese in front of Bikin have been relatively quiet since their big human wave attack failed this morning. The Chinese stopped firing their mortars when they pulled back and it's too far to the tree line for snipers. Trains can still get through if they hurry.

Now that the smoke has dissipated we can see all the casualties in the field in front of us - mostly Chinese and a lot of them. Some of them are moving. But the Russians took a heavy hit as well and the Russian casualties are overflowing the village's abandoned log houses which have been turned into aid centers. *The Russians have some medics and a bunch of stretcher bearers. I do not know how the Chinese wounded are doing but the Russians are going to lose a lot more of these kids unless something is done pretty quickly.*

Finally! There is a "come on" wave from the door of the BMD Naumenko is using as his command center. I trot over and pick up the BMD's external phone.

"Hello. Dick Evans here".... "Can you hear me, Sir?"

"Yes Sir, it's me. We are still stuck in Bikin and there's been a big Chinese attack."

"No idea, Sir. The helicopter crashed."

"It was close, Sir, but the Russians held and the railroad appears to still be usable. The Chinese tried a really stupid human wave charge. Bugles blowing and all. They used smoke for cover and got into some of the Russian positions. But then, for some reason, they stopped and pulled back."

"Yes Sir, the bridges south of Bikin are still up. At least they were about twenty minutes ago when Colonel Naumenko talked to them on one of the tank radios. They have not been hit at all."

"No Sir, we won't."

"Ah, Sir, the Russians have a couple of hundred wounded men here, teenage kids mostly, conscripts, and they do not have much in the way of medics or supplies. All they have got are some medics and orderlies. They are trying to use live blood donated by the surviving troops but that and morphine is about all they have got."

"Yes sir, it really is bad. Any chance we can get a medical drop in here?"

"Thank you, Sir. I know you will."

******

Communist Party military headquarters on Red Swallow Street is packed with senior military and party officers and their aides. Some of them are weary from a night without sleep, or maybe even two or three nights. They are all excited and generally pleased.

There had been a great deal of anxiety and concern when reports began coming in of pre-emptive Russian air strikes before the scheduled start of our attack. But they did not cause all that much damage and there is a sense of positive excitement and comradeship everywhere. It's been almost three hours since our attacks began and the initial reports look good, very good. At least that is what the staff is reporting by phone to the Politburo meeting in the small coastal resort village of Beidaihe.

"Yes, Comrade Chairman, I can confirm that we successfully defeated the enemy's preemptive air attacks and the situation is developing almost exactly as we planned. Our parachute troops have landed and destroyed the planes on every Russian airfield and our assault troops are across both of the rivers."

"Yes, Comrades, all of them. Every single one."

"Yes, Comrade Marshal, our air force has achieved air supremacy. Just a few minutes ago both of our airborne radar planes reported that there are no Russian planes in the air. No helicopters either. None at all. In contrast, our planes are either in the air engaging the enemy's ground forces or have returned to their bases and are being quickly refueled and rearmed. Some are already are attacking the Russian ground forces on their second or third missions of the war. It is a great victory for the Red Army."

* * * * * *

Things are popping at the Detachment. I was talking on two phones at the same time. On one I have got Sholakov and Lieutenant Basilof and on the other, Colonel Miskin.

Then the President interrupts both lines. According to the White House aide who placed the call, the President has the Defense Secretary and Dick Spelling on the line with him and wants to talk about the *Sian* and *Canton* and about getting more SAMs to the Russians now that the Chinese have air superiority. *What's up and why?*

To my very real surprise, the President makes it clear that he now wants the American Navy to sink the Chinese boomers that attacked Kalingrad this morning – without anyone finding out that we did it. He says he does not want to take a chance that the nuclear weapons they are reported to be carrying will be used to hit Russia. Such an attack, the President believes, might well trigger a wider nuclear war. *Wonder what caused him to change his mind?*

What he is counting on, the President says, is that the sinking will be lost in the fog of war and, even more importantly, no one will know for sure who is responsible. Then, to my surprise, he asks me if I agree or not?

"Um...Yes, Mr. President. I think I do agree." *He may be right. Probably is. But why is he telling me this instead of ordering me to do it?*

"Good. General Roberts, I am herewith giving you, as the NATO commander, permission to use the American submarines assigned to NATO to destroy any non-NATO submarines with nuclear capabilities found in NATO waters. *Permission? Verbally? Well now I know. If the Chinese ever find out it was not the Russians, the sinking of their subs can be blamed on NATO and me, not the White House.*

Dick Spelling called back a few minutes later. He has his replacement, General Talbot, on the line with him.

"You do understand what the President wants, do not you Guns?" Dick asks.

"I sure do. The orders are going out as we speak. I sent them with a NATO communications identifier instead of Washington or Campbell Barracks."

"Good man. Probably best not to actually mention it to anyone at NATO until we see what develops."

"Figured as much."

"This is probably the last time you'll be hearing from me, Guns. At least officially, that is. The Senate is going to confirm Tommy tomorrow morning and my retirement parade and press conference with the President is tomorrow afternoon. Then I guess I am gonna have to learn how to play golf. Anyhow I want you to know that I have always liked Boy Scouts like you. It's been good working with you all these years and I ... Uh... Oh hell, Chris. Good luck."

******

Captain Randall Sheets of the *Burgall* is not a happy camper on the first morning of the Chinese War. The *Burgall* is still tracking the *Sian* but he is absolutely disgusted that he did nothing when it surfaced and fired its missiles at Kalingrad. He'd spent his entire adult life preparing to command an attack sub and sink enemy ships – and never once had an opportunity to fire a shot, not even during the recent war.

"It just isn't fair," Randy is thinking when the flash NATO message comes in from the NATO commander and changes everything. It orders the *Burgall* to sink all non-NATO missile submarines in NATO waters that might have nuclear weapons on board.

I sent a similar message to the captains of the *Grayling* and *Pargo*. They have been shadowing the *Canton* for some time. Both had been nearby and been able hear the *Canton* surface and fire its missiles. All the other American and NATO subs are simultaneously sent a different message reminding them to immediately report and track any non-NATO subs they come across.

******

Alarms continue to clang as *Resolute* shudders to a halt in a great spray of water. One look through the bridge window and I know what has to be done.

"Damage control party report status," I shout into the voice tube as I throw the switch to its all-speakers setting. "The bow is gone. Are the bulkhead doors holding?"

"Engine room report status. Keep the turbines running. We've lost the bow and I am going to try to back her in."

"Harbor depth?" I shout over my shoulder to Lieutenant Shoppel as I push the wheelman aside and take the controls. "What is the depth next to the piers?" For a second Aleksandr looks at me dumbly, as if he did not understood the order. Then light dawns and he rushes to the book of harbor descriptions. It's already open to Vladivostok.

"Attention all hands. This is the Captain. Do not, repeat not, abandon ship. We are going to back the *Resolute* into the port and tie her to the dock."

My rapid fire announcements are too late for some of the men. Although only seconds had passed since the torpedo struck, two of our six big lifeboats, all loaded to the gills with infantry and all on the Starboard side, splash into the water before my order comes not to abandon ship. The boat commanders responded to the explosion by instantly throwing the launching levers that release their cables and drop them into the water.

Worse, even though I did not realize it at first, the third boat on that side also tries to drop but only the cables in the back of the boat work. That throws the men packed in it over backwards into the freezing waters - and they are mostly naval infantry without life jackets.

"Catapult starboard rafts two and three," I shout into the voice tube as the *Resolute* slowly begins to move backwards in a big circle so that its stern is pointed towards the harbor.

A couple of my deck crew take off their lifejackets and throw them into the sea as we slowly swing around and pass through the desperately waving men and bodies in the water as we slowly backed towards the harbor entrance. *Noble fellows.*

******

The briefing General Wu gives the Central Committee at its regularly scheduled noon briefing in Beidaihe is even more positive than his 0900 briefing.

"Comrades, I just got off the phone with Army Headquarters. I am pleased to inform you that all of our airbases attacked by the Russians preemptive strikes, every single one of them, are either operational or expected to be operational within the next few hours. All the Russian air bases, in contrast, have been totally closed by our paratroopers and almost all their planes have been destroyed either in the air or on the ground."

"Our situation is equally promising on the ground. Our troops have successfully placed pontoon bridges over both rivers and are continuing to advance towards Khabarovsk and Vladivostok despite fierce enemy resistance. I am also pleased to inform the Committee that both of our missile submarines in the Baltic have reported successful attacks on the Russian army staging area at Port of Kalingrad."

Then General Wu pauses and smiles before he continues. "Similarly, I can now confirm that our parachute troops took the key Russian airfields at Irkutsk and Angarsk without a single man falling to enemy fire. Their runways and facilities are undamaged and the first of our planes are landing on them as I speak. As you may recall, several squadrons of our most advanced fighters will be based on each of those fields. They will, of course, immediately begin intercepting any Russian planes which attempt to resupply the Russian forces east of Lake Baikal."

Several of the committee members clap and there are smiles all around as everyone beams at everyone else.

Then lunch is served. Chicken and rice according to the NSA.

******

A most amazing thing just happened. A troop train from Vladivostok just slowly rolled through the Biken battlefield en route to Khabarovsk and beyond.

The train came through about twenty minutes after two weird looking little hand pumped service carts and a little switch engine pushing two flat cars moved down the tracks past us at about ten miles per hour. *The two men lifting the pump handles up and down must be either very stupid or very brave.*

We all stop to watch the tiny little coal-burning locomotive as it comes past the village a couple of minutes later puffing black smoke rings into the windless air. Each of the flat cars it is pushing has a BMD parked on it and Russian Marines crouching behind a wall of sandbags. Everyone waves and hands pop up from behind the sandbags to wave back.

Ten minutes later the troop train itself comes through. It is really big and seems to take forever to pass. The troops clustered around the tanks and vehicles on its hundred or more flat cars look at us and wave.

"Jesus. Boss," Duffy exclaims as the troop train slowly clanks past, "am I seeing things?"

What really surprises me, and Duffy too, is that neither the Chinese nor Naumenko make any effort to stop the train. I look at the Colonel a bit incredulously as the train slowly rumbles through the village about two hundred meters behind our position. I am surprised because I really expected the Colonel to stop it in order to add its troops to his forces and evacuate our wounded.

"I know what you are thinking Comrade Major. I thought about stopping it. Yes I did," he sighed. "But our job is to see that as many reinforcements as possible get to the interior." *Shit, he is right. Well hell. At least we know the bridges are still up south of us.*

"Well Sir, at least we know the bridges are still up. But I am really surprised that the Chinese did not at least try to hit it with their mortars." *I wonder why they did not.*

"Yes, I am surprised about that myself. Maybe they have used up all their mortar rounds. At least I hope so. They probably did not have all that many in the first place since their troops had to carry them over the river in addition to their personal weapons and other gear. Or maybe it means they are saving what they left for their next big attack." *Of course. He is right. Jeez I sure hope they used them all up.*

An hour later Harry and I stop digging our spoons into cans of horrible Russian field rations, sardines in some kind of crème sauce to watch the first of two long and empty trains of flat cars come southbound towards Vladivostok one right after the other. They too are preceded by a hand pumper and then a single flat car pushed by a little coal-burning switch engine. The flat car the switch engine is pushing has a BMD perched on it and troops behind sandbags.

Naumenko briefly stops the first southbound train and Harry and I run to help load badly wounded Russians on the last four flatcars. There is a hospital and surgeons in Vladivostok – if they live long enough and can get there without being slaughtered along the way. We did not load the Russian dead lined up along the track. Maybe they will go on the next empty flat cars that come along.

Whoa. I am glad I am not one of the guys pumping the handles up and down on those little hand powered service cars. I am even more glad I am not one of the Russian wounded being evacuated.

******

Sian is at battle stations and rigged for silent running. After an initial spurt of high speed running towards the Russian coast an hour ago, to move away from the spot where it had earlier surfaced and fired its cruise missiles, the *Sian* is now very slowly moving north close in along the Russian shoreline. It is barely moving, making less than five knots to minimize its sound signature.

So far the captain's strategy is working. The Russian surface ships he expected to swarm to his launch site must have assumed he would run away towards deeper water instead of moving even closer to shore. His sonar men have so far only picked up the sound of one set of high speed screws. And it was moving further away from the port and its sound quickly faded away.

"Captain from sonar," is Lee Sheng's anxious call from his post on the listening devices. "Possible contact. Submarine. Possible torpedo tube doors opening bearing seventy one degrees. Estimate twenty seven thousand meters." The anxiety and fear in Lee's voice is obvious to everyone.

"Sonar. Three pings."

"Yes Captain," is the very nervous response. The pings are followed seconds later by "Sonar confirms target is submarine. Sixty eight degrees. Estimate twenty six thousand five hundred meters."

We have not heard any submarines since we got here so maybe it is the Canton. Well, no sense taking chances. I will go to maximum revolutions so it can identify us; and be ready to make a hard turn and fire a noise maker decoy if it isn't.

"All ahead maximum. Stand by to execute maximum turn to two eight two degrees. Set bow planes for maximum rise. Stand by to fire one noise maker. Come to periscope level."

"Torpedo in the water," screams the *Sian*'s sonar chief. "Two torpedoes." ... "More torpedoes."... "More torpedoes."

Captain Yee of the Sian fires all of his noise makers and makes two hard left climbing turns in a desperate effort to escape. But the outcome is inevitable - because the *Sian* had been built in a Chinese shipyard using stolen construction blueprints for a Soviet November class missile sub, a slow and noisy Soviet model that was technologically obsolete thirty years ago long before the *Sian* was launched.

At their best, the top speed submerged of the old Soviet November class of missile subs is a little less than thirty kilometers per hour. The Chinese copies cannot even do that. There is no way for the *Sian* to outrun or outmaneuver the six Mk-48 torpedoes homing in on it at over sixty miles per hour. And it does not. Twelve minutes later the *Canton* similarly does not escape a massive spread of Mk-48s fired by the *Grayling*.

Neither Chinese sub is able to surface or send a message; they just disappear.

I get the news via a NATO message about an hour later. Well, hopefully the Chinese will never know that the last of the Russian navy's operational surface vessels and submarines sailed for Vladivostok more than twenty four hours earlier. If they do, they will know that all of China's nuclear boomers, both of them, have just been sunk by

NATO submarines. But will they know that American subs did the deed and I am the one who ordered it?

Then I get back to what I was doing before the NATO message arrived and finish sending a flash order to the Marine commander at Reykjavik following up on his recent response to yesterday's inquiry.

"Effective immediately expedite movement of all able-bodied Russian airborne survivors directly to Kansk, Russia using all available means. Similarly expedite all usable captured weapons, ammunition, and parachute gear to Kansk. Ignore troops, weapons, and supplies not immediately deployable. Report shipment quantities and estimated arrival times soonest with hourly updates thereafter. Repatriation operation is code-word classified as "Rosebud Restaurant.""

And, of course, I send a copy of my order to Tommy Talbot with a request that he coordinate and support a maximum effort airlift to get the surviving Russian airborne troops and their weapons and jump gear to Kansk.

Chapter Twenty-five

Intense Fighting.

Crouching in a slit trench outside the Podovsk bunker that was now serving as Sholakov's headquarters was not exactly the best place to ask the General the questions that came in this morning from General Roberts. But the timing was perfect – neither of us would be going anywhere or doing much of anything until the Chinese air attacks stop.

"Uh, Comrade General, I received some information and inquiries from General Roberts an hour ago. I believe you will find the information encouraging."

"By all means, tell me Comrade Colonel Miskin. I really do need some encouraging news," Sholakov replied with a wry smile. "What is the news from Christopher Ivanovich?"

"He sends his regards, Sir. And he wants you know that the Chinese submarines that attacked Kalingrad this morning have apparently been attacked by Russian anti-submarine aircraft and sunk with all hands."

"He also wants you to know that a major effort is underway to repatriate and re-equip the Russian paratroopers captured at Reykjavik. They are being transported to Kansk as we speak. General Roberts says about four thousand of them should be in Kansk and available for you to use by October Twelfth."

"General Roberts also said I should respectfully suggest you consider sending a senior officer to Kansk to take command of your new airborne force. He says the men will begin arriving there in about forty eight hours, but that it is going to take at least five days to airlift in enough weapons, equipment, and ammunition to fully equip them."

"Four thousand airborne troops available at Kansk? That is good news, Comrade American Colonel. Very good news. Do you know why it is good news, Comrade Colonel?"

"I think so, Sir. The airfields at Irkutsk and Angorsk can be reached by Russian transport planes coming off Kansk, particularly if they continue on and land at your nearby auxiliary fields. On the other hand, the Chinese fighters have significantly shorter legs so that Kansk is too far for the Chinese to reach with their fighters based at Irkutsk and Angorsk."

"Exactly so. Perhaps you are a colonel after all," he says with a smile. *I just grin at him.*

"Also Sir, General Roberts requests your permission to be allowed to communicate directly with whomever you place in command of your new force of paratroopers."

"I have just the man for this, Comrade Colonel. Please tell Christopher Ivanovich that General Karatonov will be sent to Kansk immediately to take command. General Karatonov will be authorized to communicate directly with him." *And report to me immediately after each contact.*

******

"General Talbot, Chris Roberts here, Sir."

"Fine, General. Thank you for asking."

"The reason I am calling Sir, is that I need a quick intelligence update about certain Russian capabilities. Hopefully something we can get without asking Moscow or letting them know we are interested."

"Thank you, Sir, I appreciate that. Specifically, we need to know how many Kelt air to ground missiles the Russians have left and where they are located. And we need to know how many of the Tu-16 bombers or other planes that can launch them the Russians have left that are operational and where they are."

"Yes Sir, that is right. We need it yesterday and we do not want Moscow to know we are asking." *I am not going to ask Moscow and I do not want the Chairman or anyone else to ask either. I am afraid the Chinese will hear about it and figure out what Sholakov might be thinking of doing.*

******

Chinese troops and armor are now over the Amur River in force and, following a couple of hours of intense artillery preparation that is now in process, are about to launch major attack up the valley that runs from the Amur River north to Khabarovsk. The Russian artillery has remained quiet and waiting ever since it got pushed back out of range of the newly installed Chinese bridges.

As soon as the Chinese got over the Amur Lieutenant Colonel Stansky's entire battalion of tanks and infantry fighting vehicles was quickly pulled out of the initial fighting - and returned to the hull down positions the battalion prepared before it was sent forward to the Amur. At the moment it is stretched along a tree covered ridge overlooking the little village that sits astride the road running from China to Khabarovsk. *Thank God the army commander is a tanker. He understands how we should fight.*

Stransky himself is standing on his tank with his binoculars to his eyes and alternately looking down at the activity in the village and then at the faint lines he can see running across the Amur to the south – the pontoon bridges the Chinese threw across the river on either side of the destroyed railroad bridge.

The ground is still damp and muddy from the rain that fell this morning as the Chinese were storming across the Amur. Another tank battalion, the one belonging to the 112th Guards, is in a similar line of hull down positions on the ridge on the other side of the valley. *This is not like Afghanistan. Not at all.*

Stranksy is talking to his driver on the tank intercom when he notices a Jeep pull up about sixty meters away on the crest of the ridge to watch as his battalion's remaining T-62s carefully move back into their hull down positions – the positions they abandoned 48 hours earlier when they had been ordered to move closer to the river to help oppose the Chinese crossing.

Wonder who that is? Oh, it's that American tank officer who was hanging around back at the chokepoint asking all the questions. Wonder what he is doing up here. Guess I am about to find out.

"Hello Colonel Stransky" the American says through his interpreter as he walks up and salutes.

"I heard they pulled you back from the river so I thought I would come up and see how you and your battalion are doing. I am glad to see you made it back in one piece. Was it rough down there on the river?"

"Hello yourself American tank officer. I am surprised to see you. I heard all the Americans fled when the shooting started."

"Nope. No such luck. Here I am."

"Well, you better get back in your Jeep and get the hell out of here. The goddamn fuck your mother Chinese are coming and the bastards are dangerous. I lost four of my tanks and a BMD down by the river and only one of the tank crews escaped."

"No shit. Did you get any?"

"*Irina* here," Stansky said patting his tank affectionately, got one tank for sure, and maybe an armored personnel carrier, before we were ordered to pull back. "Some of my men claim they got two or three." *Mostly they lied. But they are good boys.*

"Well this position looks pretty good. You and your boys will get a lot more if the Chinese come up this side of the valley instead of up the middle. Particularly if you wait and let them get into your kill zone." *I wonder if they will wait.*

"You are right about that, Comrade American; about this side of the valley, I mean. Neither my battalion nor the one on the ridge across the way is close enough to the center of the valley to reach the road that runs up its middle - but right behind me, on the other side of this ridge, is all the heavy artillery of one of our divisions and they, so their observers claim, have the road zeroed in." *In the unlikely event the Chinese are dumb enough to use the road.*

"Where are the artillery observers," the American inquires. *I am not going to ask the Colonel how long he thinks the observers will stay before they run?*

"Down there to the right," I say as I point with a thrust of my binoculars towards a distant Jeep with big antennas on it and a couple of men standing next to it.

"It's the 314th's artillery behind me so those are their fire control observers. I do not know whose artillery is beyond the ridge on the other side of the valley. Probably the 93rd Guards." *Fuck the artillery. My job is to destroy any enemy armor and vehicles that attempt to come up this side of the valley and that, by God, is what we are going to do.*"

"Well good luck to you, Colonel, and to your men. I almost wish I could stay with you and see what happens. But I cannot. Orders. So when the Chinese make their move I will have to go. But before I do I am going to visit the artillery behind you - then I am going to get out of Dodge while I still can."

Colonel Stransky's right. It should work. Unless the artillery observers run they should be able to walk the artillery up or down the road depending on where the Chinese are massed. That'll stop the infantry but the chances of a direct hit from behind the ridge are slim - so the Russian artillery is not going to stop the Chinese tanks who come up the middle.

Then Stransky jumps down from his tank and stands next to me while he sweeps the valley with his binoculars. I get my glasses out and do the same. The Chinese artillery barrage is obscuring the view of the river. *I am glad on not down there. I sure hope the Russians pull back in time.*

We may not be able to see the river but we can see what is left of the armor and troops of the Russian infantry division stretched out below us across the floor of the valley. It's just behind the little village whose little log houses are on either side of the road. What was left of the division pulled back into that blocking position behind the village when the Chinese pushed them off the Amur. *Damn I am glad I am not down there in the valley. Those poor bastards are going to take the full brunt of the Chinese attack.*

"General Bulganin's plan is sound," Stransky tells his nervous men over and over again as I walk with him from tank to tank in the bright late morning sun.

"The division in the valley in front of us will hurt them and then fall back and hand off the fight to the 19th Guards. And our comrades in the 19th Guards, in turn, will hurt the Chinese and fall back and hand the fight off to the naval infantry behind them."

"Our job," Stransky repeatedly explains to the tank commanders and then again to the officers of the battalion's command group, "and that of the tank battalion and artillery across the valley is to hit them on the flank as they pass in front of us." *At least, that is the plan. But will it work? And how, for God's sake, will the Chinese react?*

What really bothers both Colonel Stransky and me is that there has been no Russian air support to help the army stop the Chinese advance and take out the Chinese pontoon bridges. The Russian artillery and armor got some of the bridges, but the Chinese built new ones even faster. That enabled the Chinese armor to pour across the river despite the heavy casualties the Russian tanks and the three infantry divisions inflicted on them.

What does it mean that the Russian air force is totally missing? All we've heard are rumors and snippets of information on the radios about Chinese paratroopers and big air battles.

Apparently the Russian troops have not been told anything about the absence of the Russian air force and fear the worst. Stransky's men are obviously worried to the point of hysteria at a couple of the tanks we visited. I am not exactly calm myself. It's no fun being an observer up here without a couple of inches of steel between me and the Chinese.

On the other hand, from what I'd observed, and my translator's take on the radio chatter on our jeep radio, it sounds like the SAMs of the three Russian infantry divisions in the valley made the Chinese attack helicopters and planes pay a terrible price for supporting the Chinese infantry as they came over the river – and took a lot of casualties doing it.

Obviously the Chinese infantry casualties and their helicopter and plane loses have not been enough to stop the Chinese. Hell, when the smoke clears down towards the river anyone up here on the ridge with binoculars will again be able to see the Chinese pontoon bridges and all the armor and vehicles they are steadily bringing across. It won't be long now before they reach us. I wonder who will break first. I hate to say it but I think it will be the Russians.

"Good luck, Comrade Colonel" I tell Stransky as I salute and hold out my hand to him." *I really mean it.*

And then to my interpreter.

"Come on, Simeon, it's time for to get on the other side of this here ridge and try to find a radio so I can call home with a report."

******

All day the men strung out along the little ridge stand on their tanks and watch as more and more Chinese armor and vehicles cross the river and form up on the north side. Then the sun goes down and Stransky and his men spend the entire night anxiously peering through their thermal night vision sights and waiting. Nothing.

Stransky and his men did not know it, and many of them won't live long enough to find out, but the Chinese tanks are not as well equipped as the Russian tanks. They do not have night vision sights.

A heavy Chinese artillery barrage finally begins just before dawn. The valley below is filled with flashes and explosions. The little village and the Russian lines behind it are inundated with fire for almost an hour. Initially there is a little return fire from the Russian artillery further up the valley, but not very much and it soon stops as the Chinese begin dropping counter battery fire on it. The artillery behind us and across the way remains strangely quiet. *I wonder why?*

As my men and I watch, the Russian division dug in behind the little village takes the brunt of the Chinese barrage. It has obviously already suffered serious casualties from the Chinese artillery and is barely able to defend itself by the time the massive tank-led Chinese advance starts forward at dawn. It breaks almost immediately. We watch from the ridge as the division's men and vehicles begin to stream to the rear in the midst of smoke and explosions.

******

General Bulganin, himself, stands on his command BMD and orchestrates the Russian response as the Chinese attempt to breakout of their beachhead of the north side of the Amur. He is watching from the north end of Stransky's ridge when he orders the Russian heavy artillery to commence firing and the two tank battalions on the ridges in front of the artillery to hold their fire.

Russian artillery begins raining down on the advancing Chinese. In the smoke and confusion it is difficult for the Chinese to determine where the Russian artillery fire is coming from. The helicopters they send forward to scout the Russian positions are immediately shot down by handheld Russian SAMs. As a result, the Chinese mistakenly assume the artillery fire is coming from their front and, after two or three minutes, the Chinese artillery begins firing counter battery fire over the heads of the retreating Russians and into the approaches to Kharbarovsk.

Chinese counter-battery fire continues to slam into the general area of where the Chinese think the Russian artillery might be located as the mangled Russian Guards division in front of Stransky and his tanks puts up a brief fight, a very brief fight, and then tries to pull back.

Almost immediately the entire Chinese army surges forward to move up the valley in a great mass attack. It is led by hundreds of Chinese tanks, armored personnel carriers, and self-propelled artillery – and, as they move forward without any air cover, they begin to pass directly in front of the ridge where my hull-down tanks and BDMs are dug in under their camouflage nets. The observers for the heavy artillery are positioned behind the ridge to their rear a behind us on the crest of the ridge.

This is impossible. Surely the Chinese know we are here. Is it possible they do not because their communications are so poor or our SAMs knocked down all the helicopters that came this way and might have seen us?

Bulganin repeatedly orders Colonel Stransky and his counterpart across the way to hold their fire. And each time Ivan dutifully orders his surviving forty nine T-62 tanks and twenty two BMD fighting vehicles to hold their fire.

"This is Tabriz one. Remember your orders. Hold your fire until I give the word. Pick three or four of the Chinese tanks and BMDs immediately in front of you and be ready to hit them quickly when I give the order. If your targets pass by pick three or four more. And do not forget; when I do give the order you are to keep firing anytime you have a good target."

Then Stransky remembers that the lieutenants commanding his two platoons of SAM shooters would also be listening on the battalion net. So he added "SAM shooters are, of course, to immediately fire anytime a plane or helicopter comes within range. Do not wait a second. They won't be ours." *No goddamnit they won't be ours.*

******

About ten minutes after dawn the Chinese mass begins moving up the valley. And it keeps moving until it moves through the little village and fills the valley all along the entire front of Stransky's two kilometer-long line of Russian armor on the ridge. *That is when he suddenly realized he has an uncontrollable urge to poop. Well it has been quite a while.*

Then the inevitable happens. One of Stransky's gunners cannot contain himself; or perhaps he squeezes the trigger by mistake. It does not matter. The cat is out of the bag.

"Fire," screams Stransky into the battalion radio net on his tank commander's microphone. "Fire." *And promptly forgets about his once desperate need to relieve himself.*

Stransky's tank fires and lurches backward before even before he finishes shouting his second "fire" into the mike. He knows his tank commanders will have to see what they are doing so they can make every shot count. So before the battle even starts he orders them to stay in their turrets in the open for as long as possible. Only when they begin drawing return fire are they to drop into their tanks and shut their hatches behind them. At least that is the order he is given.

Stransky has barely a moment to register the effect of his battalion's initial salvo when his tank lurches and fires again. And it continues to lurch and fire and lurch and fire until somewhere in the back of his mind he comes to realize that the battalion across the way and the artillery behind them are also firing.

He is wearing his leather helmet and the bulky earphones designed to protect his hearing but the noise is beyond anything he has ever experienced. His ears begin to ache and the noise overwhelms him.

The scene in the smoke-filled valley below is surreal, the colonel is thinking as his tank bucks and shudders under his feet. Chinese tanks and vehicles are puffing up black smoke and on fire everywhere – and those that are not destroyed merely drive around them and continue to move up the valley. *Yes, he thought, I should have become an architect.*

******

"Colonel Sir, gunner here" ... "Colonel, are you alright Sir?" ... "Colonel?" He became aware that someone is pounding on his leg.

"Oh" ... "Yes Piotr, what is it?"

"Vassily says we are running out of armor piercing ammunition, Sir. Should I start using the HE or the AP? Others are asking too, Sir?" ... "Is everything okay, Sir?"

"Oh yes. I am okay thank you." *My God, what happened?*

Then I suddenly realize I'd been staring in fascination for some time at the terrible destruction in the valley. *It was like I was hypnotized.* He is still shaking his head in surprise when the Chinese MiG flashes along the top of the ridge and unleashes the rockets that blow him to pieces.

Seconds later a Russian SAM fired by an infantry conscript from Smolensk reaches backwards from behind the line of tanks and plucks the MiG from the sky. If anyone had being looking they would have seen the light that flares as it crashes right at the snowline of the mountain beyond the ridge.

******

My Chinese railroad repair crew and I can see the locomotive of the idled train hanging over the edge of the bridge. The flat cars loaded with military equipment and troops are stretched out behind it all the way back to where the track curves its way around the side of the hill. Some of the men have dismounted and are pissing and shitting along the tracks.

The train had obviously been going slow when the engine driver saw the destroyed bridge and slammed on the brakes. That is crew supervisor Zhang's first thought. Then he sees the engine driver and his assistant waving frantically from the nose down locomotive hanging out over the water.

"Well," Zhang tells his crew as he waves back. "First things first. We will have to get Old Chou out of the locomotive before he has a heart attack." *I wonder what happened.*

******

The Chinese Central Committee members are well satisfied with what they hear later that afternoon.

"The war continues to go well, comrades," booms Marshall Wu with a satisfied smile. "I have just gotten off the phone with Red Banner Street. The runways we captured at the Irkutsk and Angarsk air fields have been cleared and are already receiving our fighters. Indeed, and well ahead of schedule, our pilots have already begun flying missions to intercept any Russian transports that might try to bring in reinforcements and supplies from Moscow and the west."

"Also I am pleased to report that the second phase of our major attacks towards Vladivostok and Khabarovsk began right on schedule at 1420 this afternoon. It is, of course, much too early to know how they are proceeding. I hope to have much more to report to you at tomorrow morning's briefing."

"Russian ground forces, as expected, have launched major efforts to retake the airfields east of Lake Baikal from our parachute volunteers. They will, as we know, succeed. But it will be at great cost and it will be too late - our men will have already destroyed all their planes, arms, and refueling facilities."

"Finally, I am pleased to report that this evening at 2100 there will be food and entertainment in the Party Pavilion. A troupe of Red Army singers will sing for us."

There are many questions but everyone seems quite pleased.

******

Dick and I jump up with our binoculars when the Russian troops around us start shouting and stand to their positions. The sun is still about an hour away from going down in the west and there appears to be movement in the tree line across the way from Bikin and the railroad line. The fourth troop train of the day clanked through the village an hour ago, its flatcars stuffed with troops and armor moving north.

According to Colonel Naumenko, if the tracks are cut beyond Bikin, the train commander's orders are to use the rails and equipment his train is carrying to repair them and keep going. If repair is totally impossible he is to dismount his men and fight his way north until he reaches the Russian forces dug in south of Khabarovsk.

It's been several hours since the Chinese in the forest across the way from us have been heard from. But they are almost certainly still there in the trees on the hill in front of us. All that movement likely means they are getting ready for another attack. Probably sometime after the sun goes down in about thirty minutes.

Wonder if they will hit us immediately or wait until it's oh dark hundred in the middle of the night. I'd just as soon get it over with. That way there'll be more hours of darkness to get away in if the Russians are overrun and Evans and I have to boogie.

Major Evans and I are eyeballing the tree line closely because Colonel Naumenko accepted Evan's suggestion that the Russians hit the Chinese with a preemptive strike if at all possible. The Russians are suddenly going to simultaneously fire all their mortars and tank tubes at the forest behind the tree line about thirty minutes after the sun goes down. With a little luck they will catch the Chinese out in the open while they are forming up for the attack we all know is coming.

Runners are passing the word for the mortar crews to bring their rounds forward and get ready. Everyone with a weapon that can reach the tree line, even the tanks, will fire ten airburst rounds as fast as possible when Colonel Naumenko fires a red smoke flare. They are to start just inside the tree line and walk their fire deeper and deeper into the trees in twenty five meter increments. The entire exercise will be repeated again in two or three hours.

******

A runner from the colonel showed up while we were peering over the top of the trench waiting for the big show to start. He chattered away with Eugene, our balding little interpreter, and then turned around and jogged back towards Naumenko's position. Eugene motioned us to follow him.

"Colonel want talk you."

Colonel Naumenko greets us with a smile and an apology. It seems that Harry and I have again been ordered to evacuate by Russian headquarters. But there is a problem, a big one - no one can come up with a way to get a helicopter in here to pick us up. At the moment, it seems, there are none available within a thousand miles.

Naumenko understands the significance of Harry and me being captured and the dim prospects of his isolated brigade. He also knows, and so do we, that sooner or later Bikin is going to be overrun. Perhaps in the next few hours. Accordingly, he orders Harry and me to retreat down the railroad line to the bridges and cross them before they are cut. Then we are to continue on south to Vladivostok and safety, legging it all the way if necessary.

"Frankly," he tells us after I walk over to see him and get the word that we are to leave, "You have been so useful I was tempted to pretend the message was not received." Then we shake hands and give each other big comradely hugs and a kiss on both cheeks. *We have known each other as men who can be depended on under fire. It's a bond that never expires.*

Harry and I talk it over and our plan is simple. As soon as it gets dark we are going to put one of the old rusty handcars on the track, throw on our weapons and some water and rations, and pump our way south towards Vladivostok as fast as we can go. We will take Eugene with us and go as far as we can on the pumper - and then start walking. *With a little luck the bridges will still be up and we won't have to swim.*

We plan to start when the second round of preemptive fire starts a couple of hours after sundown. Eugene and a Russian volunteer will go with us to help pump the little cart southward.

Naumenko is quite helpful. He uses the radio in one of the tanks to contact Major Malinovsky, the commander of the army and Spetsnaz troops at the bridges, and orders him to alert his men that we are coming and to provide whatever help he can. *Christ, I hope the bridges are still up when we get there. It's probably not too cold to swim but we will sure as hell die of hypothermia when we get out wearing wet clothes.*

"Eugene, please see if you can get a couple of cigarette lighters for each of us. Here's some money; buy them from the smokers."

* * * * * *

We get back to our equipment in the slit trench right after the sun goes down, just in time to watch the big show. We had barely reached our position when a red smoke flare zooms up from somewhere – and all hell breaks loose.

All around us we could hear the click and thump as mortar rounds are rapidly dropped into the mortar tubes and head *we hope* towards the Chinese. A few seconds later, so they would have the same time on target, the brigade's three tanks fired their cannons and the four BMDs began raking the tree line with their chain guns.

Suddenly the unseen forest behind the tree line erupts in smoke and flashes. It goes on for over a minute as every weapon that can reach the tree line discharges its allotted ten rounds. Then everything goes quiet. Ten minutes later the smoke dissipates. It's as if nothing had happened.

Harry and I will leave when Naumenko hits them again with the second barrage in about two hours.

Chapter Twenty-six

Time to move on.

We are as ready to go as we will ever be. As soon as the flare goes up and the firing for the second preemptive round of shelling begins we manhandle the hand pumper on to the nearest set of tracks, throw on our backpacks full of food and ammunition, and begin pumping like hell. Our AK-47s are slung on our backs and our pockets are stuffed with ration cans, cigarette lighters, and ammunition.

Our hand cart is moving right along when the Russians stop firing. *Damn this is sort of fun even if I cannot see where we are going.*

About thirty minutes and five or six miles later we are on the right hand track and boogying right along in the darkness towards the bridges when something suddenly dawns on me. I can actually feel the hair on the back of my neck rise.

"Jeez, Harry," I pant in a whisper, "Something just dawned on me. The goddamn Russians drive on the goddamn left side of the road. We are going south on the northbound track. Did not the colonel say that there is another troop train coming about now?"

"Christ, you are right. And the fucker will be running without lights."

"Stop," I whisper urgently. "Halt." Even the Russian who does not speak English instantly picks up the command. We coast for a few feet and stop.

"Quiet," I snap. "Everyone listen"… "Oh shit here it comes."

"Hurry," I shout needlessly as we all leap off the handcar and rush to lift it on one side in order to tip it off the tracks along with all our gear. It takes only a couple of seconds.

"Everyone off the roadbed and get down," I order in a stage whisper.

And not a moment too soon. Less than a minute later we can hear the distinctive sound of a handcar pumping its way towards us in the dark. Then, even before the hand pumper reaches us, we can hear the distinctive chuff of a coal powered steam engine coming towards us from further down the track.

"Stay down for Chrissake. Do not move" I whisper. "If they see us they will think we are fucking Chinese."

We freeze as first the hand car clatters by and then the front of a flat car with what looked like a BMD on it looms out of the darkness provided by the cloud covering the moon. There isn't a light to be seen as the long unlit train following them slowly rumbles by. Several times we hear voices without being able to see who is doing the talking.

It is so dark that even from fifteen feet away where we huddle at the bottom of the track embankment we cannot count the cars or see what they are carrying. There must have been quite a number of cars - it seems to take forever before the three big locomotives pushing them chug by and disappear into the darkness as if they are ghosts.

* * * * * *

We tipped our hand pumper back on the track, which took some doing in the darkness, and continued pumping our way south for about thirty minutes when the sky behind us was suddenly lit by flares and the sound of shooting and explosions filled the night.

Two pre-emptive barrages had not stopped the Chinese. Naumenko's little brigade of soldiers and naval infantry at Bikin is obviously once again under heavy attack. Ominously, the number of flares going up seems to diminish and several times the noise seems to get louder even as we get further and further away. *Truth be told, I feel more than a little bit guilty that Major Evans and I are not there to help.*

Naumenko's two bouts of preemptive counter fire devastate the Chinese coming out of the trees, particularly the second. Even so, the survivors had attacked on schedule. Failure to do so would have resulted in immediate and very severe punishments. In essence, they had to attack or they'd die for certain. The division commander and his political commissioner are fanatics for discipline even if they are safely out of danger themselves.

Unlike the morning attack, however, this time the Chinese charging into the open area in front of the tree line are supported by a similar mass attack from two battalions of Chinese who had spent the day infiltrating across the rail line further to the north so they could swing around and simultaneously attack the Russians positions from the rear.

Following their orders, the attackers in the rear wait in the darkness for a full three minutes after the Chinese in front of the Russians came charging out of the tree line and the shooting starts. The idea is for them to hit the Russian rear and roll it up while the Russians are fully engaged with the Chinese human wave attack coming out of the trees. It does not work.

That the Chinese would circle around behind them and attack the Russian rear is such an obvious move that Naumenko and his troops expect it. The turrets and machine guns on some of the tanks and BDMs quickly swivel around to face the rear and so do the Russian Marines and army troops in the second line of positions.

What was not expected by either side is that the train, which had passed us about half an hour earlier, would arrive as the fighting intensifies and pass right through the charging mass of Chinese hitting Naumenko's rear.

"Get on the floor and keep going." That is what the engine driver had been ordered to do if the train is attacked and that is what he does.

The men on the train, two battalions of armored infantry from 97th Guards, do not have a clue as to what is happening. All they know is that people on both sides of the train are shooting at them. So they fire back just as they have been ordered to do if the train is attacked.

In fact, no one is shooting at them. It just looks that way because they are passing through a battlefield and are in the crossfire of the two opposing forces. But it does not matter. The reality is that the train, carrying well over a hundred tanks and infantry fighting vehicles, has much more fire power than Naumenko's troops and the Chinese attackers combined. The men of the 97th fire at everything that moves as the train slowly clanks its way through the battlefield under the glare of the flares fired from the train's flat cars and gravel cars.

By the time the train passes out from under the light of the flares, the Chinese attackers have been cut to shreds and Naumenko has lost all of his tanks and BMDs and at least half of his Marines and army troops. Almost a hundred men on the train are killed or wounded.

******

Chief Matthews' offer of big money enticed all but two of the original swimmers to go out again. It probably helps that the swimmers and helicopter pilots had been immediately handed a Russian medal and packets of crisp new twenty dollar bills as soon as they returned from their first mission. Forty one of the original fifty three swimmers returned safely and several more are believed to be still on their way back.

Thirty nine of the original swimmers will go out again tonight plus one who had been too drunk to go last night and three new arrivals. They will hit more of the Chinese rail and road bridges being used to support the invasion. Those going out for the first time will be teamed with the swimmers who succeeded and came back last night.

******

"Gunfighter," Navy Lieutenant Vladimer "Vladi" Borz, and his four squadron mates of the carrier *Kiev*'s 107th squadron barely reach Podovsk in time to refuel when their squadron of Navy YAK-38s is thrown into the battle against the Chinese. Originally the "Cowboys" had been fourteen. But five did not return from the first of the two night time sorties against the Chinese and three from the second. And poor Igor, radio name "Sidekick," was lost when their AWACS controller vectored them to the dirt emergency strip twenty miles south of Podovsk after their second mission.

"It is flying at night that is the problem, not the combat," Gunfighter explained to the others in the pilots' meeting before they lift off from the emergency field for the short flight back to Podovsk. Everyone is certain he is right. They are, after all, the best of the best and famous throughout Russia - because of a news show a few years ago that made much of the radio names they adopted after watching dubbed Italian cowboy movies.

The Cowboys are sure it was the darkness and the terrible AWACs controllers who caused their casualties, not the combat. The Chinese pilots, they keep assuring each other, are not worth a damn.

Landing on the emergency field right after sunup had been a piece of cake for all them. Its length was endless compared to the short deck of the *Kiev*. Sidekick, they all agreed, had forgotten for a few seconds that there would be no arresting cable. That is why he'd run off the end of the runway and exploded his plane.

Or maybe his brakes failed. The 107th is famous for its cowboy attitude, not its maintenance. The squadron maintenance officer, God rest his soul, had preferred to fly and read girlie magazines from Romania.

Arkhara Airfield is open and ready to resume limited operations. Its ground crews and "volunteers" from its infantry defenders work all day to get it ready. And they do—they finish clearing the wreckage and debris from this morning's assault by the Chinese paratroopers by late in afternoon.

The Cowboys may be back at Arkhara and their planes may be refueled and ready, but Gunfighter and four his fellow pilots are not. He and the other pilots have been awake for more than sixty straight hours. They'd spent the day at the emergency field trying to sleep - first on the ground and then in their cockpits. But it had been impossible. Too cold.

In a word, they are totally exhausted after two nights without sleep, two incredibly tense combat missions, and an emotionally draining hour spent trying to unhook a mangled and scorched Sidekick from his ejection seat - which had not fired him high enough into the air when he tried to eject out of the flames of his crashed plane.

An officious Lieutenant Colonel tried to assign a mission to the Cowboys as soon as they landed. Vlad is the senior surviving Cowboy and the acting squadron leader. He did not exactly refuse the assignment; he just put his head down on the table and fell asleep while the colonel was telling him how important it is that he and the others fly again as soon as their planes finish being refueled and rearmed.

Six hours of sleep and a good meal later it is dark, their planes have been refueled and rearmed, and Vlad and his men are finally ready to go. *Fuck your mother, I am the senior officer and commanding the squadron. And I have got six kills already. Can it be true?*

******

Russian helicopters and tanks are back in action in front of Khabarovsk. They are counterattacking the Chinese and using their night vision sights to great effect. Vlad and his Cowboys do not know any of this – just that they are needed at Khabarovsk because all of its planes were destroyed by Chinese paratroopers.

They had taken off from Arkhara in the darkness and been sent to Khabarovsk to refuel. Finally, a little after midnight, they climb out of Khabarovsk to thirty thousand feet and report their availability to the area AWACS.

"Kiev 107 plus four."

Their AWACs controller can see from their IFF designators that they are Navy YAK-38s. *That is good.*

"Kiev 107 turn right heading 270. Descend to ten. Targets three Chinese MiG-21s at seven.

Two minutes later Vlad sees the blinking icons of two Chinese fighters appear on his radar screen and fires two Aphid missiles. Seconds later one of the icons brightens into little flecks of light and disappears. "That is seven," Gunfighter announces as he reefs his plane around in a tight turn - and collides with the Moscow Kid.

******

It's an hour or so after midnight and we are pumping away without a clue as to how close we are to the bridges south of Bikin. All we know for sure is that the bridges are somewhere up ahead of us in the darkness. That is more than a bit worrisome because the three Russian infantry companies defending the bridges are undoubtedly filled with undisciplined conscripts, terrified kids who will start shooting without thinking when they hear us coming.

I do not know about Harry and the two Russians but in addition to getting more and more worried, I am getting more and more bushed and my hands are getting seriously blistered. *Eugene is certainly smarter and colder than we are; over an hour ago he took off his shirt and wrapped it around the metal pumping bar he is holding.*

"Hold up," I finally whisper as I stop pumping. "Let's listen. We do not want to get our asses shot off by some seventeen year old kid with a gun and six weeks of basic training."

"Good idea," Harry says as we coast to a stop. "I have been thinking the same thing. But what the fuck are we going to do about it?"

The night is dark and silent. Really silent. Not even a breeze to rustle the leaves of the trees and bushes that crowd the embankment all the way up to the rails. We wait and listen for what seems like a very long time. Absolutely nothing.

Then I almost had a heart attack.

"Amerikanski?" The quiet voice comes out of the pitch black darkness.

"Da. Da." We all answer almost simultaneously, every one of us. I instinctively step off the hand cart and stumble to the ground as I fumble for my weapon. Harry is even faster. I can barely make him out even though he is only a few feet away; by the time my foot hits the ground he is already stepped off the cart. At the moment he is backing away down the side of the embankment with his weapon up.

A terse flood of Russian comes from somewhere in the darkness. Obviously a question. Eugene responds with his own question. I do not know what Eugene is saying but relief is evident in his voice.

My heart is beating a hundred miles an hour as I stand up straight and re-sling my weapon.

******

Chinese and Russians troops are not the only ones on the move tonight. At 0120 in the morning at least ten divisions of the impoverished quasi-kingdom of North Korea surge across the Russian border towards Vladivostok all along the North Korean border with Russia south of Vladivostok.

North Korea's invasion is a highly concentrated because North Korea has only seventeen kilometers of border with Russia. The North Koreans quickly get across the Tumen River both by using crude wooden boats and by marching on wooden planks laid across the Tumen River Railroad Bridge that brings the Trans-Siberian Railroad into North Korea.

The handful of surprised Russian Frontier Guards on the border do not have a chance. They are quickly overwhelmed by a massive human wave of North Korean infantry. The small and rundown Russian border city of Khasan falls instantly without a fight and the North Koreans march through it without breaking stride.

North Korea's propaganda ministry immediately goes on the air to explain that North Korea has been forced to join the war because of its mutual defense treaty with China. Their rapid response to the Russian attack, the North Koreans tell the world and those few of its citizens lucky enough to have radios, will relieve pressure on the Chinese and help assure a communist victory.

Whatever the motivation and explanations of the North Koreans, the result is that the outnumbered Russian defenders on the outskirts of Vladivostok now face another and even larger invasion force.

****** *China*

China's politicians and military leaders are equally surprised and furious. The middle of the night phone call alerting the Party Chairman about the North Korean invasion is not going well for the embarrassed general in charge Chinese intelligence whose agency had not seen it coming.

"But look at it this way Comrade Chairman," explains the embarrassed general in charge of Chinese intelligence. "We are only attacking Vladivostok to draw the Russian reserves away from Chita and the Amur River border. Now the Koreans are doing it for us. It means we can withdraw our troops and send them to Chita to join the real battle."

"Yes," fumes the Party Chairman. "That is correct. But if that goddamn little shit takes Vladivostok he'll try to hold on to it - they will replace the Russians and we will still be cut off from access to that part of the Sea of Japan."

******

Vladivostok's docks were brightly lit by their overhead floodlights. It was the second night of the war and the rumbling thunder of artillery fire could be heard both to the north from the Chinese Front and to the southwest from the new Korean Front. The level of activity at the port remained high as many of the ships of the Russian Navy were still arriving with their cargos of troops and equipment.

One long train of flatcars was on the dock spur frantically loading newly arrived troops and equipment destined for Kharbarovsk and the interior. Another long line of flatcars was standing by on a nearby spur on the dock waiting its turn.

Newly landed troops did not need to be told to hurry. They were moving fast because they can hear the distant rumble of the artillery and fear being caught out in the open by a Chinese air attack; the senior officer on the scene, who had not slept for almost seventy two hours, was pushing them hard because he fears the rail line will soon be cut. *If it isn't already.*

The major supervising the unloading of the casualties from Bikin knows exactly what the casualties and the distant thunder mean – the railroad is either cut or about to be cut. *God, I am glad they sent me here instead of with that brigade. Poor Naumenko.*

Troops continued to arrive at the port after the wounded had been removed from the train that carried them south from Bikin – but they can see the blood stains and debris and instinctively know what they mean. The troops and armor now arriving are mainly from the missile destroyer *Resolute*. The ship itself is lashed to a pier about a mile away to keep it from sinking.

Resolute's sailors do not know it yet but in an hour or so they too will double-time down to the railroad spur and be sent north to the front as infantry replacements. Only when the railroad is cut will newly arriving personnel be kept at Vladivostok and used to help shore up the port's crumbling defense lines.

******

We are picking up the last of our wounded early in morning when one of the men runs in to report a train came through heading south to the port. I order Lieutenant Gorby to flag it down. The train is an empty heading south to pick up reinforcements and equipment at Vladivostok. It may get to the port but it almost certainly won't be coming back; the railroad is effectively cut because we are out of ammunition and I have less than fifty able bodied men left here at Bikin and another three hundred and fifty at the bridges.

Whether headquarters likes it, or not, it's time to go. The Chinese are strangely silent as we hurriedly load our dead and wounded. I wish I had a radio left so I could report my decision.

Three hours later, a few minutes after the sun comes up and we make one last check of the battlefield to pick up any of our dead and wounded we missed in the darkness, the locomotive of the empty train I have taken over begins puffing big black smoke rings and we rattle our way out of Biken. We are headed south to the port with our dead and wounded. In a little while we will stop at the bridges and pick up the men on duty there.

Since I have no way to load them, I am going to order the armor and mortar trucks at the bridges to pull out immediately and drive south on the road to the port. *There is no military advantage to be gained by leaving them here now that the line is cut.*

Once we are gone the only troops remaining at the bridges and along this part of the rail line will be the Spetsnaz. I am going to order the captain commanding them to wait for his long range patrols to come in and then lead his men north to Bikin to patrol the bridges and rail line as snipers and skirmishers. Hopefully they will be able to keep the Chinese survivors away from the village and railroad for a few hours longer.

An hour later the Spetsnaz captain and three of his men stand at attention and salute as the flatcars carrying our hastily loaded men and our dead and wounded clatter over the last bridge and head for Vladivostok.

Chapter Twenty-seven

A new development.

It was late afternoon in France, just after dawn in the Russian East, when a flash message came in reporting the North Korean invasion of Russia. General Talbot called a few minutes later with the same information. *It does not make sense. Why would the Chinese want the Koreans involved?*

I called Sholakov immediately. He had already gotten the word via a number of highly agitated calls, first from the commander of the Vladivostok Front and then from assorted generals in Moscow.

And as might be expected, the Russians are surprised and furious.

"Well, now I know where the first nuclear bombs are going to go if we have to use them," is the first thing Sholakov says when I reach him.

Then he adds ominously, "and it looks like we will."

"Do not do anything rash," I caution him. "I am beginning to think it may not be as bad as it looks. I have got an idea Yuri Andreovich. Let me and my team think about it and get back to you in an hour or so."

Sholakov and the Chinese are not the only ones surprised by the North Korean invasion. We all are. It is a major intelligence failure.

Two hours later we again discuss how he might respond.

"Only one idea comes to mind at the moment," I say and explain it. "In the United States," I say after I finish explaining, "we call it making lemonade when life gives you lemons."

Then I leave him with a cheery "And Yuri Andreovich please do not use your nukes until you have a better idea of what's happening and we have a chance to talk again."

After talking to Sholakov, I call Moscow and inform Marshal Petrov of the intelligence report I have just received from the Pentagon. He, of course, already knows about the North Korean invasion and rather proudly informs me he already knows. Then I tell him that I'd just talked to General Sholakov and that he is busy stripping his units around Chita and Khabarovsk for reinforcements to send to Vladivostok to help counter the North Koreans. *It's a lie, of course, but Petrov believes it and I want the Chinese to get the message about troops being withdrawn from Chita so they will leave the railroad open for a while longer.*

In a few minutes Sholakov himself is going to call Petrov and give him more details about the "reinforcements he is hurriedly gathering to send south to beef up the Russian forces around Vladivostok."

In fact, just the reverse is true. The Kremlin and Marshal Petrov's office have serious leaks. Sholakov is going to take advantage of the leaks to try to mislead the Chinese into leaving the railroad open for as long as possible so it can "carry reinforcements south to fight the North Koreans" — *keeping the railroad line to the port open so it can be used to carry more troops and equipment north to Chita is the lemonade Sholakov is going to make from the lemon of the North Korean invasion.*

******

Right after dawn most of the surviving Russian planes return to their home fields from the auxiliary fields where they had been hurriedly dispersed. There are only a little more than a hundred planes left of the eleven hundred or so that flew off to engage the Chinese less than forty eight hours ago. They are basically all that is left of the Russian air force's fighters and fighter bombers.

Russia's airfields are not the only ones that start landing planes when the sun came up on the second day of the war. A steady stream of Chinese fighters and transport planes is coming over Mongolia and going into Irkutsk and Angarsk. And further to the west Russian and American transports are landing at Kansk with the first of the repatriated airborne troops from Reykjavik and all the other Russian paratroopers and Spetsnaz troops Moscow can scrape together.

******

In Washington the National Security Council is meeting to consider the North Korean invasion and how we might respond to the entry of the North Koreans into the Sino-Russian war. Midway through the meeting Tony Talbot mentioned that they might want to get my input. *It seems Dick Spelling told him I have a long-standing and deep personal friendship with the commander of the South Korean armed forces.*

I am just driving into the parking lot at the Detachment when an anxious Dave Shelton comes running out the door pumping his arm up and down with a clenched fist in the age-old military signal to hurry. So, instead of parking in my usual spot, I drive right up to the front door and jump out just as my mobile phone begins beeping.

"Hurry Chris, the White House is on the line."

I join the teleconference in time to hear the President report that he has just spoken to the South Korean

President and learned that the South Korean military wants to help the Russians fight the North Koreans. If they receive permission from the South Korean government they will send supplies and equipment to the Russians via an airlift and ocean shipments to Vladivostok.

Then there is a lot of meaningless discussion about this and that. The only consensus seems to be that everyone is pleased that both the Russians and the Chinese are pissed at the "Kingdom." *Yes, in private, the President often swears like a trooper.*

But military aid from South Korea is not a certainty. South Korea's Prime Minister is not convinced. His view is that South Korea should stay out of the war and let the three belligerents fight it out.

"The Chinese and Russians have constantly helped those idiots in the North threaten us; a pox on all their houses. I hope they all destroy each other." *Cannot say as I blame him.*

The "ping" as I join the meeting alerts everyone that I am on the line.

"General Roberts," I announce when the President finishes speaking.

"Ah, General Roberts. So good of you to join us. *Is he being sarcastic?* Ah, General, we are discussing last night's invasion of Russia by the North Koreans. General Talbot suggests you might have a close relationship with the Commander of the South Korean army. Is that correct?"

"Yes Mister President, that is correct. General Kim is an old and dear friend from when we were junior officers fighting together against the Chinese in Korea. He is a great friend of the United States. As you might remember, Sir, When the Soviets attacked NATO he contacted us and offered all kinds of support even before we had a chance to ask for it."

"Oh. Yes I do remember. And you are right, he is a good friend."

"Yes Sir, he is."

"Ah General, in a couple of hours the United Nations Security Council is going to meet to discuss the North Korean entry into the Sino-Russian war. Do you think you might be able to reach General Kim and get his view of the situation? In particular, does he think the North Koreans are helping the Chinese as the media suggests or are they going against the Chinese and trying to take Vladivostok for themselves?

"Yes Sir, I think I understand what you want to know. I will attempt to reach General Kim immediately."

"Excellent. Please do. We need information about the North Korean invasion so we can take an appropriate position at the Security Council meeting. Unfortunately, that part of Russia is very isolated and we have no there who can tell us what is actually happening. Even the media does not seem to have anyone there."

"Uh. Actually, Mr. President, we may have people there. Two of my aides may still be in the area. They were supposed to leave before the war started. Unfortunately, the Russian helicopter sent to extract them crashed and they are apparently still there. I will try to contact them and see if they can find out what's happening."

******

It is the second morning of the war as the Chinese Politboro assembles for their regularly scheduled morning briefing. Most of the members have already heard rumors of a "Korean problem." They ask each other what they know about it as they walk from their villas to the Party's conference center.

Even so, General Wu surprises everyone when he informs them of the size of the North Korean invasion. Other than that, the tone of the General Wu's briefing is very positive.

"Things continue to go well for us, Comrades," Wu reports. Then he described the continuing advances towards Khabarovsk and Vladivostok and provided more details about the arrival of Chinese planes at Irkutsk and Angarsk.

"Our planes coming from those fields are beginning operations this very morning to intercept the flow of reinforcements coming in by air from Moscow."

Wu is just finishing and putting down his notes when an aide comes in and hands him a note. The others watch intently as he reads it and smiles.

"We have just received more good new, Comrades. The Russians have begun moving reinforcements towards Vladivostok to help counter the Koreans. The 114th division at Bikin reports the Russians suddenly pulled out all their men and put them on a southbound train heading towards Vladivostok. Also a high level Third Department source reports that the Russians intend to move troops and armor south from Chita and Kharbarovsk. It appears our strategy is working." *I am not going to tell them the 114th has been totally destroyed and only has a handful of men left to act as observers.*

There were satisfied nods and grunts from around the table. Several members light celebratory cigarettes.

North Korea's invasion is a big exception to all the good news. To a man, the men around the table are furious with the unexpected behavior of the North Koreans and that is what they want to talk about.

"The damn dwarfs are trying to take territory that belongs to us," snarls Chairman Li after the Marshal finishes his report. The others nod in angry agreement.

"It's bad enough they do this without telling us," Li says sarcastically, "but what really angers me is that I tried to call his highness and they would not put me through."

"Such an insult after all we have done for them. It's unbelievable," the Deputy Party Secretary says with an irate tone in his voice.

"Perhaps it's time to send them a message," suggests the Premier. There are growls and nods of agreement from all around the table.

******

Later that morning Chinese planes from Irkutsk begin attempting to intercept Russian cargo planes heading east with reinforcements and supplies. They do not have much success. According to the Chinese AWACs the Russian transports are stopping at Kansk.

"They are afraid of going further," the commander of the Red Army's air force explains to the Politburo.

"It's a pity our fighters do not have the range to reach Kansk and teach them a lesson," he laments.

******

Eugene and the Spetsnaz troops who materialize out of the darkness have a brief conversation. Our volunteer pumper leans in and listens, but he does not say a word. Then the Spetsnaz huddle briefly and their leader assigns two men to lead us to their headquarters at the bridges. According to Eugene it will take about three hours of walking on the footpath along the tracks.

At the insistence of the Spetsnaz we leave the pumper behind some bushes on the side of the roadbed. Then we walk silently down the tracks. One of them says something in Russian and disappears into the darkness ahead of us. The other walks with us. Their faces, unlike ours, are blackened. If they had not said anything we would have gone right by them without seeing a thing. *Damn I wish we had some blackening cream.*

About two hours later a southbound hand pumper suddenly emerges from the darkness behind us and scares me half to death. We jump off the roadbed and then freeze while our black-faced guide calls out to the two pumpers. The startled men stop pumping and there is a lot of talking. A couple of minutes we crowd aboard and help the two pumpers frantically pump to get far enough ahead of the unseen train we can hear coming up behind us.

Our Spetsnaz guides do not say a word as the four of us climb on the handcar and begin pumping our way south. They just disappear back into the darkness. Ten minutes later we pass over the first of the bridges.

The sun is just coming up as we pump our way over the last bridge and Eugene says, "Is okay. Halt here. Train is coming." We coast to a stop and tip the hand cart off the rails like practiced professionals. A few minutes later the train coming in behind us chugs over the bridge and slows to a stop as its flat cars loaded with troops passed in front of us. They pour off morosely and began to pee and poop everywhere.

"Jesus Harry, look."

Two flat cars to my left contain an appalling sight - uniformed corpses stacked on top of each other five or six high. Russian uniforms. One of them is wearing the uniform of a major in the naval infantry. They are Naumenko's men from Bikin!

******

We walk along the train to a group of men up front by the engines. One of them is Colonel Naumenko and he is as surprised to see us as we are surprised to see him. But he gives us a brief wave and a nod.

"Wait here," he commands the men to whom he is talking as we walk up and takes a couple of steps towards us. *He is got a bandage on the side of his face and he looks exhausted.*

"I am surprised to see you" Naumenko offers as we exchange salutes and then warm handshakes. "But I am certainly glad to know you are alive. I do not have time to talk so you best get on the train and find a place. We will be pulling out as soon as the men stationed here at the bridge get loaded." Then he turns back to the two men and resumes talking to them – giving them orders from the looks of it.

Eugene is deep in conversation with some of the men who on the train. Ten minutes later we know the sad details of what happened at Bikin and a brief toot of the locomotive's horn causes the Russians to scramble to board the train.

We do not immediately board. Instead I lead our little band down the line of flat cars and gravel cars until we get past the flatcars carrying the dead and the train starts to move. Only then do we haul ourselves aboard. *We have to move; I could not stand the thought of riding into Vladivostock amidst the stacks of dead Russians.*

We swing ourselves aboard a gravel car that isn't much better; it's like all the others - loaded with men from Bikin and the bridges, many of them wounded. The idea of stoic wounded soldiers is absolute horseshit. Duffy spends most of the day holding the hand of a boy with a mangled leg that is missing a foot. Neither can understand a word the other says and they both have tears in their eyes. Periodically the boy screams when the train jerks or bumps.

Naumenko is also on the troop train. I can see him about two cars down on one of the last flatcars helping to tend to the wounded. I raise my hand in acknowledgment and he raises his in return. Then I return to periodically tightening and loosening the tourniquet on the shattered arm of another sobbing teenager. *He is going to lose it for sure if he lives.*

During most of the trip we tend to the wounded and look up at snow covered mountains as the train passes through a beautiful forest with the leaves turning color. That changes to a desolate grey industrial area dusted with slushy dirty snow as we enter the outskirts of Vladivostok.

Perhaps the engineer or someone on the train has a radio because we are absolutely swarmed with waiting troops and medics when the train finally comes to a stop at the Vladivostok dockyard. Or maybe the Spetsnaz commander had one. It really does not matter.

Further down the rail yard we can see a huge ship being pushed into place against the dock by a couple of tugs. It's got a flat deck so it must be some kind of aircraft carrier and I can see its deck packed with tanks and BMDs. The dock in front of it is covered with men, cranes, and waiting trucks and flatbed railcars.

******

"I did not expect to see you so soon," a familiar voice says and causes me to turn around as I climb rather stiffly down from the gravel car where we'd been spent the past five or six hours helping tend the Russian wounded. It is Colonel Naumenko. I do not even have a chance to respond when a Russian Jeep literally skids to a halt in front of us and an officer in a navy uniform jumps out and literally runs up to the Colonel.

The officer speaks urgently and waves his arms. He seems to be telling Naumenko to get his troops back on the train. Naumenko listens and asks a few questions. Then he shakes his head. The gesturing officer looks at him incredulously and starts gesturing and pointing once again.

I watch as Naumenko turns away and barks an order over his shoulder to one of his men. Whistles and shouting begin and the men, at least the relative handful of those who can, begin to form up in ranks. Then they suddenly break ranks and move towards the nearest trucks. Duffy and I follow them – and then stand watching as they climb in. *What the hell is going on?*

We run to catch up with the Colonel. "North Koreans," he shouts to us over his shoulder as he steps up on to the running board of one of the trucks and swings himself into its cab. "We must delay them until reinforcements arrive."

I shout a response as the three of us jog along aside of Naumenko's slowly moving truck. "We are going with you but first I have to report in to General Roberts."

Then we peel off toward a Jeep further up the dock with a driver sitting in it. Eugene shouts a bunch of Russian at the Jeep driver as we climb. *North Koreans?*

******

Thirty minutes later we are in the dingy main office of the Port trying to convince the office staff to let me use a phone so I can report in to Colonel Miskin or General Roberts. A very suspicious naval officer calls the Vladivostok Police instead.

A handcuffed ride to the local police station and twenty minutes later we are being questioned by the local police. They are not impressed by the letter from General Sholakov we each carry and Eugene's obviously sincere efforts to convince them.

"They think we are spies," said Eugene.

"Then they are fools who will soon be counting trees in Siberia if we do not get a phone," I respond. "Tell them that." He does.

"Well that did not work," I say to Duffy as the two of us get roughly pushed into a filthy jail cell and Eugene disappears. "Any ideas?"

******

NSA reports the Chinese and North Koreans are both moving troops and armor forward towards Vladivostok and that the Russians are hanging on, but barely. There are now some indications in the intercepts that the Chinese are having problems with damaged bridges but, according to the intercepts, they are being repaired.

Hmm. This is the first time bridges have even been mentioned. Yesterday I personally called the Director and asked to have all mentions of bridges flagged and immediately forwarded to me.

Another part of the latest NSA report is even more interesting. Instructions have again gone out from Red Banner Street reminding the Chinese units not to damage the railroad and not to interfere with the movement of Russian trains. The Chinese apparently think reinforcements have not yet been sent eastward to Khabarovsk and Vladivostok because the Russian communications system is in chaos.

One of the intercepted communications speculates that the Russian Command's communication center might have been damaged by the airborne operation so that General Sholakov is temporarily unable to communicate with his units.

I immediately try to call Sholakov and Miskin to give them the news. *And to get an update on the war in general and the North Koreans in particular.*

It takes a while, but I finally get through to Sholakov. I tell him about the Chinese order, without saying how I know. I also tell him that the railroad might still be open and suggest he ask Moscow for Kelt missiles and the four remaining squadrons of Tu-16s bombers for use against Irkutsk and Angarsk.

Yuri Andreovich is no dummy. He understands exactly what I mean when I suggest he hold them in the west on a one hour standby until he is ready to launch them to support a ground attack on the captured airfields using infiltrating Spetsnaz. I emphasized the word 'ground.'

Then we talk about the North Koreans and the war in general.

"As I am sure you know, Christopher Ivanovich, we are continuing to give ground to the Chinese on both fronts. But very slowly and making them pay dearly. General Bulganin just gave them a very big punch on the nose on the Amur Front and Kulibin has them stopped cold, at least for a moment, on the Ussurri."

"And the North Koreans?" I ask gently.

"Ah, those backstabbing cocksuckers," he replies bitterly. "They are a big problem."

"What's the situation?" I ask.

"The North Koreans are about twenty kilometers over the border and moving north towards the port. At the moment they are mainly using infantry. And their men are unsupported. Unsupported! Can you believe it? They are letting their men take casualties so they do not have to risk losing their tanks and planes."

"How soon do you think they will take the port and cut off your reinforcements?" I asked.

"Longer than they expect, Christopher Ivanovich, longer than they expect."

"How so?" I ask.

"Do you remember Colonel Naumenko? The man whose troops found your dead Americans?"

"Well he showed up in Vladivostok with a few hundred survivors from Bikin, including your two young officers. When he learned the North Koreans had come over the border he took his men, and some of the troops and armor he found unloading from some navy ships, and rushed them to a good blocking position about eighty kilometers south of the port. He got them there riding on civilian trucks and buses.

"Christ. They won't have a chance when the Koreans reach them. They will just be a road bump for the Koreans to run over."

"Maybe and maybe not. They are behind a big marshy area with a stream running through it - and the *Kiev* docked a couple of hours later with more than an entire division of armored infantry. They are being unloaded as we speak."

"You will probably disagree, Christopher Ivanovich. But my mind's made up. I am sending them to reinforce General Naumenko. Yes, he is a General now - and the frontal commander for the Korean Front as well. I promoted him this morning though he probably does not know it yet."

"Actually, I think I agree with you, Yuri Andreovich - both about sending the troops and about General Naumenko. But I must admit I am surprised to be hearing this from you. I wonder why my two young officers did not report in to me?"

Then after a second or so I continue.

"In any event, from everything that Major Evans told me a couple of days ago it sounds as though Naumenko is as good a commander as you've got. And, you are right about keeping the port open as long as possible. So long as it stays open and the Chinese stay stupid you can continue to land reinforcements and send them on to Chita."

"Well, let's hope it works, Christopher Ivanovich. The *Kiev* is just now docking and the helicopter carriers *Moskva* and *Leningrad* are a couple of days behind it.

Between them they are carrying the better part of three more divisions and a lot of armor. And there still are a large number of smaller ships on the way and so is the entire Black Sea Fleet including two our big landing ships packed with tanks and BDMs."

"Christopher Ivanovich, my mind's made up. I am going to send some of the Kiev's troops to Naumenko and hope he can hold off the Koreans long enough for the rest to move north."

"Yuri, my friend" I say with a smile in my voice, "the only thing that worries me is that we are in agreement about doing something Moscow is likely to approve. When we both agree with Moscow I have to ask - where has our thinking gone wrong?" We both laugh uproariously. *He needed that even if it was not much. Things have got to be getting tense out there.*

"Oh Yuri Andreovitch, I may have another idea for you, a way to fool the Chinese into keeping the railroad open."

I suggest to him that the Chinese almost certainly have observers in the hills reporting on the railroad traffic. Our intelligence, I report, thinks there might be one in the mountains about two hundred kilometers east of Chita. *We are damn sure there is; he sends a message spurt at 0227 every night.*

"You could," I suggest, "send a couple of trains loaded with armor and trucks eastward past that point several times each day; then at night, when the observer cannot see, bring them back along with the trains carrying your reinforcements coming out of Kharbarovsk. You could do the same for the line running south to the port through Bikin."

A little latter I am able to get through to Arnie Miskin with the same information. And I also tell him that I am getting worried about our guys out there, particularly Evans and Duffy. I want them to contact me as soon as they check in.

"Evans and Duffy have been seen in Vladivostok but for some reason they have not reported in. That worries me. If you hear from them, please tell them to stay with General Naumenko and be my eyes and ears on the North Korean Front."

Now it's time to drive home for dinner in my old Peugeot with a couple of Gunny Robinson's Marines following in a Jeep. Tonight it's spaghetti and meat sauce with salt bread dipped in olive oil and balsamic vinegar. The kids love it and it's my favorite meal. And then I have to fix the back door. It's sticking again.

Chapter Twenty-eight

New developments.

This morning's meeting of the combined Chinese Politburo and Military Committee is quiet, almost subdued, as General Wu reports on the progress of the war and the progress of the North Koreans.

"Things continue to go well," he tells the assembled party leaders. "Our troops advanced another twenty kilometers towards Khabarovsk yesterday and there is further confirmation that our strategy is working - one of our radio-equipped infiltration teams reported seeing an entire trainload of tanks and vehicles moving eastward from Chita to reinforce Khabarovsk and Vladivostok."

Everyone around the table looked up in surprise when General Wu goes on to say that he has ordered an end to the Vladivostok attacks and the relocation of many of the Chinese units that had been attacking the Russians.

"Our planned adjustment is basically quite simple," General Wu tells the seated men as he points to a big map an aide is in the process of pinning to the wall.

"We are going to move the bulk of our troops from here to here and let Kim's Koreans march up the coast past them. Then we are going to smash into their rear and retake the Russian land those little bastards are marching over. The North Koreans will be cut off without supplies and destroyed – and we will have both the occupied land the Russians stole from us and the port."

"And It will teach that ungrateful little shit Kim and his North Koreans a big lesson," explains Chairman Li as he nods and snuffs out his cigarette.

"What about the reports that some of our bridges have been destroyed – the bridges we will need to bring supplies and reinforcements to the Chita front," asks the wizened little man at the end of the table.

"Yes, that is true, Comrade." *How did he find out?* "Saboteurs have indeed damaged some our bridges. But they are being repaired as we speak and there is no problem – we already have more than enough men and equipment at the front. The Red Army is ready to cross the Amur and head for Chita as soon as the signal is given."

******

The Chinese–Russian battle for Vladivostok is one of the several areas in Eastern Russia on which NSA is concentrating its satellites and communications interception efforts.

Today's satellite photos instantly make it clear what the Chinese are doing. They are moving the bulk of their forces into the hills which overlook the Korean infantry that is marching towards the port. *No wonder Jack Riley called me at five o'clock this morning. He knows exactly what this means and so do I.*

It does not take a rocket scientist to figure out the Chinese plan. They have stopped attacking the Russians and are repositioning their troops so they can smash into the Korean rear and cut the North Koreans invaders off from North Korea.

It's time to call Sholakov and Miskin again. And I have got a new Russian-speaking aide to help me get through. A chaplain of all things. Captain Lonnie Farris is an American born Russian Orthodox priest. Lonnie's mother is Russian and he grew up in a Russian speaking home. His father met her when he was on the embassy staff in Moscow and somehow got her out.

******

I immediately call Miskin with the good news about Evans and Duffy getting out of Bikin and told him I wanted them to report in immediately. Two hours later, when I still had not heard from them, I tried to call Sholakov back and ended up talking through Lonnie to Colonel Durov. He is one of Sholakov's key aides and the man most likely to know.

"Where are Evans and Duffy," I asked?

My second inquiry triggers a firestorm. One of Sholakov's aides gets through to Naumenko who reports he had last seen them this morning heading off to find a phone so they could report to me. Sholakov's aide then calls the major in charge of unloading the ships who tells him there's a rumor going about that the local police have arrested several Chinese spies claiming to be Americans.

"Yes, the police have captured three Chinese spies. The Chief himself is questioning them."

"Well comrade, they are not spies. General Sholakov wants them released immediately.

******

Two hours later Miskin again calls Sholakov's office to inquire about Evans and Duffy. Once again the General's aide calls the Vladivostok police to find out why they have not yet reported in. He is told that they are not available because the police have not finished questioning them.

Sholakov goes ballistic when his aide describes the situation. He calls the political officer of the 75th Guards, one of the divisions being relocated to the newly established Korean Front.

"Get to the Vladivostok police headquarters as fast as possible and find out what happened to the two foreign officers those morons arrested this morning as spies. They are important allies and I ordered them released with apologies hours ago."

"At your orders, Comrade General. I will leave immediately."

"This is a war zone and discipline is of vital importance, even for police officers. Do you know what you must immediately do if you find my orders have been deliberately disobeyed?"

"At your orders, Comrade General. You can rely on me."

"Good. Some officers may still not fully understand that in a war orders must be obeyed. It may be that an example must be made to encourage the others."

"Also Comrade Colonel, be sure to leave a very reliable man to take charge of the police and the port if an example must be made. Tell him to concentrate on keeping the roads open and the military traffic moving. Even better, now that I think of it, you stay there yourself and take command of the police. We must get reinforcements to General Naumenko on the Korean front as fast as possible. Every minute counts."

******

The Jeep and the army truck following it skid to a stop in front of police headquarters. More than a dozen heavily armed men with grim faces follow the Colonel as he dashes up the stairs past two exiting policemen and through the door. The two policemen look on in amazement as the heavily armed men push past them. Then they hurry to their patrol car – they know trouble when they see it.

Evans and I have been tied to chairs and being slapped around and shouted at in Russian for hours. Half a dozen police stand around watching the man, obviously someone senior, who does most of the shouting. The problem is pretty basic - he just cannot get it in his head that we do not understand a word he is saying. Then the door opens and soldiers flood in.

The arrival of the soldiers obviously surprises the police. There is quite a bit of shouting back and forth and our questioner keeps pointing at us. Then the colonel commanding the new arrivals pulls out his pistol and holds it at arm's length pointing at the head of our questioner.

It suddenly gets very quiet.

Everyone, including me, is deafened by the noise when the colonel pulls the trigger and a plume of red mist sprayed out of the back of the policeman's head and splatters the dirty concrete wall. *Holy shit.* Two minutes later and we are untied and shakily on our feet with a cup of tea.

But then our rescuers have the same problem as our questioner; none of them speaks English. One of the trembling policemen says something and the colonel nods. It is almost funny to watch the trembling policeman leave. He warily walks as far away from the colonel as possible as he goes around him to get out the door. Then we all just stand there and look at each other until an equally battered and disheveled Eugene walks in trying to button his buttons and tuck in his shirt.

Things move along quickly after that. The colonel is quite solicitous. Within minutes we are ravenously wolfing down sandwiches. From the homemade look of them it's likely some policemen are going to miss supper.

The colonel who rescued us seems quite pleased when Eugene translates my request for a phone line to call General Sholakov's headquarters. He is even more pleased when Sholakov's headquarters immediately accepts the call and he hears Eugene ask to be connected to Colonel Miskin in General Sholakov's personal office, and then hands the phone to me. From that moment on he is our best friend.

******

"Change of plans, Harry. The big boss wants us to check out the North Koreans. Wants to know how long we think the Russians can hold."

Harry scoops up the remaining sandwiches as Eugene explains that we need Ak-47s and a ride down the road to where General Naumenko is waiting for the North Koreans. Our new best friend begins barking orders and a few minutes later, after long overdue visit to an absolutely filthy latrine, we are carrying AK-47s and barreling down the road in our rescuer's jeep with two truckloads of hastily conscripted Russian troops following close behind. We can see cranes unloading tanks and BMDs from the *Kiev* as we drive out of town.

Russia's "highway" south from Vladivostok towards the North Korean border runs next to the railroad tracks and periodically is framed like a picture with a great view of the ocean off to the left and snow covered mountains to the right. It's a two lane dirt road and its ruts and potholes obviously have not been graded for quite some time. *Probably since World War Two.* It is cold riding in the open jeep even with the hooded jackets and gloves we dig out of our magically reappearing duffle bags.

It's an empty dirt road. We do not see any traffic except a horse cart coming the other way piled high with a load of branches. Once I see some people walking among the scraggly spruce and pine trees; other than that, absolutely nothing. *What a shitty place to live. No wonder the Russians send their convicts and political prisoners out here.*

Finally, we came around a corner and there is a truck parked across the road with a couple of soldiers waving us to a stop. I can see from the insignia on their uniforms that we've found General Naumenko and his blocking force. I even recognize one of the men. He'd been the Naumenko's orderly and brought in the tea when we had meetings.

"The Colonel is up ahead, Comrades" he reports as we exchange warm salutes and handshakes as the lieutenant our rescuer sent with us beams his approval.

A few minutes later, and an embarrassing fall on my ass when I slip on some ice, and it is bear hugs and hot tea all around. It is quickly obvious that the General has chosen a pretty good place to stop the North Koreans. He looks at me curiously when I address him as General as he is pointing out where his men are located.

"You do not know?" I ask. He shakes his head. "Well then," I say as I salute very formally. "Let me congratulate you, General. *I emphasized the word 'General.'* I heard about it a couple of hours ago from both Colonel Miskin in General Sholakov's office and from General Roberts. And you are the frontal commander here as well."

Naumenko is dumbfounded. "Can it be true?" he finally asks as he stares at me in disbelief.

"Yes, it's true" I tell him. "And General Sholakov is sending three divisions for you to command. At least that is what Colonel Miskin told me. Two from the Chinese front on the Ussuri, where things have suddenly gotten very quiet, and one from the carrier which was just docking as we drove out of the city to come here."

* * * * * *

Trucks loaded with cold and hungry troops show up all afternoon and through the early evening. They seem to be a motley crew of clerks and jerks scrapped up from around the port. Some of them do not even have weapons. Harry and I help Naumenko and his handful of officers place them.

Everything changes for the better at about nine that evening. There is an earth shaking rumble behind us and a company of nine T-62 tanks from the *Kiev* shows up with a colonel who introduces himself as the deputy commander of the 42nd Guards Division. He knows Naumenko's name and rank from a radio message received on the ship. *I think when the colonel saluted and reported to him was the first time Naumenko really believed he'd been promoted.*

They meet in a little plywood workers shack where a rusty pump cart had been stored. A single lantern lights the shack and the colonel is mightily impressed. The obviously exhausted Naumenko has an AK-47 slung over his back, desperately needs a shave, is absolutely filthy with a ripped coat heavily splattered with blood stains, and he has a bandage on his left hand and another on his neck. He looks every inch a fighting general.

Naumenko's men are strung out in a very thin line behind a little river and the snow dusted marshy areas that run along on either side of it. He does not have listening posts out in front of his line because the water is too cold to cross. There is ice on the pools of water in the swampy area and no place for the troops to get warm except for the little bonfires that are springing up everywhere even though they begin to draw sniper fire as dawn approaches. It is so cold and windy that anyone who gets wet is almost certain to die. *Wonder how the Koreans will get across—probably either try to throw pontoon bridges over the river and the swampy area or storm the road bridge.*

Apparently the Russian political officer has taken his assignment to heart. All night long army trucks, civilian buses, and armored vehicles from the Kiev and the Chinese Front arrive in the dark and their freezing occupants are quickly assigned to places in the line along the river.

The next morning it is found to everyone's dismay that many of the nighttime arrivals are in the wrong place so that much shifting back and forth is needed. The reinforcements who arrive in the morning darkness are met and receive their assignments from the first colonel to report. He had been grabbed up by Naumenko to be his aide. Naumenko himself is sitting on an ammunition case and fast asleep with his head down on the rough wooden table that is his headquarters' only furniture.

The officers who report their arrival to the colonel are greatly impressed by his almost reverential attitude towards his new boss and what little they'd heard about him when they received their orders. They certainly harbor no illusions. The flatcars stacked five-deep with Naumenko's dead are still standing under the brutal glare of the port floodlights for all to see - they had driven past them on the way to the front.

Chapter Twenty-nine

Desperate times.

North Korean troops began to arrive just before noon. First it is skirmishers, and then a few snipers, not many but enough to keep everyone down and cause a number of campfires to be quickly put out. Within minutes numerous columns of men can be seen in the distance trudging towards the still-adjusting and still-growing Russian lines.

"Please wake up Comrade General," the colonel intones gently as he shakes his General's shoulder. "The Koreans are coming." Three worried looking major generals are crowded into the shack and watching. The difference between them in their clean uniforms and the sleeping and filthy Naumenko with his bandages and the AK-47 on his back is striking. They snap to attention and salute as he lifts his head and somehow manages to knock over the cup of hot tea they had watched the colonel reverently place in front of him moments before.

"We must stop them," are his first words as he lurches to his feet. Nothing he might have said could have endeared him more to the waiting generals.

******

Harry and I were standing outside the shack in the midst of a growing number of murmuring aides and officers when Naumenko and the generals come out. We'd seen the anxiety and uncertainty on the generals' faces as they entered. But something has changed. They came out looking confident and grimly determined.

"I do not know what they are drinking in there but I'd like to find out and get a couple of bottles," Harry says.

"You got that right. Let's try to call home and report."

A few minutes later Harry and I, with Eugene tagging along like a hungry and cold puppy, follow General Naumenko and his new generals to a radio and desk equipped BMD. One of the newly arrived division commanders had brought it for use as his headquarters. He is sharing it with Naumenko now – and it's busy. No way I am going to get a link to anywhere for a while. We can hear periodic small arms firing in the background.

"Just snipers," comments Duffy. "No one's getting across that marsh and the river without a boat or bridge."

About thirty minutes later a flare goes up and every Russian mortar and cannon fires five rounds as fast as it can. We could see explosions in the distance on the other side of the river. The Russians are going for the distant columns where the North Koreans are concentrated. The sporadic small arms firing resumes almost immediately and the columns kept coming.

Then the North Korean artillery opens up and we all dive for cover. We end up in the icy slush under a newly arrived T-62.

******

"It was sort of weird, Colonel."

It was a little after two o'clock in the morning. We finally got access to a radio phone in the headquarters BMD and here I am trying to explain the last forty eight hours to a sleepy Colonel Miskin. What I was describing was how surprised we are that the Russian generals entered the little shack looking anxious and uncertain and came out a few minutes later looking confident and absolutely determined to fight.

"Not really surprising," Miskin says. "The Russian officers lost two wars in a row and they are anxious not to lose a third and be totally disgraced. They are undoubtedly pleased as punch to find that Sholakov wants his men to stand and fight."

"Well, they are sure as hell going to fight here," I tell him. "Naumenko is determined to hold the North Koreans and he is going to have the better part of three divisions on the line by tomorrow night or the day after. And they are already pounding the Korean infantry and artillery with the artillery which showed up a couple of hours ago. They are using tracked 122s I think."

"Colonel, it looks to me as though the North Koreans are either going to have to seriously commit their armor and air or they will have to hold up here until the Russians run out of food and ammunition."

"How soon do you think that will be?" he asked. "Running out I mean."

"Not very long unless the Russians get an airlift or some ships show up with supplies. They also need some tents and winter gear to keep the troops warm in their foxholes. It's already goddamn cold out here, you know."

******

I had just gotten home that evening after picking Susan up from a homework session at a friend's house when Arnie Miskin called to tell me about Evans' report. *Thank god they are safe. If only Solomon would turn up.* I immediately call the Detachment and tell the duty NCO to recall the planning staff. As soon as I hang up I call Tony Perelli, my deputy at Seventh Army, and ask for an airlift plan from him also.

Then I call Tony Talbot's office in the Pentagon. It's Sunday just after lunchtime and the Chairman of the Joint Chiefs is a diehard golfer. So he surprises me by answering when the duty officer transfers my call to his home in Virginia. Then he really surprises me by saying that someone at the NSA had just finished reading him a transcript of the conversation between Evans and Miskin. *I wonder if he is listening to my calls. Actually that sort of worries me.*

"See ya love. Duty calls." And with that trite comment and a wave to Dorothy and the kids I set out for the Detachment.

******

Three hours and a lot of phone calls to Moscow and the United States and we have the beginnings of an airlift plan and are already beginning to put it in place. If the past is any guide, sometime tomorrow Seventh Army will also have a plan with more than a little overlap and some additional good ideas; and the Pentagon will take three of four days and come propose a course of action involving everyone including the Coast Guard, the Boy Scouts, a Presidential speech, and a couple of congressional fact finding junkets.

Captain Farris, my new interpreter, gets me through to Sholakov and Miskin a little before midnight here, morning there. There is no question about it, Major Evans is right -

Naumenko does not have three or four days. The North Koreans are bringing up motorized pontoon bridges and more heavy artillery. How do we know? We can see them on the satellite photo feeds we are continually downloading in real time.

A thought strikes me as I am talking to Arnie about Major Evans' report. "Arnie, I have got an idea. Stand by for a moment. Do not leave the line. I will call you right back if I lose you."

"Jack, how closely can you pinpoint the locations of the North Korean artillery positions?" That is the question I shout over to Jack Riley, our air force satellite expert and photo analyst, as I put the phone down on the desk instead of hanging it up.

******

Things moved quickly after I explain to Arnie what I have in mind. The Russian phone system he is using does not have a conferencing feature. So I hold and hum a little French marching song while listening to Arnie try to reach Major Evans at Naumenkos' headquarters on another line. There is lot of Russian I cannot understand so I put it on the speaker so Lonnie can listen. *If Evans can call Miskin from there it figures that Miskin should be able to call him back.*

"They have send someone to find him," Lonnie finally says. There is no talking on the line, just voices in the background.

"Hold on to both of your lines, Arnie. Keep them both open. I am going to have you relay target coordinates to Evans."

It seems like ages. Then, *finally* "I have got Major Evans on the other line, General Roberts."

"Okay. Arnie, ask Evans if he can get a line to Naumenko's artillery from where he is at? .... Yes, to their heavies, the 122s."

"Hold one, General. I will ask."

The answer came five minutes later. "Yes sir, Major Evans says he thinks Naumenko's got ground wire to his artillery. "

"Okay. Tell Evans to get the artillery on another line for a fire mission."... "Yes, damnit, a fire mission."

It seems to take forever. But then Naumenko apparently came back and Colonel Miskin is able to get him on the line. We can hear Arnie explain that he has me on his other line and that we are in contact with an observer who can see the Korean pontoon boats and some of their artillery parks.

Naumenko grasps the possibilities instantly. Miskin says he can hear him in the background giving orders.

A few minutes later we discover a big problem. The Russian maps are different from ours. They have totally different coordinates. *Hells bells.*

"Damn. Okay. Arnie, tell General Naumenko we can work around that. Ask him if one of his 122mm tubes can put a phosphorous round as close as possible to the road eight thousand meters south of the river. If so, tell him to shoot and let me know when he does. After he does that, please ask him how many 122s he can shoot for effect."

"It's on the way," reports Miskin about two minutes later. "And he says he is got twelve 122 tubes up and five more will be ready within the hour."

Moments later Jack Riley shouts and points to his satellite screen. "There it is, by God. There it is."

"Tell them up another fifteen hundred meters and left nineteen hundred. Fire another ranging round," I tell Miskin after conferring with Jack.

"There it is. Close enough. Down one hundred and left one hundred and eighty and fire for effect," Riley shouts over to me.

I repeat the adjustment to Arnie. "Have Evans suggest to General Naumenko that he make that correction and have each of his tubes fire five HE rounds for effect. Tell us when he shoots."

"Shooting orders going out now. Standby."

Everyone in the room is holding their breath and staring at the screen. Jack Riley has a pencil point at the target area. There are cheers all around when the area around the pencil point is suddenly covered in flashes. We wait impatiently to see the results.

"Jesus Christ," someone says as the smoke clears from the target area. "It worked."

"Arnie. It worked. Please tell General Naumenko our observer reports his artillery really tore up a bunch of the North Korean pontoon boats. And keep the lines open. I will have more targets shortly."

"Also please tell him our observer reports that a number of his shells fell way off the target area."

******

Using a separate line I called Sholakov with the good news that we can use our 'observer' to direct Naumenko's artillery. I also remind him that next time the North Koreans bring their bridges up they will probably hold them out of range so that they will have to be hit from the air.

On the artillery control line Miskin reports Naumenko and his staff are ecstatic about the pontoon boats being destroyed. They think it will seriously delay a Korean attack if their artillery hit enough of them. They want to know if our observer sees anything else they can hit.

"I'll ask him."

Then, while Jack and his men feverishly search the satellite downloads for more pontoon boats and other targets, we get to work on fixing the artillery problem revealed by the initial shoot. It seems that some of the Russian 122s are not properly synchronized with the other tubes in their batteries.

The fix is simple but time-consuming. Working through Miskin and Evans we have each of Naumenko's 122 tubes separately fire a phosphorous round at the Korean pontoon park. Hits Jack Riley and his men can see landing outside the target area means they are coming from an artillery tube that isn't properly synchronized with the rest of its battery. And where each errant shot lands tells us how much that particular cannon tube needs to be adjusted.

It takes a while before Naumenko's artillery finally gets each of its tubes sighted in and ready for more fire missions. While Riley watches the individual hits and calls in corrections if they are needed, the other members of his team gather around the screen with the NSA downlink and search for targets. The Russians are low on ammunition so we will wait to shoot them until we could make every round count.

There is good news in that at least two of the ammunition trucks on the *Kiev* are loaded with pallets of 122mm shells and more are on the supply trucks of the two divisions moving here from the Chinese front.

The bad news is that even after all the additional shells arrive Naumenko will only have enough for a couple of days of periodic firing. We need to get an airlift going and quickly. And it's going to be a bitch to organize because it's going to have to pick up the shells from wherever the Russians have them and carry them in some kind of roundabout route to avoid the Chinese interceptors coming out of Irkutsk and Angarsk.

******

General Talbot is pleased and relieved to hear that Evans and Duffy are safe and that the North Koreans have been temporarily stopped about half way between the Korean border and Vladivostok. And my description as to how we are using the satellite photo feeds to call in artillery strikes on the other side of the world seems to greatly interest him - he asks a lot of questions.

A couple of hours later Tommy Talbot calls back and said he is flying over an observer team to learn more about our targeting fix. I tell him they'd better hurry because the Russians are running out of ammunition. I also tell him the team should be no more than two or three men due to our lack of space. Then I leave Dave

Shelton and Jack Riley in charge of the shooting and drive home for dinner and some sleep. *It's meatloaf night.*

Jack and his guys are like kids in a candy shop. They better be. They are gonna be up all night. Dave Shelton is going to stay with them. He is been taking the night shift ever since I got back and things heated up. Lonnie is going to stay around the clock in case an interpreter is needed. He'll blow up a rubber mattress and sleep on my office floor.

******

Everything at the Detachment is alive and operational when I get back just before dawn. According to Dave, Jack and his guys have been hammering the Koreans all night despite periodically losing communications.

When I arrive, Lieutenant Basilof is sitting in for Arnie Miskin at Chita and Harry Duffy seems to have taken over from Dick sometime during the night. Otherwise we are still in business and going strong. And Talbot's observers are due to land at Riems about now. Gunny Robinson is taking a couple of civilian cars to the airport to get them.

We are in the middle of a shoot and I am leaning over Lonnie's shoulder to see the satellite picture when out of the corner of my eye I see Dave Shelton and a brigadier and a couple of colonels standing in the doorway. I motion them in without taking my eyes off the monitor.

"Recommend down two hundred and fire for effect," intones Master Sergeant Roosevelt who had taken over Jack's chair a couple of hours ago. *Jack is curled up on the floor snoring.* Major Adams, standing next to him, nods his agreement.

"Tell Basilof to drop two hundred and fire two rounds of anti-personnel from every tube," I order Lonnie.

Lonnie rattles away in Russian and holds up his hand. "Shooting," he announces a few seconds later as he drops his hand. Then every eye in the place turns to the monitor and the point of the yellow lead pencil where Adams is touching the screen.

We wait anxiously for about thirty seconds. Then the telltale flashes light up all around the pencil point.

Master Sergeant Roosevelt speaks for us all when he pushes back his chair and with a great deal of satisfaction in his voice murmurs "that'll learn them motherfuckers."

Our visitors are greatly impressed and spend the entire day watching and asking questions. They seemed amazed that we had come up with the idea and begun implementing it within the space of an hour or so. *I get the impression the Pentagon has been trying to come up with something similar and does not have much to show for it despite years of RFPs and expensive consulting contracts.*

Chapter Thirty

Uncertainty and suspicion.

"Can we really defeat both the Russians and the North Koreans at the same time?" asks the little man at the end of the table. Everyone's eyes swivel back to the Chairman. *Such a foolish question. It's time for you to retire, Peng Jie.*

"Of course we can. But that is neither our plan nor our intention, Comrade Peng. At the moment the Russians and the North Koreans are fighting each other and everything is proceeding as we expected in our efforts to recapture our stolen lands. And there is no doubt that we have fooled the Russians to our great advantage. They are moving troops towards the Koreans and towards the Khabarovsk Front as we speak."

"And the bridges, Comrade Chairman? I am told the damage is far greater than we first imagined. Is it true that our armies have been cut off from their supplies and reinforcements?"

"Of course you are somewhat correct, Comrade Peng, and your concerns are appreciated. Some of our bridges have indeed been damaged by the enemy. But they will soon be repaired. And, as you might remember, we really do not need them. Perhaps you have forgotten that General Wu assured us that our forces in front of Chita are already more than enough to get over the Amur and destroy the Russians."

I took a puff on my cigarette to give me a time to come up with the right response, and then continued.

"But why take chances? That is why we are waiting for the Russians to finish moving troops away from what they will soon learn is the main battlefield." *I will talk to the others about your growing forgetfulness, Peng. I know it is deliberate, but who put you up to these questions and what is their plan?*

******

Tonight we will all walk to the village for dinner - Dorothy and me, the kids, and our two wonderful au pairs. The Hotel du Rhone is having its Tuesday Special which, of course, we all know means chicken with mushrooms and truffles as it has been every Tuesday evening for years.

We exchange friendly greeting with at least half the people in the place and the kids immediately run outside to play with their friends from school. I am, of course, "Monsieur le Major" as I have been since I first arrived here years ago. *Being an American officer is acceptable in our little village, but being an officer of the Legion is much more significant and respected.*

Sitting next to our big round table are a couple of American men. Strangers in business suits. Expensive business suits. After they finished complaining about their hotel rooms they begin chattering away about contracts, the use of satellites for military purposes such as controlling aircraft and artillery, and how they intend to get more change orders. Tomorrow, it seems, they are going to get information from the army clods at some nearby American base and use it as an excuse to once again revise their Pentagon contract.

I lean over towards Dorothy and the two au pairs and, in French, make a request -"please only speak French so the two morons sitting next to us do not know we can understand them."

They all immediately look over at the men, of course, but the suits do not notice. When the kids came back I quickly announce, in French, "Tonight is a French language night. The first one who speaks English has to wash the dishes for the rest of the week." They giggle and play along. The chicken with mushrooms and wine sauce is superb as always.

After dinner we walk back home and I call the Seventh Army's Judge Advocate General on the secure line and describe the situation without telling him what we are doing at the Detachment. He proposes a course of action and I agree. *I think calling the officers running the program 'army clods" upset him more than their publically revealing classified information and their plans to defraud the Pentagon.*

******

The next morning I once again get up before dawn and arrive at the Detachment early to see how things are going. The latest satellite feeds and intercepts are encouraging. The North Koreans are obviously confused. After failing to silence the Russian artillery with counter-battery fire, they have begun pulling their units back out of range. According to the latest NSA intercepts the North Koreans are convinced there are Russian artillery observers hidden in the snow covered mountains overlooking the North Korean Army.

Things are not going nearly so well in front of Khabarovsk. It's only a diversion but the Chinese are continuing to take heavy casualties and move forward.

******

Sure enough. It was about nine thirty in the morning and here come the two suits from the restaurant. They flash their Pentagon IDs at the Marine guard at the gate *who knows they are coming and lets them enter* and pull into the Detachment's parking lot in a rental car. Then they walk in as if they own the place and officiously present their business cards and Pentagon IDs to Gunnery Sergeant Robinson, who is sitting at the reception desk for the occasion, and announce that they are there to meet with the Director of the Satellite Targeting Program.

"Do you have an appointment, Sir?" Gunny Robinson asks.

"Just tell the Program Manager we are here, Sergeant."

"Certainly Sir. One moment please."

A couple of minutes later the Gunny returns. "He'll be with you shortly, Sir. But first I have to see your identification. Passports, drivers licenses, Pentagon IDs, Company IDs, Insurance cards - everything including your wallets and credit cards. The usual."

"Thank you. I will copy these and be right back."

An hour later and the two men are getting increasingly anxious and complaining to the PFC who has taken Sergeant Robinson's place at the reception desk. Then three cars full of FBI agents from the Paris embassy and half a dozen MPs in plain clothes march into the reception area and take them away.

"Arrested for leaking military secrets and off to be questioned, are they? Well I guess they won't be needing these," Gunny Robinson comments with a smile as he drops their wallets and everything else they'd given him into a shredder.

Then I call Tommy Talbot and Brigadier Owens, the project officer who visited us yesterday, and explain what I have done and why. Interestingly enough, both of them say they neither informed the civilian contractors nor authorized them to obtain information about what we are doing. *Uh oh. Someone's got a leak somewhere.*

******

Both the Korean Front and the Ussuri Front are quiet today. The North Koreans have pulled back slightly while they wait for the marshes and the shallow river to finish icing up. That way precious wood won't have to be wasted building new pontoon boats.

What the North Koreans do not know, the NSA report suggests, is that the Chinese are relocating four of the divisions they have on the Ussuri Front so they can attack the Koreans; what the Chinese do not know is that Sholakov knows why the Chinese on the Ussuri River have stopped attacking the three Russian divisions facing them.

The Chinese also do not know that Sholakov has decided to take a calculated risk. Less than a quarter of Naumenko's current force will be left as a screen in front of the North Koreans with one of his major generals in command. The 122s, whose ammunition resupply may or may not be on the way, will stay with them. The rest of troops confronting the North Koreans, plus two of the three divisions now in front of the Chinese, plus the under strength division now unloading from the carrier *Moskova*, will all head to Chita with Naumenko in command - if the railroad is still open. They will be followed by the troops and armor coming in on the Russian carrier *Leningrad* and its escorts.

Sholakov's decision to move his troops is a real gamble because it will leave the defense of the port to an assortment of military odds and ends and whoever shows up on any new ship arrivals. On the other hand, the Russian navy has a lot of ships offshore and some of them, particularly the older destroyers and frigates, can provide artillery support if the Russians are forced to pull back to the port area and the city. Radio contact has already been established with the ranking naval officer, an Admiral on one of the planeless carriers, and his ships are standing by for fire missions.

******

The Chinese Army's last instruction to all its units, including the handful of men left of the 114th Division at Bikin, is to leave the railroad open until they are ordered to close it. But a closure order might come at any time, particularly if the Bikin radio reports that the Russians are moving trains north instead of south.

So far so good. The deception is working. The Chinese still have not wised up to the fact that Sholakov is sending a loaded "reinforcement" train south from Kharbarovsk during the day and then running as many as possible loaded trains north at night in the dark past Bikin. *Yes, he is pulling the same deception he is been running between Chita and Kharbarovsk to fool the Chinese observer in the hills.*

"Supposedly," said Miskin, "arrangements have been made for a Russian missile cruiser to fire a salvo of cruise missiles the next time the Chinese radio at Bikin comes on the air. If the missiles knock out the radio, the Russians might be able to keep sending reinforcements north through the Bikin battlefield until the Chinese wise up and cut the line."

The bottom line is that Chita needs all the troops and armor it can get and Sholakov has ordered Naumenko to try to get them there. Naumenko, in turn, has decided to load as many trains as possible and send them out every twenty minutes tomorrow night even if the Chinese radio is not knocked out. If the line is cut, the engine drivers will put the engines pushing the flatcars in reverse and back up all the way to the port. *It's a ballsy plan and I am an optimist. I give it about one chance in three of succeeding.*

If the trains do get through Bikin they will continue to Podovsk and wait there as needed so they can go past the Chinese observer in the dark.

Even Miskin is impressed. "If Sholakov's plan works, General Roberts, it will be like Berlin during the recent war when the Russians never stopped letting German trains leave Berlin and pass through the Russian lines on their way to Frankfurt."

******

Duffy and I are riding with one of the regimental commanders, Colonel Ikunin of the 14th Guards, in the first troop train heading north with the troops being withdrawn to form Naumenko's army. It's a very small train with a coal burning yard engine and three flat cars of loaded with three BMDs and a couple of companies of freezing and shivering naval infantry tucked down behind sand bags.

Why are we here freezing our asses off? Because General Roberts said to let him know as soon as possible if the line through Bikin is still open. We have a radio Jeep on board for communications and whatever shelter and heat it might provide.

If we get through, twelve much larger trains carrying almost twenty five thousand men and over nine hundred tanks and BMDs, the bulk of Naumenko's newly created 47th Army, will follow behind us every twenty minutes — they have been loading and forming up for almost forty eight hours and are ready to go

It's cold as hell and there are clouds covering the moon so we cannot see a thing in the dark. Everyone jumps and gets really anxious when we begin clattering over the first of the three bridges. And then we got even more anxious, at least I did, when I realize it is so dark we probably won't even know when we get to Bikin and the Chinese. At least not until the shooting starts.

We are primed and ready to bail out and walk home if the Chinese stop the train. But they do not. There isn't as much as a peep out of the Chinese. So we just keep going and going and at some point obviously shiver our way through the village. *Actually, either the clouds blocking the moon temporarily parted or I am hallucinating – a while back I was suddenly able to see the outline of a couple of shacks out of the corner of my eye and almost had a heart attack.*

Not everyone is traveling by train. General Naumenko and his staff will fly to Chita in the early morning darkness if any of his divisions get past Bikin. He is doing the right thing. It's more important he manage his entire army than personally lead a relatively small number of men who may have to make a fighting withdrawal back to the port if the railroad is cut. *We are here, on the other hand, because I climbed aboard without thinking. Harry and I should have gotten on one of the later trains.*

******

This afternoon's politburo meeting in the Beidaihe conference room starts rather smoothly. It begins with the members receiving an extensive report on the military situation. The news is good.

On the active fronts, our brave Red Army continues to advance slowly but surely towards Khabarovsk in the face of fierce Russian resistance. Similarly, there are fierce artillery duels between the North Koreans and the Russians in the south on the outskirts of Vladivostok. In contrast, the fighting in the south between our forces and the Russians has tailed off to almost nothing as our troops continue to relocate to confront the ungrateful North Koreans. *And the little bastards really are ungrateful. We've been helping that goddamn Kim with food and supplies ever since we lost so many men saving him from the fascist Americans in the 1950s.*

Most important, however, is the news that our observers in the mountains along the railroad continue to report eastbound Russian military trains coming out of Chita and Vladivostok to reinforce Khabarovsk where we are continuing to push them back. Their reports are corroborated by the observer from the 114th Division who is watching Bikin.

Army Command, General Wu reports, is elated because "every tank and soldier the Russians send east to reinforce Khabarovsk is significant; it means one less will be there to oppose us when our real invasion begins."

"I am also pleased to report," he tells the men sitting around the long table, "that our buildup of troops and supplies for our main thrust towards Chita is complete. We can proceed whenever the order is given."

"In a nutshell, Comrades. Our deception strategy is working."

"There are other interesting reports. They suggest the Russians are beginning to secretly withdraw their troops from the Ussuri front in order to use them to confront the Koreans and to reinforce Kharbarovsk."

"The Russians tried to keep their withdrawals secret but we have been able to verify them with reliable eyewitness reports. There is no question about it - the better part of the Russians forces in the south, both those confronting us on the Ussuri Front and those confronting the North Koreans, were moved by train last night to reinforce Khabarovsk."

"The Russian withdrawal is bothersome because it clears the way for the North Koreans to advance past the mountains where our Red Army troops have been repositioned and into Vladivostok itself."

Then the general drops his bombshell.

"The Military Committee is pleased by the continuing Russian withdrawal of its forces in front of our main invasion route. But it is concerned because of the likelihood that even more of our lands will be occupied by the North Koreans as a result. Accordingly, the members of the committee now believe we should remove the North Koreans while our troops are ideally positioned to do so."

The arguing and discussion continues for hours. At times it became more heated and rancorous than anyone can remember. Much of the talk is political because North Korea has been an ally in the past. In the end the military view prevails and a consensus is reached. It will be a three way war.

Chapter Thirty-one

The three-way war.

About nine this morning local time the Chinese army poured out of the mountains and fell on the North Koreans who had invaded Russia. The Russians, in turn, are shelling them both. It's a three way war and no one has tanks and other tracked vehicles capable of crossing the partially frozen stream and marshes separating the Russian lines from the Chinese and North Koreans.

But then something strange began happening. And it was being photographed and reported by the only media representative on the scene, Marcine Dupont of Reuters.

It was an amazing sight. First North Koreans begin crossing the ice and surrendering in droves to the Russians. Then more and more of the Chinese who have been attacking the North Koreans began to join them. Some of the opposing forces could even be seen walking across the ice together in an effort to escape to the Russian lines.

In many places the ice was thick enough to hold the weight of the desperate men streaming across to surrender. But it was still early in the cold season and the ice still isn't thick enough to hold the weight of vehicles. That is obvious from the pictures of the three or four North Korean trucks that fell through the ice last night when they tried.

At first it is only a few cold and starving Koreans and Chinese who come across in the dark. But by the time the sun comes up on the day after the Chinese attack on the North Koreans it is hundreds every hour. By noon thousands of desperate men can be seen struggling over the ice to reach the Russian lines.

The world media is agog at the reports and photos. They are all coming from the Reuters reporter in the isolated Russian port city of Vladivostok. Marcin's photos and her interviews with the Koreans and Chinese who reach the Russian lines are a sensation.

Within hours the Russians cannot keep up with torrent of deserters let alone get any kind of count. Hastily assembled trucks and buses shuttle them from the front to the port. There they are quickly unloaded and placed, unfed and without blankets, in the unheated tents, warehouses, and other facilities left by the recently departed Russian troops.

Soon the streets of Vladivostok are full of Chinese and North Koreans desperately seeking food and shelter. There are also dead bodies in the snow dusted streets and several buildings are blazing as a result of warming fires set by the cold and hungry men that get out of control.

By mid-morning of the second day the number of deserters, though still substantial, began to dwindle as both the Chinese and North Koreans begin shooting their deserters and reestablishing discipline. At the same time things are getting more organized to care for them because, before he left, Naumenko authorized the distribution of some of the available military rations. *They are available because they were left behind by the troops who went north on the trains.*

Marcine Dupont's sensational stories and photos have a tremendous impact. By the evening of the second day Sholakov is promoted to Marshal; the United States has announced it will begin "mercy flights" to several Russian airfields in the Vladivostok area to take out the sick and wounded of all nations; South Korea and Taiwan have offered "sanctuary" to any of the North Koreans and Chinese who wish to defect; and the Chinese and North Koreans are royally pissed and hugely embarrassed.

******

Our train pulls into the Khabarovsk station about two in the afternoon. Duffy and I are so cold and stiff we can barely climb off. And not everyone does. At least one of the Russians apparently died of hypothermia sometime in the night. He looks like a lonely bundle of leftover rags.

We and almost everyone else, including the colonel commanding our train, rush to get into the station waiting room with its promise of warmth and shelter. Others temporarily delay joining us while they pee and poop on the station platform and tracks.

The little waiting room is quickly packed and the elderly lady selling tea and sandwiches at its little kiosk is instantly overwhelmed and sold out. Most of us, including me and Harry Duffy and Eugene, have to be content with the warmth of the waiting room's coal burning potbellied stove and do without. *Christ, I am hungry.*

No one informed the station commander, an elderly lieutenant, of our train's pending arrival. But he and his men have had several weeks of experience handling much larger numbers of men on arriving and departing trains and know what to do. Within minutes two long lines of shivering soldiers are shuffling forward to have their mess kit cups filled with hot tea and be handed loaves of bread. *Wait till the lieutenant finds out how many troops are on the trains coming right behind us.*

******

Change is about to occur. The Chinese observer on the side of the mountain, a Lieutenant Tan who previously had been on the staff of the artillery school and promised a promotion for volunteering, is quite bored as he uses his powerful binoculars to watch yet another loaded train carrying Russian troops and armor east from Chita.

"Oh. Look at that," he says, talking out loud to himself even though no one is within miles. "It's exactly like the train yesterday - the BMD with the white turret cover on the second flat car is parked behind the same piece of mobile artillery with the ripped flag."

The revelation of what he just said and its implications hit Tan like a thunderbolt a few seconds later. He knows exactly what it means.

But how long has this been happening and what should I report? That is the question Lieutenant Tan pondered all day as he waits to make his nightly report. He knows full well the consequences will be extremely serious if he admits he is been sending inaccurate reports.

Tan waits until well after dark and then merely reports "no troop trains today."

Two hours later he sends another message. "Enemy closing in. Will try to escape. Long live the Red Army." Then he begins packing up his camp. Tomorrow at first light he will move deeper into the mountains.

In the dark Lieutenant Tan cannot see the train's return and the six big troop trains that follow it. Even if he had, he would not have reported them - he does not want to be "re-educated" if he gets back and he has a wife and child to protect.

The Red Army intelligence unit monitoring Tan's transmittals receives both of his messages and immediately notifies Army Headquarters that the Russians may have found the observer. The NSA analyst monitoring them both knows better. She knows there are no Russian units on the mountain and that there was an eastbound train.

"Possible but not certain Chinese may know about the fake eastbound trains" is the flash message I receive from Tommy Talbot's office while munching on a donut in the Detachment conference room. I immediately call Arnie Miskin to alert Sholakov.

******

This morning's Politburo meeting finds its members pleased by the continuing advances of the Red Army but once again filled with concern and anxious discussion and outrage due to media reports of Chinese troop defections. The rumors that the damage to the vital bridges is much greater than previously reported merely make things worse.

Neither of these problems are mentioned in the briefing notes handed out before this morning's Central Committee meeting and several of the members once again ask for more information.

"It is the North Koreans we have destroyed who are defecting to the Russians, not our troops," claims General Wu.

"Of course the Russians are parading a handful of our troops that have been captured," he explains. "Even defeated armies capture enemy troops. But it means nothing."

"The reality is," General Wu announces with some satisfaction in his voice and a nod of his head, "that we have totally defeated the North Koreans and regained some of our stolen land. We will take the rest as soon as the ice is strong enough to support our tanks."

What primarily catches the attention of the Politburo members, however, is the report that the Russians may have finally stopped shipping reinforcements eastward to the Khabarovsk front.

"Merely finding our observer does not mean they will stop sending reinforcements eastward. And even if they did find him, our deception has worked far better than we dared to hope and caused them to significantly weaken their forces in front of Chita. Comrades, the Red Army is in position and ready to proceed - now is the time to act."

According to the CIA's informant there was then much discussion as to whether or not the time was ripe for the main thrust of the invasion to commence. It takes all morning but in the end a consensus is reached. The Red Army is to proceed to retake the occupied territories.

That afternoon the order goes out to General Jian commanding the invasion force on the Chita Front. Tomorrow morning at dawn the reoccupation of the stolen

Chinese lands is to begin in earnest. In a few hours thirty two divisions of Red Army troops will storm over the Amur River and advance towards Chita.

NSA intercepts the order and within moments I am reading flash messages both from the NSA and Tommy Talbot's office.

I instantly call Sholakov. It takes Lonnie a while to get me through to him. But when he do I immediately tell the newly minted Marshal of Russia that the Chinese will attack over the Amur and begin moving towards Chita at 0527, an hour before dawn. They will also simultaneously cut the Trans-Siberian at Bikin and several other isolated locations. *And, as it turns out, they will also simultaneously launch a major attack over the Amur towards Blagoveshchenk, many hundreds of kilometers to the east of Chita, to create confusion and uncertainty.*

Sholakov and I had repeatedly discussed the various responses he might take if he has enough advance knowledge of when the main attack is coming. One of the unanswered questions had to do with when and where he might employ the paratroopers we've been repatriating from Reykjavik during the previous week.

Now there is an answer. The newly frocked marshal, my sometime friend and drinking buddy, is going to use what remains of Russia's airborne troops to hit the Irkutsk and Angarsk airfields. He is going to do it tonight in an effort to destroy Chinese planes and reopen, at least temporarily, the Russian air routes to the east.

I promptly tell Sholakov that, in my opinion, he has made exactly the right decision. It's the kind of difficult decision that comes with the territory when you are a commander. What we both assume is that the Chinese have learned from their own experiences attacking the Russian airfields and are ready to repel an airborne attack on theirs. We are wrong.

******

After contemplating the situation over a cup of tea I decide to contact Master Chief Matthews at Arkhara. I want to get his read on the state and availability of the swimmers.

What I specifically want to know is if he can get them to take out some of the new pontoon bridges the Chinese are certain to establish over the Amur when they launch their main attack. I am going to authorize him to offer another one hundred thousand dollars and U.S. citizenship to each swimmer who will go out for a third time and the pilots who take them?

That is when things start to go wrong. I cannot reach Matthews. My call arrives too late. Lonnie finally got through to someone at the Swimmers' camp who reports that Matthews pulled out to return to the States via

Moscow two hours earlier. *Wonder why he left. I will need to know before I send him back.*

Finally I call Marshal Petrov and ask him to have someone meet Matthews' plane and have him call me immediately. I tell Petrov only that Matthews is a valuable man and I need for him to return to Arkhara as soon as possible. I do not tell him why.

Late in the afternoon Matthews is patched through from the Moscow airport. He tells me he pulled out because he received a message from Arnie Miskin asking him to confirm his instructors had safely departed and telling him to close his station and leave. He'll return immediately and organize a move against the pontoon bridges; and how soon will he get the money to pay the swimmers who volunteer to go out again and what else can he promise them?

******

Finally the signal. The first song on the radio after the 2am weather forecast is "Happy Red Wind" performed by the Red Army singers of the eighth entertainment regiment. Its meaning is clear. Lieutenant Bao Wei and his Special Company are to blow the bridge over the ravine as soon as possible.

Bao immediately wakes his men and parades them in the moonlit darkness. "The Party is depending on us," he tells them. "Tomorrow afternoon we will attack and destroy an important railroad bridge. We will not fail." *Unless I can figure out a way to defect.*

Neither Bao nor his men know that the message has come too late; almost all the military trains have passed the bridge, including those carrying the men and armor that just arrived on the *Moskva* and *Leningrad*. The only exceptions are the trains now loading in the Khabarovsk yards. They are loading what is left of two of Bulganin's divisions, and almost all of his surviving armor, to carry them from the Khabarovsk Front to the Chita Front.

* * * * * *

Earlier in the afternoon Bulganin had received the order to disengage two of his divisions and most of his armor – and bring them to Chita as quickly as possible. He is been expecting the order for several days and is as ready as he could be under the circumstances. Even so, it comes as a shock both to Bulganin and to his deputy who will stay behind as the new frontal commander.

Conditions for the withdrawal are not favorable. The constant Chinese attacks have worn down all four of his divisions. Two nights ago he moved the two that are to remain back into the center of his main line of resistance. The two divisions they replaced, the ones he is going to take to Chita, moved back into the second line on the city's outskirts for as much rest and refitting as he could arrange.

Despite the problems, the majority of Bulganin's remaining armor and self-propelled artillery, the two very understrength and slightly rested and refitted divisions, and all but three of his surviving assault helicopters, are being loaded on seven very long trains of flatcars and gravel cars.

The scene in the floodlit rail yard is almost surreal. Men are everywhere running and waving or standing in ranks and stamping their feet to stay warm; tanks and BMDs and self-propelled artillery are moving up the temporary loading ramps and then clanking down the length of the flatcars to jam up against the previous vehicle that loaded; and artillery flares periodically pop and light the sky over towards the forward edge of the battle in the distance.

Overpowering everything is the din of noise as the two divisions are loaded and the smell coming from the white dusting of snow covering the ground that is increasingly pockmarked with yellow and brown stains as the men relieve themselves before they board. Even so, it does not compare to the sound of thunder coming from the frontline which is about fifteen kilometers away and periodically lit with flickering red and white lights of exploding flares and mortar and artillery rounds.

It may be my imagination, General Bulganin thinks as he stands on the hood of his jeep with his hands on hips, but I think the volume of Chinese fire has decreased significantly in the past twenty four hours. *Could it be that the Chinese are finally running low on munitions or do they know that all this fighting is merely a sideshow to the main event that will be occurring elsewhere?*

"Lieutenant Demyan," he shouts down to his aide. "Is it my imagination or has the Chinese fire lessened in the last couple of hours?" *Mother of Christ, I hope so. My boys are going to be really thin on the ground once we pull out to reinforce Chita.*

******

Transport planes carrying the Russian paratroopers lift off early in the evening from airfields far to the west, airfields thought to be much too distant to be used to attack the Chinese-held Russian fields west of Lake Baikal, or any other Chinese bases for that matter.

Controllers in the Chinese AWACS turboprop operating in northwestern China see the Russian planes take off and immediately send a report to the headquarters of the Red Army. What they think they saw, and report, are cargo planes moving men and supplies to Russian airfields closer to the eastern fronts.

Neither the AWACS crew nor anyone else suspects an attack on the Chinese-occupied airfields west of Lake Baikal. The airfields from which the Russian planes are coming are much too far away for that.

The officers on the first Chinese AWACS never do realize their mistake. They lose contact as the Russian planes move further east. The controllers on the second Chinese AWACS, the one radiating more to the east, see them coming several hours later but have already been informed that they are merely more Russian cargo flights. They ignore the Russian transports until they are well past the most eastern airfield still held by the Russians. By then it is too late.

Controllers in the second more easterly Chinese AWACS are able to get a last minute warning to Angarsk but the field at Irkutsk never receives any warning at all. The Chinese air force tower operators at Irkutsk remained blissfully ignorant of their impending doom until the dark shapes of Russian paratroopers suddenly begin dropping past their dirty rain-spattered windows.

Russia's airborne drops are timed to hit the two snow dusted airfields simultaneously. And it more or less works that way despite the murky darkness and dusting snow. The Russian paratroopers came down on the two airfields without warning. Truth be told, a goodly number of the men miss the fields completely due to the darkness and the poor performance of the pilots - but those that do make it are more than enough to overcome the totally unready Chinese.

Vicious fighting breaks out instantly with quarter neither asked nor given. The Chinese paratroopers wake up when the shooting starts and came out of their makeshift quarters in the airfields' hangars and buildings fighting to the extent they can But it is pitch black and freezing cold, and they are unprepared and without assigned positions. Worst of all, most of their ammunition is under lock and key in accordance with the peacetime regulations imposed by their officers.

Heavy fighting continues for several hours on both fields even though the issue is basically settled within the first few minutes. A good number of the heavy Russian casualties are the result of friendly fire in the darkness and broken bones from landing on buildings and equipment they did not see until it was too late.

After the Russian transports drop their paratroopers, instead of turning back to the west towards bases they do not have enough fuel to reach, the Russian transports turn on their landing lights and begin attempting landings in the sleeting rain and dark on the deserted emergency and auxiliary fields surrounding the two main airbases. About sixty percent of them landed successfully.

The United States did somewhat the same thing in World War Two. A large force of American B-24 bombers based in Italy flew far past their maximum bombing range to hit German targets on the Eastern Front. The plan was for them to continue on even further eastward and land on Russian airfields beyond the front lines. Many of them crash landed instead and most of the survivors ended up being temporarily interned by the Russians. Similarly, Doolittle's Raiders overflew Japan with the idea of bombing Tokyo and flying on to land in China. None of them made it.

Like their American predecessors, a lot of Russia's best men and a good chunk of the remaining Russian transport planes are gone - but it is well worth the sacrifice, at least according to the Moscow politicians who have themselves and their families safely out of harm's way in case the Chinese go nuclear. *If sending the transports on a one way trip turns out to be a mistake we can blame Sholakov is the consensus view.*

******

Naumenko is waiting in the Chita rail yards as the first of the trains carrying his men and equipment arrives. It pulls in immediately behind the returning dummy train which has already started unloading. Duffy and I can see Naumenko as the flatcar on which our Jeep is riding slowly moves past him and a group of his officers. I raise a hand in a friendly salute but he does not see it.

Why are Harry and Eugene and I in the Russian Jeep? Because it's damn cold out here and we can periodically turn on the engine and run the heater.

And we are not always in the Jeep – we periodically get out so some of the Russian grunts can warm up after they finish their turn at sentry duty. Then, when they are warmed up a bit, we play musical chairs and rush to change places so they climb in their sleeping bags behind the plywood sheets being used as windscreens at the front of each flatcar.

When the train finally jerks to a stop in the Chita yards we jump off to walk back to where we saw Naumenko. It's a relief to get off after two straight days and nights of sitting in a Jeep rolling through the empty Siberian countryside on a railroad flatcar. The snow covered mountains we've seen are spectacular, but damn it's cold and uncomfortable. Even the thunder of the guns to the south somehow seems fitting. *It almost seems like we are all actors in an old Russian black and white war movie. I keep waiting to see Cossacks riding horses and waving their swords.*

******

Harry and I exchanged salutes with Naumenko and then big bear hugs and cheek kisses. I do not recognize any of the officers around him. But I know exactly what he just did – he just sent a message to his staff without saying a word.

"It's good to see you again Comrade Major," He says as he looks at me briefly before turning back to watch the equipment unloading begin and shout orders to the men organizing it.

"Things are about to get difficult," he says a few minutes later as we stand together to watch the first of his trains begin to unload. "The Chinese assault battalions have been across the Amur for hours and the Chinese are already moving armor over pontoon bridges. More are under construction."

Then he turns away and begins barking orders to the men around him and greeting the officers reporting to him from the first two trains.

Harry and I quietly step back and move away from the gathering group of Russian officers. It's no wonder Naumenko has no more time for us - he is got to quickly move his troops and armor into a third defensive line before the Chinese break though the first two. He also has to unload the tanks and tank crews that the dummy train has been carrying eastward every day and returning every night. They will go into the third line he is building with his four divisions from the *Kiev* and the Korean and Chinese Fronts.

******

It took a while before it's our Jeep's turn to be driven off the loading ramp. But it finally does come off and we get in it and drive away before anyone has a chance to tell us we cannot. Then, after Eugene makes some inquiries, we head down a dirt road to where we hope to find Colonel Miskin at General Sholakov's headquarters. It's time to call home and report.

The Russian military police at the entrance to the Russian headquarters need to call an officer, and Eugene has to do a lot of talking, but we are in and a staff lieutenant in a clean uniform is taking us somewhere.

He gestures with sort of a "go in" motion at a battered wooden door. So I open the door and we walk into to a small office with unpainted concrete walls and a single electric light bulb dangling down from the ceiling. Surprise. It belongs to Colonel Miskin and is stuffed with communications equipment, sleeping bags, and personal gear. Miskin works and sleeps here and so do Andy Willow and Chief Warrant Officer Liska and his two fellow warrant officers.

Colonel Miskin, "call me Arnie," and everyone else jumps up and gives us an extremely warm welcome. It seems they have been closely following our travels and travails. Then they pepper us with questions and bring us up to date as they open cans so we can ravenously devour some of their field rations.

We've been out of touch for several days and immediately ask about the war. The big news to us is that the Chinese are over the Amur River in front of both Chita and Blagoveshchenk and the Russians have at least temporarily regained the Irkutsk and Angarsk airfields.

"Andy, will be excited to see you." Colonel Miskin tells us. "He is out running an errand and will be back shortly."

According to the Colonel, everyone else has been withdrawn or will be withdrawn shortly, even Chief Matthews and his swimming instructors; we seven are the entire American contingent – or eight if you include Captain Solomon who is still missing.

******

Harry and I, and Eugene, stack our weapons in the corner and dump our sleeping bags and packs on the floor. Then we shoot the breeze and wait while Mister Liska tries to get me through to General Roberts. It's late morning here and the middle of the night in Riems. France is ten hours earlier and General Roberts is obviously in bed asleep. He wakes up instantly.

"Evans? Are you and Harry alright? Where are you and what's happening?

"All four divisions got through? And there are three more to come and maybe more? Well that is good news and I am glad to hear it. You've done good. Real good. Okay. Let me speak to Colonel Miskin."

"Well Arnie, what do you think?

"Yeah Arnie, you are right. They might as well stay out there with Naumenko. Let me speak to Major Evans again."

"Okay Dick. I want you and Mister Duffy to stay with General Naumenko. According to Marshal Sholakov, Naumenko's men will form a third Russian line. The battle will be handed off to them if, I probably should say when, the Chinese break through the first two. I want you to keep checking in with me and Colonel Miskin at least once every day to update us."

"No. I regret we have not heard a word about Captain Solomon."

******

General Jian, the Chinese army group commander and his senior officers know their orders: Take Chita. Then continue north and take Tynda.

Taking Chita to cut the Trans-Siberian Railroad which runs south of Lake Baikal is not enough as far as Red Banner Street is concerned. General Jian is under orders to continue north and take Tynda as well.

Tynda must be occupied to cut the arctic Baikal-Amur Mainline railroad that has been under construction for years. The route of the BAM is further north than the Trans-Siberian; it goes around the northern end of Lake Baikal to Tynda and then on to Yakutsk, Magadan, and the Kamchatka Peninsula.

If the Chinese do not take Tynda, the Russians will be able to complete the new railroad line and be able to go around the north end of Lake Baikal to Yakutsk, the hub of the Russian arctic, and on to Magadan across from Alaska.

Russia's desolate arctic is sparsely populated but there are reports and rumors of astonishing oil and mineral deposits up there. The Chinese want them in addition to the cultivatable lands in the Amur drainage. Equally important, they do not want the Russians to have them.

Chapter Thirty-two

Incentives and disasters.

I left Moscow and finally reached Arkhara the next day on a special flight of a long range Bear turboprop. It was just me, a half dozen or so officers and civilians, and a bunch of nervous enlisted men, probably conscripts on their first plane ride. We finally reached Arkhara after the Bear flew far to the north in order to avoid the Chinese planes newly installed at Irkutsk and Angarsk.

As soon as we land a waiting Russian officer helped me catch a ride to the almost deserted Spetsnaz tent camp. Only the swimmers and a handful of the Spetsnaz explosive experts are still there. And they are more than a little nervous and suspicious because of my sudden departure and equally sudden return.

Everything changes when I explain I have been off to Moscow to get more money. And it really changes when I offer them each one hundred thousand dollars and American citizenship for each of them and their families — if they will make a run at the pontoon bridges the Chinese have thrown over the Amur in front of Chita. *That is what the general said I could offer them. I damn sure hope he can deliver. It's going to be my ass if he does not.*

My swimmers believe me, all twenty six of them. All but one of them instantly agrees to go again if I can line up the necessary helicopters. That is what I expected. After all, twice before they have been successful and each time a team of swimmers returned they and their pilots were immediately paid a lot of money as soon as they landed.

The only difference, which I somehow forget to mention, is that then I had the money; now I do not. I have no illusions as to what will happen to me if I try to leave before they come back or if they do their jobs and are not paid. I am toast and there's no half way about it.

Then I make the same offer to the Spetsnaz demolition guys if they will go into China by helicopter and take out a couple of bridges the swimmers cannot access. They are even more enthusiastic than the swimmers. *What the hell, how many times can they kill me?*

******

The first of the seven very long trains carrying Bulganin and initial elements of his two divisions is pulling out of Khabarovsk when Bao and his men begin their march to the bridge over the ravine. General Bulgan is on the first train because it is likely the railroad has already been cut. If it is, he and his men may have to fight their way through the Chinese to reach Chita.

Lieutenant Bao's men are just beginning to set some of the charges when an excited and shouting lookout stumbles and slides down the side of the ravine towards where Bao and his men are busy setting up the explosive charges.

"Lieutenant. Train is coming. Train is coming."

"Down," shouts Bao. "Everyone down. Let it pass."

It was the right thing to do. And it probably would have worked. But every military unit inevitably has a fool and Bao's is no exception.

Bulganin's train is already passing over the bridge when one of Bao's men decides to run to a better position where he thinks he will be less likely to be seen. It is a fatal mistake. As every soldier knows, it is movement that attracts the eye; if you freeze and do not move there is a good chance you'll never be seen.

Sure enough. Half the train has already passed and no one has seen him yet. But then he runs about twenty yards to a new position behind a thicker bush and some of the men on the train see him. They are, after all, on high alert fearing an ambush.

Two of the BMD gunners immediately open up. So do quite a number of the freezing men crouching behind the wall of sandbags that runs on both sides of each flatcar. The runner is cut to shreds and the train grinds to a halt half way over the bridge.

Trains are not supposed to stop if they are fired on. But it does. The men, at least those who can, pour off the train as they have been instructed to do if the train stops. Seconds later they see the Chinese under the bridge and open fire. The Chinese sergeant, Shen Jie, has just enough time to flip one of the timer switches before he is cut down.

The explosion shakes the train and the bridge seems to settle. But it does not go all the way down. Thirty minutes later Bulganin and several thousand of his men stand by the side of the tracks and watch intently as the train and its load of armor and self-propelled artillery very slowly inches its way across the sagging bridge with only the engineer on board.

Dead and wounded Chinese are everywhere on the cold ground under the bridge as the train moves slowly over it. Lieutenant Bao is not among them. He instinctively sprints down the ravine as soon as the first shots are fired. He'll never be found because two weeks later he will freeze to death dreaming of his family.

******

General Bulganin is the first man to re-board the train. He rushes back to his command BMD and uses the radio to contact the officers on the trains coming behind him via the radios in the tanks and BMDs.

"Attention all officers and all sergeants. This is General Bulganin. Listen carefully. The bridge over the ravine at kilometer 1617 has been damaged by the enemy but is still usable. All personnel except the engine driver are to dismount from their train before it reaches the bridge and the train is to move across the bridge very slowly. Troops are to walk through the ravine and re-board the train on the other side. Do not let your troops walk under the bridge."

"I repeat. Do not let your men ride on the train when it crosses the ravine bridge at kilometer 1617 and do not let your men walk under the bridge."

Bulganin leaves an entire company of infantry to protect the sagging bridge and care for the wounded and surrendered Chinese. The company's men are to flag down trains approaching the bridge from either direction and pass on his orders regarding its use.

Less than an hour later, the troops are reloaded and the General's train begins pulling away from the damaged bridge. As it picks up speed the men on the rear flatcars can see troops piling off a newly arriving train on the other side of the sagging bridge.

******

Transport planes carrying me and my swimmers and the Spetsnaz volunteers depart right after dark the next day. And they almost do not take off at all. It takes a late night call from an American bigwig, probably Roberts because that is who I called, to get my guys carried to Chita and enough helicopters released to carry them to their targets. But they do get released, at least that is what I have been told, and me and my guys are on our way to Chita to meet up with them. Supposedly when we get there we will find six helicopters waiting to carry my swimmers to the Amur and two for the Spetsnaz teams going into China.

At the moment I am holding my breath as the four turbo props of the old Soviet AN-12 noisily roar as we lumber down the Arkhara runway in the dark. I do not let it out until we lift off to begin a long circuitous northern route to Chita. We are not taking any chances; instead of heading west towards Chita we are going north for while in an effort to keep as far away as possible from Chinese fighters coming out of bases in China.

On board with me are about half of our teams of swimmers, Spetsnaz, and helicopter pilots and all the gear and explosives they will need for tomorrow night's insertion into the Amur. A second and similarly loaded AN-12 will follow us in about an hour with the other half. *I am no fool - I have my Russian liaison officer schedule the planes an hour apart so they will be less likely to collide in the dark.*

If all goes as planned, both planes will reach Chita and land before the sun comes up. That is where we will spend the day and hook up with the helicopters that will carry the swimmers to the Amur and the Spetsnaz engineers into China to take out two key bridges.

Admiral Morton is the one who called me with the details about the planes and helicopters. He says the army is sending the cash from Seoul to Vladivostok to Chita via a long range C-130. The plane is from a special air force squadron based at Fort Bragg. If all goes according to plan, knock on wood, it will bring the money in and then carry the survivors and me back to the States by the same route. It better get here in time or I am really fucked.

******

The helicopter carrying Russian Navy Lieutenant Commander Yakov Alksnis and eight other swimmers lifts off the snow dusted field outside Chita right after dark for the long roundabout trip to the Amur River pontoon bridges. The nine men are wearing black rubber survival suits and traveling in a rickety old Mi-8. All nine of the men came from the Russian naval base at Murmansk and they have worked together for years. Originally there were twelve but three did not make it back from their second bridge mission into China.

Stacked in the helicopter along with the nine Russian swimmers are 80 twenty liter jerry cans of fuel, two folding step ladders, and two large funnels. The Russians are sitting on the cans and the door is partially open to disperse the fumes in case they leak. It's the first time Yakov can remember that no one is smoking.

The plan is simple according to Chief Mathews. The Hip will fly to the Amur, land way upstream on an isolated section of the river bank to unload the swimmers and refuel, and then fly down the Chinese side of the Amur valley to pick them up at a similarly isolated location on the other side of the six pontoon bridges they are targeting. Five other Hips will be heading elsewhere along the river to bring swimmers to the other bridges.

"For Christ's sake," Matthews had pleaded one last time through Anatoli his interpreter before they took off, "remember that this time two teams are assigned to each group of pontoon bridges and every timer is preset to go off at the same time. So do not get excited or stop for even a second if you see someone else in the water."

******

"So far so good," Yakov shouts to his team over the engine noise as the Hip bounces and then settles on to the river bank. It tips a bit to one side as it lands in the dark but not enough to cause a problem.

"Okay," he shouts over his shoulder as he goes first out the door. "Let's go make some money."

The men haul their explosive packs to the water, adjust their scuba rebreathing units, and wade in. The Hip's three crewmen ignore them as they listen intently for a minute or so for a response to the landing. Hearing nothing, they rushed to set up the ladders and begin refilling the Hip's fuel tanks. If there had been a problem they would have left immediately and refueled somewhere else.

******

Alksnis and his swimmers quietly drift down to the first of their six target bridges just after midnight. That is where three of them including Commander Alksnis peel away in a little group to take the first two bridges. The next three men continue on down the river to take the third and fourth bridges; the final three swimmers will take bridges five and six. When they finish they will swim like hell to meet the refueled Hip at the extraction point further on down the Amur. Similar operations involving the other swimmers and their pilots are occurring simultaneously at pontoon bridge crossings elsewhere on the river.

It is easy for the Murmansk men to see the bridges across the river because the vehicles coming in a constant stream from the Chinese side of the river are using their parking lights. They can also hear outboard engines in the distance.

"It's just as Matthews told us," Yakov whispers as his two men tread water around him and the current carries them closer and closer in the darkness. "They are using skiffs to hold the pontoon boats in place against the Amur's current."

All in all attacking this bridge is going to be more difficult than last week's bridges because of the skiffs; also there are more people around and the pontoon boats are far different and much more numerous than the handful of bridge supports we exploded last week.

Then all three silently slip under the surface and let the current take them. A few minutes later, and no longer in contact with each other, they reach the first bridge. Yakov has the first of the four bridges. The men with him are each assigned one of the next two. If they can, each of the three men will slap a couple of charges on the fourth bridge as they go by.

"Shit, they are wood," Yakov says to himself as he touches the bottom of the first boat. "That means it's going to take even longer. Oh well, the money's good." Then he digs into the floating bag he is towing and pulls out the first of the many little mines with their preset timers. One for each pontoon boat.

An hour or so later he drifts down to put the three charges he has left on the fourth bridge. So far he has not seen or heard another swimmer. And it is taking much longer than he expected. Matthews warned them that the boats holding up the bridges would be rising and falling as tanks and vehicles moved over them. But he had not expected such large and sudden moves. It makes placing each of the little explosive charges much more time consuming, but not impossible.

* * * * * *

Duffy and I are on the side of little ridge looking down into the Amur Valley. It's a cool crisp sunlit morning. With our binoculars we can clearly see what's left of the first Russian line and the very intense forward edge of the battle running all along the second line. At the moment we are with Naumenko in the Russian General's incomplete third line. It runs all the way across the valley through which a spur line of the Trans-Siberian runs down from Chita towards the Chinese city of Manzhouli on the other side of the Amur.

From up here it appears that some parts of the Russian first line are still intact. But not many. The Chinese have obviously rolled over most of it and around the rest. Now they are assaulting the Russians' second line with everything they can bring up. *Damn I am glad we are not down there. Those guys look to be in deep shit.*

What we are looking down at is almost surreal. Artillery flashes and smoke are everywhere from here to the river. Periodically a streak of light and smoke goes up from one side or the other – and quite often the result is an exploding plane or helicopter.

Casualties must be tremendous on both sides. A few minutes ago Harry counted well over a hundred burning tanks and armored vehicles. And that is just on the small part of the front we can see.

******

We stayed awake and watched as the intense fighting continued all night and, if anything, grows in volume and intensity as it moves closer and closer to us. And it does not seem to be going all that well for the Russians. The disorganized and suffering survivors of the initial Chinese attacks have been coming through Naumenko's positions all night long. As the sun came up the next morning we can see what appear to be significant Chinese breakthroughs in several parts of the second line.

Naumenko's four seriously understrength divisions are next if the second line goes down. Marshal Sholakov just came in to tell him he is got to hold the Chinese long enough for the survivors coming through our lines to set up a new main line of resistance further back along the valley. That is where the Russian artillery has already been relocated and that is where we will go ourselves if the Chinese break through here.

Sure enough. By sundown the Russian second line begins to crumble and survivors begin flooding through our lines under the bright light of the flares being fired by both sides so they do not have to fight in the dark. Sometimes the retreating Russians come through in some semblance of order with their surviving tanks and vehicles; sometimes they do not. We can see them clearly because the flares are frequently lighting the battlefield in front of us as brightly as if it is daytime.

******

There is a brief lull in the fighting as the sun comes up the next morning. Individual stragglers are still coming through our lines but for the most part, the Russians in front of us who could retreat have already done so. About ten in the morning Harry and I crouch with our translator in a hurriedly dug new hole as intermittent Chinese artillery rounds begin falling all along the Russians' latest defensive line.

Looking through a narrow gap in the sandbags we'd piled three high around our hole we can see masses, huge masses, of Chinese troops and armor in the distance – and moving towards us. *No more casually standing up to look at the battlefield to see what's going on. The Chinese are too close. If we can see them, they can see us. Interestingly enough, we do not see nearly as many*

Chinese planes and helicopters as we saw yesterday. There are not as many of the Russians' either.

"Harry, is it my imagination or are there nowhere near as many Chinese planes and helicopters in the air today?"

"Yeah. And not as many tanks and personnel carriers either. Figures. They must have lost a shit pot full of stuff the last couple of days."

We are using our binoculars to look carefully through the gap in the sandbags at the Chinese men and tanks in the distance when a breathless Eugene jumps in our hole to rejoin us.

"General tell Amerikanski comrades be ready go further up the valley. Is better. General tell Amerikanski comrades talk to General. You come."

******

Naumenko is on the phone in his headquarters BMD parked behind a rocky outcropping when Eugene pounds on the door and it opens. Somehow he had found time to shave and someone had gotten him into a clean shirt and slapped a clean bandage on his face where the mortar fragment had sliced him at Bikin. His pants and boots are even more torn and filthy than they were when we saw him several days ago.

"Ah, my American Comrades," Naumenko greeted us as he hung up the phone. "How do things look on the other side of the ridge?"

"The Chinese seem to have broken through the line in front of you in a couple of places. It looks like they will be handing off to you in a couple of hours."

"Yes, that is the report I received from Marshal Sholakov himself about an hour ago. He and his staff are trying to organize another line behind us with the troops that have been withdrawing and a couple of General Bulganin's divisions that are just arriving."

"There is one thing Harry and I noticed, General. It may be our imagination but it seems that the Chinese air and artillery support has been declining ever since yesterday afternoon."

******

That night we call in to report to General Roberts and then watch from a new hole on the top of the ridge as Naumenko's men on the slopes below us are hit with wave after wave of Chinese human wave attacks. They hold all night. Then, just before dawn, the surviving Russians use up the last of their ammunition and run for their lives under the light of artillery and mortar flares.

It is almost quiet as the sun came up. Perhaps because both armies are totally exhausted after three days of some of the most intensive fighting in the history of warfare; perhaps because on both sides of the front line the troops and armor ran out of ammunition.

Who knows why the lull occurred. Whatever the reason, it was a godsend for the Russians. They had time to reorganize their exhausted troops and two new divisions, the last two to arrive, came up with their armor and artillery under a General Bulganin to strengthen the Russian line. There may be, we are told, as many as three more of the Vladivostok divisions coming – if they can make it past Bikin.

That afternoon the Chinese launch two suicidal infantry attacks with little or no armor or artillery support. The Russians easily beat them back. We watch the whole thing. *I cannot put my finger on it but the Chinese seem to be desperate. Almost as if they are engaging in the do or die "forlorn hopes" of the eighteenth and nineteenth century British army.*

Late that afternoon Sholakov launches a small counterattack using the newly arrived troops and armor of General Bulganin's two divisions. It works. The Chinese just melt away in front of them. By the time darkness falls the Russians have pushed half way to the Amur and reoccupied a lot of the land they'd lost in the past seventy two hours.

Chapter Thirty-three

Confusion and change.

The morning's Chinese Politburo meeting opened in chaos for the first time since Lin Piao and Mao's widow tried to grab power so they could continue the 'cultural revolution.' All the news was bad no matter how much Chairman Li and General Wu attempted to spin it as "most temporary and easily reversible."

Members of the Politburo are not without their own sources. They spent most of the previous night calling their military contacts and comparing notes. The picture that emerges is beyond grim.

By the time the meeting begins promptly at nine in the morning the Politburo members know the troops north of the Amur are rapidly running out of supplies and reinforcements due to the destruction of pontoon bridges; they know the Russian airfields west of Lake Baikal have been recaptured by the Russians along with every airfield east of the lake; they know about the destruction of inbound tankers and the loss of the coastal petroleum storage areas; they know about the loss of almost all the Chinese submarines; and they know the Red Army has been defeated in front of Chita and many of their troops are surrendering.

Li and Wu arrive at the morning meeting hoping no one would know how badly the war is going. They are mistaken. A majority of the Politburo members realize the war is lost—and one after another they began to denounce General Wu and Chairman Li for losing it and misleading them.

First Wu and then Li abruptly decide to leave the meeting as the questions and accusations continue to increase. Wu did so after announcing that he is going to fly to the Front to see for himself what is going on and to take command if necessary. A few minutes later Chairman Li stands up and announces that he too will be flying out to the Front to help rally the troops.

General Wu's first thought is not to rally the troops, it is to save himself by organizing a military coup. But that idea does not generate the necessary support among the demoralized and fearful senior staff at Red Banner Street. So he announces to his staff that he is going to personally fly to the front and take command. That is when Chairman Li decides to go with him. *If Wu thinks we've lost it's time to run.*

Four hours later the air force transport plane General Wu and Chairman Li are using in an effort to escape to India is shot down at the order of Hua Guofeng, the newly elected Party Chairman.

******

Initially the United States knows none of this and everyone is confused, particularly me. First the NSA intercepts suggest General Wu and Chairman Li have been arrested. Then they suggest that one or both of them tried to escape by flying to India. Then the CIA reports that their plane has been shot down and they are dead.

No one knows what the hell is happening. What we do know from Colonel Miskin and Major Evans is that the Chinese north of the Amur have been defeated and are surrendering in droves.

******

Three days later and the Chinese north of the Amur have either retreated by paddling boats across the river or surrendered. The war is effectively over even though sporadic fighting continues at various places along the border. And I am off to China as part of an American peace delegation to meet China's new Party Chairman and new Defense Minister.

We are, it seems, to shuttle back and forth between Moscow and Beijing as part of a United Nations attempt to broker a peace agreement.

Our first stop is Beijing to meet with the new interim leader of China, Hua Guofeng. He'll hold the office of Party Chairman until a successor is selected by the Central Committee or whoever is making such decisions in China these days. Hua's the old guy who filled the post temporarily when Mao died.

The Vice President is leading the American contingent in the peace delegation and for some reason he has asked for me to be among the various and sundry officials who will accompany him. Secretary of State Hoffman is not going. She resigned last week to prepare for the presidential primaries.

Epilogue

Not everything and everyone is accompanied by planeloads of media and involved in great events and monumental undertakings. While we were flying to China to promote world peace and assorted political careers, Chief Matthews was welcoming a C-130 delivery out of Tokyo with bundles and bundles of shrink wrapped one hundred dollar bills and a dozen or so Special Operations troops to guard them.

Matthews had a big smile on his face the next day when he said hello to Evans, Duffy, and Willow as he ushered some of his cash-rich swimmers and Spetsnaz aboard the plane to join them for its return trip to America. Some of the Russian pilots and his interpreter are with him because they too want to start a new life somewhere else.

One reason for the Chief's big smile might be the two hundred or so pounds of nice new hundred dollar bills in his three personal duffle bags.

****

****

****

Please read more.

All of the other action-packed books in this great military saga are also available as eBooks. You can find them by going to Amazon or Google and searching for *Martin Archer fiction.* The first three books are also available as an ebook collection in *The Soldiers and Marines Trilogy.*

And a word from Martin:

I hope you enjoyed reading *War in the East* as much as I enjoyed writing it. If so, I respectfully request a favourable review on Amazon and elsewhere with as many stars as possible in order to encourage other readers. And I would also very much like to know your thoughts about the story. I can be reached at martinarcherV@gmail.com. /S/ Martin Archer.

Amazon eBooks in Martin Archer's exciting and action-packed *Soldier and Marines* saga:

Soldier and Marines

Peace and Conflict

War Breaks Out

Our Next War

Israel's Next War

Amazon eBooks in Martin Archer's exciting and action-packed *The Company of Archers* saga:

The Archer

The Archers' Castle

The Archers' Return

The Archers' War

Rescuing the Hostages

Kings and Crusaders

The Archers' Gold

The Missing Treasure

Castling the King

The Sea Warriors

The Captain's Men

Gulling the Kings

The Magna Carta Decision

The War of the Kings

The Company's Revenge

The Ransom

The New Commander

The Gold Coins

The Emperor has no Gold

Fatal Mistakes

The Alchemist's Revenge

The Venetian Gambit

Today's Friends

The English Gambit

Collections

Soldiers and Marines Trilogy – books I, II, III

The Archer's Stories - books I, II, III, IV, V, VI

The Archer's Stories II - books VII, VIII, IX, X,

The Archer's Stories III – books XI, XII, XIII

The Archer's Stories IV – books XIV, XV, XVI, XVII

The Archer' Stories V – books XVIII, XIX, XX

Other eBooks you might enjoy:

Cage's Crew by Martin Archer writing as Raymond Casey

America's Next War by Michael Cameron Adams – an adaption of *War Breaks Out* to set it in our immediate future when a war breaks out over the refugee crisis in Europe.

THE NEXT BOOK IN THIS SAGA

Israel's Next War – sample pages

.... Lights came on in the homes throughout the neighborhood and the family's neighbors, almost all reservists as most Israelis are, rushed for their weapons. It does not take a rocket scientist to know that bursts of automatic weapons fire in their quiet residential neighborhood meant something was seriously wrong. And fighting back is drummed into every Israeli beginning on his or her first day of basic training and every day thereafter - go for the attackers and go fast and hard.

The first man to try to reach the family's little home was their neighbor from two doors down the street. He is a taxi driver who, of all things, serves in the relatively small Israeli navy when his reserve time comes up each year.

His wife was already on the phone calling the police when he steps out of his front door trying to simultaneously get a clip into his Uzi submachine gun and hold up his pajama bottoms. He hesitates for a second as he steps off his porch. Where did the shooting come from? The night is totally silent and the two street lights on the block are lighting the quiet residential street with a yellowish glow. Everything looks normal.

A split second later the door immediately across the street opens and the taxi driver sees the heavy set older man who lives there alone with two little dogs rush out wearing absolutely nothing except a Galil assault rifle. He heads straight for the house next door on the taxi driver's side of the street.

The taxi driver instinctively starts that way too, although he almost falls when his loosely tied pajamas start to slide down below his waist and he steps on the cuff of one of his pajama legs. He hops on one leg to pull them up with one hand while holding his old navy-issued Uzi in the other. Lights are going on and doors banging everywhere up and down the street. Somewhere in the background he can hear shouting.

The older man had gotten to the middle of the street, and is clearly illuminated by the two street lights, when the muzzle flames and chattering roar of an automatic weapon reach out towards him from one of the windows of the house he is charging. The older man goes over backwards in sort of a somersault and his weapon skids away with a metallic clatter as it hits the asphalted street.

That is more than enough for the now-running taxi driver – he stops and fires a long burst into the window where the muzzle flashes came from. Then, as his pajama bottoms begin to fall down around his knees again, he dives awkwardly to his right and rolls behind his wife's car which is parked in front of his house. He is a modest man and his first move is to pull up his pajama pants again as he peeks around the back of the car.

The first of many police cars arrives two or three minutes later. By that time half a dozen armed neighbors in various stages of dress from only wearing underpants to fully clothed are already crouching up against the walls of the victims' home. Even before their car begins to screech to a stop the two policemen can see the partially dressed neighbors carrying guns and carefully avoiding the windows of the little house. They instinctively know exactly what it means.

The driver of the police car can also see the naked body sprawled in the street. He takes in the scene in an instant. Then he accelerates again and skids to a stop to place his car between the body and the house.

The arrival of the police car changes everything. It is almost as if the people in the house have been waiting for it to arrive. Once again an automatic weapon chatters and once again red muzzle flashes come out of a window. A different window.

The police car is peppered - both of its occupants wounded before they can finish diving out on the safe side away from the house, the driver quite seriously.

The second round of firing from the house really surprises the high school social studies teacher who lives next door. He is the one the police saw standing in his boxer shorts with his back against the wall next to the window from where the firing came. So his head is only a foot or so from the roar of the shooting and the muzzle flames when the terrorist, or whatever he turns out to be, begins firing at the police car.

The school teacher jerks back instinctively when the shooting starts, but only for a couple of seconds. As soon as the shooter stops firing he quickly leans forward, twists his Uzi around so he is holding it as far out in front of himself as he can and uses his left thumb to awkwardly fire a burst back in towards the window where the muzzle flashes came from. Then he dives to the ground up against the house and cuts his face on a protruding water faucet.

"Did you get him?" someone shouts. The school teacher does not respond. He cannot hear the question; he is temporarily deafened by his own firing and the firing from the window. He just lays there, unmoving and holding his face for so long that some of his neighbors think he is been hit.

******

The street in front of the house is absolute chaos as more and more police cars and armed neighbors arrive. Several brave souls use the shot up police car for cover as they crawl from behind the older man's house in an attempt to reach him and the two policemen on the street. They do not draw fire and are able to get to them despite serious scrapes and cuts to their bare knees and other tender places.

A few moments later one of the men sheltering behind the police car shouts out what he intends to do.

"I am going to shoot out the street lights."

Without waiting for anyone to answer he fires three or four short bursts until he shoots out the two nearest street lights. In the resulting darkness, and carefully keeping the police car between themselves and the house, the two men each grab the seriously wounded police office by the collar of his uniform shirt and began crawling backward towing him on his back between them. There is nothing they can do for their naked neighbor.

As the seriously wounded policeman is being retrieved, his slightly wounded partner winces from the pain in his leg as he leans around the rear tire of the patrol car and slowly and deliberately empties his pistol into the shooter's window in an attempt to cover the rescue effort. Several of the men across the street understand what he is doing and do the same. The wounded policeman had to use his pistol because the automatic weapon every Israeli police car carries is still clamped to the dashboard where he and partner left it when they dove out on the passenger side.

There is a lot of shouting back and forth. Everybody is shouting questions and giving orders to everybody else. The confusion and uncertainty is inevitable. There isn't much of a moon and without the street lights it is a scene of absolute bedlam in the dark. No one knows for sure what is happening and no one knows how many terrorists are in the house.

The would-be rescuers also do not know the state of the family living there. But they all understand the initial burst of firing probably means some of the people in the house are casualties. But they cannot be sure and within seconds every new arrival knows there are two little girls in there along with their mother and father.

A military quick reaction force arrives from the sprawling Tel Aviv army base about fifteen minutes later along with a helicopter equipped with a searchlight.

The helicopter searchlight is a mistake and the men crawling toward the house know it as soon as they see its beam of light snaking along the ground towards them. Sure enough, three or four bursts of automatic fire come from the house within seconds of the helicopter illuminating the police and neighbors who have previously been moving forward in the dark. The helicopter itself takes a couple of hits and several more of the suddenly visible Israelis go down including a neighbor rushing to the scene several blocks away and a newly arrived policeman sheltering behind the door of his car.

"There are at least two of them in there," the force commander unnecessarily shouts to his men. They did not hear him and did not need to; they'd seen the muzzle flames for themselves and open up with everything they have.

******

The standoff lasted for more than three hours without a word from anyone in the house. During those hours the neighborhood is evacuated, the dead and wounded retrieved and rushed off to the nearest trauma center, and the armed neighbors withdrawn and replaced with snipers and special troops with night sights on their weapons. Finally, an Arabic-speaking officer with a bullhorn roars out one last call for everyone in the house to come out with their hands up. Once again there is no response.

So be it thinks the incident control supervisor who has taken charge of the scene. He shouts an order, explosive charges are slapped onto the front and back doors and exploded, and a volley of tear gas grenades is fired through a number of windows. Then the team of heavily armored special troops pours through the doors and rushes into the house.

The tremendous explosion occurs about ten seconds after the first of the special troops dashes in through the front and rear doors. What is left of the windows blow out, the roof appears to lift up, and the observers can see two great flashes of red light inside even before they hear the tremendous explosions. The waiting medics and firemen instantly rush into the house and do their best.

******

"How many?" asks the Prime Minister into the phone as he paces the floor in his residence barefoot wearing only his pants. He desperately wants a cigarette and his ulcer is hurting again. His wife with her hand over her mouth is listening intently from the chair where she is sitting in her nightgown.

"Eight of ours and three terrorists. Five more of ours wounded. The little girls and their parents all have multiple gunshot wounds."

"Goddamn them to hell. Deliberately shooting children. Those fucking bastards. We are going to retaliate really big this time."

"Well here's the thing, Prime Minister. We've identified one of the men on the beach. He is an Iranian."

****

****